"...an unusually realistic novel about the beginning of America's involvement in Southeast Asia..."
- KIRKUS REVIEW

OPERATION WHITE STAR

by
Richard O. Sutton

Daring Publishing Group, Inc.
DARING BOOKS • LIFE ENRICHMENT PUBLISHERS
CANTON • OHIO

Copyright © 1990 by Richard O. Sutton

All rights reserved. No part of this book may be reproduced or transmitted in any form or by any means, electronic or mechanical, including photocopying, recording or by any information storage and retrieval system, without permission in writing from the Publisher.

Published by Daring Books
P.O. Box 20050, Canton, Ohio 44701

Library of Congress Cataloging-in-Publication Data

Sutton, Richard O., 1938-
    Operation White Star / by Richard O. Sutton
      p. cm.
    ISBN 0-938936-91-3
    1. United States. Army. Special Forces--Fiction.
2. Vietnamese Conflict, 1961-1975--Fiction. I. Title.
PS3569.U8974064 1989
813'54--dc20   89-23606
                                                                     CIP

Daring Publishing Group offers special discounts for bulk purchases of its products to be used for fund-raising, premium gifts, sales promotions, educational use, etc. Book excerpts or special editions can be produced to specification. For information contact the **Special Sales Department, Daring Publishing Group, 913 Tuscarawas Street West, Canton, Ohio 44702. Or call 1-800-445-6321.**

---

10 9 8 7 6 5 4 3 2 1

Printed in the United States of America

This book is dedicated to my son,

JEFFERSON DAVIS

who wouldn't let Ed Meadows rest

until his story was told.

Table of Contents

1. DASL's 7
2. The Convoy Commander 26
3. The Tale Of Two Hunters 36
4. The Frogman 53
5. The Green Berets 61
6. Otto Nottus 67
7. These Boots Are Made For Walking 77
8. Shadows 84
9. Briggs' Boys 90
10. I Love How You Love Me 96
11. The Lonesome Polecat 102
12. The "A" Detachment 110
13. What Is "White Star"? 116
14. Behind Closed Doors 122
15. Shake, Rattle, And Roll 129
16. Skinny, Flat, And Ugly 135
17. Unwritten Rules 141
18. Down On The Banks Of The Hanky-Pank 149
19. Snap, Crackle, Pop 154
20. Turn About's Fair Play 161
21. Burning Your Bridges 167
22. The Quick And The Dead 173
23. Who You Gonna Believe? 185

24	Payday	192
25	Viva La France	198
26	Who Could Know Such A Thing	203
27	A Workman Is Worthy Of His Hire	209
28	Tweaking A Beard	215
29	And Away We Go	221
30	When The Going Gets Tough...	229
31	...The Tough Get Going	235
32	A Winner Never Quits...	243
33	And A Quitter Never Wins	251
34	Story Tellers	256
35	Among The Hmong	262
36	Rice	268
37	When Your Hair Stands Up On End	274
38	Vang Pao	283
39	Air Boss	287
40	Med Evac	293

1

DASL's

If there was one thing in this world that LTC B.B. Briggs hated more than second lieutenants, the personnel assigned to the 7th Special Forces Group (Airborne) were not aware of it. For this reason it was especially cruel when they played the joke on 2 LT Ed Meadows during his checking in procedures at their enclave on Smoke Bomb Hill at Ft. Bragg, NC. The morning had been long, and it was already getting hot despite the fact that it was only May. Then in came this second lieutenant, spiffed up with shiny brass, and flashing the big West Point ring on his left hand. Said he had orders to report to the 7th Special Forces Group (Airborne), on this date, at this time, in this place for his new duty station. SP4 Brinkley tried to explain to the Lieutenant that he must be in the wrong place, they weren't expecting any new personnel in today and the Lieutenant probably wanted the Personnel Section of the 82d Airborne Division which was right on down the road about two miles and thank you for stopping in, Lieutenant, sorry we can't help you.

LT Meadows was persistent. He had a copy of his orders right here in his briefcase, and would the clerk be so kind as to direct him to the Reception Area so he could get all this In-Processing crap out of the way and go sign up for a BOQ assignment?

SP4 Brinkley was insistent. He understood that the Lieutenant *THOUGHT* he had orders for the Group, but he was quite sure there was a mistake somewhere, for there weren't any TO&E* slots for second lieutenants in the Group. However (in his most condescending and exasperated tone), if the Lieutenant would just show him the orders, perhaps Brinkley could sort out this trouble and direct the Lieutenant on his way, SIR!

Meadows unzipped the plastic document case he'd bought just before he left Ft. Sill and pulled out one of the hundreds of copies of the orders he'd been issued. He presented the paper to Brinkley the way you'd expect a conqueror to wave the document of surrender to the vanquished. "Here you are, Specialist Brinkley!" Meadows read from the uniform nametag in front of him. "I think you'll find that I am at the right place and I'd appreciate your help in In-Processing."

Brinkley took the proferred document, breathed a loud sigh of REAL exasperation, and leaned on his elbows on the desk top to look over the orders. "Alright, Sir, just give me a minute to look these over and I'll see if I can help you"

Damn these lieutenants, thought Brinkley. *You'd think they'd teach these guys to read a set of orders up there at Hudson High rather than spending all their time shining shoes and brass, and all that marching.* His eyes scanned the sheet to insure that it had the correct style, and LOOKED right, then he settled in to read the cryptic message contained in the most correct military abbreviated format. "Direction of the Pres--, Sec't Defense---DP, Par 2a---2d Lt Meadows, Edward R. is directed to proceed----etc, Ft. Bragg, NC, further assignment 7th SpFrcsGp(Arbn)---". *Wait just a minute. This looks like this Lieutenant is assigned to the Group! Can't be! There isn't any TO&E slot for a second lieutenant in Special Forces!* Something was obviously wrong with these orders, but SP4 Brinkley wasn't able to spot what it was. "Sir," mumbled Brinkley in his most concerned tone, "I'll have to get the Sergeant Major to look at these. There has been a mistake made somewhere but I'd better let him explain it to you." The fact of the matter was that Brinkley had no idea what to do next and he figured calling in the Sergeant Major was the wisest thing to do at this point.

Brinkley knocked and then entered the Sergeant Major's office. "Sergeant Major, we got a problem out at the front desk. We got a

---

*TO&E - Table of Organization & Equipment

Second Lieutenant thinks he's been assigned to Group, and the problem is, he's got these orders to prove it!"

"Gimme the orders!" growled the sergeant major. "Obviously, there's been a screw-up somewhere. Let's see where the hell it is." He looked over the sheet of paper. "What the fuck? Brinkley, where'd you get these orders? Is this some sort of joke or what? What the hell are you showing me? These orders say there are SEVENTEEN damned second lieutenants due in here today and assigned to Group. Somebody's messed up. Holy Shit, the colonel's gonna pop his gasket when he sees this! I know he don't know about this cause we were talking about manpower at Report an hour ago. Holy Shit! I gotta take this over to the Old Man!" Kicking the chair he'd been sitting in against the wall a good ten feet behind him, the SGM stood up and started moving toward the door, snatching his "Old Ironsides" fatigue cap from the rack as he passed it. "Whatever you do, Brinkley, don't tell Colonel Briggs about this crap until I get back from the Old Man's office!"

"Wait a minute, Sergeant Major," wailed Brinkley. "What do you want me to do with this Second Looie till you get back?"

"I don't care what you do with him. Invite him to have a cup of coffee. Ask him to have a seat. Send him over to sit awhile at the Cannoneers' Club. I don't care what you do with him; just don't let Briggs see him or his orders. I gotta get to the colonel's office before some more of these guys show up. Just do something with him!"

"Yes, Sergeant Major!" replied Brinkley, as the cruelest of cruel jokes began to take form in his mind. "I'll do something with him!"

LT Meadows was looking at the framed pictures of parachutes, and paratroopers, and C-119's, C-123's and a couple of C-130's on the wall of the office when Brinkley came back in. "Sorry to keep you waiting, Sir, and it seems I owe you an apology. They don't tell Spec 4's everything around here. The Sergeant Major said your orders are in good shape and you're right, you are supposed to report here. He said there's a whole bunch of new lieutenants due in today. My mistake, Sir, and I apologize. Just that we've never had second lieutenants before. This is all new to me. Anyway, they're expecting you, just didn't tell me about it. They're going to take care of your inprocessing a little later after you all sign in. You're a little early."

"Right, Brinkley, I wanted to be early," said Meadows. "And if they've only got one BOQ room on Post, I want that, too. When is this processing going to take place?"

"Just a little while, Sir, probably right before lunch. But they don't want you to have to hang around here. One of the officers has arranged for y'all to be his guests in his quarters until the processing can get started. Name's Colonel Briggs, and he's the Deputy CO of the Group. He had to go out for awhile, but he left word for the sergeant major to tell y'all to go on over to his quarters, Room 220 next door there, and he'll meet y'all there. And, Sir, the sergeant major said something about a refrigerator full of beer in the BOQ. Said the colonel said for y'all to help yourselves and make yourselves at home until he got back. It's that building right there, Sir," said Brinkley and he motioned toward the wooden barracks-turned-executive-BOQ next door. "I'll send your buddies over as soon as they arrive, and I'll tell Colonel Briggs y'all are here when he checks back in. Glad to have you join us and welcome to Special Forces, Lieutenant."

Meadows found the room just as Brinkley had directed. The door was unlocked, just as Brinkley had said. The refrigerator was full of Budweiser bottles, just as Brinkley had hinted. So Ed took out a bottle, bent the cap off with the churchkey hanging on the door, and loosened his tie just as Brinkley had offered. Taking a swig of the icy brew, he sat down in one of the big, overstuffed chairs of the sitting room portion of the apartment, and began looking at the current issue of Playboy he found lying nearby. They'd told him back at Ft. Sill that when he got to his regular unit, it would be different than signing in to Ft. Benning for Airborne and Ranger schools, or to Ft. Sill for Cannoneer's training, and, *believe you me,* thought Ed, *Viva la difference!* He wasn't even through with the beer before there was a gentle knock at the door, followed by Sam Dynamis, his classmate and a fellow second lieutenant, entering the room. "C'mon in, Sam," yelled Ed. "Have a brew. Make yourself at home. This 'Sneaky Pete' living is all right! Pull up a chair." Ed was quite the effusive host.

No one knew for sure why Briggs hated second lieutenants so. Some said it was because he had been one for so long. Others said it was because he had been busted as a enlisted man by a second lieutenant. Still others said it was because he was just a mean sonofabitch who hated second lieutenants. Whatever the reason, he could not tolerate the presence of these officers when a stray from the Division or

DIVARTY* wandered into the Group area. And whenever he got mad, he took it out on second lieutenants, usually at the Officers' Club, and usually at night. He was an obnoxious, abrasive, aggressive sonofabitch.

By 1100 hours, ten of the expected Lieutenants had checked in and Brinkley had dispatched them all to Briggs' quarters. The sergeant major had called to say that the Old Man was just as confused as everyone else, and was checking with DC on what the hell was going on. In the meantime, could Brinkley hold down the fort? He'd be back as soon as the Colonel found out what was going on. Yes sirree, Brinkley was doing just fine, Sergeant Major. We'll hold down the fort. The SP4 clerk-typist had no sooner hung up the phone than LTC Briggs entered the Group Administration office. "Where's Top?" he growled at no one in particular.

"He's gone up to Group," replied Brinkley.

"Tell him to get his ass over to my hooch when he gets back." Another growl. "We gotta do something about this frigging training schedule. Too much loose ends. Too many folks wandering around screwing up during duty hours." With that, he went stomping out and over to his BOQ. A minute passed. Then...it wasn't a growl or a moan; it was more like the scream of a panther in distress, or mad, or lost, or pierced to the soul with a flaming iron. They *knew* Briggs was in his apartment.

There was no TO&E slot in Special Forces for a second lieutenant. Just in case anyone in the world didn't already know that, all they had to do was wander onto Smoke Bomb Hill and the word would be shortly forthcoming, Ed was sure. He couldn't go to the mess hall for a cup of coffee without hearing it, he couldn't attend a formation without hearing it, he couldn't even take a crap without hearing it. That wasn't all he heard. He could still hear Colonel Briggs' lambasting that first day, I mean, a real bomb blast! He thought the guy was going to stroke out the way he turned red and the veins bulged in his temples and neck, and even across his forehead. Ed knew, for that forehead had been very close to him for a long time during Briggs' tirade. Couldn't figure out why he'd been singled out from among the seventeen Dumb-Ass Second Lieutenants, or "DASL's" as the

---

*DIVARTY - Division Artillery

lieutenants now referred to themselves. Briggs might have picked on Ed because he was the one who'd shouted for him to drive on in and have a brew, or a shot of the Colonel's whiskey they'd found, pull up a seat and wait for Good Ol' LTC Briggs, who was hosting this fete! Heck, Ed thought it was another classmate arriving; he didn't know it was *the Colonel*. He knew now, and he doubted he'd ever forget.

After Briggs had regained control of himself and the group commander had arrived with the sergeant major to restrain him; sanity prevailed briefly and the group commander, Colonel Remington, had told the lieutenants there was no TO&E slot for a second lieutenant in Group (again), and he'd see to it that they got whatever assignments they desired if they'd just request their orders be rescinded. Seemed like the thing to do at the time, but after discussing it with his fellow DASL's over a pitcher of beer at the O Club Annex later; Ed decided he was going to become a Sneaky Pete, whatever in hell that was, and he wasn't leaving. As a matter of fact, every one of the DASL's decided to stay. Their arrival had evidently been unexpected, but the lieutenants really didn't know what to expect from Group, either.

Ed had been heading for an 8" Self-Propelled Howitzer unit in Germany when he finished his training at the Artillery Center at Ft. Sill, OK. It was a "leg"...non-airborne slot, but that was alright with him. He wanted to get to Europe and see the frauleins. About a week before their class, 1961-2, graduated, their Tac Officer, Captain Bjornstad, had called a special class meeting to make an announcement. The Department of the Army had a special requirement for up to 21 second lieutenants to join Special Forces. He didn't exactly know what Special Forces was, but he'd found a newspaper clipping—a magazine, actually, which described the unit as a new kind of commando, or something on that order. It was an Airborne slot, at Ft. Bragg, and was a Permanent Change of Station (PCS). Anyone interested could talk to him after the meeting, but he had to send the list in tomorrow night, so it was a short-fuze opportunity. That meant you had to decide right away. Everybody laughed and started yelling, "AIRBORNE, ALL THE WAY" and no one volunteered, but after the meeting was over, Ed went up to read the article.

There were a bunch of guys reading the article. The Special Forces were the guys who used to wear green berets as a special designation, but the rumor was that they had screwed up the maneuvers in Louisiana in '54 or '56, or sometime so badly that they'd lost the berets and had never gotten them back. They'd nearly ceased to exist, but had somehow managed to stay alive on a small and very quiet scale. They were referred to as, "Sneaky Petes" and the article said they were "good soldiers, fine cutthroats". *What the hell*, Ed thought, he could use the extra $110 per month jump pay and could always get to Europe later. He was the seventh to sign up. Seventeen volunteered all together. All were airborne qualified: prefix 7-on their Military Occupational Speciality (MOS) code, and all were Small-Unit Artillery Leaders, MOS 1193, so they were all listed as 71193's. The slot at Bragg was for a 31542. Ed had no idea what the prefix 3-was, but the 1542 was Infantry Small Unit Leader...a Grunt, a Gravelcruncher, a Beetlesmasher. Oh, well, it couldn't possibly be worse than Ranger School and he'd survived that, even finished 6th in his class of 96 motivated lieutenants. So, here he was and here he was going to stay.

When government bureaucracy get into a situation out of the ordinary, they begin the "Stall and Shift" maneuver. Make the offending party fill out some more forms; tell them they have to be in triplicate, tell 'em to come back tomorrow, and then send 'em to another department, cause you don't deal with that here. That's what Group tried first when they tried to get the young officers to request reassignment. No dice. Okay, if the S&S maneuver doesn't work, send them to school. That's what happened next. Sheffield and Ridgeway were dispatched to the Language School at Monterrey, California, for a year to learn Swahili; Dixon and Temple and Hooper were sent to Jumpmaster School in the Division; Wheat went off to Ft. Holabird, Maryland, for an Intelligence course of some type; Spivet and Everett and Goings and Bowlin started the Special Warfare Officers' Course that was just beginning; and Prusser, Vincent, Hickman, and Adams were dispatched to the Uwharrie National Forest Area for an FTX—a Field Training Exercise, which seemed like a good deal except they were attached to the Aggressor Forces—a Company from the 82d, and were only observers. Meadows, Castlemount, and Smith were given their choices of which of the basic skills Enlisted Men's course they wanted to attend: Weapons, Communications, Medical, Demolitions, or Operations and Intelligence. Each course was three weeks long and all were at Ft. Bragg. Ed chose Weapons, and the class was starting this morning—his third day at Ft. Bragg. A Sergeant Kelso was instructing:

"Men, welcome to yoah weapons training indoctrination course. We are pleased to have one of da new lieutenants in our course with us this cycle. We ain't never had an officer attend dis course before because dere is no TO&E slot for a second lieutenant in Group. We'll try to keep it simple so da lieutenant can keep up with us." (Laughter, not from Ed). "What y'all will get out of dis course is determined by what y'all put into it. You screw-up and don't pay attention, and y'all will get yoah ass killed and probably some of dose around you; PLUS, yoah ass will be sent to a leg outfit so fast you won't even have time to finish dying." (He made the "leg" assignment seem a lot worse than the dying part.) "We will present to you da basic US and foreign weapons you can expect to encounter if you are inserted on an Unconventional Warfare mission anywhere in da world. You will disassemble dese weapons, clean dese weapons, fire dese weapons, and fix dese weapons in case of minor malfunctions. Y'all will graduate with passing grades or I will personally kick yoah ass out of Group and on to a 'leg' outfit in Corps. Except da lieutenant. There ain't no TO&E slot for a second lieutenant in Group, so I will allow da colonel to kick his ass. Any querstions? Okay men, off yoah ass and on yoah feet. You, too, Lieutenant. Move into da building in a rapid, but orderly manner and find you a seat dat doesn't already have someone's ass in it. Two men to a table. Lieutenant, you'll work with Sgt. Vickers. We ain't never had an officer take dis course before, but I t'ink Vickers will be able to help you. Alright, MOVE OUT!" (Hell, with a command like that, it was a wonder the pine trees didn't move a little bit, too!) There was one other thing Ed had noticed. Brinkley, up at the Orderly Room, was the only E-4 he'd seen; everyone else was an E-5 or higher. And there weren't very many youngsters. There weren't a lot of native-born Americans, either, and if you didn't speak with a gutteral or Latin accent, you were definitely in the minority.

Lying there on the table in front of Ed and Vickers was a Kalishnikov assault rifle, better known as an AK-47, country of origin—one of the Eastern European nations, but actually a product of the Soviet Union. Nothing like starting off with the prime weapon of the prime enemy. Ed had never held an AK before, although he was familiar with it from various places he'd been over the last couple of years at the Academy and in his travels during the summers. He picked it up and was surprised at how front-heavy it was. "Pretty good weapon, Sir," offered Vickers. "You'll find a lot of them when you get over to Boogeyland." There, he'd said it: *Boogeyland*. Ever since arriving here, Ed and the other DASL's had heard an undercurrent about the operation in "Boogeyland." But none of them had been able to find out exactly who, or which land was the boogey. Between them they had tried to find out from various sources exactly where this operation was, and, better yet, *WHAT* it was, but to date they'd drawn a blank. On the spur of the moment, Ed decided to try a new tactic. He knew it was Asia somewhere, and the smart money said it was either Taiwan or Korea. He played a hunch.

"Yeah, my Dad made it to Korea about ten years ago, and he said the gooks were using a lot of AK's then. In fact," said Ed, waxing bold, "he said that more of their troops had AK's than had Simonov's."

"That may be, I don't know about Korea. I ain't never been there. And I don't know about Simonov's, either, cause I ain't never seen one," said Vickers, "but in Boogeyland, there ain't a lot of guys with AK's; just a few. But you'll see 'em."

Scratch Korea. Looked like Taiwan, for sure.

During the next two weeks, Ed learned more about the disassembly and reassembly of small arms than he'd have ever learned even if he'd memorized WHB Smith's book, **Small Arms of the World**. That was their textbook and he'd bought a copy at the Post Book Store; but by far, the majority of knowledge disseminated from the cadre was obviously gleaned from the beds of their personal knowledge. Russian, French, German, U.S., British, Czech, even some Japanese weapons were introduced, samples were provided for each pair of trainees, and the rudiments of use and any idiosyncracies gone over. At the end of each day there was both a written and a practical test on each weapon covered. Ed was a good and willing student, and he did well on all the tests. More importantly, he *knew* these weapons. He studied about them at night and practiced on them in the daytime. He got to be quite adept at weapons' handling. At no time, however, day or night, did he approach the level of familiarity with them Vickers displayed. That guy was a whiz. He never hesitated a second when disassembling one of them, never faltered, never dropped a piece.

He was always in command of his weapon. "Damn, Sargeant, you're good on these pieces!" commented Ed one day.

"Aw, hell, Sir, I ain't so good. Just that I did this all day, every day, for six months last trip to Boogeyland and it gets to be old hat."

"Say, Sarge, do you speak Chinese, too?"

"Hell, naw, but you don't need that in Boogeyland, either."

Scratch Taiwan.

They went out on the ranges the third week. All day, every day, ten hours a day, five days of the week, they fired weapons. They fired till they got tired. Ammunition didn't seem to be a problem; you wanted some more, they gave you some more. They fired the Brno and the Bren, the Maxim and the Madsen, the AR-15 and the AK-47, the Chatellerault and the Schmeisser. They fired full-automatic and semi-automatic. In groups and individually. They fired and fired and fired. Nearly everyone in the class was a "gun nut" of some degree, but when they finally shut down the firing line at 1700 hrs on Friday, even the most gung-ho had shot enough for one week. Ed had several weapons that impressed him. The Russian Mosin-Negant carbine kicked the hell out of him and he quit shooting it after only five rounds. The American BAR was a fine weapon, shot smoothly, but was heavy, same for the British Bren. But he really liked the AK. Not the Soviet's PPS nor the PPSh; they were nothing but junk, but the AK was nice. Too bad the bad guys had it. While they policed up the brass and gathered the weapons together, Ed thought he'd try Vickers one last time to reveal Boogeyland. "Say, Sarge, they don't make you pick the brass up off the beaches in Boogeyland, do they?"

"Don't guess so, since there ain't a frigging beach in the whole damn country."

Now we're making progress. The country was landlocked. Back to the Goode's World atlas tonight.

Several hours later, after a cleaning session during which no one was interested in talking about anything except "gimme some powder solvent," or "throw me some fucking rags," and an occasional "Fuck!", Ed was all cleaned and shined and shaven and smelling like a canoe, or kayak, or dory, or some other small boat. He got the Southern Comfort bottle, poured a glassful, and recapped it. Then he added a lime Fizzie, waited for it to stop fizzing before he sat down with his drink, his clean body, and his Goode's World Atlas to do some research. According to Goode, there are only six really landlocked countries in Asia. Assuming that you could believe Vickers, and Ed believed you could, Boogeyland had to be one of those countries. There was Afghanistan, but the people there are really Arabs, or at least Middle Eastern, and the natives in Boogeyland were called "slopes" or "slant-eyes" by the old heads, so Afghanistan was out. There was Tibet, Nepal, Sikkim, and Bhutan. Ed didn't know much about the folks there, they might be "slopes", but he doubted it. Besides, you don't think of jungle when you think of Tibet, and Boogeyland had jungle. That left Laos. Laos, why, hell, yes; it had to be Laos!

For his big research paper his last year at West Point, Ed had done a study on Laos and arrived at the conclusion that we could be involved in a war in Laos within the next decade unless things changed in the international relations arena. He had failed on that paper because his instructor said he arrived at an invalid conclusion. The S.O.B.! Unknown to either of them, at the very moment he was failing on his paper, U.S. troops were engaged in some kind of surreptious mission in Laos that smacked of warfare. *IF* Boogeyland was Laos, and *if* Vickers wasn't lying, and *if* a lot of other things. Undeterred by the "ifs," Ed dug out his notebooks from his senior year in the bookbox under his bed and found the one with the failing paper in it. Refilling his Fizzie and Comfort, he was up until the wee hours refreshing his memory about the little nation of Laos, locked away over there between the nasty neighbors of China, Vietnam, Cambodia, Burma, and Thailand. *Damn!* thought Ed. *Tomorrow night at Ronnie's I'm gonna blow their minds. That bunch of DASL's are gonna wonder where the hell I found out about Boogeyland.* Revelling in his impending triumph, Ed spilled the Fizzie and Comfort and ruined the failing paper on Laos forever. No matter. He'd gotten all he wanted out of it, anyway.

It was Saturday night, and that meant it was time for all the DASL's, all single, to gather at the Officers' Club annex called, Ronnie's, and to act like they were the epitome of the swinging bachelor as depicted in *Playboy*. The truth of the matter was that each of them was pretty lonesome; they knew hardly anyone at Ft. Bragg or in Fayetteville; and their busy schedules of schooling pretty much kept them so busy they weren't able to meet many people. So, instead of dating, or running off to DC, or even to Myrtle Beach, they met at Ronnie's and tried to impress all their classmates in the Division who were, they were positive, living a much more mundane existence than the troops from Smoke Bomb Hill. They would laugh loudly, and let the word, "Boogeyland" slip out loudly enough for their classmates to hear, but certainly not loudly enough to cause any revelations. Heck, if you didn't know what Boogeyland was, it was hard to leak information out on it. Until tonight. This was to be the night of the "big revelation."

Ed felt like he was St. John on the island of Patmos because he knew so much about Laos. He waited until all the quorum of DASL's had assembled before he called them politely together: "Hey, Shit Heads, hang your knobs over here and give a listen. Are there any Division Poopy-Troopers around?" he asked, and after they had ascertained that there were not, he continued, with the refinement befitting one of the Guardians of America, "While you fuckers have been fucking off all over this post, sucking your thumbs or some other appendage, I have been doing a lot of fucking listening to some of the old heads who have let me in on a thing or two." The reference to the Old Heads was, of course, a lie, for the veterans of Special Forces had no more to do with Ed than they had to to do with any of the rest of the DASL's. But it had the desired effect; you could almost see the ears prick up as his fellow travellers leaned forward to listen. "First of all, you Shit Heads have got to keep your fucking mouths shut as to where you heard this cause I could be in deep shit if the heads found out I told y'all."

"Cut out the crap, Meadows," growled Smith. "Do you know something or are you fixing to blow smoke up our butts?"

"Okay, okay, listen to this and tell me what you think. First of all, the reason we ain't been able to find out nothing about Boogeyland is because we ain't been listening to the right people. Now, this week while I was at the range firing weapons, I got the straight stuff." (Ed was determined to get as much prestige out of this event as he could.) "We know that Boogeyland is in Asia, right?" Nods of assent. "Okay, we also know that it's got jungle, the natives are slant eyes, and it goes through the monsoon cycle. That ain't all. I found out that the place is landlocked, the Mekong runs through it (he lied; Ed ASSUMED the Mekong ran through it), and it has a lot of mountains. Okay, DASL's, where does that have to be? It has to be Laos!

That's right, Laos! And listen to this; the country has fewer than 100 miles of paved roads, no railroads at all, both a king and a premier, has a three-headed government, and is the location for the largest opium growing operation in the world. The United Nations estimated they exported 22 TONS of heroin illegally last year. I found out a lot of other stuff if you're still interested." Ed leaned back to enjoy his moment of glory. It was Smith who spoke again.

"Old heads, my eye. You sound just like that monograph you messed up on last year at school. I typed it for you, and I've heard every word of this crap before. Who the hell do you think you're kidding? Your idea about Laos sounds good, but there ain't no old head who told you shit. You just warmed up that same crock of crap you tried to sell to ole Captain Karney up at 'Woo Poo,' and I might add, you failed miserably, just like you're failing now. Old heads my ass. Meadows, you're as full of shit as a Christmas turkey!" (Peals and gales of laughter...not from Ed.) "Hell, Meadows," continued Smith, "I'm gonna buy you a beer for the tallest tale of 1961! Old heads...you bald-faced liar!"

Ed still liked his idea about Laos. Damn, he'd forgotten about Smith typing his paper! He decided that if he was going to be a good liar in the future, he was going to have to learn to type.

The summer of 1961 passed rapidly for Meadows. Following the three weeks of weapons training, he went through another three-week cycle, of Medical training this time, and he was just as fascinated by what he learned there as he was by the previous cycle. He learned that a fully-trained Special Forces medic was actually qualified far beyond what he would have expected. There were instances mentioned of medics "in the field" (on a mission) actually doing appendectomies and the patient survived, and amputations were evidently commonplace occurences among the indigenous troops they dealt with.

Little by little, Ed was gaining a great deal of respect for the members of this elite force he had joined. Then there were the airborne operations: jumps, as they were called. Nearly every day of the week there was a jump for one of the units of the Group, and "strap-hangers"—personnel who wanted to jump but were not on the manifest, were always welcome and would be added to the manifest and allowed to jump if there were any spare chutes. There were always spare chutes. It got to be a macho thing among the DASL's to see who could get in the most jumps. You couldn't miss any of your training, but since all the jumps were in the evening, if you were willing to stay up late, you could get in a jump at least every week.

You needed 30 jumps, plus Jumpmaster school, plus two years on Airborne status to get your Senior wings, and Ed easily had the required number of jumps before the summer was over. It was on one of these straphanger outings that Ed saw his first streamer. They had jumped from a C-119, a real beautiful experience, and had rolled up their chutes out on Sicily drop zone and gathered over to one side to await the deuce-and-a-half trucks for the ride back to post, when a formation of C-130's came flying over the drop zone at 1250 feet. The Division was having a jump, and the sight of several hundred parachutes in the sky all at once was awesome. Special Forces jumps were one plane-load, about 40 troopers at a time. As they watched the sky filling with chutes, one of the chutes failed to inflate and they watched in horror as the trooper fell earthward at three times the survivable rate. Ed, along with everyone else around him, yelled futilely for the trooper to activate his reserve, but he never did, and the sickening sound of his body smashing into the ground was something Ed would never forget. Sometimes, when all your jumps were going well, it was hard to remember why you got extra money for being a paratrooper, but the element of danger was real and ever-present. That was a sick, sick sound. Meadows jumped again the next night, and, later he wondered why he felt compelled to jump again so soon. Daring death, probably. It was good to be immortal, even if it wasn't forever.

Ed matriculated through the Special Warfare Officers Course, much to the displeasure of LTC Briggs. As fall rolled around, another season of Army football began. He and the other DASL's had begun to be accepted by the NCO's of the Seventh Group. They'd also learned that Boogeyland was, in fact, Laos, and that it did export 22 tons of illegal heroin per year. They had also learned what "the cage" was.

Situated right in the middle of Smoke Bomb Hill, surrounded by a double fence of ten-foot high barbed wire, was an enclave of three barracks buildings, an Orderly Room, and a small mess hall. Most of the time that was all there was, but about every two weeks, the place became occupied. You could tell because there were MP's patrolling between the fences 24 hours a day, spotlights all over the place all night, and no one was seen entering or leaving the compound. Then there would be a night when some covered trucks would back up to the gate, troops and baggage would be loaded on, and the next day the MP's would be gone, the lights would be off, and another team or teams, would have departed on a mission somewhere in the world. Meadows yearned to be in "the cage."

It was a brisk autumn Saturday morning when Meadows was introduced to "the Bear Pit." They'd had a called Company formation, something rare for Saturdays, and after a few announcements, the Sergeant Major had taken the stand to boom out the news that they were having "Company Stakes" that day. All the NCO's had whooped and hollered, and begun to clap and whistle. Ed had no idea what to expect. Then the SGM continued that the last man in the pit would get a three-day pass, and everyone who participated would get free beer as long as the kegs he motioned toward lasted. There were six kegs. That's a lot of beer. "Okay, men, everyone to the pit and anyone who don't want to play can pick up his transfer to Division at the Orderly Room. With a roar, the formation disbanded and flowed toward a large hole in the ground, about six feet deep, vertical sides, circular in shape, maybe thirty feet across. Ed flowed with them, not so much because he wanted to, but because he had no choice, he was carried along. Into the hole the crowd jumped—a hundred men stuffed into a muddy hole. The sergeant major yelled for silence. "Okay, men, listen to the company commander!"

LTC Askins, a stringbean of a man with grey hair cropped close to his head, was someone with whom Ed had little contact and hardly knew. He didn't especially desire contact with the company commander. For all Ed knew, all Lt. Colonels were like Briggs, and he'd already met him. "Men," began Askins, "we don't want anyone killed and try not to break anyone. Here's your chance for three days of wine, women, and song at government expense. Try not to get thrown out of the hole. Okay, Sergeant Major, let the games begin."

Damn, thought Ed, *you'd think this was the Olympics.*

The sergeant major blew a whistle, and all hell broke loose. Bodies went flying everywhere. There were grunts, and smacks, and groans, and yells, and cussing, and hollering like Meadows had never experienced before. It became obvious very quickly that this was not a gentleman's game and it was also obvious there were no rules. The object seemed to be that you were to throw everybody else out of the hole while trying to prevent being thrown out yourself. Having survived the initial upheaval, Ed teamed with an unknown giant of a man who was having a lot of success tossing people out. Together, they defended and attacked as an unspoken team, and though each was soon bloodied and bruised, the crowd in the pit got a lot thinner and still the two of them remained. It was tough going, non-stop, brutal, but Meadows survived and fought on. Finally, there were only three men left in the pit: Meadows, the Giant, and another Sergeant who looked a lot like Goliath. "Get his legs, Lieutenant," whispered Giant, and Ed drove a picture-perfect tackle into Goliath's thighs. Goliath grabbed Ed's chest and began to crush the life out of him very rapidly. That's when Giant hit Goliath right on the jaw with as hard a right hand punch as Ed had ever heard delivered. Goliath sagged, then collapsed in a heap, smothering Meadows. Ed squirmed out of the grasp of the fallen Philistine, and between the two of them, he and Giant rolled the unconscious form onto the lip of the pit. Now there were two.

Ed backed off a little bit to face Giant. *Sonofabitch, this guy was huge*, and, as experience had shown, he was also mean. There was no way Ed was going to throw this guy anywhere, but, dammit, he could at least put up a fight. Recalling the sound of the right hand punch, Ed assumed his best "On Guard" position from Ranger school and prepared for hand to hand combat. Giant chuckled, brushed aside the side-wheeling kick Ed tried to deliver, grabbed him by the scruff of the neck and the seat of his pants, and ignominiously tossed Ed far out of the pit. He hit the ground with a thud as the crowd roared its approval, and Giant leapt out of the pit and raised his hands in triumph. Amid the cheers of the Company members, Giant quaffed the beer someone handed him, then someone handed him another. Walking over to the battered, bruised and beaten lieutenant, Giant held the beer toward him. "Have a beer, Lieutenant. You done good." The bruises lasted for several days, the aches even longer, but neither lasted as long as the glow of pride Ed felt after that Saturday. Giant was one of the old heads, and Giant said he done good. To hell with the English lessons, the conjugations, and the grammar, when you done good, dammit, *you done good*.

There was a brisk crispness in the air and you could see the little clouds of steam escaping your mouth with every breath as you finished the morning run around the perimeter of the hill that bright October morning. Ed was panting, as he was wont to do, for running in any form or fashion had never been his forte. Even though the run had been only a couple of miles, he hated beginning it earlier, he hated doing it, and he loved stopping when they finished. Actually, he may have stopped a few feet short of the finish line, but not so short as to attract attention. When you're five-foot, ten-inches tall and weigh 180 pounds with a lot of the weight below the waist level, running isn't usually your forte. "LT Meadows!" yelled the sergeant major. "The Old Man wants to see you in his office NOW!"

Damn. Ed knew he had stopped a few feet short on the run, but he didn't think it was *that* short. What the hell can they do to you for stopping short on the run...make you an aide to Briggs? Lieutenant colonels didn't have aides, but, then, they'd never had second lieutenants in Group before, and there was no TO&E slot for a second lieutenant, so that's probably exactly what they intended to do. " 'What did you do in the war, Daddy?' I was an aide to the meanest sonofabitch that ever lived because there was no TO&E slot for me anywhere else in the world." Ed took a few deep breaths to try and catch his breath, entered the orderly room, cast a glance at the sergeant major who motioned him on over to the colonel's door. Then the SGM stuck his head in the room and announced, "Sir, Lieutenant Meadows is here now. He just finished PT and ain't got no clothes on."

"Send him in, Sergeant Major," came the muffled reply. "And close the door after him."

That's it. Aide to Briggs. Probably assigned to the division to boot. All because of a few feet on the run. Ed entered the commander's office, approached to within two paces of the front of the desk, snapped to attention in his gym shorts, tee shirt, and combat boots, and rendered a smart, precise, hand salute. "Lieutenant Meadows reporting, Sir."

LTC Askins returned the salute. "Stand at ease, Lieutenant," he said and Ed assumed the position of Parade Rest smartly. "Relax, Lieutenant," and Meadows let one shoulder sag slightly. *How the hell can you relax when you're about to be sent to Devil's Island to be the aide of Satan himself? Stupid run.* "Don't you have a Top Secret clearance?" asked the colonel.

"It is still being processed, Sir," said Ed. "The last I heard I was still Secret with an Interim Top Secret."

"It's final now," said Askins. "What I'm going to tell you now is classified Top Secret, so listen and act accordingly. Use this information on a 'Need To Know' basis only." *Who could possibly need to know about Satan's Gofer?* "I'm sure that you've heard a lot of talk about Boogeyland, and I'm sure that you think you know a hell of a lot about our operation there," continued the colonel, "but what I'm going to tell you now is new poop that we just received from DA. As you probably already know, we are training troops of the Forces Armee Royale in Laos for their conflict against the communist Pathet Lao under the name of 'White Star Mobile Training Team.' Until now, our operation has been rather small, one B team and four A teams in country, but DA has just directed us to increase our commitment there to a C team, three B teams, and twelve A teams. Frankly, we are not prepared to meet that requirement. We simply don't have enough trained troops, what with our other covert commitments. Our Company—A Company, has been given the mission of training troops in a hurry to meet this requirement. We'll meet that requirement here at Bragg. We figure we can turn out two A teams every two weeks ready for Laos. In a month, we should be able to increase that to four teams every two weeks. We've decided that, with this tight a schedule, we need a shake-down exercise for the teams before we send them over there. So, we're setting up a Maneuver Field Control at Eglin Air Force Base, Hurlburt Field. Major Galahad Kreeger will be in charge of this MFC and he flew down there with the advance party yesterday.

"You, Lieutenant Prusser, and two non-coms will be assigned to the MFC to act as indigenous personnel on the ground to guide the teams through ten days of a practice exercise when they're rotated down there. It will be a TDY assignment of indeterminate length, but less than six months. You need to get your gear together and be ready to leave here in the morning at 0600 hrs for the trip down there. You can go by POV* and we'll buy the gas. I don't care if you ride together or separately, you and Prusser, but the Sergeants will take care of themselves. Now, Meadows, we never had Second Lieutenants in Group before, so a lot of people will be watching how you do to see if you mess up. Most of them *want* you to mess up. Sending you

---

*POV - Privately Owned Vehicle

there was not my idea—I think you'll screw up all over the place, but the colonel says that since we have no TO&E slots for second lieutenants, this will be a good place to hide you. Take off the rest of the day and get ready. Sergeant Major will take care of getting your orders cut and they'll be ready in the morning. And, Lieutenant, the other DASL's have no need to know about this assignment. That's all."

Ed snapped to attention and saluted. Askins waved a reply. Meadows turned on his heel, walked over to open the door, and left. "Leave the door open, Lieutenant," hollered Askins. Ed did. He walked out of the orderly room into the brisk morning and found the sergeant major standing on the steps.

"Lieutenant," said the top, "don't let the Old Man fool you. It was his idea to send you to Florida. A lot of the old heads around here think you DASL's have done a damn fine job so far, and they're pulling for you. I personally picked you, and I don't make mistakes. I liked the Bear Pit. Give 'em hell, Lieutenant, and, Lieutenant, DON'T FUCK UP!" The eternal salutation of DASLhood.

2

The Convoy Commander

There was one change Ed discovered when he arrived at the company area at 0530 hrs the next morning. The MFC had called the previous evening and given the company a shopping list of the supplies and equipment they needed down in Florida, so instead of two POV's making the trip down, there would also be three 2 1/2-ton trucks, a jeep, and a three-quarter with a radio van on the back. Plus, two 2 1/2-ton trailers and fifteen enlisted men and non-coms. LTC Askins called the two lieutenants into his office. "Which one of you guys has date of rank?" he asked.

"We have the same date of rank, Sir," answered Prusser.

"Okay, then, I'm appointing you as the convoy commander today, and LT Meadows will be commander tomorrow. You'll RON (remain over night) at Ft. Gordon. Top has called down there and you'll be met by the MP's when you get there and escorted to an area with a barracks to spend the night. The MP's will provide security for your vehicles. Here's a credit card for fuel for all the vehicles, including your cars. Supply your own rations: in other words, buy your own meals. I wouldn't eat at the mess hall at Gordon, even if they offer. Despite the fact that anyone in the world can see this convoy, and there isn't much to see, remember that your mission is classified Top Secret, so don't be talking to anybody, especially the bunch of legs at Ft. Gordon. Any questions?" There were none. "Okay, Lieutenant

Prusser, your convoy is due to leave at 0600. You'd better get your butt in gear. And, Lieutenant...(Ed knew what was coming before Askins ever mouthed the words)...don't fuck up."

"Yes, SIR," replied Prusser, his jaw tight, his lips pursed, his body standing at rigid attention. Ed knew that Prusser was taking his position of authority very seriously. They left the Orderly Room and Meadows asked what plan Prusser had for the convoy. "I think I can handle it," replied the fellow lieutenant-turned convoy commander. "If you'll just get your vehicle ready to go and bring up the rear, I'll get the rest of the men organized and select the route. I'll lead the way. Too bad they don't have radios for POV's so we could communicate."

"Yep, too bad. Okay, I'll ride drag. I figure I can keep up with a duece-and-a-half." Ed could see there was no sense in trying to help Prusser, for anything he did would be interpreted as a threat to the "Convoy Commander's" authority. It looked like a long day dawning. Ed cranked up his Valiant and drove around to the motor pool area. There was a lot of activity here, for, in addition to this convoy leaving, there were the usual training requirements of the company going on. He parked outside the gate, turned off the engine, and waited. He could see Prusser striding around inside the compound, erect, stiff, in his most Teutonic manner. Actually, Dan Prusser wasn't a bad fellow. He had been in Company C-2 at West Point, and Ed was in D-2, so they had all their classes together for the whole four years. Prusser was from New Jersey and usually pretty quiet, but always took his assignments extremely seriously. The pursed lip, set-jaw look was nothing new to Ed. They were not close friends, but four years of college, Ranger School, Airborne School, and five months of Artillery School together had made them at least close acquaintances.

Meadows was from Memphis, Tennessee. Actually, he was born in Arkansas, had lived in New Orleans, but had spent his high school years in Memphis attending South Side High School, so he called Memphis home. Besides, his folks still lived there. He was a Son of the South, and had come under a great deal of criticism for the fervor with which he defended the Confederacy, Ole Miss Rebels, and Dixie. But, Ed reasoned, if you can't be proud of your heritage, what can you be proud of? Prusser was not fervent in his admiration of the Union during their study of the War Between the States, but he did insist that it had been the Civil War. He also said it was history, when everyone in Memphis would gladly have pointed out that they had only paused to reload.

Right at 0600 hrs, Prusser's blue Falcon pulled out of the Motor Pool. The 3/4-ton with the radio van and a 3/4-ton trailer was next. All the canvas was down on the trailer, so it was impossible to see what it was carrying. Next came a 2 1/2-ton with an engineer boat inverted on its bed and looking like a great, green whale. This truck was pulling a shrouded trailer and was also belching black smoke, lurching and grinding and coughing. It was going to be a long day. The next truck and trailer was surprisingly normal in its appearance; next came a 2 1/2-ton without a trailer, but with its curtains drawn; and, finally, the 1/4-ton, jeep, and a 1/4-ton trailer. Meadows noted the disparity between what Askins had said would be going and what was actually going, but he had learned enough about the workings of Group not to be surprised. As the jeep passed, the driver waved, and Ed recognized him as SGT Vickers, from Weapons training. He waved back as he started his engine, Vickers smiled real big, flipped Ed the finger, and the Great Whale Convoy (Top Secret) was on its way to the land of sunshine, beaches, broads, and beer.

It was a long day, and it was only noon. Belcher, the whale-carrying truck, was capable of about ten miles between breakdowns. Meadows found out the reason for the jeep trailer at the first stop. It carried spare parts for the vehicles—particularly Belcher. SFC Shoulders was driving Belcher, and he was some sort of shade-tree mechanic. He crawled out of the cab, flipped open the hood, and began to dig around in the truck's innards. He also began to cuss. Now, Ed had heard sailors cuss when he was aboard the Tarawa, and the Iwo Jima, and the Saipan: carriers that he had spent time on in training in the past, and sailors could cuss. Sergeants in the Army cuss pretty well, too, but for pure poetry in motion—absolute purity of form in the art of cussing, nobody, but nobody, surpassed a good truck mechanic. Shoulders was a genius, both at fixing Belcher, and at cussing. He only took about twenty minutes to get the 6x6 running again that first time, but the trail of black smoke from Belcher's stack continued. The second stop lasted a little longer, the third even longer, and after six hours, the Great Whale Convoy (Top Secret) was exactly 150 miles from Bragg. As Shoulders was exercising his art forms, Prusser came back to where

The Convoy Commander

Ed was chewing on roadside weeds and talking with SGT Vickers. "Lieutenant Meadows, could I speak to you a moment?"

Lieutenant Meadows? What's with this crap? "Yes, Sir, Convoy Commander. Excuse me, Sergeant, I have to talk with the Convoy Commander." Rising to his feet, he walked with Prusser a few meters away from where Vickers remained sitting in the grass eating a weed.

"I think we need to be official around the men," began Prusser.

"Bullcrap."

"Well, I think we should, so I would appreciate it if you would honor my desires while I am Convoy Commander."

"Bullcrap."

"We haven't made as much progress as I had planned," said Convoy Commander, "and I think the men need a break for lunch. Sergeant Shoulders says he'll have the 2 1/2-ton truck running again in about twenty minutes. I'm going to drive on ahead to the next town and find us a suitable place to eat. When the vehicle is fixed, you lead the troops on into town and I'll meet you at the city limits and guide them the rest of the way."

"Good idea, Dan, I'll do just that. See you in a half-hour or so." With that, Convoy Commander strode away and marched back to the front on the convoy where his steed awaited. Soon his Falcon disappeared from sight. *That guy is a pain in the behind,* thought Ed as he rejoined Vickers, *but his ideas are right.*

Not long after their conversation, Belcher belched a cloud of especially dense smoke, coughed, chugged, burped, and then began a rhythmic rumbling that signified its willingness to continue the journey. Ed drove Arvak—his affectionately named Valiant, along the convoy, telling the drivers to follow him. When he got to SFC Shoulders, he saw that a lot of the dense black smoke had settled on the Sergeant's face. "Follow me, Sarge, as fast as your great green whale can swim."

Prusser was right by a sign which read, "City Limits." He led them to a little restaurant in the heart of this small South Carolina town, and when they had parked, the majority of the town square's parking places were filled. The men crawled out of the trucks and strolled into the building. It was a nice, clean little dining room, about ten tables with red-checkered tablecloths, linen napkins, and a couple of clean, but extremely homely waitresses. When they asked for your order, there was molasses all over their words. Ed loved it. He and Prusser sat together, along with Shoulders and SSG Peter J. Brinkman, the only black soldier in their detachment. When it came time for Brinkman to order, the waitress sweetly informed him that he would have to eat in the kitchen. Ed had a sick feeling crawl into the pit of his stomach. He looked at Prusser. Prusser looked at him. Brinkley started to get up. "Well, let's go, men," said Ed, blatantly usurping the Convoy Commander's authority, " we're going to eat in the kitchen."

"Oh, land naw, all y'all don't have to go, just the colored man," giggled the waitress.

"Honey," replied Ed, "we're all colored. He's black, we're pink, or brown, but we're all colored, and we're all eating together." Turning to Prusser, Ed continued, "Lieutenant, is there a drive-in place around here?"

"There sure is, and that's where we're going." Assuming his mantle of authority once again, Dan led the exodus from the restaurant to a place on the far side of town called, *McDonalds*, which bragged of over 2 million served. They ate at picnic tables in front of the drive-in, and they made it to Gordon before dark. The rest of the day went better than the first had gone. But for Ed, it had been a tragedy. He was so proud of the South and of being a Southerner, and he wanted everyone to see that it wasn't really the bad place so many media people called it. He had never dreamed there would be this kind of trouble, never for one minute expected something like this to happen. In all his life, he had never heard something like this said before. Never. But, as he mulled it over in his mind during the afternoon, maybe the reason why he'd never heard it before was because he hadn't been listening. The thought that his beloved South still permitted such to occur was making Ed literally sick to his stomach. He still loved the South, was still proud of his Southern heritage, but, to tell the truth, a little bit of the Glory of the Grey died that day, slain on a restaurant-battlefield in South Carolina.

In their barracks building at Ft. Gordon, the trucks secured outside with periodic MP patrols, most of the men were showered and cleaned up and sitting around swapping lies before turning in for the night. There were no sheets on the bunks, nor were there any mattresses. No matter, they'd sleep on the floor with a blanket apiece and be content. Meadows had found a corner bunk and had spread out his blanket next to it. A trip is hard work. It is easier to hike with a rucksack all day than it is to ride in a vehicle, any vehicle. SFC Shoulders ambled over and hunkered down. "Lieutenant, we seen what you did today, and I thought I'd let you know we support you one-hundred-per-cent. There's a lot of us from the South, but we got no time for that kind of shit. Brinkman won't never say nothing to you, but he appreciated it, too, and he won't forget. Donnie Vickers is a good friend of mine and he says you might make a good officer someday. Welcome to Group," he concluded, extending his hand. Ed shook the proferred hand and replied.

"Thanks, Sarge, I appreciate that."

"By the way, Lieutenant, who's the Convoy Commander now?"

"Hell, Sarge, I don't know. Why?"

"Well, I think we ought to provide our own security for those trucks outside. I ain't never met an MP worth a nickel, and we got all them radio crystals in the commo van, plus about a million dollars' worth of other stuff. We got a weapon or two here and there and this is a TS mission."

"Sergeant, you're right. I'll see to it." Meadows walked down the aisle to where Prusser was lying on the floor poring over a map of Georgia. Still had his Official Convoy Commander face on. *This is gonna be tough.* He was thinking, trying to find a way to mention the security aspect to the Convoy Commander when Prusser spoke first.

"Ed (oh, it's Ed now, is it? I must be in charge), you handled that situation in the restaurant well today. I was impressed, and I'd like to shake your hand." *Well, I'll be damned.*

"Thanks. Just seemed like the thing to do. Listen, since I want to be sharp tomorrow for my tour as Convoy Commander, I'd like to volunteer to pull the first guard tour on the vehicles outside. Me and Sergeant Vickers. Then I can still get a good night's sleep. These guys are all worried about their radio crystals. I've got my Highway Patrolman and I'm sure Vickers has a club or something. Then you could assign someone to relieve us at 2200."

"Damn fine idea. I'll have a roster made up for the entire night. We don't want just anyone snooping around our stuff."

That was easier than Meadows envisioned. He and Vickers caught no one snooping around the stuff, but they also saw no MP's snooping for snoopers. Shoulders and Brinkman relieved them at 2200 hrs. "G'night, Lieutenant," said the two, almost together. "Brinkman is gonna get in the commo van and try to raise Bragg, or the MFC. Something about the ionosphere and this time of night. If we get any hot poop, we'll let you know."

"Thanks, Sergeant, I appreciate that, but for crying out loud, please let the Convoy Commander know, too. We all gotta live together." Brinkman crawled into the commo van, Shoulders dragged a shotgun out of Belcher, and Ed went to bed and to sleep, in that order, but separated by only a microsecond.

They got started again at 0630, not too bad considering they had no formal wakeup. Meadows mapped out their route and sent Prusser ahead as the scout. He was to wait for them every hour, or at any particularly tricky intersection or detour. They'd gas up every two hours, or on demand of Belcher. The trip went well. They were at Columbus, Georgia, by 1400, and Ed discussed the option of spending the night at Ft. Benning with Shoulders, the ranking NCO, and Prusser, but decided to go on to Eglin. Nothing could happen at Benning but bad. They were at Dothan before dark and still pushing on. Belcher devoured 50 gallons or so of gas every two hours, but he kept right on belching. They pulled up to the AP at the gate of Hurlburt Field at about 2200 hrs. The young Air Policeman walked up to Belcher and looked at SFC Shoulders. "You guys must be with the Army bunch here. They're expecting you. Building T3309, two streets down, turn left, first building on the left. It's an old mess hall. By the way, Sarge, what'cha got in your truck, a whale?"

Building T3309 was right where it was supposed to be. The MFC people were, in fact, expecting them: they had a washtub full of iced-down beer and a desk full of sandwiches. They were also very happy to see the beleagered detachment. SGM Noel was obviously in charge. "Lieutenants, here's the keys to your BOQ rooms. When you're finished eating, I'll detail someone to take you over there. We'll take care of the equipment. The major wanted to be here, but when it got so late, he went on into town to see the ladies. He'll meet with you at 0800 tomorrow."

Meadows took a bottle of Bud, declined the sandwich, and said he was ready to go. One of the MFC personnel in civilian clothes hopped on a motor scooter outside and led Arvak to the BOQ. He waved goodbye and Ed went to his room. Prusser had decided to stay and eat. There were clean sheets on the bed, even a mattress, and clean towels in the bathroom he and Dan would share. This Air Force living was all right. The shower was hot, the towels soft, the bed welcome, and the Bud unopened when Ed closed his eyes and checked out for the day.

At 0600 hrs, Ed was up, cleaned, brushed, shaven, had splashed on a dash or two of Old Smell 'Em Good, and was walking with Prusser to the MFC building for directions to the nearest mess hall. The walk was about an half mile, but they had both felt like walking rather than driving any further. It was cool this time of day, and, to tell the truth, it didn't heat up as much in the daytime as Ed thought it would down here in Florida. Sure, they were in the panhandle of Florida and probably closer to Alabama than to any sizeable Florida town, but it was still Florida, still on the Gulf, and should have been warm. Once at the MFC, the Duty NCO pointed them to a building adjoining T3309 where there were airmen entering, obviously intent on having breakfast. The airman at the door checking ration cards didn't know quite what to make of a couple of army lieutenants, so he waved them on through rather than go through the hassle of trying to find out what the correct price was for a visiting army company grade officer to eat breakfast. Probably saved himself a good twenty minute question and answer period. They collected plates of grits, eggs, and bacon, mugs of steaming, fragrant coffee, and sought a table where they could talk. No one from the MFC was here yet, so they found a table by the window and sat down. Ed broke the silence, "Say, Dan, what do you know about Kreeger?" he asked, referring to the major they were going to meet in a little while.

"Not too much. He is supposed to be an old major and I understand he's first generation removed from the old country, in this case, Germany. That's about all. Couldn't pick up anything last night; no one seems to know much about what we're doing."

"That ain't hard to believe. Hell, I don't know what we're doing, so I can't expect anyone else to know anything."

"There was one thing the sergeant major said last night after you left," added Prusser. "He said for us not to be late under any circumstances at all." They ate the rest of their meal in silence, and were over at T3309 by 0730. There still wasn't anything but a coffee pot active here, so Ed got them each a cup and they sat down to wait. It was 0755hrs when the sergeant major walked in.

"Lieutenants, the major will be here in about a minute. Come on into his office and I'll tell him you're here." (Fool me once, shame on you; fool me twice, shame on me. Meadows remembered another day when he had been told to just go into someone's room and wait; a certain LTC Briggs. Not this time, SGM!)

"That's okay, Top; we'll just wait out here." Prusser was caught in a half-up, half-down attitude; he didn't know what to think. He had missed the pleasure of Briggs' company that first day, but he sat back down. That's when the major came in.

"Well, well, well,..heh, heh, heh,... here's our young lieutenants. Heh, heh, heh,...come on into the office. You, too, Top. Heh, heh, heh." The man doing all the laughing was about six feet tall, 220#, and the majority (no pun intended) of his weight was around his middle. Somehow, the laughing was not reassuring to Meadows. "Sit down, sit down, heh, heh, heh, we don't go for all that West Point rank crap here. Heh, heh, heh. Meadows, ain't you the wiseass that got into ole Briggs' whiskey? You little thief, heh, heh, heh. He told me all about you, Sonny Boy, so you better watch your self here. Prusser? Heh, heh, heh. You ain't done shit since you got in Group, have you? Jerking spit and polish, heh, heh, heh. We'll give you a chance to fuck up, too, right, Top?"

"Fucking A, Sir."

"Well, heh, heh, heh, we ain't got no TO&E slot for a second lieutenant here, so we had to find a place to stick your butts till they call you back to Bragg. Heh, heh, heh. Tell 'em, Top. I gotta go get some fucking breakfast. Heh, heh, heh. These little air force wives wear an old soldier out, heh, heh, heh." With the last triplet of heh-heh-heh's, he got up and left the room. He'd never even taken his hat off, much less said, "Hello." *Whatever they have in mind for us,* thought Ed, *it ain't gonna be good.*

"The major and I come up with a fine place for you two to spend your vacation in Florida. Since we are due to receive our first teams down here in three weeks, we figured the best thing for you to do is to get to know the land, so we're assigning you each a NCO and sending your hides out to the woods for 18 days. We'll arrange for some message drops every couple of days, and we'll bring you in a couple of days before the first teams get here. You'll each have a rucksack with whatever you want to carry in it. I asked the major about rations, and he said to 'survive.' The sergeants assigned to you are each old heads who can teach you a thing or two if you'll listen. Meadows, you got Leontine; Prusser, you got Kazam. You can get your gear together and be back here ready to leave at 1300. That's it. Heh, heh, heh, except for what the major said; SURVIVE!"

3

The Tale Of Two Hunters

Meeting Staff Sergeant Pompeo G. Leontine was a lot like not experiencing anything at all. He was short, less than 5'9", balding, old (anyone past thirty was old to Ed at this stage in his life), very reluctant to talk, and, after shaking hands with Meadows when they were introduced to each other by the SGM, he didn't. Kazam was also a staff sergeant (E6), definitely slovakian in derivation, and he expressed a big, wide grin across his broad face. His stature was even less than Leontine's, being on the order of 5'5", or so. Kazam was assigned to Prusser and they were going to Sector HILL, while Leontine and Meadows went to Sector TREE. The MFC Operations and Training Section had arbitrarily divided Eglin's reservation into six operational areas, or sectors, and had also designated three drop zones, or DZ's, within the reservation boundaries. The names of the sectors all had four letters, and, clockwise from Hurlburt, they were Area TREE, Area PINE, Area HILL, Area DIRT, Area MOSS, and Area SAND. The DZ's had five-lettered names; KELLY, in Area PINE; IRISH in Area HILL; and DUTCH in Area MOSS. With the size of the Eglin ranges and the sizes of the respective areas, it was highly unlikely that you could expect to meet anyone while getting to know your area.

The two teams left in separate jeeps: the operational personnel, the lieutenants and their sergeant partners sitting in the back holding their rucksacks on their laps, and a driver and helper from the MFC ccupying the front seats. By taking the roads and staying on reservation property, the trip to their drop point in TREE would be about 40 miles, and it took them an hour to make it. Finally, the jeep pulled over to the side of the two-lane, blacktop road and stopped. Leontine had said not one word during the trip; Ed tried to comment on some aircraft they had seen at Hurlburt, but dropped the subject when the sergeant hardly blinked.

The Rider turned around in his seat. Driver looked straight ahead. Rider was wearing civilian clothes, so Ed didn't know who he was. "Here's your maps," Rider said, handing both of the backseat passengers topo maps. "The six Areas and the DZ's are marked. We're right here at the fire tower in Area PINE. Your Area is all west of here. We'll drop your first message in a RED DOT match box at the base of that speed limit sign up ahead tomorrow sometime before 1600. It'll have instructions for the next drop and anything else the major needs to tell you. You are to remain tactical. There are no friendly forces in this area, so don't talk to anyone. The game wardens and AP's should leave you alone since they've been told you'll be here. If you do get picked up, or in trouble, or anything else, say nothing to nobody. Your business here is Top Secret. Ask for them to contact the MFC. Tell them nothing, not your name, nothing. Best thing to do is don't get caught. Evade. One more thing, Lieutenant, the major said for me to tell you, 'don't fuck up'. Adios, Compadres, have a ball in the woods."

Leontine threw his rucksack onto the ground and climbed out of the jeep. Ed did the same. The jeep made a "U" turn and headed back to Hurlburt. Meadows picked up his pack and began struggling into the shoulder straps. "Hey, Sarge, ain't you coming?" he asked.

"Wit' all due respect to your rank, Sir, I t'ink we oughta sit here and wait a bit. Dose guys from the "Mother Fuckers" Club are probably gonna be right back to try and find out which way we headed. Les jist pull dese sacks over inta da brush and take a break. I'm gonna take a crap." With that, he pulled his rucksack over under some bushes, took a roll of toilet paper out of the inside, and wandered off into Area PINE to the east.

Meadows dragged his heavily-laden pack into a clump of bushes near Leontine's, then he sat down under a tree nearby. Fifteen minutes passed. Pompeo returned, stuck the TP back into his rucksack, and likewise sat down next to a tree. Fifteen more minutes. Nothing happened. The only thing Ed had learned from Leontine so far was a new name for the MFC. He was to learn many more. "Sergeant Leontine, you awake?" whispered Ed.

"Yes, Lootenant, I'm awake."

"Sarge, there ain't nothing happening. It's nearly 1500. If we're gonna make camp and try to scare up something to eat before dark, we better get a move on."

"Lootenant, wit' all due respect to your rank, Sir, you ain't gonna live ta be old bein' in too big a hurry. Jist wait a while. Dem mu'fuckers ain't far away. When dey come back, if we get a chance, take everyting you can find in da jeep. Dere might be a bottle of hootch, or a map, or no telling what. Maybe even some food. Give 'em time to get somethin' ta eat and get back here. Dey'll come."

An hour passed, no mu'fuckers. Another hour. It was 1700 and getting dark. There had been several vehicles passing on the road, but the sound of a jeep engine is distinctive, and when they heard it, Ed's ears pricked up. The light was poor, so Leontine could have acknowledged the sound, but Ed saw no movement from the sergeant at all. The jeep approached from the south and was driving with its blackout lights. It pulled up to the area where they had gotten out earlier and stopped. Ed was about fifty meters away, so he couldn't hear what Rider and Driver were saying, but they killed the engine and got out. Each of them had a rifle, an M1, with the bulge of blank adapters silhouetted against the darkening sky. They also had flashlights, and when they crossed the road, they switched on the lights and began searching for something, *probably our tracks,* thought Ed. He looked over at Leontine, but the sergeant wasn't against his tree. Meadows looked around and caught the movement of Leontine, on his belly, crawling toward the jeep. Meadows did the same. They reached the jeep together as the MFC people continued their search on the other side of the road. Leontine rose to his knees and began passing things to Ed. There were two six packs of Coke, a brown paper sack full of something, a map case, and then Pompeo whispered to Ed, lisping in the approved tactical manner, "Take thith thit and thuff it in yo' thack. Get ready to move out."

Meadows crawled back with his load. He stuffed the parcels in the top of his rucksack and squirmed into the shoulder straps. He waited.

It was only a minute before Leontine appeared, walking upright. "C'mon, Lootenant," he whispered, "let's make tracks," and he was gone, heading east. The mu'fuckers were still thrashing around across the road. Ed got up and hustled after the disappearing figure of Leontine. They walked through the woods of Area PINE for about twenty or thirty minutes before the Sergeant stopped. "Let's take a breather and see what we got," said Pompeo. Ed was more than happy to comply. He shrugged off the pack and set it down. Both of them were breathing hard as they sat down, too.

"What you figure they aimed to do, Sarge?"

"Ah, dem bugfuggers probably planned to shoot us up and steal all our goods, maybe turn us over to da police and make us call da MFC to come bail us out. Bunch of mu'fuckers. You wan' a beer?" he continued, handing Meadows a fairly cool Bud from a six pack he pulled out of his rucksack. "Nice of dem to tink about us." They drank a beer apiece, then started a second before Leontine spoke again. "What all'd you get?"

"Hell, I don't know." Meadows opened his pack. "Some Cokes, a map case, sack of something, feels cold." He opened the sack. "Damn, Sarge, they brought us supper. We got some sliced meat, pickles, that's it."

"Not too bad for mu'fuckers. I got some beer, loaf of bread, batteries, canteen, that's all. Let's eat all da meat, bread, if you like, Cokes. Dem Cokes is too heavy to carry far, easier to piss 'em out than carry 'em. Wit' all due respect to your rank, Sir, I'd suggest we make a cold camp here tonight and see where we stand in da morning. We'll take a look at dem maps then. Dem mu'fuckers ain't gonna stay out here all night."

"Sarge, you know we're in Area PINE. We're supposed to be in TREE."

"I know 'dat, you know 'dat, but dem mu'fuckers don't know dat. We're better off 'dem not knowing. Dem fuckers is treacherous, I don't trust 'em." They made a cold camp, got out their sleeping bags, affectionately known as, "fart sacks," and went to sleep.

Pompeo already had a fire going when Ed woke up the next morning. "Morning, Sarge, am I late?"

"Nah, Lootenant, I'm jist gettin' da coffee goin'. See if you can find us some mo' wood." Ed got up, stretched out the wrinkles from a night on the cold ground, and began picking up sticks from under the trees they were camped in. "Lootenant, you got any gloves?"

"Yeah, I got some field gloves in my rucksack."

"Better put 'em on when you're picking up wood. It ain't too late for ole 'Mister No Shoulders' ta be laying around." Meadows got his gloves and put them on. October may be the Fall, and it may be cool, but it was Florida, and he really didn't have any desire to come across a snake unprepared. He was also more careful in his wood picking up. They drank coffee brewed in a number 10 can over an open fire, pouring in a little cold water to settle the grounds before serving. It was delicious. The Cokes were cool and they drank three apiece, then put the other six pack in the stream nearby. "We may come back dis way again, and dem Cokes'll stay nice and cold. I don't t'ink we have to worry about the Magnificent Fellows Club coming out to look for 'em."

After the coffee-Coke breakfast, they went through the map case. It contained detailed topo maps of their area with the intended drop points all nicely marked. There were also maps of PINE, HILL, and SAND. The last mentioned was down on the beach at Santa Rosa Sound, and the campsite marked was at Hammock Point. "That's probably where da boat training will be," said Leontine. "Let's go over to Area TREE and see what our house looks like."

The next week passed quickly. They found a nice place next to a clear, cold stream called Turkey Gobbler Creek, and established their base camp. Each day they stashed their gear under some brush and explored their area carrying only their canteens, compasses and maps. Meadows had brought his Model 28 Smith & Wesson Highway Patrolman .357 magnum and he wore this as well. Leontine had a similar weapon, a Smith Model 19 .357 Combat Magnum, and he wore this. They spent all day every day exploring the lay of the land in Area TREE. They also spent all day everyday in school, for Pompeo was a master of the woods, and Ed was wise enough to be an excellent student. Leontine knew the ways of the Group, of Unconventional Warfare, he knew when to do what and how, and he knew that a pair of pliers is as essential to woods' living as is a number 10 can. During the week they became very good friends, an unusual combination: Meadows—the West Point graduate from a very protected and conservative Southern Baptist background—a Christian who read his Bible sometime every day and kept a diary; Leontine—a first generation Bostonian of Italian immigrant parents, who had served time on a P-farm in Texas, had fought in Korea and participated in the quelling of the Koje-do riots over there, married a Japanese bride and father of a two-year-old girl and a six-year-old boy. His political views were non-descript and his religion about the same. He supposed he was a Catholic, but didn't want to be quoted on that. Whatever the differences, their personalities meshed and they worked well together. One day, at one of their drop points, they found a chicken and a sack of potatoes. The fowl was tied up but still alive and the vegetables were not quite rotten. There was a message there for them to run a recon on the Auxillary Field up in Area PINE the next day, and then make their way down to Hammock Point in Area SAND two days later. "Sunnybitch," said Leontine, "we gonna eat well tonight. I'm tired of C's and roots. I'll fix us up some stew like my wife fixes chicken and we'll crawl inta our sacks full tonight."

Back at the camp, Leontine stirred up the fire and started the blaze going again. Meadows, who had been carrying the chicken, offered to wring its neck and skin it. "Lootenant, we're surviving," said Pompeo. "You don't waste nothing when you're surviving. Let me show you how the Japanese do chickens." He took the miserable, scraggly little chicken and broke its neck with a rabbit punch. Then he began to meticulously pluck off the feathers. "The Japs ain't found a way ta eat feathers yet, but dey probably will."

When the bird was free of feathers, Leontine cut off the skin and sliced it into strips, putting the strips into his canteen cup which also contained a little water. Next, he gutted the carcass and asked Ed to separate the viscera (he said, 'guts') into the separate organs. Ed started to throw the intestines away, but they were cleaned out and put into the pot, too. Pompeo diced the meat into little squares, dropped them into the pot and added the head with the comb still attached, and the feet, too, with the nails still sticking out of the toes. All this preparation took about two hours, but at last the stew was simmering on the fire and smelling good. Smelling, yes; looking, no. It was hard to get excited about watching chicken heads and feet turning over in a pot of stew. Finally, it was about ready. "Get ready, Lootenant, you're about to have have Japanese-Italian-Turkey Gobbler chicken stew."

"Lemme get my mess gear," said Meadows, getting up, stumbling, and kicking over the canteen cup full of stew. They tried to right the mess and salvage as much chicken stew as they could, but Meadows nearly kicked over their friendship as well as their stew that night.

Field 6 was an auxillary field on the Eglin reservation not too far south of Defuniak Springs, Florida. It had a single north-south runway, paved, with a fire house and truck serving as the control facility. There was another building, a house, north of the fire house, and there were clothes on a line in back of that house. Every once in a while, a woman could be seen entering and leaving the house, taking out wash to hang and bringing in that which had been out there. All this could be seen from the tree line south of the field where Leontine and Meadows were lying early the next morning. "Probably got a fireman living here with his family," muttered the sergeant.

"Yeah, I suppose so. Wonder what they use this field for? It ain't big enough for any jets to land on, and you know they don't use it for target practice with those people there," whispered Meadows.

"No matter. Dey probably got some plan at da Magnificent Fellows' Club for a raid when da teams come down here. Let's look it over. I'll make my way down da west side and look over da house. You circle to da east and see what's over there. Be awake for hunters over there, like dem we seen on da way over here. Dey ain't supposed to be on da reservation, but dis is awful close ta civilian territory. Lootenant, you might make a good officer someday, and I'd hate for you ta have your butt shot-off looking like a deer. We'll meet back here in an hour. It's a long way to SAND, so we need ta get going."

"Okay, Sarge, meet you here at the rucksacks at, let's see," looking at his watch, "1000 hrs. Adios."

There was a drainage ditch which ran the length of the runway on the east side of the field and a berm behind that which was probably created when they dug the ditch. At this time of year, the ditch was dry, although the mud was a bit soft on the bottom, Ed discovered when he tried walking in the ditch. He could skirt the low bushes growing on both sides by staying about five meters away from the ditch proper, and if he stayed to the east of the drain, the berm behind him provided a fairly concealed route toward the buildings. Ed moved slowly, pausing often, playing like he was out hunting deer and had seen some up ahead. He knew that any sudden move would spook his prey just as discovery of his presence by the firefighters would arouse their suspicion. Every once in a while he caught sight of Pompeo moving furtively down the west side of the field, and he was pleased to note that their rates of progress were about the same.

When Meadows was directly opposite the fire station, he took the small notebook out of his pocket which every lieutenant carries, and made a sketch of the compound, estimating sizes and distances, but he felt his estimates were pretty accurate. Then he went on to the very end of the cleared area north of the structures and looked it over. Not much to see. It was 0930; time to get started back. The biggest, and most serious, even potentially fatal problem patrol members face on the return to their bases is the natural tendency to let down their guards a little bit, to move too rapidly, to be less alert than they were on the trip out. The urge was there to hustle back to the rucksacks and wait for Leontine there. Ed knew there wasn't anything between here and there that he hadn't passed by and checked out already, but he forced himself to move with the same, or similar, caution to that which he had exhibited on the way down. It was no problem avoiding the personnel of the fire house, just stay east of the bushes and try though he might to move slowly, by 0945, Ed was practically back at the rucksacks. He crawled into the brush along the ditch, lay down on his belly, and waited.

Leontine had a little more difficulty in reaching his objective unseen than Ed did. It was easy enough to remain unseen and keep something between himself and the fire house initially, but for the last 100 meters or so, there was nothing to hide behind. He had squatted in the treeline and was contemplating his options when the door of the firehouse opened and two people came out. One was a female and one a male and they walked to the house behind the fire house together. Assuming they were husband and wife, Pompeo decided to take a chance. He stood up and walked right up to the door of the station and turned the knob. It was unlocked, so he went in. There was a desk and a couple of chairs, a TV that was turned off, and two telephones on the desk, a field phone and a commercial telephone. There were also a lot of papers on the desk, including a manila folder that had SOI scrawled on the front, Standard Operating Instructions, so Leontine appropriated that folder and stuck it into his shirt. Nothing else particularly attracted his attention, so he decided to get out of there. He opened the door an inch, looked around, then opened it widely and left, closing the door behind him. Walking quickly, he covered the 100 meters back to the tree line and got down on one knee to survey the vicinity. Nothing moving, nothing different. It was 0940 by his Timex, so he started back to meet the lieutenant. Leontine wasn't careless, but he wasn't especially watchful, either, yet still nothing bothered him while he made his way back to the rucksacks, sat down, and fished out a Lucky Strike for a smoke.

At 0955, Ed had about decided to join Leontine when he heard some voices behind him. There were two, possibly three different males talking just on the other side of the berm, and as Ed slowly turned his head to look, two men climbed to the top of the mound. They were wearing civilian hunting clothes, but civvies were no strangers to this reservation, Meadows was discovering. The men also had on orange vests and caps and were carrying shotguns. Evidently, they were hunters either lost or poaching, and they had spotted Leontine. Perhaps they wanted directions, Ed kidded himself, but self didn't believe that. They were carrying beer cans, too, and judging from the way one of them was weaving, these weren't their first cans of the day. Leontine had spotted them, too, but they were too close to evade without leaving their gear behind, so he sat there and quietly smoked his cigarette.

"Hey, Soldier-boy!" shouted one of the hunters. "Hold on there a minute; we wanta talk to you." With that they walked down the hill and over to Pompeo, passing within 5 meters of Meadows but never seeing him. "What'cha doing out here?" asked the larger of the two men in a belligerent tone.

"Who wants to know?" said Pompeo as he field stripped his smoke.

"Me, Soldier-boy, me, that's who. What'cha doing here? This area is Off Limits during hunting season. You're lucky we didn't shoot your ass off. What'cha think of that?"

"I t'ink I'll be going den. Hope you fellers have a good hunt."

"Hold on there a minute, Buddy, it ain't that easy. You a sergeant, eh? I was in the Army once and I didn't like sergeants. Right, Teddy?" he asked to his smaller companion.

"Damned right, Joe Don. You always said you was gonna kick some Sarge ass when you got out." Leontine was picking up his rucksack and starting to put it on. That's when they saw the .357 in the holster on his belt.

"Stop what you're doing, Sarge, and get your fucking hands up!" ordered the big guy. "What you doing with a pistol? Keep him covered, Teddy, and if he moves, shoot holes in him. Raise your hands, Sarge, NOW!" Pompeo did. Big Guy reached out and took the pistol out of Pompeo's holster. "A .357, big deal. Well, Sarge, it's just you and us now, and I'm gonna kick your ass for carrying a pistol. You're all alone now, Sarge."

The roar of the .357 firing off a round directly over Big Guy's head stopped all action. "Not quite alone," said Ed, his voice hoarse and his throat dry. "Both y'all drop your guns or I'll kill you where you stand." It sounded tough and the men dropped their guns, but Meadows wasn't sure what he'd have done if they hadn't complied. Leontine wasn't equivocal about his actions. He picked up his Smith where Big Guy had dropped it, blew the dust off, and stuck it back in the holster. Then he kicked Joe Don square in the groin with a bodacious swipe of his combat boot. The hunter screamed, rolled himself into a ball, laid down on the ground and began crying with loud and tearful sobs. His interest in what was happening around him was slight at this point. Pompeo picked up Big Guy's shotgun, walked over to Teddy, and smashed the butt of the gun into his face. From where Meadows was lying, he could see the spray of blood that flew out and the splat of the blow reminded Ed of the sound of the dying paratrooper hitting the ground back at Bragg. Only louder. Teddy was out like a light, flat on his back.

"Okay, Lootenant, I t'ink you can come out now. Ole Billy Bob, or Bobby Joe, or whatever da hell his name is don't care what we do now." Glancing at the writhing form of Big Guy, Ed could believe Leontine.

"Damnation, Sarge, you really hurt these guys, I mean really. Sonofabitch. I don't believe this. No one will believe this. Is this one dead?"

"Nah, he's taking a break, da lazy mu'fucker. He'll wake up," and to emphasize his point, Leontine kicked Teddy's side. The injured man moaned, and rolled away from the kick. "See dere, da lazy bastard's playing possum." If possums were bleeding like he was, they weren't playing.

"What'll we do with them? We can't let 'em stroll out of here, and the AP's will never believe our story."

"Let's kill 'em," said Leontine. "Hey, feller," he shouted at Joe Don. "You wan' me ta kill you?"

Joe Don moaned and cried louder than before. "Nooooooo, nooooooo, please, Sarge, have mercy, please don't kill us!"

"Maybe we can do something else," offered Ed.

Leontine was adamant. "Nah, let's kill 'em."

"What if they had a truck? We could ride down to SAND, then tie 'em to a tree."

"Or kill 'em down dere. Good idea, Lootenant." Turning to Big Guy on the ground, Pompeo said, "Hey, you dere. Shut up a minute. You got a truck?" Joe Don shut up and nodded. "Where?" pressed Leontine.

"Just the other side of the berm."

"Okay, Wiseass, take off your clothes."

"WHAT?"

"Your clothes, take 'em off. NOW!"

Joe Don started undressing. "You got two minutes to be naked or I shoot you right between da running lights." Joe Don undressed in a hurry. "Okay, Billy Bob, you got five minutes to be back here wit' de truck. You're late, I make ol' Teddy jist half a man. You're two minutes late, no man at all; three minutes and ole Teddy squats to pee forever. Four minutes and I blow his brains out. From below. It's messy for ole Teddy. Get da pickup truck."

"Sarge, could I get the keys from my pocket?"

"Get da keys and get your ass out of here."

As soon as Joe Don left, the two soldiers turned their attention to Teddy. He was waking up and looking better, but he was never going to look good again. They made him strip buck naked and sit on the ground until Joe Don returned. "Five minutes and fifteen seconds, Bobby Don," said Pompeo to Joe Don. "I hardly had time to nick Teddy's bag."

They rolled the clothes into two separate balls and set them on the tail gate of the truck. The shotguns were placed in the bed near the tailgate. Ed loaded their rucksacks into the back while Pompeo positioned the two stark naked hunters in the cab. Joe Don was to drive, Teddy was to hold his face together, if he could. "Okay, Bob Ben, Joe Bob, what da hell…drive," instructed Leontine. "Don't get no speeding tickets, don't do nothin' dumb. I'll be right behind you, and it would give me great pleasure ta blow your redneck head off."

They drove down to Niceville in about thirty minutes. In the middle of town, Pompeo had them pull over to the curb and the two soldiers got out of the back, hefting their rucksacks and holstering the weapons they had both kept drawn throughout the drive. "Drive nice and slow and I may not kill you," said Leontine to Joe Don. "Now get your ass out of here. Your buddy needs a doctor. And don't let me catch you poaching no more," he concluded, and the truck sprang into motion and drove off on down the street.

As they watched it drive away, Ed asked, "Would you really have killed them, Pompeo?"

Leontine was silent for a minute. The truck disappeared around a corner and Meadows and Leontine started walking off to the south. "You bet your sweet bippy, Lootenant." Ed believed him.

Once the truck was out of sight, the two men turned the first corner they came to and found themselves walking in front of a row of shops that included a grocery store. "Say, Pompeo, how would you like an Eskimo Pie?"

"Dat'd be fine wit' me. Besides, we need ta get off da streets just in case dose guys decide to do sumpt'in dumb like calling da Police, or worse yet, trying ta get even. Let's go in dis store and get dese packs off." And so they did. They stood their rucksacks up against the wall near the door, fairly certain that no one would bother them. It was too late to hide their pistols, so they wore them just like they were supposed to have Magnums strapped on. When you are in the woods for two weeks with only an occasional splash in Turkey Gobbler Creek to rinse away the grime, you don't realize how the smells of the campfire and grungy uniforms tend to create a certain aura about you. Both Ed and Leontine noticed that they seemed to be the only ones on whichever row they were pushing their cart down, and at first Ed attributed this to a lack of business on the part of the storekeeper, but as he noticed the other rows filled with shoppers, and especially when he saw the distasteful face one of the ladies made when she happened to be caught downwind of them, it dawned on Meadows that they stank. So he tried to catch a whiff of Pompeo. It wasn't hard. It also wasn't hard for Pompeo to catch a whiff of Ed. "Say, Lootenant, one of us stinks, and I tink, wit' all due respect to your rank, Sir, dat it's you."

"Why, Sergeant Leontine, I'm ashamed of you. I thought you knew more about the Army than that. I am an Officer and a Gentleman, by an act of Congress, and I'm sure the one I smell is you."

"Sir, wit' all due respect to your rank, you smell like a skunk dipped in manure."

"I distinctly catch the odour of Eau de Rearend." They were both giggling like schoolgirls when they reached the ice cream section, abandoned their shopping cart and picked out a fresh Eskimo Pie apiece. At the check-out station, there was a woman with a small boy in front of them, and the kid was fascinated by the soldiers. Meadows tried to smile at the child, but the little one was not making any friendly gestures. He stared as his mother paid the tab for $43.57 worth of groceries, then tugged at her sleeve.

"Mommy, Mommy,...what are those men?" Looking at Leontine and Meadows for the first time, the lady actually seemed horrified by what she saw.

"Come on, Edward, those are Nasty Old Things," and with that, she gathered her bags of groceries and her boy and hustled out the door, keeping her eyes glued to the two men as though afraid they were going to bite her, or growl, or eat her child. But Ed knew she wasn't alone in her opinion of them when he tried to hand the clerk a dollar bill to pay for their ice cream, and the man refused to take it from Meadow's hand. He dropped the bill on the counter, the clerk retrieved it, made change from the cash register, and deposited the coins on the counter. No telling what germs you could catch from a Nasty Old Thing. They sat on the curb to eat their treats, then loaded on their packs and headed north out of town. As soon as they saw the palmetto thickets across the road, they crossed and entered the woods, feeling much more at home than they had felt in the town. Not only at home, but much safer, too. "Leontine, you Nasty Old Thing, why don't you take a bath?"

"It's my Lootenant, Sir, dat won't let anyone smell better dan him and he smells like a skunk dipped in manure."

"That's the trouble with officers nowadays,... they got no class. Do you know that they're letting second lieutenants in Group now?"

"Yeah, but dere ain't no TO&E slot for dem and dey'll just screw up, anyway." To be honest, what they had just said wasn't that funny, but it was funny to them at the time, and they sat down on the ground and laughed till they cried.

"Pompeo, let's wait till dark and walk over to the Albatross Club. You know the major'll be there sniffing bicycle seats, and let's go tell him the civilians called two of America's defenders of freedom, 'Nasty Old Things.' Maybe he'll buy us a drink, or at least a sandwich."

"Okay wit' me, Sir. He's gonna be pissed if we do dat. Probably screw up his chances wit' one of da dames for da night."

"What've we got to lose? The bastard kicks us out in the woods for three weeks without so much as a chicken (the memory of which was painful for Ed) while he sniffs around every night and chuckles. I think he owes us a meal."

"I don't give a shit, Lootenant, I been a' E6 before, anyway. You wanta say hello da the major, we'll say hello to da major. He probably tinks we're queer for each other, anyway, we may as well." They leaned against their rucksacks to await nightfall.

The police car pulled off the road and in among the palmetto shrubs just before dark. The driver killed the engine and turned off the lights. He had parked the car in such a way that he could have an easy survey of the traffic going both north out of Niceville and south into Niceville. Where the patrolman sat slouching behind the wheel was not fifteen meters from where Pompeo and Ed were stuporously awaiting nightfall. It was so close to them that they could hear the squawking and cracking of his radio. "Hey, Tharge," lisped Ed quietly, "do you thee what I thee?"

"Yea, I thee a Boy Thcout lithening to hith radio. Let'th thee if we can find out what he'th here for."

"You mean go athk him?"

"NO, I don't mean go athk him. Lithen to hith radio." If they concentrated hard, they could make out what the dispatcher was saying, but it wasn't very interesting. Darkness fell and the policeman stayed right there and they hadn't heard anything to alarm them, so they were getting ready to go when they heard the radio crackle one more time.

Crackle..siss...static..."All units"...static...crackle..."we have an update on the assault suspects reported earlier...they were identified at the H.G. Hill store early this afternoon...suspects are armed and should be considered extremely dangerous...the two assault victims have been released from the hospital but one of them is going to require surgery after his wounds clear a little...be on the alert for suspicious persons especially on the north side of town..." static...siss...crackle.

"Maybe we better not bother the major tonight," whispered Meadows.

"Naw, Lootenant, wit' all due rethpect ta your rank, dat wath a dumb idea all da time. Let'th get da hell out of here and go down to Thoulderth' place at Hammock Point." They headed east into the thicket and away from town. Their intention was to stay at least one hundred meters from the highway, for they figured there might be other police cars in other locations watching other entrances and exits from the town. There was, one that they could vouch for, on the east side of Niceville, about a half a mile from town. They heard the crackle of its radio long before either of them saw it, but when they did catch sight of it, they were well concealed by a lot of intervening bushes, scrub oaks, and palmetto. Not much happened the rest of the way down to about where they figured Hammock Point would be on the other side of the road.

"Let's go down ta da road and look for a turnoff heading toward da beach. I guarantee you Shoulders ain't roughing it," said Leontine.

"How well do you know Shoulders?" asked Ed as they began making their way toward Highway 98.

"I knowed him a long time. We go back a long way. He was in da 173rd at Koje Do. He's a good head and can be a mean son'fabitch. You won't find a better man. I asked him about you when I found out you and me was gonna be together, and he said you might make a good officer someday. Be a good man ta have as a friend."

Meadows grunted. They reached the highway and split up, Meadows heading east and Leontine west, with the agreement to meet back here in thirty minutes. Ed kept a thin screen of bushes between himself and the road, which had a lot of traffic on it. Every time he saw the lights of a car approaching, he stopped and crouched down, so in fifteen minutes he hadn't gone very far. There had been no roads heading south, so he was turning to head back to their rendezvous when he heard the growling and sputtering of a truck coming out of the woods south of the highway a little ahead of him. It was Belcher, good ole Belcher, there was no mistaking that noise. The olive drab truck emerged from the brush, stopped to check the traffic, then pulled onto the highway and headed west. Meadows couldn't tell for sure who was driving, but it looked like Vickers. It was good to see a friendly face, even if he couldn't see his face.

Back at the meeting place a few minutes later, he told Leontine about the road and they walked down to where Ed had seen Belcher come out of the woods. Sure enough, there was a road and when they found a long enough interval in the traffic to be sure they could cross the road without being discovered, they ran across Highway 98 and into the woods on the south side. They didn't walk on the dirt road, but instead walked parallel to it for about a hundred meters, and they were on the beach. There was a fire burning in the middle of a rather large and elaborate campsite and several men sitting around the fire having a pretty good time. At least, they seemed to be having a pretty good time. They were drinking something and eating something, and laughing at something. "Think we ought to go in?" asked Ed.

"Let's get a little closer and see who it is for sure." It was their destination. They saw Shoulders, and some other guys Ed didn't know, and Brinkman, and they could see that their friends were drinking beer and eating oysters from a GI can and laughing at what Shoulders was saying.

"...and those guys musta really walked all over those civilians. Top said one of them had a busted face, all of it, and the other was gonna sing soprano for awhile. (laughter) I bet they messed around with ole Leontine and he played a tune on them. That guy ain't one to jerk around. Hope they know the whole world is looking for them. Maybe we oughta drive up north tomorrow and see if we can find them and bring them in."

One of the men who had been sitting down stood up, and it took him a long time to stand up. It was Giant! *Damn,* thought Ed, *I didn't know he was down here.*

"I'll tell you something," said Giant. "That Lieutenant ain't no one to mess with, either. He was a tough sonofabitch in the Bear Pit. I'll bet he fit right in. I'm turning in. If you guys decide to go looking for them, wake me up."

When Pompeo burst out of the woods, it scared Ed half to death. "Spicer, you eat bugs," said Leontine. He strode over to Giant and they hugged each other briefly.

"Sonofabitch!" exclaimed Giant, who was now named Spicer. "You stink, Sergeant. Where's your partner in crime?"

"He's over dere in da woods covering me and fixing ta shoot all your asses off if you ain't nice ta me and offer me a beer."

"You guys are in a world of shit," said Shoulders as Ed walked out of the woods. "The whole State of Florida is looking for you. What the hell happened with those civilians?"

"First da beer, den da talk," laughed Leontine. There was plenty of beer. There were also lots of oysters, and fresh bread, and some fried chicken that wasn't too cold, and then they talked. Leontine did most of the talking, and he didn't elaborate very much on the Tale of the Two Hunters. All the men around the fire were interested in what he had to say, and when he had finished, they started a question and answer period that lasted until they were satisfied that they had most of the facts. Shoulders, who was the obvious leader here, ended the discussion.

"Well, like I was saying, y'all are in a world of shit, cause that ain't the way the cops heard it. I think the best thing to do is let y'all sleep here tonight, and then we'll get you back to Field 9 in the morning where you can get cleaned up and shave and not look like yourselves in case the cops come back down here looking for you. They ain't exactly sure you're one of us, cause the Base Commander verified our story that we ain't got no people in that area right now. Good thing y'all were supposed to be in TREE. You can sleep in your fartsacks over in the woods; we don't want the smell stinking up our tent. Vickers'll be back with the truck in the morning and we'll get you in somehow. I'll take care of Top, and you'll have to handle the major if he asks, Lieutenant. Just tell the truth; he ain't dumb. Put the fire out, Brinkman, let's go to sleep.

As they got their sleeping bags out and settled on soft spots in the sandy soil, Pompeo said to Ed, "You done good, Lieutenant. Goodnight." For a DASL, that was a rare compliment.

4

The Frogman

Hot water. Clean towels. Smell'um Good. Stinkalot McSmellworser. It felt so good to be clean again, and shaven with Foamy and hot water, and rinsed with hot water, and showered in hot water, with lots of Dial suds, and a hot water rinse, and more suds, and more rinse. Shampoo and rinse, and soap all over everything and more rinsing. It felt good to be clean. Brushing his teeth even felt good to Ed, so he brushed for a long time trying to get all the yellow off, swished some Lavoris around to get his mouth tingling, then ran a comb through his hair and put on some clean, fresh-smelling underwear. Next, a set of starched fatigues with all the nametags and patches and insignia, and then a change of boots with fresh, soft, and especially dry socks. He got his other Louisville Spring-Up to wear, took out his other field jacket, and figured that he looked as little like the fellow who had come in here as he could. The major had told him, and Leontine, too, to be back at the MFC in an hour and most of that time was already gone. Ed had been surprised at how understanding the major had been when they related their story to him. He'd merely chuckled a few times, told Top to see about getting them some different sleeping bags, and to get them back out to Shoulders' place as soon as possible. He didn't want the cops coming around and finding them in the MFC; there was less chance of them snooping around Hammock Point so much. It really surprised Ed that the major was so reasonable.

What Meadows didn't know was that the major was actually pleased the incident had occured, especially since no one had been hurt too badly and there were no fatalities. "Might be the best thing ever happened to us, Top," he'd said. "The word is already all over the post, and pretty soon the word'll be out in the community...don't mess around with the Army guys from Hurlburt. That's all we want, after all, to be left alone. Yep, heh, heh, heh, might be the best thing ever happened to us!"

One of the first things Ed had learned last summer when he was going through that traumatic time of helping the 7th Special Forces Group (Airborne) adjust to life with second lieutenants, was that you never asked someone where something came from. If you did, all you'd get in reply was that a good agent never divulges his source of supply; therefore, Ed didn't ask that silly question when he picked up his brand-new, Air Force Artic sleeping bag with waterproof cover, zip-out, down insert and wolf fur collar around the face opening. This was a lot nicer than the mountain bag he had been issued and that had served him so well but, when last seen, could be smelled as far as it could be seen. It was even nicer than any of the other bags he had been "issued" and that his room back at Bragg was storing. There were also some other goodies in the pile the Top had waiting for him; a skeletonized survival rifle in .22 Hornet calibre (stamped U.S. Air Force), a box of rounds for it, a nice Kabar knife (stamped the same way), and a light-weight rucksack with a metal frame that was far, far lighter than the multi-pocketed, heavy-duty canvas bag he'd left out at Hammock Point with his goods. Meadows presumed he'd have to sign for all this stuff, but nobody mentioned it, so he didn't, either. Leontine had a similar pile, but no survival rifle. Seemed he'd already been engaged in the timeless service process of barter and had gotten some cooking equipment, instead. Virgin, lightweight, of course.

Meadows hardly recognized his partner. He had on a fresh, starched uniform with stripes and patches and insignia all over the place. Instead of a "Nasty Old Thing," Pompeo looked like a recruiting poster. That seemed like a good name for him, so on the ride back out to the beach in Belcher with Vickers, he said to Leontine, "Sergeant, I wonder if I could sign on with your outfit?"

"Hell, no, Lootenant, wit' all due respect to your rank, Sir, we ain't got no TO&E slots for Second Lieutenants in da Group. We are da elite of America's fighting men; we take only da cream of da crop for volunteers, and only t'ree out of a hundred dat starts out in our outfit finishes da training. Sorry, Lootenant, but we can't use you. Maybe you oughta try for da 82d Airborne Division. Dey make night jumps in da daytime," he replied, alluding to the widely held belief that all troopers in the Division jumped with their eyes closed. All three men laughed as they roared through Ft. Walton Beach. When they entered Niceville, Ed had a brainstorm.

"Hey, Sergeant Vickers, drive around to that grocery store up ahead. Let's see if Pompeo and I can pass inspection." Vickers stopped the beast in front of the H.G. Hill store and Ed and Leontine piled out. They strolled into the store and up the aisles to the ice cream section, where they picked up three Eskimo Pies. At the check-out counter, Ed handed the same clerk a dollar bill. The man took it from his hand and placed his change right in the palm Ed extended. "Mister, I understand y'all had some excitement here a couple of days ago."

"You're right, Sir," replied the clerk. "We had those men in here that the police are looking for. I knew right away they were some kind of criminals. They were dressed up like servicemen, but it didn't fool me, not for one second. I think the police are wasting their time looking for them around here; they're probably on their way to California by now. To tell you the truth, I think they intended to rob me, but we had so many shoppers that they got scared off. Yes, Sir, they were some kind of criminals. Thank you, and come again." Nodding, Ed and Leontine left and got back in the truck waiting outside. They handed Vickers his ice cream and drove off. It's wonderful what a little soap and water does for desperados.

Life at Shoulders' place was different from life on Turkey Gobbler Creek. This was to be the small boat training area for the teams and was equipped for providing that training. The Whale was here, but now it had a 40hp Mercury motor on it and it was sitting in the water looking like a boat instead of a beached whale. This craft was used for zipping around Santa Rosa Sound in what was dubbed, "training," but was actually scouting for likely fishing sites. There were two big rubber assault boats like Ed had used in Ranger School that the men of Hammock Point used when they went fishing. They had big motors on them, too, making them a lot nicer than the paddle propulsion Meadows was familiar with. Shoulders, whose name for the team problem was Cap'n Cruze, had a whole bunch of SCUBA gear down here, too. He was a graduate of the Navy Scuba Course they conducted down at Key West, and the gear was available for everyone to play with. Ed was introduced to the wet suit and the regulator, and he became adept at fishing, Cap'n Cruze style. They'd go out to a previously located site, don the gear and take spear guns down in search of fish. The majority of what they harvested was Sergeant Major fish, sheepheads, a cute fellow with vertical stripes who had teeth in his mouth that looked just like baby teeth. They cooked up good and constituted a great portion of the Cruze family diet. There were oysters, too, millions of them, and they would fill a GI can every day for consumption by the members of the beach party every night. Most of the oysters were gathered from around the half-submerged hull of an old freighter about a mile out from camp. It was easy living for a week. Someone from the MFC visited every day and they had runs into Hurlburt daily, but mostly they were left alone.

Shoulders called the group together one afternoon. "Listen, Gang," he began. "I know everybody's working their butt off (laughter - Ed included), but we gonna have to do something to let the major know we're training down here. So listen up. I know everyone knows how to conduct a submarine extraction (Ed didn't, but he figured he was going to learn), so tonight I've invited the major and Top out to see how good we're going to train the teams. We'll have a couple of guys go out to the wreck with a case of C rations before dark, then about 2300 they'll sent "V's" with a flashlight with a green filter. We'll have a team here on shore answer with "C's" and no filter. The shore party will row out to the wreck and swap the C rations for a member of the group, then they'll row back. The signals will be exchanged every two minutes. Everything will be tactical, camouflage, all that shit. Put on a good show, and Top'll be happy and they'll leave us alone. Lieutenant, you ever done this?"

"No, Sergeant, I haven't."

"Okay, then, you and Leontine will be the submarine. Take one of the boats and some stuff to keep you occupied and go out to the wreck about 1700. Tie up on the far side where you ain't visible from here. Get a compass bearing on us here, cause we ain't gonna have any lights showing tonight. Come around and tie up on this side of the ship after dark and start sending at precisely 2300 hrs. Send three sets of V's, wait two minutes, then send again. Do this until 2400 hrs, then if the team ain't reached you, come on back in. Me and Vickers and Spicer and Randall will be the shore party. Brinkman, we're sending you back to Africa, so you're the exchange man. I want everyone to play the game, lots of warpaint and blacked out uniforms and lots of quiet, all that crap. Okay, the show starts at 2300. Lieutenant, there ain't no need for you and Leontine to get all dressed up, ain't no one gonna see you, anyway."

The first discovery Ed made concerning the equipment they were to carry to simulate a submarine was what exactly was going to keep them occupied. Beer...a case of Bud. Where all this beer came from, he was at a loss to explain. There had been no contributions requested for the beer fund, and he knew that it wasn't Government Issue. He also knew that the members of the 7th Group were not hesitant to request same, and they couldn't stand free-loaders. Probably some more of that good agent stuff. They took some food, what, he didn't know, for Pompeo provided that. Flashlight, compass, spare batteries, and he slipped on the .357 when he saw Leontine wearing his. "Da Russians are in Cuba," was Leontine's reply when he asked about it. What he could do about the Russians at this range with a 4″ barrel on his pistol, Ed didn't know, but he'd learned to trust the judgement of his sergeant. The shore party pushed them out into the Sound a few minutes after 1700, and after a few pulls on the rope, the motor sputtered to life and they were on their way. Running the Mercury wide open gave them a top speed of about twenty miles per hour, so in less than five minutes they were at the wreck and Pompeo had secured a line to the hull on the southeast side. Then the waiting began, along with the beer drinking.

As contrasted to the first time they had been together, Pompeo was not reluctant to talk at all. He talked about Korea, and the riots at Koje-Do. The chinese had infiltrated a colonel into the prison camp to organize the riots, and the prisoners had manufactured gas masks for themselves so that tear gas had been ineffective. An army general had allowed himself to be taken hostage, and they had finally called on the 173rd Regimental Combat Team to go in and eliminate the rioters. Eliminate was the right word. It had evidently been a bloody mess, and it was there that Leontine had gotten to know Shoulders, and Spicer, and a whole bunch of other people who were now in Group.

Meadows was amazed at the insight Pompeo had concerning the operation, and he was even more amazed at the respect Leontine had for orientals, all of them. He wasn't too sure about the Laotians, but he said the Vietnamese, the Viet Minh, had conducted a classic operation in throwing the French out of Indochina. The sergeant hated the French, had nothing good to say about them at all. Ed asked about the Foreign Legion, and Leontine explained to him that damn few of the Legionaires were French; most were Germans from WWII, a few other nationalities thrown in. Leontine was very well read, and Meadows decided he was a source of knowledge they could tap for teaching Military Art classes at West Point. Somehow, though, Meadows just couldn't see Sergeant Leontine instructing the Corps of Cadets. Bloody shame. By 2000 hrs, it was fully dark, so Pompeo suggested they pull out to the other side of the wreck and tie up. They did.

It got cold out there on the water, but with their field jackets and all that beer, it wasn't too bad. There was a breeze blowing and the waves were slapping against the side of the boat in almost a romantic fashion when they noticed that a fog was building up. By 2200, the fog was pretty thick, so they doubted the troops on shore could see their signal, but waited anyway. Right at 2300 hrs, Leontine crouched in the bow of the boat, pointed the flashlight toward the general direction of the camp (they had neglected to take a compass reading, but they knew about where the shore party was), and pressed the button on the light three times in rapid succession, then one long blink. Morse code for, "V." He did this three times, then paused. Both men strained their eyes for the answering flashes, a dah-dit-dah-dit, but they saw nothing. After two minutes, he repeated the procedure. Still nothing. For half an hour they went through this routine, but they saw nothing in return.

"You think they can see us, Sarge?"

"No way, fog's too t'ick. I t'ink maybe dey'll push out and head in dis direction until dey can see our signal and get dis ting over wit'. Maybe. If dey ain't too drunk by now."

Ed giggled. Speaking of drunk, he had to take a leak. "Hey Pompeo,

I'm gonna take a leak."

"Be my guest, Lootenant, just go downwind, please." Meadows stood up and leaned over the side of the bouncing boat. He tried to match his rhythm to that of the wave movements, but a lot of the water splashing into the rubber boat did not come from the Gulf. He sat back down in a new spot well away from his site of urination, and they continued their vigil. 2345. Ed thought he heard something.

"Leontine! you hear that?"

"Hear what?"

"Listen. I thought I heard something." They listened. They heard the water slapping against their boat, and against the hull of the ship, and they heard their boat bumping against the ship, but that was about all. Then he heard it again. Soft. He couldn't make out what it was. "You hear it that time?"

"I ain't heard nuttin' but you pissin' in da boat."

"Then listen. I know I heard something." Pompeo kept sending V's. There it was again, closer, this time, and this time Leontine heard it.

"What was dat?" he whispered.

"Damn if I know. Sounded like air, or blowing, or something." The waves weren't romantic anymore, and it was uncomfortably cold, field jackets notwithstanding. Pompeo had stopped sending V's. There it was again, much closer, and it was definitely air moving, like someone breathing, no doubt about it.

"You got your piece out?" whispered Pompeo.

"Yea," replied Ed as he drew his Smith. All kinds of thoughts rushed through his mind, but the one that stuck was predicated upon what Leontine had said earlier about the Russians being in Cuba. What was to keep them from running infiltrators into Florida like this, or spying, or, worse yet, from wasting two guys from Special Forces sitting in a rubber boat in the middle of the night in the fog? Sonofabitch. Here I am twenty-three years old and the damn Russians are gonna kill me and they'll never know what to tell my folks. Sonofabitch. This time the sound was unmistakable, it was breathing, two deep breaths, then a splash, then nothing.

"Lootenant?"

Ed nearly fell overboard, he was so startled by the sound. "Yeah?" he croaked, his voice dry, his tongue sandy.

"Whoever it is knows we're here. Dis ain't no game. If you see him, kill him. Waste him good, two rounds, at least. If it's one of our guys playing tricks, too bad." They listened. They waited. It was oh, so cold, and Ed was scared worse than on his first jump, worse than on his first anything.

Suddenly, there was a loud splash at the side of the boat and both men pointed their pistols at the sound. A large, dark figure broke the water and the porpoise took a couple of deep breaths through his blow hole before he re-submerged. "Sonofabitch," whispered both men in unison as they uncocked their pistols. "We nearly had a dead dolphin." said Ed.

"Start da motor, Lootenant, we're going in," stated Pompeo as he untied the boat. Ed did, and ten minutes later they were met by the beach party on shore. As they beached the boat, Leontine whispered to Meadows, "Dat damn fish made me piss in my pants."

With a selfish pride, Ed noted how dry his pants were. The operation had been called off at 2200 when the fog got too thick, and the major and Top had headed back to the Albatross.

"Guess we better have some radios next time," was all Shoulders said. As for the story of the Russian frogmen-turned-porpoise, Leontine and Meadows decided to let that one lie, but Ed wasn't going to forget the dry pants part.

5

The Green Berets

The word came to the troops at Hammock Point by way of the daily MFC run that the first teams scheduled to arrive for the problem at Eglin would be delayed for at least a week. It seemed that President Kennedy was paying Fort Bragg a visit, and every available trooper had been pressed into duty for the myriad of demonstrations and displays planned for the president. This left a gap in the schedule of the field troops, but at Hammock Point it didn't matter. Prusser and Kazam had arrived to partake of the easy living, and from the way Dan talked, you'd have thought he was the only one out in the woods this past couple of weeks. The troops took turns riding in to Field 9 with Belcher to shower, shave, shine up and each man could count on a bodily cleaning session about every third day. It was Meadows' turn toward the end of the extra week, and he had just gotten off the truck with a sergeant named, Valentine, whom he'd been talking to when Top stuck his head out of the door of the MFC. "Lieutenant Meadows, the Old Man wants to see you 'toota-suite.' He's inside now, Sir."

Ed spoke no French, but he knew the expression, "toot-sweet," or, "toota-suite" was alleged to mean, "very quickly," in French. So he went into the office of the major very quickly. "Lieutenant Meadows reporting, Sir," he blurted out as he snapped to attention and rendered a smart hand salute.

The major waved back. "Relax, Lieutenant, stand at ease. Heh-heh-heh. You been living like a fat cat out there with old Shoulders, heh-heh-heh. But you'll be back to surviving soon enough up there in TREE. Next time we put your butt in an area, you stay in that area and don't go wandering off beating up on civilians, heh-heh-heh!"

Meadows was tempted to argue the point about their orders to run a recon on the airfield, but decided instead to adopt the old plebe lines of, "Yes, Sir, no, Sir, no excuse, Sir." So he said, "Yes, Sir."

"Right, Lieutenant. Whatcha doing right now?"

"I came in to clean up, Sir."

"Plenty of time for that later. There's a plane due in from Bragg in about three hours that's gonna drop us a couple of people and some supplies. Top is getting together a DZ crew and I'm putting you in charge. Get your ass up to DZ Kelly and set up the DZ for them. If you get a move on, you can just about have it ready before they get here. And, Lieutenant (Meadows knew the next line by heart), don't fuck up, heh-heh-heh. Get your ass out of here."

"Yes, Sir." Another smart hand salute. He was tempted again, this time to salute with only the longest finger of his right hand, but he passed that temptation, too. Outside, there was a deuce-and-a-half being loaded and about a half-dozen men lounging around in a group. One of the men walked over to Ed and saluted.

"Sir, I'm Sergeant Dodge, the NCOIC of this detail."

"Pleased to meet you, Sergeant," replied Ed as he returned the salute and then shook hands. "I presume you've done this before?" Ed had learned a long time ago to "presume" instead of "assume" since the latter made an "ass out of u and me."

"Yes, Sir, lots of times."

"Good. I'll just tag along then."

"Okay, Sir, I'll get the men aboard and we'll get going. Why don't you get in the cab?"

"Will do, Sergeant," and Meadows mounted the truck. He settled into the seat as the driver climbed aboard from the other side. Ed couldn't be sure, but the driver looked a lot like another driver he'd seen one night not too long ago in a jeep that lost its load of beer and batteries to Pompeo and him. Ed nodded, and the driver did the same. Then Dodge climbed in next to Ed.

"Let's go, Johnson," said Dodge. "I'll protect your jewels from the

Lieutenant." They all three laughed and the ice was broken. They talked about nothing in particular for a few minutes, then all of them lapsed into the stupor that soldiers adopt when riding in trucks. Johnson manuevered the big vehicle expertly through the streets of Ft. Walton Beach and on north out of town. It took them an hour to reach Kelly, and the truck ground to a halt at the south end of the clearing.

"What do you want me to do, Sergeant?" asked Ed as they dismounted.

"Why don't you stay here at the truck and take a wind reading, Sir? We'll get the panels out."

"Okay, Sarge, have at it." The reference to the wind reading concerned the Regulations concerning airborne operations in the Army. Whenever there was to be a personnel drop, you were supposed to have an anemometer on the DZ and were supposed to take a wind velocity reading just before the drop to ensure that the winds were less than 15 knots for purposes of safety. If they were too strong, the jump would be called off because of safety considerations. There was an anemometer in the cab of the truck, but they seldom used it. Instead, you stood outside, and if the wind didn't blow you down, then they were reported as "3-5 knots, gusting to 8." Meadows couldn't remember a single jump when the winds were reported as otherwise. Of course, if a bunch of guys got hurt, the OIC would have to answer about the wind readings. That never happened, either, at least, not in Group. So Ed licked his index finger, held it up, and satisfied himself that the winds were "3-5 gusting to 8." Then he sat down, leaned against the front wheel of the truck and watched Dodge at work.

The sergeant led the men several hundred meters out into the clearing. Each member of the party had a large cloth panel, about three by five feet, which was fluorescent orange on one side and red on the other. He lined the first four men up exactly 50 meters apart in a straight line. The next two men were placed at right angles to the last man in the row and they were spaced 50 meters apart, too, forming a large inverted "L." Then each of the troopers staked down his panel with the orange side up, long axis of the panel at right angles to the "L." The aircraft was to approach the DZ along the long leg of the "L," and when it reached the cross arm, the first trooper in the aircraft would exit. Should anyone see an unsafe condition on the DZ, such as a vehicle crossing, or a sudden gust of high wind, he would reverse his panel to show red and abort the drop. Any or all red signified the same thing to the Jumpmaster in the plane: don't drop. To be correct, there was a formula for computing where to place the "L," two formulae, in fact, which read: Altitude (Hundreds of feet) X Wind velocity (MPH) X 4.5 (constant for the T-10 parachute) = wind drift in yards; and 1/2 speed of the aircraft (MPH) X exit time in seconds = dispersion pattern in yards. Practically speaking, they placed the "L" in the middle of the Drop Zone. Nothing like following the Axiom of the Army...KISS (Keep It Simple, Stupid). The pattern was in place and still they had an hour before the aircraft was to arrive.

The First Air Commandos, the Air Force unit based at Hurlburt, flew a variety of aircraft, but mostly C-46's and C-47's—old World War II birds painted grey with a minimum of other markings. This unit had a policy which dictated that whenever they took off on a mission, they had to fly for at least four hours before landing. Not only that, but they flew mostly at 50 feet over the surrounding terrain. It was an adventure flying with them, and most of the troopers were only too happy to exit the aircraft when they popped up to 1250 feet for the drop. The aircrews were among the best in the Air Force, and probably in the world. When they were supposed to reach a certain point for a drop or whatever, they were supposed to arrive plus or minus two minutes from the scheduled time, and they usually did. There was no sense in looking for them now, so Meadows got up and went out to the angle of the "L" where Dodge was waiting with Driver (Sgt Johnson). They had an AN/GRC 19 radio set up to communicate with the aircraft when it did arrive.

"I got lonesome, Sarge," he said.

"Pull up some sand and take a load off, Lieutenant. Have a chew," he added, flipping Ed a pack of Levi Garrett chewing tobacco. Meadows didn't really enjoy chewing, but the invitation was as much a dare as a friendly gesture, so he opened the pack and took out a wad of the vile-looking stuff. He formed the wad into a ball, stuck it in his mouth and handed the package back to Dodge.

"Thanks," he muttered as he began chewing.

"Lieutenant, you got any beer or sandwiches left over?" asked Johnson.

"Naw, Sarge, we did all that stuff in. Next time, I wish you'd buy

Schlitz." They sat in silence after that. Finally, a few minutes before 1700, Dodge spoke to Johnson.

"Turn on the radio and see if you can raise 'em, Sarge." Driver fiddled with the dials and the radio began to screech and hum.

"Uncle, Uncle, this is Poor Boy, Over," he said into the mike, using the pre-arranged call signs. Screech, hum. "Uncle, Uncle, this is Poor Boy, come in, please, over."

"Poor Boy, this is Uncle. We have the DZ in sight, should be at your location right on the button, over."

"Roger, Uncle, we are set to receive visitors, over."

"Two minutes, Poor Boy, out." End of transmission. Ed strained his eyes to pick up the plane, and there it was, coming out of the haze and heading straight for them. It was already at 1250 feet and right on target. It was a C-47, a Gooney-Bird. They watched as the plane lumbered up the line of panels in the "L," and when it was directly overhead, the first bundle dropped out of the door. Another bundle followed, then the first jumper appeared before any of the chutes opened. Another trooper followed, and that was all.

"See you later, Poor Boy, over."

"Roger that, Uncle. Poor Boy out," and the plane was gone. The chutes were open now and there were two green cargo chutes and two olive T-10 personnel chutes. The wind really was negligible, and the parachutes descended almost straight down. The cargo bundles hit first, followed by the troopers who landed softly, one near each bundle. Meadows watched as the men rolled up their chutes and stuffed them into their Aviator's Kit Bag. The cargo bundles were not large, so they didn't require any help dragging them in to the Control Point, Ed's location. The DZ party, meanwhile, had rolled up their panels and they were heading for the CP, also.

When everyone had assembled, Sergeant Dodge said, "A couple of you guys help with the bundles. Let's go home."

"Wait a minute, Sarge," said one of the new men. "Look what we got." They both took off their helmets and reached inside their shirts, pulling out some funny green caps and putting them on their heads. "Kennedy was impressed as hell at what he saw at Bragg. He gave us our berets back!"

There was a cheer from the troops, and everyone began talking excitedly. "Wait a minute," said New Guy One. "What you think we got in these bags? We got berets for everyone!" Another cheer, and the bundles were torn open. Ed grabbed one of the treasured headpieces and tried it on. He looked around, and his impression was that everyone looked like Donald Duck, but he wasn't about to say it. It was obvious this was a significant moment for the troops. No more Louisville Spring-Ups, no more Old Ironsides; they had the berets back. Sonofabitch, Ed was feeling proud. No matter that he hadn't voted for Kennedy, that he wasn't a Catholic, that he wasn't a liberal, or even a Democrat; by Golly, he was a Green Beret!

6

Otto Nottus

The time had finally come to get on with the reason for their being: team training. All the troops were called in from the field for some photographs. These were individual shots which would be sent back to Ft. Bragg and given to the team leaders so they would be able to identify as authentic the reception committee which would meet them when they parachuted into Florida. Each man was given the option of choosing a name he would be known as, and Ed selected, "Otto Nottus," in honor of a very close friend of his from bygone days. A cover story was created for each man as well as for the problem as a whole. Meadows' story went something like this: he was an aeronautical engineer in a country which had been conquered by a foreign, communistic, power. He wasn't in agreement with this new government, so he, along with some of his friends, had fled to the woods and organized a resistance movement that had met with some minor successes in opposing the communists. They were in need of formal training in the art of guerrilla warfare and were especially in need of supplies, equipment, and arms to continue their resistance. Therefore, they had requested help from the Americans, who had promised to respond with some teams skilled in guerrilla fighting. Politically, this country was opposed to the American way as well as communism, but the current situation demanded help from whomever it could be obtained, and "Uncle Sugar" seemed the wisest choice. Once the resistance succeeded in overthrowing the communistic government, they wanted the Americans to go home, too, so their alliance with America was tentative, at best. That was the story.

The mission of the troops from the 7th Special Forces Group (Abn) was to convince the guerrillas of the advantages of democracy as well as providing arms and training. How well they succeeded would determine their grade in this part of the problem.

For the picture, Meadows, alias Nottus, posed wearing dark sunglasses, a suede leather jacket, and a black wool watchcap. Except for the sunglasses, these were the clothes he'd wear when he met the troops at the DZ. There was an elaborate system of code words and challenges and replies which he had to memorize, and drop sites for receiving communications from the MFC were selected.

As for Leontine, he became Beau Buckskin, Otto's lieutenant, and the remainder of their command consisted of simulated, make-believe, guerrillas. Ed had played soldiers and cowboys all his life, so having a simulated command was nothing new to him.

The teams were to drop in at 2200 hrs on Sunday night, so early that Sunday morning, the major and Top had everyone in for a final meeting. The major spoke first. "Well, men, heh-heh-heh, you finally get a chance to play gorrillas, heh-heh-heh." He emphasized the G-O. "You have been briefed on the problem, and you should know the terrain, except, of course, ole Meadows and Leontine who know Area PINE a hell of a lot better than Area TREE, heh-heh-heh. You'll spend ten days in your areas working with the teams. They'll have their own instructions, but your job is to act like guerillas really act, heh-heh-heh. Then you have one day to move down to Shoulders' place, where they'll get small boat training and a simulated submarine exfiltration. Then we'll bring everyone back here for critique and to ship them back to Bragg. Now remember, this is play for you, but these men will be going to "White Star" within a month, so it should be serious business for them. Do it right. That's all I have, your turn, Top."

"Most of you have played this sort of thing before, so you know the problems you may run into. The team leaders will be captains and you'll probably know most of them as well as members of the teams. Don't screw around with them, play the game. It is a tactical exercise, and you're to remain tactical (make-believe). Don't let them badger you into turning administrative. This is your country and they're your guests. Take notes so you can brief them at the end of the problem. Any criticism you make now could save their life later. Any questions?" There were none. "Okay, Prusser and Kazam, take a jeep out to your camp and drop your gear off, then go to DZ IRISH and get ready to receive your team. The MFC will provide the DZ crew and pick up the jeep, but they won't help you and they'll pull out as soon as the troops are on the ground. They'll bring the jeep back, along with any casualties from the drop. Meadows, you and Leontine do the same thing, but go to TREE after your drop on KELLY. Now, stay in your areas. The Air Force will be utilizing parts of the base for gunnery training, so you go wandering around, you'll probably get your ass shot off and I'll have to write a bunch of fucking reports. Let's have a good problem, a good, SAFE, problem. Go."

Will wonders never cease, they were trusting us with a jeep, thought Ed as he joined Leontine. "You ready to go, Sarge?" he said to his buddy.

"Bet your butt, Nottus. Let's get away from dis Magnificent Fellows' Club." The jeeps were parked outside the building, full tanks of gas, ready to go. They loaded their gear and Meadows decided to drive. That was fine with Leontine. Down the street, through the gate, and on toward Ft. Walton Beach. "Step on it, Lootenant, we just about got time ta go up ta Crestview and get us some goodies before we drop da gear off. Never know when a couple of cases of beer and some food might come in handy."

They stopped at a grocery store in Crestview and stocked up on beer, canned goods, Sterno, matches, and lots of sardines. And Tabasco sauce. A drop or two of that stuff made even C rations taste good. Then they drove to the small bridge over Turkey Gobbler Creek and offloaded. Making several trips, they stashed their goods at the campsite they'd previously used. From there, it was fifteen klicks (kilometers) as the crow flies to KELLY. Of course, it would be closer to 20 klicks as the troops walked to get back. They parked the jeep at dusk right on the edge of the DZ and walked about two hundred meters away to wait. From there, they could see the troops setting up the "L" some half-mile away. Donning his gloves, even though it was late November, Ed took precautions against No Shoulders and helped Leontine gather enough wood for a fire that would last well into the night. This was the signal the team would look for after they were on the ground and ready to meet their hosts. Then, they waited. It seemed to Meadows like they spent the biggest part of their time waiting.

As the chill of the night began to be felt, Leontine started the fire and they started to play the game. "Sarge, do you know who's coming down?" Ed asked.

"Yeah, da New Guys told me. One team is ole Joe Johnson's team. He's not a bad guy, pretty good officer, but don't talk much. He'll have his team all organized and he'll play the game. His O&I Sergeant is Kowalski, a big Polack you and Spicer met in the Pit. Good man. Used to be in the Wehrmacht. Dey didn't know who else was on the team. Da other team is Whiskey Young's team. He's an alcoholic who ain't took a sober breath in years. He's a sonofabitch who will be a real problem. I asked Top which one we'd get and the son'fabitch wouldn't tell me. His Team Sergeant is Tallamino, a fellow paisano, who's a good head, but he's got ulcers and drinks AmphoGel like it's going out of style. Don't know how effective he'll be with ole Whiskey running da show. We better hope we get Johnson. Let your buddy, Prusser, have da drunk." They talked about other things and did some more waiting. Ed's watch pointed to 10 on the dot when they heard the plane. "Well, Lootenant...'scuse me, Colonel Nottus, here we go."

They could make out the silhouette as the aircraft passed overhead, and seconds later, they could count the chutes that had blossomed. Fourteen. Probably twelve men and two bundles. Then it got very silent. Fifteen minutes passed. They heard the trucks start up and drive away from the other end of the DZ as the reception party headed back to Hurlburt. Their jeep left, too, and now it was really quiet. "Listen ta dose guys," muttered Pompeo. "Dey sound like a herd of elephants coming our way."

They must have been elephants walking on mice feet, for Meadows heard nothing. Just as the long hand pointed to 6, a figure emerged from the darkness and walked toward their fire. It was Whiskey Bill Young, in the flesh.

"Hey, there, you fellers," said the captain. "Are you hunting around here?"

"We were, but dey's too many people stomping t'rough da woods for us ta do any good," replied Leontine. The challenge word was "fire" and the answer was to be "water", then the challenge would be "red deer" and the password "water" again. If all that came out right, then the guerrillas would acknowledge the team and start the problem.

"Well, I was just wondering since I saw your fire over here."

"Yeah, we probably ought to pour some water on it and cool it off."

"If you do that, it's a cinch the red deer will stay away."

"They'll go wherever the water is."

"You must be Beau Buckskin. I'm Captain Young, from the United States of America. We're here to help you. Is Colonel Nottus around?"

"He ain't far away, but where are your men? We're supposed to have a whole bunch of people here, not one guy."

"My men are right here. I didn't think it would be wise for them to all gather around the fire."

"You're right, Cap'n, it ain't. We got a long way to go tonight, so if your men are ready, I'd suggest we get going."

"They're ready, Sergeant," Young said into the darkness, "Saddle the men up and let's move out." There was some movement among the dark bushes as the Special Forces troops gathered their packs and prepared to move out. Leontine kicked dirt on the fire until it was smothered. Captain Young moved over to where Ed had been sitting throughout the preceeding conversation and said to him, "Meadows, you should have been the one to meet us, not your sergeant."

"Are you talking to me?" Ed asked. "My name is not Meadows and I'm not a lieutenant. You must have the wrong person."

"Don't give me that shit, Lieutenant. You know damned well who I'm talking to."

"Captain Young, or whatever your name is, for your information, my name is Nottus, COLONEL Nottus, and I don't like your attitude very much. I'd suggest you get your gear and get ready. As Mr. Buckskin said, we have a long way to go tonight." With that, Ed rose up and walked over to Leontine. "Let's go, Beau. Seems like the Americans sent us a wise-ass to help us. Let's see if the wise-ass can walk."

Since their gear was already stored on the banks of Turkey Gobbler Creek, Leontine and Meadows had nothing to carry except their walking sticks, while the American team was heavily laden with supplies and equipment. This made for some tough walking as the two guerrillas stomped off through the sand and the Americans tried to stay abreast. Captain Young dogged Ed's footsteps for the first fifteen minutes, but then he began to lag a little behind, then a little more behind, and after thirty minutes of trudging through the sand, Young was very far behind. It was about this time that SFC Tallamino pulled up alongside Leontine and said to the guerrilla, "LT Buckskin, our men are travelling with a lot of gear, and we really need to adjust some of it. Is there any place where we could stop for a few minutes to adjust some of these packs?"

"Why, sure, Sarge. We can take a break right here," said Pompeo and right there he stopped and sat down. This was more like playing the game. In reality, the two rebels had intended to stop after about an half-hour to see if the team was alert enough to post sentries when taking a break. They were.

"Munoz, you post out front about 100 meters and keep watch," said Tallamino. "Howell, you drop back about the same distance from the last man in the column and watch our rear. Beaumont, left flank 50 meters; Everbaum, right. The rest of you stop in place and adjust your gear." Tallamino was disgustingly efficient. Captain Young had caught up by this time.

"Good job, Sergeant. Say, Meadows," he said, addressing Ed, "What the hell you trying to do? These men are tired from a long flight and loaded down with equipment. If you don't get off your hobby horse and show some sense, I'll have your ass when this exercise is over."

Ed was seething. He thought about stopping the problem right there and heading for the fire station at Field 6 to call the MFC and informing the major. Probably be exactly what the major would want, and he'd probably be shipped back to Bragg in disgrace. No way. So he held his tongue and sat down next to Leontine. "Say, Beau," he said in a voice loud enough for the captain to hear, "These Americans ain't in very good shape. Maybe they ain't what we need to help us against the government."

"Ah, Colonel, some of 'em are doin' okay. It's jist da fat ones having trouble." It was Young's turn to boil for he was a little chubby.

"Okay, Assholes, I'll play your silly fucking game, but your ass is grass when I see ole Kreeger. He knows what the score is. Fucking tin soldiers. Fucking West Point. You're gonna see what the real world is like soon enough." So saying, he took off his big rucksack and sat down. When he did, Leontine stood up.

"Colonel, we better get moving. We got a long way to go before daylight."

"Right, Beau. Captain, get your men on their feet. Let's go," and he and Leontine started walking. The team members struggled to their feet and followed, Captain Young bringing up the rear. They walked as far as the Niceville road where Leontine presented the problem of crossing to Tallamino.

"Da government patrols dis road pretty frequently. We'd better be careful crossing it. We usually run across, but wit' so many troops, I don't know if dat would be a good idea. What do you tink?" Captain Young had caught up by this time, so the team sergeant presented the problem to his CO.

"Ain't no problem, Sarge. Get Lieutenant Allen up here. Spread the men out along the road. When I give the word, we'll all cross at once." The solution was okay, so the team was still doing well, in spite of Ed's wish that Young would screw it up. They crossed the road, reassembled in the woods on the other side, and headed on toward Turkey Gobbler Creek. The light was just beginning to break in the eastern sky when they reached the campsite.

"Captain Young," Ed addressed the officer, "This is our camp. My men are all around us so it's safe. You can put your men over there by the creek. Don't let them wander off, cause my men will shoot anyone they don't know, and they don't know you. I'm going to get some sleep, and we'll talk in the morning when I wake up. I want to see what you have to offer us. You look like you could use some rest, too. Sorry, but no fires. There are government patrols all over these woods. Good night," and with that, Ed went over across the creek to where Leontine waited.

"We got a problem, Sir," Pompeo said, "and its name is Young."

"Right. Let's get some sleep. Let him stew for awhile. We'll think of something in the morning."

But, they didn't. In every conversation they had with the captain, he referred to Meadows as Lieutenant and to Leontine as Sarge. The other team members tried to play the game for the most part, but it wasn't a very good situation. Ed and Pompeo kept notes on the progress of the training, but even these notations soon took on the tone of accusations against the stubborn Captain. They weren't having fun. On the evening of the fourth day of the problem, they were supposed to pick up a message at one of the drop points where they could leave one of their own. When this time arrived, Meadows and Leontine told Tallamino they had to meet some of the other guerrilla leaders in the region, so they'd be gone for a few hours. Taking their pistols and little else, they then started off for the little bridge carrying the Ranger Road over Turkey Hen Creek a couple of miles away.

"What we gonna say, Sarge?" asked Meadows as they walked through the woods in the dark.

"I dunno, Sir. Dese guys is doing okay on da problem, it's jist dat fucking Captain. I toll you he was bad news. He oughta have an accident."

"Yeah, I know that, but he ain't had an accident and we gotta tell the MFC something. We can't say everything is fine, cause that guy ain't played the game yet. Let's let the major know."

"Sir, wit' all due respect to your rank, I don't t'ink dat's a good idea. I t'ink we oughta cover our ass by taking notes and tell what happened at da end of da problem. Let da major decide what to do den."

"You're probably right, but that guy really frosts my balls. He is a son-of-a-bitch."

"Agreed. Let's get on over ta da drop and see what da Mother Fuckers Club has left us." They walked the rest of the way in silence.

The supports of a bridge are favorite places for drop sites in unconventional warfare, and the eastern support of this bridge was the conventional unconventional site pre-selected for this drop. Meadows and Leontine approached the area warily, remembering the way they'd been set up on their initial entrance into this tactical area, and it wasn't above the MFC to arrange a welcoming party for them on this occasion. So their progress over the last couple of hundred meters was slow as they strained their senses for any untoward sound or sight or smell. It was the sense of hearing which alerted them first. Meadows was about ten feet ahead of Pompeo as they crouched and watched the drop for the prescribed thirty minutes by the clock when he heard a faint scratching in the woods north of the bridge. He couldn't be sure what it was, but he was sure he had heard something. "Tharge?" he lisp-whispered.

"I heard it. Lithen." They waited a few minutes before they heard it again, closer this time. Ed thought of the porpoise.

"Think it'th a fithth?"

"It ain't no fithth, but there thure ath hell ith thomething over there. You got your pieth?"

"I got it," replied Ed as he drew his weapon, "but I ain't thooting no fithth." It was hard to suppress a giggle. They waited. Now they could tell that the sound was a man coming down the road toward them, but try as they might, they still could see nothing.

"Lootenant, if it'th a Ranger, let him go, but if it'th thomeone elthe, thoot hith athth." More waiting. Leontine was the first to spot the figure moving along the side of the road. "There'th the bathtard," he whispered.

It was a man carrying a rifle and trying to stay concealed somewhat by the roadside brush as he approached the bridge. He had a somewhat familiar gait. He also had a somewhat familiar gut pouching over his beltline. "Hell, Tharge, it'th Captain Young," muttered Ed.

"Thay down, Lootenant," whispered Leontine. From the corner of his eye, Ed saw Pompeo raise his pistol and heard him slowly cock the hammer.

"THARGE!" whispered Meadows excitedly. "It'th Captain Young. Put your weapon down!"

"Hold tight, Lootenant," and Ed could see the pistol trained on the figure about twenty-five meters away.

"THARGE, DAMMIT, IT'TH YOUNG! PUT YOUR GUN UP!"

"Hold tight, Thir. He ain't thuppothed to be here," and the pistol remained trained on the figure.

Meadows knew Leontine was going to shoot Captain Young. He had to stop it, somehow. Damnation, he was an American! Rising out of his crouch, he hollered at the figure, "Hey, you, what the fuck you doing here?"

Young was surprised by the sound. He turned around and faced Ed as the lieutenant walked up. Meadows heard Leontine lower the hammer carefully. "Why, Lieutenant Meadows, there you are. I thought you and your buddy got lost. This is always the site we use for a drop down here and I thought I'd just tag along and see what you fellers found out." Captain Young was smiling. "You assholes might need some help talking to ole Kreeger. Too bad he ain't here."

"Captain Young," began Ed, "You are not supposed to leave the camp…"

"Knock off that shit, Meadows. Let's see what we got." There was a small cage by the bridge and inside it were six chickens. There was also a sack of potatoes and a can of coffee, compliments of the MFC. A Red Dot match box lay next to the chickens, but it was empty. "What the hell," said Captain Young, "This ain't worth the walk. You guys can carry this shit back, you want to play the game so fucking much. I'm going back to camp," and off he walked.

Ed stood next to Leontine as they watched him head off back through the woods. "That son-of-a-bitch. What the hell are we going to do, Pompeo? He's making a farce of this whole thing."

"Wit' all due respect to your rank, Sir, you fucked up."

"How do you figure that, Sarge?"

"You should have let him have an accident, Sir, and me and Mr. Smith and Wesson was gonna give him one."

7

These Boots Are Made For Walking

By the time seven days had passed, the conflict between Meadows and Captain Young had almost erupted into open warfare. Ed got to the point where he could hardly stand to see the man coming to talk over the plans the team had formulated for training the guerrillas. Pompeo had maintained some semblance of rationality, and had taken over most of the tasks of inspecting the work of the team and arriving at their grades. Despite the open hostility between their leader and the guerrilla chief, the team was performing well, held together by the strong will of Sergeant Tallamino. Just as Pompeo had predicted, the team sergeant lived on a diet of AmphoGel, but he did his job extremely well, and Meadows was impressed. They got a message at one of their drops to have the team run a recon on the airfield over in Area Pine on Day 8 and then proceed down to Hammock Point on the following day to meet with Captain Cruze. Meadows was ready for that, because then he would be relieved of the burden of Captain Young and he and Pompeo could prepare their case on trying to get him relieved of his team. Leontine and Meadows consulted the SOI from Field 6 that they had confiscated, and discovered that it was standard practice to run a fire drill and test the truck and hoses every other Sunday morning between 1000 hrs and 1200 hrs. With any luck at all, this would be the other Sunday morning.

"Captain Young," said Ed at their evening strategy discussion, "one of the nearby guerrilla chiefs has sent me word that the government has an airstrip in his area, and we would be welcome to use it for receiving your supplies, for a small fee, of course, like some weapons and instruction on their use by your team. I know this man well, and he is reliable. If you'd like to take your team over there and look the place over, Beau and I could direct you tomorrow." It was an effort for Meadows to be civil, much less play the game.

"Lieutenant Meadows, is this the airfield recon we're supposed to run down here?" queried Whiskey Bill.

"Captain Young, I am asking you for the last time not to call me by that nickname. My name is Colonel Nottus, but you may call me, 'Colonel,' for short. Do you wish to see the airfield or not?"

"Hell, yes, Lieutenant, we'll run a fucking recon on the field. When do we get down to the beach and get some oysters?" To make matters worse, Young had managed to smuggle some booze down here with him and it hadn't gotten broken in the jump. Too bad, Ed would have enjoyed watching a good case of the DT's. As it was, the Captain was about half-loaded all the time.

"Captain, if you'll have your men ready at 0400 hrs with all their gear, we'll take you to the airfield. Now we ought to get some sleep." Ed left his seat by the small fire they had allowed after the fifth day, and began fixing up his fartsack for another night. He and Pompeo had already packed, and Leontine had the alarm set for 0330 hrs, so Meadows crawled into the bag, zipped it up and went to sleep. Leontine and Captain Young were still sitting by the fire when Ed checked out.

No matter how long you've been in the Army, 0330 hrs comes too early every day; no matter how many problems you've been on, it's still early. It was early when the little alarm went off and Meadows and Leontine crawled out of their sacks to start the day. Pompeo kicked the ashes of the fire around, added some wood, and they soon had a sizeable blaze. "May as well have some hot coffee on our last day here," he'd explained, to no one in particular. "Lootenant, where's your cup?"

"In my hand, Sarge," returned Ed as he offered his cup to the sergeant.

"Dis is da last of our coffee, Sir. I'm gonna shitcan dis Number 10 can so remind me ta get us another before we come back out here."

"What the hell, I'm tired of your coffee anyway, Sarge. I want some stirred with a swizzle stick and smelling like turkeys ought to smell in a bottle. Like, wild."

"I don't know about da smell, but I'm sure yo' buddy da cap'n could supply you wit' da booze." Both men laughed.

"You know, Pompeo, I really can't stand that bastard. Be just my luck to get over to Laos and have the son-of-a-bitch for a Team Leader."

"Hell, Sir, accidents is easy to happen in Laos. One little round between his running lights and your troubles would be over."

"Hell, I'd probably only wound him." Whiskey Bill himself suddenly walked into the light from their fire.

"So, you fuckers been holding out on me. Gimme some of that coffee."

"Right, Sir," said Leontine as he rose to take the captain's cup. Leaning forward, he moved his foot to keep his balance and kicked over the coffee. The fire sizzled and smoked and sputtered in rebellion at the invasion of water into its realm. "Damn, Sir, I'm sorry 'bout dat. We ain't got no more. Sorry, Sir."

"Fucking assholes," murmured Young as he walked off.

"Say, Pompeo, was that an accident?" asked Meadows.

"Damn right, Sir. Little trick I learned from my Lootenant: how to kick things into the fire."

"Leontine, you're a mean sonofabitch."

"Fucking A, Sir. Let's take dese guys ta a fire drill."

For the two erstwhile guerrilla leaders, the trip to the airfield was old hat, but for the team members, who had no idea how far they had to go, it was a struggle through the sand. Leontine led the way first, and he set a brutal pace. When Ed's turn came, he showed no tendency to slacken it. Not only that, but they took a most circuitous route to "avoid the government patrols." In fact, it was 0930 hrs before they reached the vicinity of the airfield.

"There it is, Captain Young. Can you tell all you need from here?" quizzed Ed.

"Hell, no, Lieutenant. I'll have Tallamino organize a recon patrol, and I'll just sit here with you guys and relax. You got any beer?"

"No," replied the two men in unison. They'd planned on easing off to the creek not 300 meters away and retrieving their Cokes donated by the ambush party from the MFC that other night, but that idea was dropped. Leave 'em. They could get them another day. SGT Tallamino got the recon patrol organized, and they shoved off, planning on reassembling at 1100 hrs. Meadows and Leontine waited. They didn't talk, not with Young around, and the captain seemed to be snoozing. They watched the men of the patrol as they crept toward the airstrip, and then the men were lost from sight in the woods. These men were no novices, they knew their business. Still, Meadows and Leontine waited.

Sitting on the ground here among the bushes, they could just barely make out the door of the firehouse nearly a mile away, but they could see it well enough to tell when the fireman went inside. Could be he was just making a phone call. Then the big door to the truck stall opened, and the two guerrillas held their breath. Maybe they were in luck, maybe it was the other Sunday. There was a wail, and the flashing of lights, and the fire truck came lumbering out of its garage. It gathered speed as it headed toward the south end of the runway, lights flashing, siren screaming. When it got to the end of the paved strip, the driver turned it toward the pavement and braked it to a halt. He sprang out, manned the water cannon mounted on the back, and hosed down the woods all around that end of the field. Almost, but not quite, the stream of water reached the three observers. First, Leontine giggled, then Ed laughed, then they cried as they laughed so hard, but they just kept laughing. "Captain Young," managed Ed between convulsions of glee, "looks like your patrol has been discovered." Then they laughed some more.

"You fucking dipshit!" yelled Captain Young. "You childish bastard. Do you think this is funny? You're supposed to be training men for combat, and you play this silly-ass game. You knew that fucking truck was gonna come down here. You shithead! Is that all you learned at fucking West Point, how to fuck off? Well, Lieutenant, is it?"

"No, Captain, it isn't," answered Meadows still intermittently giggling. "We learned to be officers, too, but not drunks."

"You tin soldier shithead. You try to walk us into the ground wandering over here, then you pull this shit. You ain't got the sense God gave a goose."

"Captain, if the walk was too strenuous for you, all you had to do was say so."

"You fucking ring-knocker. I can walk your fucking ass into the ground any fucking day you please."

"Sir, you're wrong. You can't walk me into the ground." As mad as Ed was on general principles, Young was furious. He was irrational. Meadows thought he was gonna have a stroke, or whatever old alcoholics had.

"Asshole, you pick the time and place and I'll show your ass!" stormed the captain.

"Why not right now? We're supposed to move down to the beach by tomorrow morning. Why don't you and me just go on ahead and let Beau Buckskin bring the rest of your men? It ain't that far, about 20 miles. Are you game?"

"Fucking right, Asshole. With or without rucksacks?"

"With everything. Get your gear, Captain." Meadows went over to get his stuff, and Leontine accompanied him.

"Lemme help you, Lootenant." Then, in a whisper barely audible, he added, "You fucked up, Sir, wit' all due respect to your rank. Dis fucker used ta walk a lot. Too late to worry now, just set a fast pace, and don't never let up. Whatever you do, don't stop."

Before he could ask, "why?", the captain walked up, all loaded and ready to go. "If you lovebirds can break it up now, we can get this show on the road. Didn't they teach you the difference between boys and girls at West Point, Lieutenant? Fucking queers, whispering sweet nothings. C'mon, Asshole, let's go!"

"After you, Captain. I wouldn't want to take advantage of you because of your age."

It was easy getting back into the rhythm of walking since they'd warmed up with the stroll through the woods earlier that morning. Ed's pack fit well and he felt good. He was used to walking in the sand, and he had on a good pair of well-broken-in boots. *These boots were made for walking,* he thought, as they headed down the trail to the south. *Yep, time to step right out.*

On the other hand, Captain Young was having a hard time getting going. His rucksack was very heavy, making him almost top-heavy, and it seemed that with every step he took, his boots slid sideways in the sand, providing him poor traction, indeed. He was breathing hard and sweating profusely, and they'd only been going for a few minutes. He struggled to stay abreast of Meadows.

When they reached the little bridge across the creek separating Area

PINE from Area HILL, Ed was twenty-five meters ahead. Thirty minutes later, the gap was fifty meters. Captain Young looked bad. He was walking all bent over, leaning heavily on a walking stick he'd picked up somewhere, and sweating to the extent that his uniform was drenched. He was laboring in his breathing, gasping and panting. Meadows began to worry a little about him. Sonofabitch, what if the guy dropped dead out here? How would Ed ever explain it to the major? What if he had heat stroke, or passed out, or something? *This was a dumb idea*, thought Ed. Still, they kept walking. At the ten mile point, they came to another auxillary field where a lot of old aircraft carcasses were stored. There were B-29's with the engines torn off, a couple of F-80 hulls with broken canopies, and an assortment of other relics of by-gone days. They kept walking.

Now Ed was really worried about the Captain, for he was a good 500 meters behind and struggling. "Crap!" exclaimed Ed to himself. "I can't have the guy dying out here. I'd better check on him." With this thought in mind, Ed slacked off on his pace. He didn't stop, he just slowed down and started taking smaller steps. Captain Young began to close the gap, but not quickly. He closed it so slowly, in fact, that Ed was forced to stop and wait for him when they reached the fifteen mile point.

"Are you okay, Captain?" asked the lieutenant. "You don't look so good."

"Yeah," panted Young, "I'm okay, but I could use a break. Need a smoke and to catch my breath. How much further?"

"About five miles. We can take a break, if you like. We've been walking pretty fast."

"Yeah, let's take a break. I need a smoke." They found a shady spot under some trees and sat down. As Ed slipped out of the rucksack harness, Young sat on the ground still attached to his bag. He was red-faced, and sweat was dripping off of him, and he was breathing so hard he was blowing, but still he managed to get a soggy pack of cigarettes out of his pocket and succeeded in firing one up. Meadows drank from his canteen and offered it to Captain Young. "Want some water?"

All Young did was shake his head. He finished his cigarette while Ed fished a fresh pair of socks from his rucksack and exchanged them for the ones he'd been wearing. They felt good. Captain Young was still blowing. "Ready to go?" asked Ed.

Young nodded. He struggled to his feet as Meadows donned his pack, and Ed thought he was going to have to help the captain up. They started walking slowly and Ed determined to stay close to his competition long enough to make sure Whiskey Bill was alright. The pace picked up. Captain Young was doing better. Ed decided to move on out, so he quickened his steps and lengthened his stride. Young stayed right with him. Ed was walking so rapidly now that his feet were slipping sideways in the sand, but he wasn't pulling ahead of the captain. To tell the truth, Ed was starting to fall behind. Not much, just a couple of yards, and he knew he could make that up, but he kept waiting for the captain to collapse, or stroke out, or something, but he didn't. Instead, Whiskey Bill began steadily pulling away. Meadows tried to trot to catch back up, but in the sand and with all his gear, it was impossible. Captain Young was standing up straight, and striding right along, and leaving Meadows in his wake.

"This can't be happening!" Ed said to himself. "C'mon, Gang (to his feet), let's move it." His feet tried. Ed tried, but they couldn't catch the captain. As they approached Highway 98, Young was a good 200 meters ahead. He crossed, and Ed tried one last time to catch up by running toward the road, but he merely slipped and slid in the sand. There wasn't a lot of traffic, so Ed crossed without delay, but Captain Young was already out of sight in the woods. When he reached Shoulders' camp, Captain Young was sitting on a camp stool, drinking a beer, and telling everyone his version of what happened. He saw Ed coming.

"Well, well, well, what have we here? A fucking Tin Soldier sucking his thumb? Look at your future leader, men, a fucking loser to an old man. Would you follow him into combat? Fucking shithead, you can give 'em a free education, but you can't make 'em smart."

As Ed dropped off his pack and looked for a place to sit, he cursed himself under his breath. "I was stupid. I fucked up in waiting for him. I'm a dummy. But my biggest fuck-up was stopping Pompeo from killing the sonofabitch."

8

Shadows

There wasn't much left for Pompeo and Ed to do when they returned to the MFC except to compile their notes and organize them into some sort of order before they met with the major and Top to give a preview of the upcoming critique for the team. They talked about Captain Young and the way he'd acted throughout the problem, but when they made their final recommendation that the captain be relieved of his command, the major only laughed.

"Lieutenant, heh-heh-heh, I think you're just pissed off because old Young whipped your ass on the little marathon you organized, heh-heh-heh. Maybe you learned something, do you good, heh-heh-heh. I don't want no mention of that when you give your critique. You can fuss about him not playing the game, but don't say nothing about a failing grade. The team passed, you got your ass kicked, and that's all there was to it, heh-heh-heh. That the way you seen it, Top?"

"Well, yes, Sir, I agree, old Tallamino did a good job. Maybe Captain Young did okay, we know he can walk, but maybe we ought to recommend he be sent to one of the "B" teams instead of commanding an "A" detachment. Personally, Sir, I wouldn't want to be in his team."

"That may be, Top, but Young's in trouble because of his drinking. If we give him a bad recommendation on this problem, they'll shit-can him at Group. No, we are going to say they're ready for Laos. Tallamino'll see them through, heh-heh-heh. That's what good NCO's are for, isn't it, Top?"

"You're right, Sir," and that's what they did. The team got a passing grade, Captain Young got very drunk and was virtually poured onto the plane when they left, and Meadows was left to lick his wounds. He wouldn't have long to lick them if they followed the schedule, for another team would be coming down in a few days. But there was a change in the schedule.

There may have been a conflict going on in Laos, or Lebanon, or China, but it was November in the United States, and if another team came down now to go through the problem, they'd be out in the field over Thanksgiving, and that just isn't done, not in this day and age. So the schedule was adjusted to allow for a couple of week's training time to be used for reviewing and refining the problem. Translated, that meant that the MFC crew could play around for awhile until after Thanksgiving. The major let the married troops return to Bragg to be with their families and the single people matched out to see who had to stay and who got to go home for the holiday. Ed lost, Prusser went home. There were enough people left at the Florida outpost to keep the beach site open, mainly because of the desire for oysters which abated little and also because Sergeant Shoulders didn't go home. Instead, he conducted real classes on hydrographic survey and a little on techniques of SCUBA diving for anyone interested. That included Ed.

The lieutenant didn't spend the nights down on the beach, he enjoyed his BOQ room too much for that, but he'd drive his Valiant down there every afternoon that he wasn't the Duty Officer and drink beer and shoot the breeze with the troops. And he did some SCUBA diving, too, It was on one such afternoon visit that Shoulders offered him a proposition. If Meadows was interested, the next day he could join Shoulders, Vickers, Valentine, and a couple of others who were going across the bridge in Ft. Walton Beach to Santa Rosa Island and do some survey out in the Gulf itself, rather than just in the Sound. It would be a lot more exciting than the rather bland conditions in the still waters of the Sound and was contingent, of course, upon the weather. Meadows was definitely interested.

The next morning, which was the Saturday after Thanksgiving, dawned bright, crisp, and crystal clear; Belcher was loaded with one of the 14-foot rubber boats and its attached motor and copious fuel tanks, a couple of cases of beer, four sets of compressed air tanks, wet suits, a couple of dry suits, some other sundry items including paddles, and eight of them set out to explore the Gulf of Mexico like Cortez and Pizarro never dreamed possible.

If you're flying over this part of the Gulf, there is a change in the color of the water from a brown tint to the green of deep water which you can easily see. It occurs at a variable distance from the shore, but on the average it is a couple of hundred meters. Ed didn't know what real sailors called it, but back in Ranger School, it was referred to as the Green Bank. It marks a drop-off in the depth of the water that is rather sudden, and the resulting undertow generated has spelled the doom of many swimmers through the years. During the Ranger raid on the Aggressor CP, they had left the old LCU (an Army vehicle) and had paddled over the Green Bank. Just a couple of cycles before Ed went through that training, they had lost five Rangers in a boating accident there. When Shoulders announced that they were going to work off the Bank, Ed wasn't thrilled. Although many of the officers and a few of the top NCO's treated the second lieutenants as DASL's, by far the majority of the NCO's and men were very tolerant of these men for which there were no TO&E slots in the Group. Therefore, it was no surprise when Ed was offered the chance to be one of the first men to participate in this adventure.

On a Navy boat (Meadows loved to refer to all watercraft as "boats:" it seemed to bother sailors), there may have been facilities for frogmen to change into their wetsuits, but on this craft you donned your gear right out there in front of God and everybody. Presently, there weren't any other observers as Ed shucked down to his bare birthday suit and pulled on the neoprene. It was quite brisk, or, as Shoulders called it, colder than a well-digger's ass when they finally got dressed. Ed and the sergeant jumped into the water to get wet and start the process of allowing their body heat to warm the water trapped in the rubber suits. Shoulders changed his mind: now it was colder than a witch's tit. They slipped their arms through the harnesses of the Scuba tanks as the other men held them over the side for them, put on their masks and a lead-weight belt, checked the fit of the mouth pieces and turned the valves of the tanks on and checked out their breathing. Swishing some water around the inside of the mask, Meadows put it on and was all set. Shoulders, holding onto the side of the boat, suggested Ed might want his fins on, too, so Ed had the men in the boat help him back out of the water and onto the side of the inflatable boat where he put on the fins. Now he really was ready. Back into the water, still cold as the witch or the well-digger, take your pick. They swam around on the surface for a few minutes, warming up and getting comfortable with the mouth breathing-on-demand process before going back to the side of the boat and deciding what they would do. The boat was to stay right where it was. They had put out a small anchor which would keep them in about the same position, plus an inflated life vest serving as a sea anchor to keep them pointed in the same direction. Shoulders would lead the way, and Ed would follow him and abide by the sergeant's hand and arm signals under water. There was supposed to be an hour's worth of air in their tanks, but to be on the safe side, they planned on staying down for no more than forty-five minutes. Shoulders had a diver's watch strapped on his wrist and he was responsible for keeping up with the time. After these two had taken their turn, they'd switch and let someone else play for awhile.

"You ready, Lieutenant?" asked Shoulders.

"I reckon so, Sarge. When do I get warm?"

"Don't worry about it, Sir. It ain't gonna bother you. Okay, let's go. Now, Sir, if you have any trouble at all, for any reason, let me know. Don't hesitate. If we don't use our heads, this can be just as hostile an environment as Laos ever will be. See you at the bottom," he said, lowering his mask and biting his mouthpiece, and he was gone. Ed followed.

All the diving they had done in the Sound had been in shallow water, not more than fifteen feet deep. When Ed followed Shoulders down, it was a new experience to turn tail up and swim vertically down. It was surprising how well Ed could see, for the water out here was not nearly so murky as that in the Sound. They went down for several seconds, Meadows wasn't sure exactly how many, but they descended far enough that it made a difference to Ed's ears and he had to squeeze his nose and blow to equalize the pressure. At the bottom, Meadows was relieved to see no vegetation, for it scared him to death to think of swimming around in seaweed. Shoulders seemed to be at home down here, and he glanced over at Meadows frequently and smiled around the mouthpiece. It was a funny-looking smile, but it did reassure Ed. Shoulders pointed at the bottom, and Ed looked down. The sand was only a couple of feet below him and he could see a fine cloud of silt and sand flowing seaward. The current was rather strong, requiring Ed to keep swimming just to maintain his position, and it was easy to see how a regular swimmer could find himself in trouble were he to be caught in this undertow. Meadows glanced upward to see if he could find the boat, and with the bright sunlight providing a backdrop, he could easily make out the shadow of the bobbing craft.

They moved shoreward a little way and the current became much stronger. After about fifty meters, they came to a virtual wall of sand, a very precipitous drop, the old Green Bank itself. Now it was all Ed could do to keep alongside Shoulders. Not only was the current strong, but it was turbulent as well, and Meadows found himself being twisted and turned continually by the force of the water. He looked up to see if he could make out the top of the bank, and when he did, he saw the shadow of the boat passing overhead, parallel with the shoreline. What the hell was going on? They were supposed to stay where they were left! He looked over at Shoulders, but the sergeant was busy writing something on the board he'd brought along for making notes. Meadows glanced back to where the boat was supposed to be, and there it was, the shadow bobbing with the waves. Wait just a minute. Were there two boats out here now? Ed knew they'd only brought one, and none of the other guys from the MFC were planning on coming out here. Of course, this was a free country, and someone else could be fooling around up there, but they hadn't seen anyone while they were on the surface. He looked around, trying to locate the other shadow, and there it was, about fifty meters away, now passing parallel to the way Ed was aligned. Not only that, but it wasn't on the surface, it was below the surface by a considerable amount.

When Ed was much younger and just learning to hunt, shoot and walk through the woods, he was aware of the fact that snakes lived in the woods. He liked studying snakes, they were fascinating creatures. He used to catch a lot of little DeKay's snakes on the banks of the railroad cut just off East Trigg Avenue back home in Memphis. He and his friends loved to scare the wits out of less-informed people, translated, "girls," with these little reptiles. All the while they handled these snakes, however, they were aware of the fact that not all snakes were to be handled: like rattlers, and Ed had wondered at the time if he would recognize the sound of a rattler rattling when he heard it. There had been that fateful day near Nonconnah Creek when he'd stumbled across a rattlesnake and the fellow had set to buzzing, and there was no mistaking a rattler when it was rattling. Of late, he had wondered if he'd know a shark when he saw one. He did, and this was one. This was a big one.

Meadows grabbed Shoulders by the arm, and pointed at the animal. Shoulders gave him that funny looking mouthpiece smile and shook his head. Ed pointed again. Shoulders smiled again. Ed pointed a third time, but this time he pointed at the boat, released the Sergeant's arm, and turned around and swam upward toward the boat. He kicked his feet vigorously, swimming as fast as he possibly could. No stopping early this time, like he had on the run back at Bragg; he kicked and swam as hard as he could all the way to the boat. Breaking the surface next to the boat, Meadows required no help from anyone as he clambered aboard and took off the tanks, spitting out the mouthpiece and jerking off his mask.

"What's wrong, Lieutenant?" asked Valentine. "You still got thirty minutes' air left."

"Shark. There's a big fucking shark down there."

"What kind?" asked Vickers.

"The kind that eats people!" replied Meadows.

"Aw, Sir, there ain't no man-eaters around here this time of year." Vickers was a graduate of the Navy school, too.

"He looked like a man-eater to me. He had a gleam in his eye when he looked at me."

"Shit, Sir, you still got thirty minutes' air left."

"You can have them. Be my guest." And right there Ed made a vow. If all the sharks in the world promised to stay off dry land, Ed promised to stay out of wet water.

9

Briggs' Boys

There was only going to be one cycle during December because of the holidays—Christmas and New Year's, just as the cycles for November were interrupted for Thanksgiving. Yep, getting ready for war here at the end of the year was tough. Pompeo returned from Bragg and he and Meadows headed back to Area TREE, but there were a few changes. Two more DASL's were dispatched to the MFC and they were assigned sergeants and planned to open up Areas MOSS and DIRT to complement TREE and HILL. Prusser went back to HILL with Kazam, and Jack Hickman took SGT Dodge to MOSS, while Art Venice took SGT Russell to DIRT. Hickman and Venice were two of Ed's best friends, but he barely had a chance to say "Hello" before they were off to the field.

Leontine had brought a couple of shelter-halfs with him from Bragg, four of them, to be exact, so now the two friends had a pup tent apiece for their quarters instead of sleeping under the stars all the time. Or the rain, as it turned out, for their spell of fair weather turned sour and it was misting or raining nearly all the time now. They had two days alone in the field to get everything set up before the MFC sent word that the new teams would be arriving on the 2nd of December, Saturday evening at 2200 hrs by parachute, on DZ KELLY. In case of inclement weather, they'd land on Field 6 at the same hour. Great. Meadows and Leontine decided to walk on over to KELLY on the first and from there they could make it to Field 6 in about an hour should the need arise.

Another fire, another period of waiting, and the DZ crew from the MFC arrived with word that the weather was supposed to be good enough for a drop. The DZ was set up, darkness fell on time, the fire felt good in the moist, cool air, and at 2200 hrs they heard the sound of the aircraft engines. At 2202 hrs, just barely making the time limit, the blossoming chutes in the night air heralded the start of another training cycle. This time their team was commanded by a Captain Jackson, whom neither Ed nor Pompeo knew, but he made the correct contact, introduced Lieutenant Smith, his Executive Officer, and the whole bunch of them started the walk back to Area TREE. Smith held the distinction of being a FIRST Lieutenant, for which there were TO&E slots in the Group. Jackson was a big, friendly man who played the game to the hilt. He never failed to refer to Meadows as Colonel Nottus, or to Leontine as LT Buckskin, so they started out on the right foot.

The entire problem went so much better than the first cycle. The team members worked hard, their NCO's cooperated with Leontine, and Jackson and Smith were each a pleasure to work with. Training schedules for the guerrillas were devised: a raid against the Government outpost in Crestview was planned, and by the ninth of the month, Day 8 of the problem, every objective of the TREE phase of the problem had been accomplished. Pompeo and Ed were to pick up a drop that night at the Turkey Hen bridge, and they both expected it to be their orders to proceed down to Cruze's place. So, when suppertime came, they invited Jackson and Smith over to their campfire to have dinner with them. Ed declared the situation "administrative," meaning that they could drop the sham names, and enjoy a little camaraderie with some fellow members of their parent Group. It was a nice evening. Meadows was talking with Smith, and for the sake of something new to talk about, he asked how LTC Briggs was doing.

"Haven't you heard?" asked Smith.

"Heard what?"

"Hell, man, Colonel Briggs got the shit kicked out of him by some big dude over in DIVARTY. He was getting drunk at the Cannoneers Club the other night, and he got to talking about DASL's. In his usual fashion, he was saying how they were the worst things to happen to this earth, the dumbest, all his usual shit, and this big moose of a Captain from DIVARTY joined in telling how bad Brigg's DASL's were. Well, Briggs took exception to that, since the guy was from the Artillery and not in Group, so he asked this guy where he got the right to criticize Brigg's DASL's. He said that his DASL's could beat the shit out of the artillery DASL's, and, as a matter of fact, he could beat the shit out of any captain from the Artillery. The captain took him up on that and they went outside and the captain beat ole Briggs like a drum. He beat him really bad, but Briggs never would admit that his DASL's couldn't beat the shit out of the artillery DASL's. It was brutal."

"Well, I'll be damned." said Ed. "I'll just be damned. I never would have dreamed that I was one of Brigg's Boys. Who'd a' thunk it?"

"That old bastard is really kinda proud of you guys," Smith continued, "but don't tell him I said so."

"Yeah, well, look, Pompeo and I gotta go pick up a message, so we'll see you in the morning. Your team is really doing well, you're knocking the shit out of this problem. Have a good night. Guess it's time to revert to tactical. G'night." The two officers of the team left to return to their sacks, and Leontine and Meadows struck out for the bridge. Having made the trip a couple of times before made it seem shorter than it had with Young tailing them. They reached the site, went through the usual precautions, and picked up the message from the match box. Pompeo opened it after they were safely back in the woods.

"What's it say, Pompeo?" asked Ed as he lit a match and held it so Leontine could read.

"LT Meadows to Field 6, 0800 10 Dec."

"What else does it say?"

"That's all. There ain't anything else. What you t'ink's going on?"

"Damn if I know. What'da you think?"

"I dunno, but I don' like it. Let's go get your gear together. I t'ink it'd be a good idea for you to mosey on up dere tonight and have a chance to look da place over early in da morning. See if dem bastards from da Magnificent Fellows Club have a surprise for you. C'mon, Lootenant, you got a long walk t'night."

They decided to leave the tents by Turkey Gobbler, so Ed hefted up his packed rucksack, said he'd be sure to be on his toes, and said goodnight to Leontine. Away into the darkness he went.

It's always darkest just before the dawn, but it always a damn sight darker at night when you're alone. Ed walked along the sandy trail winding toward the Niceville Road and Field 6 beyond. The light from the fire alongside the creek faded rapidly, and all Ed could hear was the sound of his boots shuffling through the sand. At least, that's all he could hear that he was sure of. There was a virtual cacophony of sound from the night. A rabbit squealed in terror as it was caught by some unseen predator off to his left, a sound he'd heard a lot since being in Florida, but tonight the scream seemed to have a special element of terror in it. Ya' know, woods are eerie at night. Not scary, mind you, not for an Airborne Ranger, Special Forces-trained killer, but they were eerie. Well...okay, maybe just a little bit scary. It was 0200 when Meadows spotted the lights of a vehicle moving down the road toward Niceville, so he became especially wary as he approached the road. If the MFC had any monkey business in mind, they'd most likely pull it near a road. Those folks didn't like the woods very much. He moved up until he could see the blacktop surface plainly, then he eased down to the ground to watch for awhile. The glow of a cigarette, the sound of talking, the smell of gasoline, anything out of the ordinary would alert him to the presence of something that didn't belong. He sat and watched the road for ten minutes and saw, heard, and smelled nothing wrong. But he *FELT* something wrong. Something just wasn't right, so he waited awhile longer. Still, nothing, nothing at all to alert him, but the hair on the back of his neck was standing up now. There was something behind him, he could feel it. Very slowly, he slipped his arms out of the rucksack straps and drew his weapon. He slid down until he was lying on his back, the rucksack shielding him from anyone or anything behind him, and then he turned ever so cautiously and quietly onto his stomach.

"Don't shoot, Lootenant, it's me."

Remember the dry pants after the porpoise episode? Forget them. "Pompeo. What the fuck you doing here?" Ed hoped the sergeant didn't pick up the quiver in his voice as he mouthed the words.

"Hell, Lootenant, you don't t'ink I'd send you off alone, do you? You might get scared of da dark. Ya' know, you might make a good officer some day. You done good. C'mon, let's cross da road. Dere ain't no one here."

On the other side and safe in the woods again, they decided to retrieve their cached Cokes and take a break. The colas were ice cold and tasted good and they drank all six of them before they continued on toward Field 6. By 0400 hrs, they were at the spot where the "Tale of Two Hunters" began. "Let's jist wait here till light," Pompeo said, so they unloaded their shoulders and sat down. Neither of them said anything, and Ed was glad, because he was afraid he'd let on how glad he was to see ole Leontine. Damn, that guy was a real friend.

When daylight came, it was well after 0600 hrs. There was nothing unusual going on, but they stayed concealed in the bushes and kept watching, anyway. About 0700 hrs, a jeep drove up to the firehouse, and the one man in it got out and went inside. A few minutes later, they saw a figure making his way down the east side of the strip toward the house. It was Venice, and he was walking like he didn't have a care in the world. He crossed the field, and he, too, went into the firehouse. Then Prusser and Hickman came strolling out of the woods near Ed and walked to the firehouse.

"Damnation, Lootenant, looks like a convention. You better go on in dere. I'll just hang around and keep my eyes peeled. Leave your gear here." When Meadows got to the house, all the other people were inside. The man in the jeep was Top, and he said he didn't know why they were there, but he was supposed to be there at 0800 hrs, too. So the four lieutenants and Top sat around and talked until 0800 hrs. Nothing happened then, either. At 0815 hrs, Venice looked up suddenly and said, "Listen!"

They all listened. There was an airplane coming, a prop job, and coming in low. It had started to rain, but they all went outside anyway and scanned the skies. A white, single engine airplane was coming in for a landing and Meadows identified it as a T-28, a trainer in the Air Force. The pilot put the gear down and landed the aircraft smoothly, then taxied up to the firehouse. There were two men inside, and when the plane stopped and the engine sputtered out of life, the rear canopy opened and the figure inside began climbing out. He took off his helmet and put on a beret before jumping down from the wing. Sonofabitch. It was LTC B.B. Briggs.

The colonel walked up to the group of huddled figures and Top called them to attention. "Good morning, Colonel, good to see you," he said and all five of them saluted in unison. Briggs ignored their greeting.

"Sergeant Major, you got them fucking DASL's here?"

"Yes, Sir, they're all present and accounted for."

"Good. At least they can do something right. Listen here, you dumb-ass Second Lieutenants (it had been a long time since they were addressed so formally). We got some orders from DA that I brought for you. Those dumb bastards in the Pentagon don't know what worthless sonsofbitches you are. They sent you orders just like you was people." Meadows held his breath. Could it be that they were on the next increment for Laos? Damn, he hoped so.

"LT Meadows!" growled the colonel. "Get your ass out here." Ed got his ass out there in front of the colonel.

"Yes, Sir?"

"Either you ain't fucked up enough, or else DA ain't heard of it, because these orders say you are now a *First* lieutenant." Smiling for the first time Ed could remember, the Colonel held out his hand. "Congratulations, Lieutenant, welcome to the Officer Corps."

Well, I'll be a sonofabitch! If this ain't the shits? I'll bet there has never been another promotion to equal this one, thought Ed as he shook hands. Each of the others received congratulations, too, and then Top produced some silver bars and the Colonel pinned them on the lieutenants. Top also produced a bottle of champagne, and they all celebrated for a little while.

"Okay, Lieutenants, get your butts back in the woods," said Briggs, and the revelry ceased. Top went back to the MFC, the aircraft took off for somewhere, and Ed went back to meet Leontine.

A first lieutenant. Sonofabitch! thought Meadows. Actually, he knew that rank among lieutenants is like virtue among prostitutes. He would miss being a DASL. Then, with a smile to himself, he thought, *I won't miss being a DASL. I'll always be one of the DASL's. We were a pretty good bunch, not to have a TO&E slot in the Group. And he was sure they could kick the shit out of any lieutenant in Artillery, whether First or DASL.*

10

I Love How You Love Me

The remainder of the training cycle with Captain Jackson's team was a breeze. There was no marathon walk down to the beach, but a leisurely stroll consuming the better part of two days, instead. This time SGT Shoulders had the team set up their camp in Area MOSS on the north side of Highway 98 instead of on the beach. The MFC personnel supplied a goat for the team to do with as they wished, and what they wished was barbequed goat. The team members set to work digging a pit and filling it with logs of oak cut down nearby, then they slowly cooked the entire animal over the coals, giving it a full 24 hours of heat before inviting all the personnel from the beach party over for a goat roast. All the goat was cooked except for the head, which they skinned and stuck on a pole about ten feet high right in the middle of their camp. That was some primordial-looking creature, that goat head, devoid of its hairy skin, naked, impaled on a stick, with its big yellow eyes staring grotesquely down when the group gathered for the party.

Even the major showed up, heh-heh-heh-ing around and looking very out of place in this field setting. The meat was delicious, the oyster appetizers nice and salty, and, would you believe it, not one can or bottle of beer? No, this time there were two kegs which appeared on cue from someone. Everyone denied obtaining them, but Shoulders confided to Spicer, who confided to Leontine, who confided to Meadows that the major himself arranged for them. Wonders, in the world of the Special Forces trooper, never ceased. It was a good party. It was a good cycle, a good team, and a good feeling for the guerrillas when they put the team on the C-46 for the trip back to Bragg. This bunch would do well in Laos.

The guerrillas spent a couple of days closing down the beach site, then joined with the MFC members in shutting that headquarters down to caretaker status as all the men prepared to go on leave over the Christmas Holidays. Those returning to Bragg would be leaving on the 18th as the 1st Air Commandos arranged a training mission to coincide with their return, while the rest would go wherever they wanted to go by POV, bus, train, plane, or boat. Ed was going home to Memphis, and he invited both Venice and Hickman to go with him since they lived such a long way off—Nevada and Nebraska—respectively, but they elected to go on home. So Meadows prepared for the trip to Tennessee scheduled to begin on the 18th. The four lieutenants sponsored a big beer bust for the MFC members at a local pub to celebrate their promotions on the evening of 17 December. It went about as all beer busts do with a good time had by all, and on 18 December, every member of the Florida detachment left on leave with a hangover.

Since receiving his beret, Ed had not been home, so he decided to make this trip in uniform. The only outfit he had with him was fatigues, so he got out a nice, fresh-smelling and fresh-looking pair, carefully bloused his boots over his Corcorans, snapped the camouflage neckerchief around his neck, and tucked it into his shirt. Pausing in front of the mirror, he checked to insure that his beret was at the correct jaunty angle, that his lieutenant's bar was white and not yellow, and then strutted out to the previously loaded Arvak for the 10-hour drive to Memphis.

There is a small river near the Alabama-Florida border called the River Styx, which sports a sign on its bridge that reads "Charon Retired!" Ed was stopped there as traffic had been brought to a standstill while some wreckers and policemen removed the remains of a wreck that day. Ed had gotten out of his car and was lounging against the door when someone from a car further back came walking up to see what was going on. When he saw Ed, he stopped and stared at the lieutenant. Meadows waited for him to say something, and when he didn't speak but continued to stare, Ed smiled and nodded.

"How do?"

"Hello," replied the man. "You in the service?"

"Yes, I am," said Ed, slowly straightening up to stand more like a soldier.

"I was wondering. I used to be in the Army, but I ain't never seen a uniform like that before. What Branch you in?"

"Army. Special Forces," stated Ed with all the pride he could muster.

"Oh, yeah? Who's army?"

"The United States Army. American."

"They sure have changed," said Man From Further Back. "I thought you might be a Boy Scout leader or a Mexican. Well, see you," muttered Man as he went on toward the wreck.

Dumb civilian. What can you expect from the uneducated? The authorities got the road cleared and Ed continued on his journey. He took off his beret and set it on the seat next to him. He felt uncomfortable with the New York license plates he still had on Arvak, and there was no sense in causing some Alabama or Mississippi State Trooper to think some New York Puerto Rican was invading their hallowed ground. A Southern accent wasn't always enough to stay out of trouble down here. He passed through Mobile, turned north toward Meridian on Highway 45 and sped on toward home. There were Christmas decorations out in all the little towns on this balmy December day, causing Ed to remember another trip home at Christmas time.

He was a senior at the Academy, a First Classman, as the three stripes on his cuff proclaimed, and that was about as high as you could go in his world at that time. There was a saying at West Point that Plebes believed in God, Yearlings were doubtful, Cows were atheists, and Firsties thought they were God; and while Ed had no delusions to that effect, he did think being a senior was pretty hot stuff. The Tennessee Air National Guard had managed to schedule a C-47 on a training flight to Stewart Air Force Base at Newburgh, New York, just north of West Point, and on the return flight there just happened to be enough places for all the Tennessee cadets to hop a ride home. They had landed at Knoxville and Nashville and were now headed for Memphis, it had gotten dark, and as Ed looked out of the window at the ground below, the Christmas lights of all the little towns had been winking up at him. It was beautiful. They landed at Memphis, and the four cadets still on the plane had dressed each other off, making sure the capes of their long grey overcoats were properly turned back, their caps squared away, and they were looking good, before they exited the aircraft when it rolled to a stop. A national guardsman rolled some steps to the door, and out stepped the future members of the Long Grey Line.

"Say," said the guardsman, "y'all are really looking sharp. You from the Citadel?" Talk about a low blow.

That was two years ago, but the Great American Public hadn't been educated much about the army in the meantime. At Corinth, Ed stopped for fuel and a Coke (no beer at home), then turned west on Highway 78 for the final leg to Memphis. He'd be glad to get to Tennessee, there was something ominous about Mississippi in the early sixties. Arvak crossed the state line and turned west on Shelby drive. At Highway 51 he turned north for a block, then west on Richland, veering left at the fork, and there ahead of him was Windham Road and 5155, home. Pulling his little car into the driveway, Ed put on his beret, shut Arvak down, and got out. The house was dark, but when he knocked on the back door, he heard movement almost immediately, and there was his dad, smiling as always, opening the door to let him in.

"Hello, Ed, good to see you," Dad said, hugging him as always. "Come on in. We thought you might be home tonight. Your mom has some food still on the table for you." When you came home, there was food for you. If it wasn't on the table, it was nearby, and that food was meant to be eaten. Then there was more food, and that was to be eaten, too. Always.

"Hello, Eddie," said his mom as she came into the kitchen. "We're glad you're home. I've got some supper for you. Come on and sit down. You want some milk or coffee?" It may be DASL, or Lootenant, or even Special Forces Airborne Ranger Trooper Sir, have a beer elsewhere, but it was, "Eddie, sit down and eat" at home. It was an awfully good feeling.

While he ate, they talked, and his dad was first to notice the white bar on his collar. Ed was congratulated, his mom wondered where he had gotten that Donald Duck hat, and when his obligations were fulfilled and his stomach stuffed, Ed wanted to make a phone call.

"I thought you might want to call someone," said his Dad. "She's probably anxious to hear from you."

Complimenting his mother on the meal, Ed excused himself from the table and went to the phone in the den. Seven turns of the rotary dial and there was the sound of a phone ringing. Once. Then there was a sweet, cheerful, definitely Whitehaven-flavored voice saying, "Hello?" Just the usual answer caused Ed to feel a thrill.

"Denise? This is Ed."

"Eddie. I knew it was you. Where are you?"

"I'm at home. Are you busy?"

"No. Are you coming over?"

"Well, I'd like to, if you don't have anything planned. I have to clean up and change clothes first."

"Okay, but hurry. I'm dying to see you."

"Be there in fifteen minutes." No red-blooded American boy would stand idly by and let a sweet young thing die. He was cleaned, changed, and over at the house on Lydgate in fourteen minutes. Sometimes you have to move a little faster than you did on the banks of Turkey Gobbler Creek.

Denise's real name was Michelle Denise Waltham, and Ed liked the name, "Michelle," but Denise and all her family called her, Denise. There was no percentage in bucking those odds. She opened the door when he knocked and Ed hugged her. He would like to have kissed her, too, maybe a couple of times, heck (a change of vocabulary always occurs at home), maybe even a few times, but the presence of her Momma, Daddy, and a couple of brothers, a sister, and a bunch of in-laws in the background intimidated the blood and guts trooper. He went in and the family and Ed exchanged pleasantries. Meadows was not as much at ease here as he had been with Pompeo on the Turkey Gobbler. There was talk about the church Christmas program upcoming, and the weather, and more tid-bits, before Ed had a chance to speak directly to Denise.

"Are y'all planning to do anything tonight?" he asked.

"No, why?"

"Well, I thought you might want to go get a Coke or something."

"I'd love to," Denise replied enthusiastically. "Let me get a sweater." Then, turning to her mother, she continued in the same breath, "Is it all right if I go out for a Pepsi with Ed for a little while?" Michelle

Denise could get more words out of a breath than Pompeo could. It was all right, she got the sweater, and they were soon on the road toward town and Leonard's. You only had to date Denise once or twice to know where she wanted to go and what she wanted to eat and drink. She wanted to go to Leonard's Bar-B-Que, eat a Miss White Pig and a bean pot, and drink a Pepsi. All that, and she still weighed only 112 lbs. Leonard's was in South Memphis, the home of South Side High School, Ed's former stomping grounds, and it took them about ten minutes to reach it from Whitehaven. They parked in the back parking lot, as they had done many times before and waited for curb service, as they had waited many times before. He got the kiss he had wanted, the couple of kisses he had contemplated, heck, he even got the few he had hoped for. They were cuddled up pretty close...just talking, the radio was playing softly, and Ed felt very comfortable with this girl in his arms. He felt so comfortable that he said, on the spur of the moment, something he probably wouldn't have said if he'd stopped to think about it.

"You know, I'll probably wind up marrying you."

"Aw, that's just a line. You probably say that to...hey, wait. Turn the radio up. Listen. I just love this song."

Ed dutifully turned the radio volume up, and there was a sweet-sounding song playing with a catchy little phrase in it about, "squeeze me, tease me, please me..." and Meadows liked both the tune and the words a lot. "What's the name of that?"

"*I Love How You Love Me*. They play it all the time. I like it." There was that burst of too many words from one breath again.

"Yeah, I like it, too. We ought to make it our song. I Love How You Love Me. I love to love you, Denise. I bet I do wind up marrying you." And, he did, but not that trip home. Not for a long time, as a matter of fact, and what happened in between that night and the altar would fill a lot of pages just in the telling of it!

11

The Lonesome Polecat

It was a long way from Windham Road in Whitehaven, Tennessee, to the woods outside Ft. Walton Beach, Florida. The trip home which had required ten hours in making was accomplished in eight and a half in returning, and that included fifteen minutes spent in listening to an explanation of the traffic laws of the State of Mississippi while the trooper filled out the citation for exceeding 60 mph in a 50 mph zone. Ed had listened patiently and had not even contested the ticket, for the last time he had glanced at Arvak's meters, the long red hand was about at 85 on the round dial. He was guilty of exceeding 50 mph, all right. Meadows was in a hurry to return to Hurlburt because he wanted to write a letter to Denise. He liked writing letters, a lot better than talking on the phone, for instance, because you had an opportunity to edit what you said in a letter. Besides that, he was thinking of Denise constantly, and he thought a spell in the woods would allow him to sort out his thoughts. Ed knew he was getting on toward the marrying age, after all, Bud Robocker and Butch Nobles were already married and Bob Castleman was getting pretty serious about that Helen girl in Dallas. Ole Turkey Gobbler Creek never lied. Not many people knew that, for not many people knew about Turkey Gobbler, but the murmuring of its waters always carried the sound of truth.

The MFC orderly room was nearly deserted when Ed entered to

sign in. The forlorn little Christmas tree someone had put up on the desk of the duty NCO still sat there. It was blue, and all the ornaments were silver, and it may have been pretty at one time, but it wasn't pretty now. Meadows hollered to see if anyone was around, and one of the commo men who worked with Brinkman came out of the sleeping room where he had obviously been doing what the room was designated for doing.

"Happy New Year, Sir. Welcome back to sunny Florida. Ain't nobody else here but me and four other NCO's. Alabama beat Arkansas, LSU beat Ole Miss, no, make that Texas beat Ole Miss, LSU beat Colorado; we're all going to get together here tonight and try to stay drunk; the Major gets back tomorrow; have a good evening, Sir, good night," and he disappeared into the sleeping room, evidently to prepare for the next hourly, recorded broadcast. It was a pretty good broadcast, come to think of it, for it told Ed about all he needed to know. He signed in, drove over to the BOQ and unloaded Arvak, then sat down and read the most current issue of Aviation Week magazine he could find in the stack of periodicals in the lobby. It was a good magazine. There were a bunch of civilians staying in the BOQ, driving cars advertising the Marquardt Corporation. Meadows wondered what they were doing here, and on page 34 of the December 18 issue, he read that they were engaged in work on ramjet powerplants at Eglin AFB. Nice magazine, to tell you about your neighbors. Wonder which magazine they read to find out about him?

At supper time a couple of hours later, Meadows drove down to the Spin Drift Restaurant in Ft. Walton Beach and had a nice meal of turkey breasts and green beans, but he was thinking of a certain girl who liked Miss White Pig sandwiches and a bean pot with Vienna bread on the side. And a Pepsi. He considered ordering a Pepsi in her honor, but that was one drink he couldn't stomach. Besides, he wasn't at home anymore, so he ordered coffee.

About 2100 hrs, Ed wandered into the orderly room, and the attempt to stay drunk was well underway for the commo man and his buddies, who now included SGT Padillo—a medic from Cuba whom Ed really liked. As usual, Padillo had a radio tuned to a Cuban broadcast and was cussing out Fidel. Although Ed spoke Spanish and was considered fluent enough to carry such a rating, he was not familiar with the words Padillo was using. They didn't teach those at West

Point. There was plenty of beer, and still there was no request for any funds to feed the beer kitty. He decided to take a chance.

"Where does all this free beer come from?" he asked no one in particular.

"The Air Force donates it," came the reply from no one in particular. 'Nuff said. Meadows joined in the drinking of the Air Force-furnished libation. By midnight, the entire bunch of them was drunk, as they would say in Whitehaven; or "shit-faced" as they said in the Army. That was when they all decided to get their left ears pierced, and Padillo performed the honors, using Xylocaine for anesthesia and sterile technique. He tied a strand of nylon suture through the holes and then applied a band-aid to conceal his handiwork. There they were, six drunk soldiers, all with band-aids on their left ears. Hell, it was time to go home. They had to be at a meeting in the orderly room in just four hours to begin Cycle Three of the training for Laotian-bound teams, so Ed was going to have to sleep fast.

The major didn't make it back for the meeting, nor, for that matter, did several other members of the group, but all the Band-Aid Bunch was there. They weren't in very good shape, but they were there. Top dispatched the teams to the field, but he gave them twenty-four hours to get ready. By then, everyone was present or accounted for. The major was accounted for. There was no monkey business when the jeep took Pompeo and Meadows to TREE, driving them all the way to Turkey Gobbler, and this time it took the two men three trips apiece to carry all their stuff in. Their camp was taking on more and more of the comforts of home. You don't have to practice being miserable.

During the two days they had to await the arrival of the new teams, Ed talked a lot about Denise to Pompeo. She was on his mind a lot. He cut a new walking stick, and as they sat around the fire and talked at night, he whittled on the stick. On one side, he cut the name, "Michelle," through the bark, and on the other, "Denise." Then he cut rings, and "x's," and stripes. Leontine listened like a good father should but had little to say in the way of advice. Once, he did make a comment about love-sick lieutenants and compared them to "lonesome polecats," but that was about all.

They were to run two cycles during January, and they both went well. Pompeo and Ed were in the field for the entire month, but that was where they felt like they belonged, so they really didn't mind.

The last increment was put aboard a plane at Hurlburt on the 30th, and all the guerrillas were brought in for some Care and Cleaning on the same date. By this time, the major was also back, and he announced to the whole group in the MFC that they were going to have a jump in the morning since several of them were in danger of losing their jump pay. You have to jump at least once every three months to draw your extra $110 per month, $55 for the NCO's and EM's.

This wasn't just going to be a jump, it was going to be a coordinated effort between a planeload of new people arriving from Bragg and the folks already at Hurlburt. There would be three planes arriving within a six-minute time interval, one from Bragg and two from Florida, but each would have been in the air for a minimum of two hours. In other words, in the language of the troops, they were going to have a "mass grabass." Almost without fail, something would go wrong in one of these operations, usually resulting in someone getting hurt, and Ed had a weird premonition that he was going to die. He didn't know why, but he was sure something was destined to go wrong and he would not survive the drop. Of course, he said nothing about this feeling, it was relatively common for troopers to have such unctions—the only problem was many times they came true. He considered volunteering for the DZ crew, but that wasn't the way you got around such an experience. No, if it was your time to go, you may as well check out in a 1250' fall as any other way, so instead of volunteering for the DZ crew, he asked to be first in the stick on the first airplane. This request presented no problem at all for Top as he wrote out the manifest and Meadows was duly listed.

The big C-46 was perched on its gear waiting for the troopers to board and the T-10 parachutes, T-6 reserves, and kit bags were lined up in a neat row on the tarmac outside the door. Procedures in the Group were relatively informal on jumps, and instead of going through all the jumpmaster checks before boarding, each man merely picked up his gear and carried it onto the plane with him. Two hours was a long time to sit all strapped up waiting to jump. The door was left open as the plane fired up and taxied to the end of Hurlburt's runway—in fact, it wasn't even there. The aircrew had stowed the door somewhere. Meadows took a seat next to the open doorway and buckled on his seatbelt. With a final revving of the engines, the plane turned onto the runway, wound the engines up to their full power and roared into the air.

But not much air. About an hundred feet of altitude was all they gained before levelling off, reducing power and beginning the series of dog-legs across southern Alabama and Georgia which would consume two hours' flying time. Through the doorway, Ed could see farms and a couple of small towns they flew over at a couple of hundred miles per hour. Several times they passed over wooded areas where the trees were tall enough to almost brush the underside of the fuselage. Maybe they were going to crash and that was how Ed was to meet his fate. He had no premonition of whether or not the rest of the troopers were going to die, just that he was. Thirty minutes from the scheduled drop time, SGT Valentine, who was serving as the Jumpmaster, got everybody up and they started donning their chutes. Meadows slipped his arms through the shoulder straps of the T-10 and hefted it onto his back. Settling it there, he reached between his legs and grabbed the leg straps, insuring that they were not crossed. A good way to join the soprano section of the choir was to jump with your leg straps crossed. He threaded the strapping through the loops of the harness and pulled the safety clip out of the release box, then rotated the plate so it snapped out to the safe position. Then he replaced the clip. One shoulder strap was permanently attached to the box, the other he snapped into place. Both leg strap buckles were snapped in and he was chuted up. By pulling the adjustment straps, you tightened the harness and most everyone, including Meadows, did this while crouched over to make sure of a tight fit. Next step was to check the rip-cord of the reserve, turn this chute so that the handle was on the right side, and snap it onto the two "D" rings of the harness. He'd placed the kit bag next to his body and secured its handles to the shoulder strap before he snapped that strap into the release box. You have to wear a helmet to jump, so all the men had brought theirs along. Time to take off the beret, stuff it into a pocket somewhere, and you were ready. Almost. You were still not hooked up, so a buddy was required to hand you your static line from the back of the main parachute, laying it over your shoulder. All this took fifteen minutes.

Valentine checked out each trooper—the quick-release boxes, the reserves, the Capewell devices which could release your risers if you were being dragged along the ground by the wind after landing, the helmets and their chinstraps. Then, since talking was very difficult due to the roaring of the engines, he slapped you on the shoulder to indicate that you were ready to go. Nothing left to do but sit back down.

Five minutes out, it was time to initiate the jump sequence and the series of jump commands known so well by every paratrooper. Valentine walked to the back of the cabin, hooked his static line to the anchor line cable near the ceiling, and turned to face the anxious troops. Utilizing hand and arm signals as well as shouting the commands, he began.

"STAND UP." Everyone struggled to their feet and turned to face the rear of the plane and the Jumpmaster.

"HOOK UP." The snaps were fastened to the anchor line cable and the safety wires inserted through the little holes which prevented the snap from coming open. It was always cold about this time...you had goose bumps normally, but Meadows had an extra bunch this go-round.

"CHECK YO' STATIC LINES." You ran your fingers along the line as far as your shoulder, then the man behind you checked its course the rest of the way to its attachment to the main chute.

"CHECK EQUIPMENT." Since they were jumping "Hollywood," without rucksacks or weapons, there was nothing to do but look down at your release box.

"SOUND OFF EQUIPMENT CHECK." The last man in the stick slapped the behind of the man in front of him and shouted his number and the word "Okay!" and since there were only ten men in this stick, that didn't take long. "Ten Okay, Nine Okay, Eight Okay, Seven Okay, Six Okay, Five Okay, Four Okay, Three Okay, Two Okay," and Meadows felt the sting of a slap on his rear.

"One Okay," he shouted at Valentine. The red light next to the door flashed on as the plane suddenly jerked and began the climb to 1250' for this peacetime training drop. Were the jump for real, they would have dispensed with the reserve chutes and exited from 500'. No time to activate a reserve from that altitude. When the aircraft levelled off, Valentine continued.

"STAND IN THE DOOR," he yelled as he pointed to the doorway. Ed turned into the doorway, placing one open palm on each side of the opening and the toe of one boot outside, his head up, gazing at the horizon, knees flexed, back straight. The next command would be to "Go!" There would be another slap on his fanny, and he would leap out to his certain doom. Meadows thought about Denise, about his folks, wondered if he'd feel his body striking the ground, remembered the guy from the 82d who augered in, and then he saw the light change to green on the wall of the cabin next to his head. Most units would jump on green, but in Special Forces, all that means is that the pilot is ready for the drop. The Jumpmaster controlled a Group jump.

"DON'T JUMP!" shouted Valentine, grabbing Ed by the backpack. "RED PANEL!" he hollered in Ed's ear as he motioned toward the ground. Meadows looked down, and there on the sand below him, slipping out of sight beneath the tail of the air plane, the bottom panel of the "L" was red instead of orange. *Saved by the panel,* thought Ed as he watched the ground whipping by. "We'll go around." said the Jumpmaster. "The other planes are late, anyway." The Air Commandos were never late. Meadows hoped they wouldn't jump so he could cheat death.

It took five minutes to line the plane up again with the DZ, and then they were set to go again. Ed shuffled to the door in an abbreviated command sequence, assumed the position, and the green light came back on. "GO!" yelled Valentine, and his slap helped catapult Ed out of the plane. Locking his feet together, his elbows tucked in to his side, his chin on his chest, Meadows determined he was going to hit the ground in a good body position. He also kept his eyes open. When he hit, he wanted to see it all. Silently counting to four, Meadows was surprised to feel the tug of the chute opening and jerking at his harness.

"Probably a streamer," he muttered as he glanced up instinctively to check the chute. No, it wasn't a streamer, nor a Mae West, it wasn't even twisted. The canopy was open fine. Ed floated down on one of the nicest jumps he'd ever experienced and landed with a soft collapse in the sand, unhurt. So much for premonitions.

The other two planes made their passes and the exercise was finished with no casualties at all. Ed turned his chutes in at the truck parked off the side of KELLY and waited while the other men assembled. One of the men from the Bragg group was Lieutenant Wilson, an old head who had gotten a commission through OCS and had been in Group for years, but had always been kind to Meadows during his DASL days. He spied Meadows standing near the truck and hollered at him.

"Hey, Meadows. We got some news for you. You got three days to get back to Bragg. You've been picked for a mission."

Ed couldn't even reply. He was going. He was going on a mission. He was finally going to war. Who knows, maybe his premonition would come true, after all.

12

The "A" Detachment

Meadows drove through the Fayetteville gate to Ft. Bragg late in the afternoon. He had gone by Memphis to see his folks and Denise, spent the night, then drove all the next day to get to Bragg. If they ever got the Interstate system finished, specifically I-40, the trip between Memphis and Fayetteville would be a snap, but it wasn't finished, and sometimes it made more sense to go by way of Atlanta so you could pick up the Interstates north from there. To be honest, there just wasn't a good way to get here from there! He drove to Smoke Bomb Hill, carefully abiding by the speed limit since the MP's would get you by either Radar or Vascar, and they allowed no tolerance at all. In the four months Meadows had been gone, nothing had changed at Ft. Bragg, at least, nothing he could see. The pungent smell of coal smoke hung like a pall over the Hill as he parked Arvak in the B Company parking lot and walked up to the orderly room to sign in. No sense in being charged leave time. Some buck sergeant (E5) whom Ed didn't know was on duty as the troops had shut down for the day on this Thursday, the first day of February, 1962, and he asked Ed where he was coming from when Meadows filled in the sign-in book.

"I've been down in Florida," replied Ed.

"Were you with the MFC at Eglin?"

"Yeah, but I was one of the guerrillas." Meadows wanted to make sure the sergeant knew the distinction, for he didn't want to be considered one of the Magnificent Fellows, or a Mother Fucker, either.

"Really? Which one were you? We've heard all about you guys."

"I was Nottus. You hear of him?" asked Ed.

"Oh, yeah, damn right we've heard of you. You were with Leontine, weren't you? One of the DASL's. You're the guy who tried to get Captain Young shitcanned. Too bad you didn't succeed. He left with his team for White Star a couple of weeks ago. What're you back for?"

Ed wasn't sure how much of this upcoming mission was classified, so he decided to be a little evasive. "I really don't know. Orders from Group to get back here."

"Probably going on a mission. I wish to hell I could get on one of the increments. I'm tired of all this Mickey Mouse shit here. I'd give my left nut to go somewhere."

Meadows remembered how anxious he was to go somewhere, himself. "I hope so. I hope to hell I ain't back here just to play grabass while someone else goes. Well, Sarge, mind the fort," said Ed as he waved at the duty NCO and left the room.

The old two-story wooden building in the Spring Lake area of the post which had been converted to a BOQ looked the same to Ed, too, when he parked his car under the big pine trees. There were a couple of other cars there, but he saw no one. Going up to the second floor and reaching the door of his room, Ed unlocked the Master lock and wondered if he had been ripped off while he was gone. He hadn't been. His room was suffocatingly hot, so he opened a couple of windows before going through the adjoining bath to see if Hooper was home, or if he even lived there anymore. It was obvious someone lived there, but no one was home. He looked at the fatigues hanging up in starched formation in the closet and saw that they belonged to Hooper, and that made him feel good. Jim would have taken care of his stuff for him.

Meadows unpacked Arvak in several trips, by which time it was fully dark, and still no one had arrived in Hooper's room. It was time to get something to eat, for Ed seldom ate much when he was driving. He decided to have a good meal, so he fired up ole Arvak and made the drive into Fayetteville, to the Hamont Grill where several of the DASL's frequently went for a real meal instead of the more usual fare at Ronnie's. He ate a country fried steak with some vegetables and a slice of lemon ice-box pie, then bought a five-pack of Marsh Wheeling stogies to take back to his BOQ with him.

Hooper's white Chevrolet was parked in the lot when he returned to Spring Lake area, and the two men were glad to see each other. They stayed up until the wee hours updating the data banks on all that had been going on at Bragg and in Florida. Not much of any significance had occurred.

At 0600 hrs the next morning, 1st Lieutenant Meadows was in formation with the rest of B Company when the first sergeant called the unit to attention for Report. He saluted each of the "B" Detachment Commanders as they reported all present or accounted for, then he saluted the Commander of B Company, who was not the one Ed had four months ago. The new CO was a LTC Suomi, a Finn, who was well-known throughout the Group as a former general in the Finnish Army who fought the Russians during WW II. The colonel returned the salute, told the first sergeant to publish the orders, and the colonel went back into the orderly room. The first sergeant took care of a lot of housekeeping requirements, then he said something that really mattered.

"LT Meadows? Is he here?" asked the first sergeant.

"Yo," hollered Ed from his position at the rear of the formation.

"Welcome back, Sir. You're being assigned to A-26. You can meet them at the Team Room after formation." More bullshit followed, but Ed had heard what he needed to know. At least he was assigned to an A team. Now if only that team was in an increment for Laos, or anywhere else, for that matter. He'd gladly go to the Congo, if that was to be their mission. It was a possibility.

The upstairs of the barracks buildings in the B Company area had been converted into a series of stalls, or alcoves, which had big bins for storage of rucksacks and other pieces of equipment belonging to the team members. A-26's stall was located in just such a place, and it was to here that Ed was directed when he asked directions to the Team Room. There were several NCO's sitting around when Ed entered, none of whom he knew, and they rose to attention when he came in.

"At Ease," said Ed quickly, and they all sat back down. "I'm LT Meadows, and I've been assigned to A-26. Is this the right place?"

"Right, Sir," replied a Master Sergeant Bradley. "I'm Sergeant Bradley, assistant team sergeant, this here's Sergeant Riley, the medic, that there's Sergeant Bushman, demo, and this here's Spec 4 Kidd, commo. The rest of the team should be here shortly. Glad to have you aboard, Sir."

Meadows shook hands all around. Sure was a lot different from the last time he'd checked in at Ft. Bragg. They talked a little as the other team members arrived, followed by the captain, and Ed was formally introduced to the members of Detachment A-26.

T. Michael Johnson, the Detachment CO, was a captain who had been commissioned through the OCS program. He was married, the father of two girls, 25-years old, well over six-feet tall and a little pudgy. His native state was Florida and he liked to talk about all the water skiing he used to do. He was not particularly bothered by the fact that Ed was a Ring-Knocker (West Pointer), and was generally friendly.

Meadows was the Detachment XO. Ed already knew himself. Master Sergeant (MSG) Flagstone was the team sergeant, first name Raymond, but he went by, "Ray," or, "Flag." He was 36-years old, a skinny little man not over 5'8" tall, had a bushy, reddish mustache and a lot of nervous energy. His home was the Army, but he'd grown up in Boston and still carried the trace of an accent. He wasn't real friendly, was cordial enough, but somehow made Meadows feel ill-at-ease.

Master Sergeant Bradley, the man Ed first met, was, in fact, the assistant team sergeant. He was 35-years old, at least as tall as the captain, blonde-headed, and moved slowly. Bradley was very quiet, but a hard worker, and the men seemed to like him. Meadows reserved judgement for the time being.

Sergeant First Class (SFC) Burt Thomas was the senior weapons specialist. He was 32-years old, short and stocky, built a lot like Ed was, but very muscular. He was married and had a couple of kids, was from Utah—a Morman, and exhibited the laconic style and wit of a true western cowboy. Ed liked him right off the bat.

The assistant weapons specialist was Buck Sergeant (SGT) Frank Beaudreau, whom Ed immediately didn't like. He had black, thick hair, swarthy complexion, hailed from Jersey City, and was an obvious bullshit artist. Beaudreau was single, but the women from

Tangiers to Timbuctu were all after him, to hear him tell it, but he knew his weapons and could tear down a Maxim in no time flat. Beaudreau was 28-years old.

Staff Sergeant (SSG) Harold Riley was the medic. He, too, was built like Meadows and Thomas, but Riley's weight ran to fat. He was always sweating profusely, spent a lot of time with his medical gear, especially when the team was doing hard work, but had finished first in his class at the Dog Lab. (We can't talk about the Dog Lab, that enclosure in the old hospital area where medics were trained to treat real gunshot wounds in real, live patients who responded with tail-wagging instead of smiles when treated kindly. There were lots of animal rights' activists who would have had apoplexy had they known about the Dog Lab.) Riley was 32-years old, and had previously reached the rank of E-7, twice, as a matter of fact. Harold was divorced, but still in love with his wife, who had remarried.

The ass't medical specialist was SGT Len Pickett, a young, brash Texan who worshipped and adored the Texas Aggies. Pickett was stocky, too, but by no means fat, shorter than Meadows by a couple of inches, had a brand new man-child presented by his wife of ten months, and made a perfect pair with Thomas. He was 25. His standing in the Dog Lab class was not discussed.

The two communications specialists were both very young and were both specialist fourth class (Sp4), called "Speedy Fours" by the troops. Ricky Eason was a tall, gangling, skinny 24-year-old former hippie from San Francisco. No one ever figured out how he ever got in the Army, much less in an all-volunteer outfit like the Group. Eason was a whiz with the Morse Code key and was very easy-going. He had some political connections back in California that were evidently pretty strong, but he didn't like to talk about them, so the Team didn't ask.

Pete Kidd, the other commo man, was also 24-years old, but he was short and quiet, almost a duplicate of SFC Thomas. You'd never guess he was from Texas after you'd met the other Texan, Pickett, but he was. Pete was skillful with the key, too, and probably the hardest worker Ed had ever seen. The Team never did anything that Kidd wasn't in the middle of it. No wife for Pete: he longed to get back out west somewhere and live with a string of horses.

Then there were the demolitions men, the most interesting of the lot by far. Among the members of the Group, demo men were considered the strangest of a strange lot, and these two made you understand why. SSG Francis Bushman was the senior of the two. He was 40-years old, at least, and had gotten that age by trying to drink at least a quart of some alcoholic beverage every day that he could remember. Short, slight, with bug eyes, a crooked smile, and crooked teeth, Bushman delighted in playing the part of town drunk, but there was something about him which made you think that what you were seeing was only what he wanted you to see. Francis, called, "Frank," had been married several times and was currently between wives, but not between women. For all his avowed prowess, Beaudreau could not hold a candle to Bushman when it came to womanizing.

Tom Svoboda was the final member of A-26. Freckle-faced, short, but built like a weightlifter, Svoboda was 24-years old, a "Speedy Four" from Illinois who liked to blow things up. His training was definitely mediocre until they put a blasting cap in his hands, and from that point on, he had become a real example of the Demo Man. He ate, drank, and slept demolitions, and was clever enough to figure out a lot of novel uses for C-4, the primary explosive used in the Group. Svoboda got along well with the rest of the detachment, but when the work was over, he disappeared and didn't reappear until the work started again. He rode a motorcycle, that much the Team knew, but where he rode it and what he did once he got there was Tom's business and Tom's alone.

That was it, the members of Detachment A-26. For better or worse, this was the outfit Ed was committing his life to for the duration of their mission, whenever and wherever it might be.

13

What Is "White Star"?

It was official, they were going to Laos, so said the captain after all the team members had assembled and gotten introduced. Their increment would consist of three A detachments, which would replace three teams already over there. They would be assigned to the White Star Mobile Training Team, WSMTT, or simply, White Star, which was, in turn, nominally under the control of the Military Assistance Advisory Group-Laos, or MAAG-Laos. In truth, the Special Forces units were controlled by no one but the Special Warfare Center at Ft. Bragg, but for paperwork purposes, they were associated with MAAG-Laos. It was not known just exactly where they would be going, but their mission would be more akin to Counter-Insurgency than to Unconventional Warfare. So much for the guerrillas. There was one other fact known; one of the A Teams would be split when they got there into two Field Training Teams, FTT's, but no one knew which team would be so split. Captain Johnson would be the ranking officer in this increment, and he confided in Ed that he was going to try and get A-26 that assignment. Be good for Ed to command a team, Johnson felt. *Be good for Ed to command a team,* Ed knew. Tentatively, their departure was scheduled for the first week in March, so there wasn't much time. Meadows wondered if they were going to go through the Florida training, and was informed there wasn't enough time for that. Probably just as well. Ed would probably have turned out to be at least as bothersome to the guerrillas as Young had been.

The team went onto an intensive training schedule during the day time, to update their Ready folders and get their requirements for passports, international drivers' licenses, immunizations, small arms qualifications, parachute jumps, and physical conditioning. They had Area Study every night until 2200 hrs, as they tried to learn about the geography, politics, history, and customs of their host country. The training began with a jump from a C-130 that very evening. Ed had no premonitions about this drop, but when the prop-wash from the big Allison turboprops hit him as he exited the door, he felt like he should have had. All's well that ends well, I suppose, and the drop ended well with no injuries. They had to make two more jumps before leaving for White Star.

The Area Studies were interesting. For their purposes, the instructors began with the history of Indo-China following the defeat of the French at Dien Bien Phu. All European influence was supposedly removed with the departure of the "frogs," as the French were known, and there had been a period of relative quiet. The tiny, landlocked Kingdom of Laos existed under a government which followed the old "troika" system that the Russians liked so much: one "neutral" leader, one communist, and one "pro-Western." As is the usual case, the neutral was a socialist, if not a communist, and the pro-Western was a corrupt dictator who milked his section of the country for all he could get out of it. The King was supposedly above politics, reigning from the royal capitol of Luang Prabang, while the corrupt politicians worked out of Vientiane. Bordering on China and North Viet Nam, as it did, Laos was heavily "influenced" by those countries, especially near the borders. The Viet Minh-North Vietnamese, claimed they had no troops in Laos, an obvious lie which all but the most naive of the United Nations knew to be such, but there was little territorial exchange going on. The bad guys—the Viet Minh, controlled the border provinces, Thai bandits and Burmese warlords controlled the areas bordering them, and down south the Cambodians dictated the terms of habitation. That was only the superficial politics—it got more complicated up close.

Geographically, it was easier to define Laos. It was bordered on the north by China, on the east by North Vietnam and South Vietnam, on the south by Cambodia, and on the west by Thailand and

Burma. Only a cursory examination revealed this country was the key to all of Southeast Asia, a fact the bad guys seemed to grasp but the good guys didn't. The Mekong split the country in two until it reached the Thai border, then it served as the line of division between those two nations as far as Cambodia. There were mountains in the north, the Plain of Jars in the middle, a few more mountains, some jungle, and finally the Plateau de Bolovens in the south. Here was the last outpost of the Indian gaur—the largest ox in the world—surely destined for extinction.

Ethnically, there were four classes of peoples: The Laotians, or Lao, lived in the towns and along the waterways at the low altitudes. They were the most plentiful, the most peaceful, the most corrupt of the classes. They were the poorest soldiers and composed the bulk of the Forces Armee Royale, the FAR, the folks Ed would be training. Next up the scale, which corresponded to the altitude, were the Black Thai and the White Thai. These people weren't from Thailand, but were closely akin to the Siamese. There weren't many of them—they were pretty hardy souls who did some slash-burn agriculture, but mostly engaged in trade between the other classes of Laotian citizens.

Next up, the Lao Tung, primitive and poorly-organized, they were feared and hated by the Laotians, treated as slaves whenever the Lao could get hold of them, and a fertile recruiting ground for the Viet Minh. In stature, they were a little taller than either the Thai or the Lao, but they were subject to the higher dwellers of the mountain peaks, the Meo. It was the Meo who grew the poppies which they converted into opium and enslaved the Lao Tung with the drug, who in turn did the bidding of the Meo, who hated the Lao. The Meo were pure descendents of the Chinese, fiercely independent, vicious fighters, who wanted to be left alone to grow poppies. Both the good guys and the bad guys wanted to win the hearts and minds of the Meo, but the Meo wanted to grow poppies. Simple, huh?!

The language of Laos was Laotian, both written and spoken, and it was similar to Thai as Portugese is to Spanish: if you speak one, you can probably get along in the other. Their alphabet was akin to Sanskrit, or Thai, or something from the third ring of Saturn, so little effort was expended in learning to read, write, or speak Lao. Instead, the teams learned the rudiments of French, for it was still taught in all the schools and was required for training as an officer in the FAR. Not all European influence was gone.

Militarily, the situation was also crystal clear. The bad guys were supplied by the French, who had been kicked out by the same bad guys; and the French flew American-manufactured airplanes full of American-manufactured clothes and goods to the bad guys to use against the FAR, which was trained and assisted by the Americans. The Viet Minh provided the training and officers for the Pathet Lao...the Red Lao...the PL's...the bad guys, while the French supplied them. Ed began to wonder if he really was ready for war. Whatever happened to the white hats and the black hats?

The plot thickened: there were the Kong Le forces—the KL. Kong Le was an Airborne commander who had the best troops in the entire country fighting for the FAR, but he got disenchanted with the corruption he saw, so he switched sides, along with his forces. Then he got mad at the PL, so he declared himself neutral, but kept his army. He would fight for whichever side made him the best offer, and right now the PL, with their buddies the Viet Minh—supplied by the French with U.S. arms and equipment, were making the best offer. Time to study French.

Most of the time the Army works like a giant slug, slow to respond and extremely difficult to convince of the need for anything. On occasion, however, it can be a friend par excellence. Whomever had arranged this training schedule had known the correct buttons to push, for all of Ft. Bragg seemed to be at the disposal of the A Detachments preparing for Laos. It was possible to get ranges opened up on Saturday, so they could qualify with their M-1 rifles, the .30 calibre carbine, the Browning Automatic Rifle, BAR, the .45 calibre pistol, and the 1919A6 .30 calibre machine gun. Magic, that's what it was. Ed qualified as an "Expert" with each and every weapon, as did all the personnel the pit crews liked. A lead pencil shoved through a target makes a .30 calibre hole and even leaves a rim of lead around the hole, just like a bullet. The M-1 pencil, it was called, and it ran rampant throughout their qualifying. Shooting the .45 pistol was harder, but Ed was a good shot, anyway, and he qualified "Expert" for real. Time passed rapidly at this pace, and the month of February was gone. Their folders were ready, their shots were given, their equipment packed, and it was Friday, the second of March, when Captain Johnson had a dinner over at his house for all the team members and their families. Meadows, of course, went alone.

"You can't quote me on this," Johnson said to the assembled host, "but I have an idea that this may be the last time we all have a chance to get together for awhile." There was a lot of guffawing and chuckling, Ed included. It was nice to be in the know. "My wife and I wanted to have you all over sometime before we shoved off, *IF* we're shoving off, (more guffawing) so we want everyone to have a good time, let all your families meet one another, just in case there were to be some kind of troop movement next weekend." So much for National Security. Hell, they were keeping this Top Secret about as well as most Top Secrets are kept. Then everyone followed Captain Johnson's suggestion and got to know each other. Bushman got to know Beaudreau's date very well, it seemed, while others seemed to mix and mingle and disappear and reappear on a thirty minute cycle, each time with a different member of A-26. The social interactions between members of the Detachment and the wives of other members was confusing. *Just something to get us ready for Laotian politics,* Meadows reasoned. *Y'know, that's about what it was. War makes strange bedfellows, too.*

On the Sunday following the party on Friday night, Ed drove Arvak up to Martinsville, Virginia, to leave him with his sister and her family there. He ate Sunday dinner with them, but wasn't very talkative, and at dusk they put him on a bus for the trip back to Ft. Bragg. It was cold, the sky was threatening, and a penetrating wind rocked the old dog (Greyhound) around as it rolled through the Carolina night. When they reached Spring Lake, Ed asked the bus driver if he'd let him out once they got on post. From there, he could walk to his BOQ and avoid having Hooper come pick him up at the bus station in Fayetteville. Since he had no baggage, the driver agreed, and Meadows stepped off the bus just inside the gate at the Spring Lake area of post.

He turned up the collar of his woolly coat to block some of the wind and started walking toward his BOQ, about an half-mile distant. As the wind whipped around him, the cold seemed to bite clear to his bones. Meadows thought of another night when he had been a cadet at the Academy. He'd been up on the cross-country trail to watch his roommate run against Fordham, and as he walked down the hill above the protestant chapel, he saw all the lights shining on the plain below him. The foreboding grey battlements of the buildings stood as if on guard, and he had thought about how many men before him had made that same walk, seen that same sight, and graduated to go off and become heroes as they defended their country against all enemies, foreign and domestic. He'd wondered back then if he'd ever go off to do battle with the foes of his way of life; if he'd ever become a hero of his country.

Ed didn't feel like an impending hero that night in the Spring Lake area, but it was true that he was going off, possibly, yea, even probably, to do battle with someone: he guessed it would be an enemy of his country. Maybe things would become more clear by the time he got over there. They hadn't for the last couple of eons, but, "Quien sabe?"

At the BOQ, Hooper was home and so was Jim Opal, another of the DASL Detachment whom Ed knew pretty well and liked even better. Once, during the five-day mountain problem in Ranger School, Opal had decided to kill Meadows. Opal had been trying to sleep, and Meadows kept waking him up, and Jim had decided to eliminate Ed on the next wake-up trip, but before he could carry out his plan, they'd changed patrol leaders and Ed hadn't passed his way again. Opal was kinda like the Demo men in Group, he was a little bit on the different side. Come to think of it, he liked demolitions, too. The three lieutenants talked well into the night, more or less just passing the time with Ed. The feeling was pretty prevalent that he would be leaving soon. How soon, they didn't know for sure, nor did Meadows, but he did know something the other two didn't know. At 1100 hrs tomorrow, Ed, along with the rest of A-26, A-25, and A-27, would be entering "the Cage."

14

Behind Closed Doors

The members of Detachment A-26 were all assembled at the most secure of all places, the B Company Mess Hall at 0900 hrs the next morning. Captain Johnson was addressing them. "I hope you have all completed everything there is to complete. LT Meadows and I have gone over your personal folders with Sergeants Flagstone and Bradley, and, as near as we can determine, we've done everything there is to do. I hope so. I've been in a classified briefing with the colonel up at Group Headquarters this morning, and I can tell you we are entering the Cage at 1100 hrs. That much is unclassified. From now on, you are to talk to no one about what is going on. Once we get inside that wire, you ain't coming out until we all come out, or you're scratched from the mission. No exceptions. I hope you've all said your goodbyes to all your women folks and kids, cause there ain't no phone in the Cage. At 1000 hrs, there'll be a truck at the barracks for us to load all our stuff on, so some of you need to be there to help, at least four should be enough. The rest of you be there at 1050 hrs. Don't be late. We'll ride in the truck to the Cage, unload it, and that's it, you can't come out. I have verified that personal weapons will be authorized, so you can bring your hog-legs along. Any questions? Okay, who's gonna help load?" Everyone was. Hell, they knew all this already, and Ed had brought his Smith & Wesson, his Bible, and even secreted his diary in the rucksack stowed in the team room.

So had everyone else brought his possibles, as the mountain men of the old west referred to their personal items.

A few men from other detachments came by to have a cup of coffee and share a few words with the A-26 members, but mostly they just sat there waiting for the time to pass. Finally, it was 0930 and Flagstone stood up.

"I'm going on to the team room. There ain't no point in sitting here mooning around. What the hell, men, let's go to war." With that, he turned and walked out of the mess hall with the rest of the team following. It was cold outside, so the field jacket felt good to Ed; he only wished he'd zipped the liner into it. They didn't have to walk far to the barracks, and the deuce-and-a-half was already there, but there was no driver. No matter, all twelve of them could drive anywhere in the civilized world with their international drivers' licenses. Loading the truck was no problem with all of them participating, even SSG Riley. Besides their individual rucksacks, they each had a big duffel bag full of stuff, and there was the team box...an eight-foot long monster packed with all kinds of goodies, and a second, slightly smaller box Riley and Pickett had filled up with medical supplies. Ten o'clock, one hour to wait. This time it was Captain Johnson who was tired of waiting.

"Any objections to going on in?" he asked. There were none. Flagstone appointed himself the driver and the captain got up front with him. Ed and the others loaded into the back. The drive down to the Cage took about two minutes. Flag backed the vehicle expertly up to the fence, to the gate, which was locked with a surly MP standing on the other side.

"What the hell you men want?" he asked, then, seeing the captain climb out of the cab, he added, "Sir?"

"We're one of the groups supposed to enter today," Johnson informed him.

"I gotta see your passports, dogtags, and ID cards, Sir," said the military policeman, asserting his authority as policemen are wont to do. "Once I admit you, you can't go back out for no reason. You'll leave your passports here with me, they'll be returned when you leave. I would suggest that the ones unloading the truck stay outside until it's all done, then they can come in."

"We'll all just unload the truck and carry the stuff in with us. Make your job easy, Sarge," replied Captain Johnson.

"That'll be fine, Sir." The detachment members unloaded the truck, piled all their stuff on top of the boxes, then lined up for "the Authority" to make his checks. Unlocking the gate, the MP called to a companion standing nearby, and instructed him to stand behind the team. *Probably so he could shoot someone if they tried to get away,* thought Ed, as though anyone would want to get away now. *Didn't they understand how hard we had worked to get a mission? Who the hell would try to get away now?*

The MP looked closely at each man's dogtags, which they had conveniently hung outside their jackets, checked their ID card pictures with their faces, and asked each man his Serial Number. He compared passport photos with ID card pictures with faces, returned the ID cards, keeping the passports, and, one by one, admitted the men to his sacred ground inside the enclosure. They lugged in their gear, then left the team boxes in the care of their "Authority" while they carried their packs into the middle of the three barracks buildings. They were to sleep upstairs with the first floor reserved for their classes, which would begin soon, after dinner. Then the team boxes were carried upstairs. It was 1100 hrs.

Their quarters were actually pretty nice. Each officer had his own room upstairs, and the rest of the men had individual alcoves, which provided them some manner of privacy. The head was clean, there was hot water ready for showering, and even the mirrors above the sinks were clean. They could see the men of A-25 and A-27 checking in with "the Authority," and he was no friendlier to them than he had been to A-26. Must be trained into MP's to behave like jackasses. Chow in the little mess hall was a surprise, too. There were fresh flowers on the tables, tablecloths, and real dishes instead of the MelMac stuff in the usual mess hall. Not only that—the food was very good and there was a lot of it. The mess personnel were from Group, but they weren't from B Company. And suprisingly, they were friendly.

After dinner, their reason for being in the Cage became clear. No more were they introduced to the broad brush treatment of Laos, now they got down to brass tacks. Detachment A-26 was to be split into two FTT's: FTT-17, with the captain in charge, and FTT-19, commanded by 1st Lieutenant Edward Meadows. The division of the

Detachment would be left up to the members of A-26.

As for FTT-19, they would be relieving a similar team currently assigned as advisors to the 11th Battalion Parachute—the 11th BP, located near Thakhet, Laos. It was commanded by one LTC Khom, an excellent officer who had distinguished himself in battle against the Viet Minh up in Phong Saly province after the fall of Dien Bien Phu just across the border. He was supposedly straight, that is, not corrupt, and was considered to be one of the best officers the FAR had to offer. As for FTT-17, they were being assigned to advise the 1st Regiment Parachute—the 1st RP, of which the 11th BP was a part. They, too were currently located near Thakhet. The action in this area had been sporadic of late, but opposing them were elements of the KL battalions who were supposed to be pretty good soldiers. Many of the men of the 11th BP had served with the KL before the latter defected, and vice-versa, so there seemed to be a certain reluctance on each side to engage in much combat. The Americans currently serving there had met with little success in getting their units to do anything, and the reports coming back to the Special Warfare Center were not encouraging. It seemed there was a possibility the Kong Le troops might re-defect, but it also seemed that the possibility of the 11th joining them was quite distinct. Colonel Khom had been offered the opportunity to keep his rank and command a similar unit on the other side by Kong Le, himself. And himself and Colonel Khom were buddies from way back. Lovely. Any more good news before bedtime? This detailed briefing lasted until suppertime, then concluded for the day. There would be more tomorrow, but the night could be used by the team to do whatever they wanted within the confines of the Cage.

After supper, Captain Johnson called Meadows and Sergeants Flagstone and Bradley into his room. "We've got to divide the Detachment up, and we may as well do it now so we can benefit the most from these briefings. How do you propose we do it, Lieutenant?"

"I guess we ought to go through the specialties and pick one for your team and one for mine of each. Flagstone and Bradley know the men better than we do, so they can provide their input as far as personalities and capabilities go. Is that all right with you, Sir?"

"That was the same thing I was thinking. Now, Sarge," he said, addressing both the master sergeants, "don't be shy. We need your help, so speak right up. If there's some mismatch somewhere, say so, okay?" They nodded okay. "Let's start with the O&I sergeants, you two. Any preferences?"

"I'll go with the lieutenant," said Flagstone, "if that's alright."

"Fine by me," said Ed.

"Me, too," muttered Bradley.

"Okay, that's okay with me," said the captain. "Listen, why don't you two go over to your room and come up with a division of the troops. Sergeant Bradley and I will do the same here. We'll get together after breakfast and work out the solution together. I'm tired as hell, it's late, and we need to think about this awhile."

"Yes, Sir, I agree," said Ed. "We'll see you tomorrow. Flag, come on over to my room and we'll talk about this. Oh, Sir, one more thing. Is there any beer, or at least some Cokes, around here?"

"Damn, Lieutenant, I forgot. The refrigerator downstairs is supposed to be full of that stuff. Tell the men to help themselves." Seemed like a good way to end a long day.

The only trouble was that the day couldn't end there, not for Ed and Flagstone. They got some beer and retired to Meadows' room. Flag shut the door. "Every swinging dick in this detachment knows what the hell we're doing, Sir, and there ain't no sense in them knowing how we're doing it."

"Right, Sergeant, you're right. Well, let's get to work. First of all, I don't know shit about anyone here, not even you, as a matter of fact. Do you know everybody?"

"Fairly well. I know Bushman and Riley good; the others are pretty young and haven't been around much. I talked with Leontine about you. We were in the 187th together and he's a good head." (Just how many men did the 187th have in it? Either it had ten or twelve thousand, or else every man-jack of them had joined the Special Forces Groups.) "That's why I volunteered for your team. Ole Pompeo said you might make a good officer someday."

"Okay, then let's pick 'em. By the way, I think Leontine is one hell of a good soldier. I'd hate to have him after me."

"You're right about that. The way I see it, we want Bushman on our team. He's crosstrained in O&I* and has a lot of experience in

---

O&I - Operations and Intelligence

S-2 (Intelligence) stuff. He'll be able to get us all kind of stuff. Couple of years ago, he went to the DAEE and DAME course at Holabird and there ain't a lock around he can't pick."

"I hate to seem stupid, Sarge, but what is DAEE and DAME?"

"Defense Against Electronic Equipment and Defense Against Mechanical Equipment, bugging and lock-picking, or de-bugging and locking, whichever. Okay, we want Bushman at all costs. The commo guys are both young, so it don't matter to me. Let's ask for Kidd, but if we have to swap him to keep Bushman, do it, but act like it hurts."

"What about the medics? Is Sergeant Riley any good?"

"He's probably the best medic of the two, but the jerk is always whining about something and he don't help out worth a shit. Let's ask for him, but let them make us take Pickett. He's a loud-mouth, but at least he works."

Ed felt like he had to say something, make some kind of a contribution, since he was "the Leader." "I like Thomas for the Weapons man; how about you?"

"Damn right, Lieutenant, he's one of the best men in the Group. No way are we gonna get Bushman and Thomas both, Bradley's too smart for that. We can ask, but we ain't gonna receive. We're either gonna get Bushman or Thomas, but not both, and I think it'll be Bushman. Bradley thinks he's a drunk and he won't pick him. We can live with Beaudreau. I think he's an asshole, and I think he's trouble, but if he's too much of a pain in the ass, we'll get rid of him over there."

"Leontine would suggest an 'accident.' He says they happen all the time in Laos."

"They do, Lieutenant, they do. By the way, we can't go through life calling you, 'Lieutenant.' Since you're the youngest man on the team, you can't be the Old Man. What're we gonna call you?"

Meadows thought back to the Customs and Courtesies classes at West Point, and the concept of 'Social Distance,' and the fact that some of these men might die while under his command. He didn't think "Ed" was appropriate. "I dunno. Do you have any ideas? I don't think my first name is appropriate. How about 'Meadows'?"

"Nah. When I was a lieutenant in Korea, they called me 'Boss,' and I liked that. How about, 'Boss'?"

"If you don't think the men will mind, I don't mind. Say, I didn't know you used to be a lieutenant."

"Hell, Boss, there's a lot of things you don't know. I'll tell you about it sometime, but not now. Let's finish up, I'm tired."

"I think we're done. You, me, Bushman, Thomas—if we can get him, Kidd, if we can get him, and Riley, if we can't get Pickett. Isn't that about it?"

"Yeah. Let's knock off for today. See you in the morning, Boss."

Ed liked the moniker, but somehow he felt kinda like a warden at some Mississippi penal farm instead of a commander of troops.

15

Shake, Rattle, And Roll

Flagstone was right, Bradley didn't want Bushman and he wouldn't let Thomas go. The captain didn't seem to care either way, but he backed up his team sergeant, and Meadows got Bushman and Beaudreau. He also got Riley for the asking, and that disturbed him. He'd have liked it better if they had dickered awhile for the senior medical specialist. Bradley said that Thomas and Eason couldn't live with each other, so Meadows got Eason. That was fine, no problem. Lined up in order and by rank, FTT-19 consisted of:

1st LT Ed Meadows, Team Commander

MSG (E8) Raymond Flagstone, Team Sergeant, Operations & Intelligence

SSG (E6) Francis Bushman, Demolitions, O&I, and Scrounge

SSG (E6) Harold Riley, Medical Specialist

SGT (E5) Frank Beaudreau, Weapons Specialist

SP4 (E4) Ricky Eason, Communications Specialist and Resident Hippie.

It wasn't a bad team. FTT-17 had Captain Johnson, Bradley, Thomas, Pickett, Svoboda, and Kidd, and, of the two, Ed felt it was about a draw, except he thought Flagstone was better than Bradley and, naturally, he was better than Johnson! Continuing his game of team rating, Bushman was supposedly better than Svoboda, Kidd and Eason were even, Thomas beat Beaudreau, and Riley and Pickett were even.

Final score: FTT-19, 3; FTT-17, 1; and 2 even. We win.

Flagstone gathered the FTT together and introduced Ed to the members as, "Boss," and from that point on, you'd have thought he had been named Boss by his mother, it was used so freely. Their training was divided, as well as their detachment, and the briefings given to the members of FTT-19 were different from those given to FTT-17. The briefings were in the mornings, four hours' worth, everyday, on everything from gummy rice to ke kwi. That's Laotian for, "bull shit." In the afternoons, the men worked on their equipment, cleaning, packing, recleaning, repacking, and the nights were occupied with French lessons for the officers and Laotian for the men. Ed liked Laotian better than French, and he soon mastered the phrase, "Chou me makke fi, boi?" That asks if you have a match. Then there was "Boi pin yang," equivalent to "no sweat," the most popular phrase in all of Laos. The French used to have a saying about the peoples of Indo-China, which went something like this; "The Vietnamese plant rice, the Cambodians harvest rice, the Laotians listen to it grow." Meadows was going to war with the listeners. Wonderful. Time passed quickly, and on Saturday night, after the language classes, Captain Johnson called a detachment meeting of the entire A-26 complement.

"Men, the waiting is over. We leave in the morning from Pope Air Force Base on a C-124. We'll be the only team on the plane, along with 33 tons of medical supplies for Thailand, or somewhere. Due to the requirements for crew rest and the slow speed of the airplane, we'll be stopping at Tinker, Travis, Hickham, Wake, Guam, Clark, and Bangkok before we get to Laos. Have some civilian clothes ready, cause we'll be allowed off post at each stop, and uniforms will not be allowed off post. We'll get a wake up call at 0400 hrs and the plane is scheduled to leave at 0900 hrs. The Air Force will load the supplies; we'll load our stuff. For the trip, we'll travel as one detachment with our usual chain of command. Better get some sleep."

Easier said than done, for Ed. Months of anticipation, weeks of training, days of briefings, and now down to hours of waiting. There were a lot of things on the lieutenant's mind. How would he perform in combat? Would he freeze up, and decompensate? Would the men follow him? Was he going to get killed? What was it like to be shot at? Lots of questions, but no answers; only time would reveal these to him. Meadows closed his eyes and tried to go to sleep, but he couldn't. Was this all a mistake? He didn't have to go to war, he could stay home. The United States wasn't at war; most Americans hadn't even heard of Laos. All his classmates were doing their various duties in the Army without going to war. His head was a whirling maelstrom which robbed him of the sleep the captain said he needed. Ed prayed that night. He prayed for safety—for himself and his men; he prayed for wisdom, as promised in the first chapter of James; he prayed for guidance, but most of all, he prayed for help in performing his duty. After all, wasn't that what it was all about: Duty, Honor, Country? It wasn't a motto anymore, but an assignment—the assignment he'd accepted that day long ago at Trophy Point when he'd raised his right hand and been sworn into the service of his Country. Duty, with Honor, for his Country. It wasn't a bad goal. When Flagstone came in to wake him up, it was dark and cold and rainy outside. "Let's go get 'em, Boss. See you downstairs in a few minutes. I'll have the men there." Meadows got up, took a quick shower, shaved, brushed his teeth, and was downstairs in ten minutes.

   The lights which had been on all around the Cage were off now, and they loaded the truck parked by the gate in the dark. A couple of MP's stood guard over the vehicle while the team ate breakfast, and the rest of Smoke Bomb Hill slept. It was Sunday and no training was scheduled. At 0530 hrs, they loaded into the truck and the canvas was closed around them. No one was talking much. By 0600 hrs, they were at Pope and the big bumblebee—the C-124, was squatting outside a hanger on the far side of the field. Air Force personnel were loading the medical supplies and the Army truck drove right inside the hanger where the men were allowed to get out, but not to leave the building. Everyone sat around looking at everyone else until 0800 hours when the Air Force finished their loading. Captain Johnson motioned for them to start loading their own gear, which was stowed and tied down by 0830 hours. Fifteen minutes later, at 0845 hrs on the button, the detachment lined up under one wing of the Globemaster II and a jeep drove up to where they were assembled. Colonel Richards, the new CO of the Seventh Group, got out, along with LTC Suomi, who would be taking command of White Star in two months, and, unbelievably, LTC Briggs. As the team stood at attention, the officers lined up in front of Captain Johnson. Colonel Richards returned his salute, shook hands, and said something to him.

Then Richards turned to Meadows, returned his salute, shook hands, and said, "Lieutenant, remember that you're representing the United States of America over there. Make us proud of you."

Colonel Suomi was next. "I vill be seeing you in two months, Lieutenant. Take care of yourself and of zese men."

It was Briggs' turn. As they shook hands, Meadows knew what was coming without a doubt. He knew the words by heart, but Briggs gave him his tender blessings, anyway. "Meadows, don't fuck up." And it was off to the sound of the guns.

As the big radial engines growled to life, the airplane began to shake. When they taxied to the end of the Pope runway, the airplane rattled. With the gathering of speed on the runway, the C-124 developed a rolling motion much like a boat in a heavy sea. Breaking free of the concrete, the lumbering giant of a cargo craft tucked its wheels, withdrew its flaps, and sped for the other side of the world just slightly faster than Ed had maneuvered Arvak through Mississippi. For six hours, the team tried to get comfortable as "Old Shakey," flew westward. The landing at Tinker Field was uneventful, and the men dismounted the bird dressed in civilian clothes. They had a nice barracks for the night, and a retired major took Captain Johnson and Ed into Oklahoma City for supper. They were back at the barracks by 2000 hrs. The poker game which had started on the plane was suspended when they landed, but the men had vowed that it would continue until they returned to Ft. Bragg.

Flying to Travis the next day was another experience of shaking, rattling, and rolling. They flew over the Plains of Oklahoma and Texas, the Badlands of New Mexico, the Great Crater and Grand Canyon of Arizona, all snow-covered, and the Sierra Nevadas before landing at the California Air Force base. Supper was taken by the whole detachment at the NCO club there.

Getting away from Travis was another problem. They were delayed for a couple of hours while the gizmo was reattached to the snorkel-rod, or something like that, and during their wait, a Flying Tiger Super Constellation—L-1049, loaded up with 107 Army personnel headed for MAAG duty in Viet Nam. The men were mostly legs—non-airborne soldiers, and they were travelling first class, stewardesses and all. Damn legs. Finally, the gizmo was fixed, and Detachment A-26 took off. The poker game had hardly begun when they were informed by the pilot that the gizmo was loose again, and they were returning to Travis. Damn gizmo. Two more hours on the ground before they tried to slip the bonds of the continent, and this time they succeeded. The Constellation was long gone.

It was raining when they landed at Hickham Field, where part of the filming for the movie *From Here To Eternity* took place. Ed, Flagstone, Svoboda, Pickett, and Captain Johnson rented a car and saw the sights of Honolulu that evening. Well, some of the sights. They saw two night clubs. But the next day they got to see a lot more, cause that damn gizmo still didn't work and they were all delayed twenty-four hours while a new gizmo was flown in from Travis. *Wonderful. Wonder if that gizmo is essential for keeping the plane in the air?*

At 0400 hrs the following day, detachment A-26 was enabled to continue the poker game on the way to Wake Island. They flew over a hell of a lot of water, but thanks to the new gizmo, they did stay over, and not in it. Ed's first view of storied Wake Island encompassed the entire island. Hell, it was nothing but a sand bar, or a coral atoll, to be more precise. There was nothing to it. Why would they make movies of this dinky thing? Dinky or not, it had a big fuel depot to replenish the parched tanks of Old Shakey, so she could continue her odyssey. Choices of a spot to eat supper were slim; the team ate in *THE* mess hall, then slept in one of the (few) buildings present for that purpose. The poker game continued all night long. Before boarding Old Shakey early next morning, they learned that the Lockheed Constellation was missing and presumed lost between Guam and the Philippines.

It took all morning to reach Agana Naval Air Station, Guam, Marianas Islands, where they refueled, then they flew for three hours as part of the search pattern looking for the Constellation. No trace was ever found. *Poor guys,* Ed felt bad for the legs. At Clark Field, the air was surprisingly cool, very humid, but not unpleasant. Meadows halfway expected to see General MacArthur, or at least Jonathon Wainwright on hand to welcome them, but they weren't. Checking in at the barracks, Ed declined an invitation to visit Manila, but chose instead to write a letter to Denise after supper and go to bed early. The shaky plane ride had something to do with it, the lost Constellation affected him, but mostly, the prospect of arriving in

Southeast Asia on the morrow made Meadows tired.

The final legs of their trip went smoothly. The Globemaster II dutifully deposited the detachment at Don Muang airfield in Bangkok. With scarcely an hour's delay, they loaded their gear, minus the medical supplies, into a venerable old (unmarked) C-47 flown by a red-headed civilian named, appropriately enough, "Red," and took off for Savannahkhet, Laos. He flew with a certain reckless abandon, you might say, reading a paperback book, his feet propped up on the instrument panel. There was no co-pilot, no crew, just Red, but he managed to bounce the plane down safely on the short strip in Savannahkhet. It lurched and jerked, and rolled to a stop, and the men of detachment A-26 prepared to disembark.

As Ed jumped down to the ground (there were no air stairs, much less a jetway), he really didn't know what to expect. It was hot, that didn't surprise him, but there were no explosions, no whistling shells, no bursts of cordite smoke, no running for cover. He had finally arrived in the war zone, and it was the most peaceful town he'd ever visited in his life.

16

Skinny, Flat, And Ugly

An American came wheeling up in a three-quarter ton truck, a 3/4, with an attached trailer, slammed the vehicle to a stop, killing the engine, and jumped out. He asked for Captain Johnson, which seemed an unnecessary query since there was only one man standing there with captain's bars on his collar. "I'm Johnson," said the captain stepping forward.

"Glad to meet you, Sir," said the man offering his hand to the captain. "We don't salute in public here so as not to identify the officers to a sniper. I'm Sergeant Yeomans and I'm here to pick y'all up and take you to the team house. Major Murphy is in a briefing, or he'd have come along. If you'll load your gear in the truck and pile in, we'll get going."

Ed noticed there were no markings on the truck other than the directions for fueling and a warning not to overfill, to allow for expansion. They threw all their gear, including the team boxes, into the trailer, then, as Yeomans had directed, they piled into the truck, he fired up the engine, and with a lurch and a sputter, they were off for the team house.

Savannahkhet was a large city by Laotian standards, but it was small stuff to the Americans. The airfield was located on the southeast edge of town, but there was a paved road leading into the city. The road became the main street with buildings on either side. Describing the prevalent architecture would be a chore, for there was no prevailing style. Most of the houses seemed to be some sort of dirty stucco on the outside and they bordered right on the street. Interspersed with the stucco were more or less "rattan" buildings, which sported grass roofs, and every so often there were big, white, square-looking two-story buildings with walls around them which looked definitely European in derivation. The downtown area consisted of a string of shops with open air fronts; the shops joined together in one seemingly single unit, which stretched for an entire block. Well, at least there was some commerce here. Nearly every man Ed saw had on a uniform, or part of a uniform—the most common color being some shade of green. The women wore mostly black or faded plaid skirts which reached to the ground and were wrap-arounds. As for the kids, their clothing bills must have been cheap, for they wore a tiny cotton shirt and nothing else. Telling the little boys from the little girls was no problem.

About a quarter of a mile past the downtown area was the team house, one of those big white buildings with a wall around it, but this one was three stories high. The sight of U.S. fatigues and teal blue and gold shoulder patches was welcome to Meadows. All the men piled out and went inside where there was a makeshift orderly room and a sign-in book much like the one at B Company on Smoke Bomb Hill. Each man was required to sign in before he could officially begin playing war. Major Murphy, the CO of this B Team, was on hand to welcome them. He said Captain Johnson and Lieutenant Meadows could spend the night at the team house, but the rest of the men would be quartered downtown. They'd be going out to their field locations in the morning.

Ed hefted his rucksack and duffel bag onto his shoulders, and followed the captain, who followed the sergeant, who led them to their cots on the third floor. There were four cots in the room, a bathroom with a bidet and a shower, and the weirdest little commode that Ed had ever seen. But the most interesting fact was that there were mosquito nettings over all the beds, called "mosquito bars." Meadows dumped his stuff on the cot and sat down. It was hot outside, very hot, but inside the building it was surprisingly cool. The windows, which were really doors, were wide open, catching any errant breeze that happened along.

"Captain Johnson, it *is* hot!" exclaimed Ed.

The captain, who was sweating like a racehorse, nodded agreement. "And this is the cool part of the day. I'm gonna take a shower."

While Johnson showered, Ed relaxed on the cot and pondered his fate. He didn't like being here in town. It was obvious this wasn't where the war was, and it was just as obvious the B Team didn't have enough room for them here. Maybe things would look better tomorrow. Another thing which bothered Ed was the fact that he hadn't seen a single weapon carried by anyone on the trip in from the airport. What kind of war were they running here, anyway? He and Leontine had carried their pistols in the friendly confines of the swamp in Florida; it seemed that someone should be armed here. The captain finished and returned to the room, his towel wrapped around him in the fashion of the skirts of the Laotian women. "Damn, captain, you're going to fit right in here if you dress like that."

Johnson laughed. "Yeah, but my dress is white and their's is black. Guess that makes me a good guy. Why don't you get cleaned up and let's go into town?"

"Be right with you," replied Ed, getting up and beginning to undress. "Think we ought to wear civvies?"

"Hell, yes. Major Murphy said they're authorized downtown."

Ed tried the hot water handle of the shower and cold water came out of the head, so he tried the cold handle and cold water came out. Guess these handles don't speak English. He rinsed the grime of the day off of his body, then got out and towelled off. One thing you can say for a shower that doesn't speak English: it's invigorating!

The style of dress here seemed to be trousers with a shirt worn out and that's how both the men dressed. Meadows dug around in his rucksack until he found his Smith, slipped it out of the holster, and opened the cylinder. Each chamber was full. He stuck the holster back into the bag and stuffed the pistol into his waistband, covering the handle with his shirt. Now he felt dressed. "Captain, are we gonna get any guns over here?"

"Damn if I know. They'll probably tell us about that tomorrow. C'mon, let's go see what Laos is all about." They walked down the stairs, asked the sergeant standing near the door where they should go for some food and drink, and the sergeant directed them to the Constellation, a night club where the team was staying. Even though it was getting close to dark, they decided to walk on into town rather than wait for someone to come by with a jeep, and off they went. As they passed some natives on the road, Ed remembered what he'd heard about the women over here. The veterans back at Bragg said they were dark, flat, ugly, and skinny when you first got here, but the longer you stayed, the lighter, more buxom, prettier, and fatter they got. On his first day in the country, the former description definitely applied.

The Constellation was reached without incident. It was one of those stucco houses, but was two stories high and sported a big sign which read "Constellation" outside. The entire front of the place was the door, and once inside, it was difficult to see. What lights there were consisted of candles on the tables spread around the room and their smoke only added to the pall hanging from the ceiling. As Meadows' eyes adjusted to the dim surroundings, he made out most of his team sitting at tables with girls, who were mostly dark, flat, ugly, and skinny. The men seemed to be enjoying their company; maybe they'd been in country longer than Ed. Captain Johnson found them a table and the two sat down. Almost immediately there were two girls sitting down in the other two chairs at the table. They were dark, flat, ugly, and skinny.

"Whoa, there, Wild Bill," said the captain. "Can we help you ladies?" The girls giggled. "What's going on here?" pursued Johnson. More giggles.

A man walked up and said something to the girls in a foreign language, or maybe in the native tongue of Laos. The giggling ceased. "Ah, Sir," he said in halting English. "You want dancing girls?"

"What are dancing girls, Bucko?" asked the captain.

"You new in country, Yes?" not waiting for an answer, he continued, "These girls sit your table with you, smile you, drink beer with you. Have lot of cold Budweiser."

"And just what do we do for these girls?"

"Ah, that not bad. You pay one hundred kip every hour girls sit with you. Not too bad, pretty cheap."

"What happens when we finish sitting?" asked the wary captain.

"You like girl, you take home with you, your home, her home, same-same. One thousand kip, all night."

"Well, thanks anyway, but we'll let these girls go tonight. We're new in country, just as you said, maybe next time." Turning to the girls, the captain made pushing motions with his hand. "Shoo, shoo, run along ladies. Maybe next time." The girls left, but the pimp was persistent.

"Not like these girls, boi pin yang, have plenty more, you see."

"Look, Pal, we appreciate all your trouble, but not tonight. See you next time around." The procurer left. Throughout this entire exchange, Ed had sat speechless. Never before in his life had he seen such open invitations to buy some time with a whore. Even in Juarez they weren't this flagrant. It was something new and amazing to the young lieutenant, something they had forgotten to mention in their detailed briefings back in the Cage.

"Have you ever?" he asked Johnson.

"Hell, yes, Lieutenant, happens all the time in Korea. That bit about the dancing is a new twist. These girls are whores, plain and simple, don't let all this jazz about dancing throw you. Be careful of them. If you gotta dip your wick, be better to wait for Bangkok, you're not as likely to get rolled there. The Thai police are tough."

Meadows had no intention of dipping his wick. That wasn't what he came over here for. They drank a couple of beers, ate some stuff called "bif-stek" which was a product of some poor cow somewhere, but certainly wasn't beef steak, watched a terrible guitarist assault a terrible guitar while grinding out some song that had a faintly familiar overtone, then it came time to leave and pay up. They realized that they had nothing but dollars to pay with, and the currency of the country was kip. Eighty kip equalled one dollar, officially, but the waiter offered them an exchange rate of 130 kip/$1, and they accepted his offer. Their bill came to exactly 520k each. A nice round number, four bucks. Probably just a coincidence.

Outside, Meadows spotted Flagstone and Bushman walking down the street. "Hey, Flag, where y'all going?" he hollered.

"Hi, ya, Boss. Good evening, Captain. Glad to see you're both sober. We're going over to the Sensabay Hotel. They got a club over there where the Air America pilots hang out. Supposed to be the nicest place in town. Care to join us?"

"Count us in, Sergeant," said Captain Johnson, and the four of them walked the two blocks to Savannahkhet's finest hotel—its only hotel, the Sensabay. Like the team house, this building was three stories tall and built in a square, but was much, much larger than the team house. Up on the top floor they had a club called the Boi Pin Yang and that was where the four men were directed by the doorman. As they climbed the stairs, Ed was amazed by how nice this hotel was. It was clean, there were lights everywhere, folks wore jackets and ties—it was a different world.

Even the club was nice. A long wooden bar ran the length of one wall and it was crowded by people Ed recognized from the team house. Red, The Relaxed Pilot, was there, as were a lot of men with hair too long, who were speaking French. Frogs, no doubt. Bushman selected a table in one of the corners and they all sat down. A relatively pretty girl with a relatively pretty smile, speaking relatively good English took their order for four beers and they sat back to see what was going on.

Down at the far end of the bar, two guys were arguing, and it appeared that they might come to blows any minute. Red, The Relaxed Pilot, was telling several of the guys around him about some hair-raising flying adventure, and the Frogs were snickering and sneering in pious self-righteousness. Meadows didn't like the Frogs. Flag and Bushman talked a little, but Johnson was quiet as they drank their first beers and ordered refills. Ed noticed that there weren't any dancing girls here; in fact, except for the waitress, there weren't any women at all. Suddenly that changed.

She came through the door, and all conversation in the room ceased. Tall, at least 5'8", long black hair hanging down to the middle of her back, almond shaped eyes in an oval face, HUGE boobs which jiggled when she walked, a dress so tight that the slit in the legs was the only thing allowing her to breathe, and that slit didn't stop at the knee, not at the mid-thigh, but ran all the way up to her behind, she swept across the room toward the bar with every eye in the place dancing to the twisting of her hips. *Sonofabitch,* thought Ed, *I've been here longer than I thought.*

The object of everyone's attention flowed up to Red, The Relaxed Pilot, and applied herself to his arm, to his chest, to his side, to his legs. Hell, she applied herself everywhere. Red merely grinned and was still grinning when the four soldiers left a little later. *One of these days,* mused Meadows, *I'm gonna have to learn to fly an airplane.*

17

Unwritten Rules

There was a message on the bulletin board at the team house for the members of Detachment A-26 which stated there was to be a briefing at 0700 hours tomorrow in the conference room at the team house, duly noted by Captain Johnson and Lieutenant Meadows when they returned from seeing what Laos was all about. They trudged up the stairs to their third floor roost and crawled into their cots, pulling down the mosquito netting and tucking it under the blanket which served as a mattress. Ed felt like he was a member of Tarzan's crew as he bedded down for the night. The captain was the last one in bed, so he turned out the light and the first night in this strange, seemingly peaceful country, was turned out with it. Meadows wondered if he'd have trouble falling asleep, but he didn't wonder very long.

The conference room had a lot of chairs arranged in rows in front of a large canvas which obviously covered a map. Precisely at 0700 hours, the detachment was assembled, Major Murphy stepped up in front of them and began the briefing. There were a few differences from what they'd heard back in the Cage. To begin with, the designation of FTT-17 was changed to FTT-13 and they were being assigned to the 15th Group Mobile—the 15th GM, which was now the parent unit of the 11th BP to which FTT-19 was being assigned. These teams were to serve as ADVISORS, not Special Action Forces, not combatants, not Rangers, to their respective units. Captain Johnson would command the new FTT-13, and Meadows was to command FTT-19. Whatever breakdown of personnel the two officers had agreed upon would still be honored. Turning the briefing over to Captain Vosser, his S-3, the Major left to continue his duties with his B detachment. Captain Vosser removed the canvas from the wall map and continued the briefing.

"The 15th GM Headquarters is currently located at Taket," he said, indicating the location of a spot on the map slightly south and slightly east of the larger city of Thakhet, "and is the parent unit for three battalions located in this general vicinity," circumscribing a larger circle on the map with his pointer. "The 11th BP is located along the banks of the Xe Bangfai—the west bank: three companies on the front with one company in reserve. Opposing them to the east are units of the 55th BP which have joined the Kong Le forces currently aligned with the Pathet Lao. These Kong Le troops have been showing some aggressive tendencies lately, and last week a company of the 33rd Battalion Infantry was overrun here," indicating a location further north of the 11th's, "with about twenty casualties. The U.S. team was isolated and managed to Escape and Evade until picked up by friendly forces the next morning. The men of that detachment felt they were the reason for the attack—that the enemy was trying to obtain some U.S. prisoners. You guys with the 11th BP had better watch your asses." Ed had every intention of watching his ass, and those of his men, as well. "We have been trying to get the 11th to run nightly patrols across the river but to date they have cooperated very poorly. Captain McKinter currently commands FTT-19 whom you'll be replacing. We have no advisors with the other two battalions of the 15th GM, but we hope to have some soon with the build-up we've been promised from Bragg. Since these two battalions are on the flanks of the 11th, should they collapse, as they are suspect of doing, it would leave the 11th isolated and put you men in extreme peril. You need to work out an E&E plan when you get on the ground and make it known to us in detail so we can provide you with the quickest and strongest assistance, should the need arise."

The briefing continued, but it was mostly concerning the future of the 15th GM, and Ed's interest was riveted to the situation as it applied to his FTT. This was some plight to be in. If the FAR units north and south of the BP collapsed, he'd be sitting out there with the river to his front, and the enemy on the other side of that river, the enemy to the north, south, and probably the west! Just him and his team, along with several hundred men who didn't speak his language, were of questionable loyalty, and didn't even know his name. This is commonly known as being surrounded. *Well, Lieutenant, you wanted a war, you got a war. What the hell, let's go get 'em.*

By 0800 hrs, the briefing was over. They were released to draw weapons from the S-4 warehouse near the team house, or Captain McKinter had indicated he would turn over his team's weapons if the new team desired. After consulting with Flagstone, they decided to accept McKinter's offer. His men had been here for six months, and they probably had a good idea of which arms each man would benefit the most from carrying. Had he chosen for himself, Ed would probably have selected an M2 Carbine.

There would be no reason for carrying civvies up there, nor the team box, at least not to start with. Better to travel light and feel your way around first. After combining the contents of his rucksack and the duffel-bag to eliminate all the niceties and carry only the combat paraphenalia, Meadows took the duffel-bag over to the S-4 warehouse where a section had been set aside for the teams in the field to store their extra gear. This was supposedly a secure building, and it did have 24-hour, around-the-clock guards. At Flag's suggestion, all the members of FTT-19 had gotten out their personal weapons and strapped them on. Meadows had his trusty Smith; Flagstone carried a Colt .32 automatic—a thoroughly useless gun, if you asked Ed, but Flag didn't ask Ed; and Bushman had a huge Ruger .44 Magnum Super Blackhawk with a barrel that seemed to be thirty inches long; SSG Riley had brought a Smith & Wesson .38 Special with a 2″ barrel; Beaudreau wore a sawed-off 12-gauge Mossberg bolt action shotgun in a swivel rig which allowed it to be fired from the hip; and Eason had a standard Army .45 in a shoulder holster. Some army Ed was commanding. It looked like it might be good on a movie set, but there wasn't much uniformity for war. Ed also had an ammo pouch with 100 extra rounds for the .357.

The two FTT's were to leave from the airfield by helicopter at 1000 hrs to join their units, but there was only one chopper, and it would have to make two trips. Captain Johnson elected to take his team in first. He was as anxious to see some action as Ed, and "RHIP"—

Rank Hath Its Privileges. They rode out to the strip with Yeomans, who was also armed today, and there they met the aircraft which they would get to know well during their stay in Laos.

It was an H-34, a big, bulbous-nosed craft with a noisy engine that flew at about 100 miles per hour when the wind was blowing right. The chopper was painted a lime green with yellow lettering on the side, but the lettering was in Laotian, so Meadows had no idea what it said. Up on the tail rotor spar were the letters H-X, and its call sign was Hotel X-ray. The crew consisted of the pilot, a civilian, and the crew chief, also a civilian, and they both sported big handle-bar mustaches. The pilot was armed with a .45, while the crew chief had a Thompson submachine gun with the shoulder stock removed. More like a machine pistol. FTT newly designated 13 crawled aboard, the pilot mounted the landing gear strut and then climbed up into the cockpit and began flipping switches. The crew chief made sure everyone was on board, then he walked out front where the pilot could see him, waved his hand in a circular motion, and the engine began coughing and sputtering to life. As the tail rotor started whirling and the blades began to move on the main rotor, Ed thought of the joke about the Italian helicopter that had two rotors—a little one in the back that said "Guinea, guinea, guinea" and the big one on top that said, "Wop, wop, wop." The crew chief got in, a cloud of dust stung the skin and blinded the eyes of the men left behind, and the big craft rose up and began guinea-wopping off to the north. Meadows watched it for a couple of minutes until it disappeared from sight in the morning sky.

Flagstone was standing nearby, and in the silence following the departure of the helicopter, he walked over and talked to Ed.

"How you doing, Boss?" he asked.

"Well enough, I guess. How long till he gets back?"

"Yeomans says it'll be at least an hour. Takes about thirty minutes to get up to Taket from here. They'll have to refuel when they return, so it'll probably be a couple of hours till we get out of here."

"How's everyone else?"

"They're okay. May be a little puckering going on, but they'll be fine. Beaudreau's all hung over. Eason's scared. They're okay."

"Tell you the truth, Sarge, I'm a little uneasy myself. Sounds like we're going into a real party situation. We could find ourselves in a hell of a mess pretty quick."

"Ah, you can't believe everything these assholes here tell you. They always try to scare the piss out of you. It won't be so bad."

Regardless of the fact that Flag was an old soldier and knew the ways of war much better than Meadows, Ed still felt uneasy. He sat down, using his rucksack as a backrest, got out one of his Marsh Wheelings, and had a smoke. Flagstone joined him and smoked a Camel—smoked three Camels before Ed finished his stogie. Maybe Flag wasn't concerned, but Ed never knew him to smoke so much before. They talked a little, Bushman joined them, and the three senior members of the FTT decided to make up an emergency Bug-Out plan they could use if they got hit before having an opportunity to formulate an official E&E plan later. They divided the team into three elements of two men each which would bug-out if the situation dictated, and try to make their way to the Mekong River to the west and thence to Thailand where the population was friendly. Meadows and Flag were one element, Bushman and Eason the second, and Riley and Beaudreau the third. Calling the rest of the men over, Ed explained the plan to them.

"What do you think?" the lieutenant asked.

"Sounds good to me," said Riley.

Beaudreau burped, but nodded his head.

"I don't care," said Eason. "I'll do whatever you guys decide. I just think that the guy with the radio and the guy with the generator should be together."

"Fuck the radio, and the generator," said Flagstone. "Leave 'em. We're talking about a real emergency situation where you're trying to save your ass. Leave everything but your weapon and your buddy. You might leave some of these Kong Le hot shits around, too. Kill all you can, then bug out. Only me or the Boss will make the decision to activate the Bug-Out plan. When we do, you can bet your ass that you're going to be in a world of hurt. Listen, I think I hear the chopper."

He did, and so did the others. It roared in toward their position, hovered briefly, then settled to the ground with a bump, bounced back up, and settled down again, remaining ground-bound this time. Pilot shut the engine down, Crew Chief got out and took a leak, and Yeomans reeled out the hose from the fuel tank behind them to begin refueling the bird. All smoking materials were extinguished. The tank of the chopper gulped down enough gasoline to fuel Arvak for a couple of years, then the nozzle was removed, the hose reeled back in, and the members of FTT-19 got aboard. There was a repeat of the previous departure sequence, and soon enough, they were in the air and climbing to 1000', headed north by northeast.

The air was a lot cooler up here than it had been on the ground at the airfield and it felt good. Meadows watched the city slip away beneath him, and they were over what appeared to be a solid carpet of jungle. Here and there he saw some rice paddies, dry now—brown, with a few kwi (water buffalos) browsing in them. On his map, the town of Ban Na Deng should be ahead of them, and after a few minutes, there it was, nothing more than a clearing with a few grass huts and some surrounding rice paddies. He could see no one. More jungle, another small village or two, and up ahead of them rose a rocky hill, easily identifiable from their altitude, where the village of Taket was supposed to be. Pilot directed the craft downward, and they were soon barely above the tree tops. Travelling at 80 knots at tree top level was a lot different from travelling at 80 knots at 1000'. The chopper slowed, the tail began dropping, and Pilot deposited the H-34 in a small rice paddy near some big ant mounds. Crew Chief motioned the men out, so all the members of FTT-19 got out. The rotor blades never stopped turning as the men dismounted, and in seconds Hotel X-ray was gone, curling over the tree tops as he headed back for Savannahkhet. Sergeant Pickett appeared out of the dust cloud that remained.

"C'mon, you guys. Follow me. Let's get away from this field," and he started off at a fast walk. Ed and the others hustled to catch up. They moved out of the open into the woods which bordered the paddy before Pickett stopped. "There was some sniper fire earlier today, before we got here, so we don't want to stand around in the open. Our team is over there," he said, indicating the rocky outcropping that was nearby. "That's Taket. Your bunch is down the road about a mile from here on the river. We ain't been down there, but one of their men is supposed to be here to pick you up. He'll guide you in. I gotta get back to the team and meet some of our troops. Y'all take care, I'll see you later." When Pickett left, despite the presence of the other team members, Meadows felt very much alone.

"Flag," he said to his team sergeant, "get the men to spread out in a perimeter and let's at least look like we know what we're doing. Ain't no sense in dying in a bunch." Flagstone quickly arranged the troops in a rough circle about 20 feet in diameter. Each man laid down behind his rucksack, facing outward. They waited for an escort they didn't know, who would arrive from a direction they didn't know, with instructions they didn't know. It was a most comforting way to enter their area of operations—kinda like Pompeo and Meadows had entered Area TREE.

The watch on Ed's wrist indicated it was 1300 hrs before a man came walking across the rice paddy toward the team's position. He was definitely an American, you could tell by his size, but he was wearing a green cowboy hat, unbloused trousers, and his shirt wasn't tucked in. Not only that, but it was a short sleeve shirt. He carried an M-1 rifle slung over his shoulder, and he obviously wasn't worried about snipers. Seeing the lieutenant standing up, the man altered his course to arrive at Ed's position. "Lieutenant Meadows? Sorry it took so long for one of us to get here. I'm Thomas, from the 11th BP. We're mighty happy to have you guys get here. If you'll follow me, we have about two klicks to walk."

Ed shook hands with the sergeant, and Flag knew him. The team sergeant said, "Thomas, you old sonofabitch, good to see you." They shook hands, then Bushman, who also knew Thomas, greeted him in just about the same endearing words. Riley followed, also with those words of refinement, and then Beaudreau growled at the guide.

"Thomas, I'll bet the 11th will be glad to get rid of your ass and get some real soldiers in here."

Thomas only laughed. "You guys are gonna have your hands full. Let's get going; we can't leave till y'all get there and we got hot dates in Savan tonight." "Savan" was GI for Savannahkhet. Ed introduced Eason to the sergeant and they started out. Only Eason and Ed were the odd-balls, not knowing Thomas.

There was a dusty road through the forest, or jungle, whichever you wanted to call it, that the team went walking down in single file. Thomas was obviously in a hurry, so their pace was rapid. Ed walked second in line and he had Flagstone bring up the rear. It would have been easy for anyone to spring an ambush on them as they hurried along, but the veteran Thomas evidently wasn't worried. "Sarge," asked

Ed, "how close are we to the enemy right now?"

"Well, Sir, when we get to the team positions, we'll be about three hundred meters from the river, and they're on the other side."

"What keeps them on the other side?"

"Common consent, Sir. Our guys don't go over there, and they don't come over here. Unwritten rule." Meadows wondered how strong unwritten rules were. They approached a little clearing in the woods, and there, under the trees, were the other members of the old FTT-19, packed and ready to leave.

18

Down On The Banks Of The Hanky-Pank

Captain McKinter was a bespectacled, kind-looking man whom Ed had known vaguely from West Point. K.K., as he was called, was a couple of years ahead of Ed, so they hadn't been friends by any means, but if Ed's memory served him well, K.K. had also been a Sunday School teacher there, and that may have been how they knew each other. Whatever the circumstances of their previous acquaintance, this afternoon in Laos they were glad to see each other. The two men shook hands, then K.K. put his arm around Ed's shoulder and squeezed real hard. "I'm glad you'll be replacing me here. It should be a good tour for you. Let's sit a spell and talk. First, though, I've instructed my men to brief your guys on their respective areas, so if it's okay with you, I'll have them pair up while we talk."

"Sounds like a good idea, Sir," said Ed.

"Call me, K.K. That's my name."

"I'm Ed." K.K. told his team sergeant to proceed with their plan, then he and Ed found a shady spot beneath some trees and sat down for a pow-wow. The captain was quite thorough in his brief rundown of their situation. LTC Khom was up with one of the companies on the river and would be spending the night up there. He'd be back in the morning. The reserve company, which was the weapons company, was located about 50 meters away in the woods, and that was where the colonel's HQ was located. There had been no fighting to speak of lately, but in the previous months, the 11th had been in several actions and had acquitted itself pretty well. McKinter didn't think there was much danger of the battalion defecting, but he did believe Kong Le was anxious to get some American prisoners. The captain thought he wanted them to bargain with in exchange for rejoining the FAR, but you couldn't be sure, he might want them for trading to the PL for a promotion. Best not to get captured.

There were some rumblings from the GM about the 11th moving down to Xeno, the paratrooper training base near Savannahkhet, and, if so, McKinter felt sure the FTT would accompany them there. Not much else was happening. They had one interpreter, named Charlie, a Thai, who was probably an agent of the Thai Army being used for gathering intel on the KL's and PL's, but he, too, was absent. About once a week he had to go to Thailand, to visit his ailing mother, he said, but probably to report to his superiors, and that was where he was now. A couple of the tahans spoke a little English, and they'd be coming up to meet Ed and his men after awhile. McKinter gave Ed his weapon, a Remington 870 Wingmaster 12-gauge shotgun with a 30-inch barrel, and two boxes of 00 Buck ammunition in brass cases. He said the B Team was pretty good about supplying them with whatever they needed, especially ammunition, and there was at least one chopper run every day to bring in mail and supplies to the GM.

The battalion had one vehicle, an old Dodge 3/4-ton, but the colonel had it tonight. The FTT had three .30 calibre machine guns which they loaned to the battalion in reward for doing something for the FTT, such as running a patrol. Right now the machineguns were in the possession of the FTT so Ed could do with them as he desired. McKinter offered to spend a couple of days up here with Ed since they weren't supposed to leave Savannahkhet quite yet, but the lieutenant declined he offer, although he did appreciate it. *Better to start with an entirely clean slate,* he thought. The old FTT had two six-packs of Kirin beer left over, one of the Japanese beers that was available here, and they passed the twelve cans around to drink a toast celebrating their departure and the new team's arrival. The toasting done, McKinter and his men shook hands all around, loaded up with their gear, and left. Just before he disappeared from sight down the trail, Sergeant Thomas stopped, looked back at Meadows' team, smiled broadly, flipped them the finger, and then he was gone.

Meadows called the team together. "What have we got for armament?" he asked. Flagstone had an M-1 rifle, his favorite weapon, Bushman had a BAR, which was his choice, Riley also had an M-1, Eason had an M-1 Carbine, and Beaudreau had an M-3 "Grease-gun," with which they were all satisfied. Ed spoke to Flagstone. "Have the men find locations for sleeping tonight on the edge of the BP company's position. Set up a rotation for guard duty tonight with two man shifts so we're at 33% alert at all times. I'm gonna take Bushman with me and go down to have a look at the river as soon as those tahans who speak English get here. See if you can get some grenades from the tahans and give everyone at least two. Make a note that we want to get some for ourselves, and some various smoke grenades as well to go with our Bug-Out plan. See if you can get the tahans to understand that since this is our first night in country, we don't want any visitors tonight. I'm determined that we ain't going to get captured, Sarge," he concluded.

"Wise, Boss, I'll take care of it. I took some notes from their sergeant, and I want to go over them with you tomorrow. There's several things we need here. Don't do nothing dumb down at the river, and don't get yourself shot. You're too heavy to carry out." Although the admonition was not necessary, Ed appreciated it a lot more than the prior warnings "not to fuck up."

The two tahans came over a few minutes later. Their knowledge of English was a little better than Ed's was of Laotian, but not much. To his surprise, Bushman began speaking to them in French, a tongue they obviously understood. Soon, the four men were on their way to the river. "Sarge," said Ed, "I didn't know you spoke Frog."

"There's a lot of things you don't know, Boss, but you're learning." The road down to the river was a lot less travelled than it was from the GM to the BP HQ, and it rapidly petered out until it was only a dim trail. In just a few minutes the tahans stopped and spoke to Bushman. "This is as far as they go, Boss," said the Sergeant. "From here on we're on our own. Follow me."

Bushman took the heavy BAR from his shoulder and handled it like a rifle. Ed checked his shotgun to make sure that a round was chambered and the safety on, then he followed Bushman. His Remington held five rounds, and it was crammed full. It was hot, Meadows was sweating, but some of the sweat on his palms wasn't from the temperature. Bushman moved slowly and stealthily, pausing to listen every few steps, and Meadows tried to follow suite. There were lots of noises from the insects around them, and Meadows discovered that the mosquitos in Laos don't wait for dark to begin their assaults. Stopping behind some tangled vines, Bushman dropped down and began crawling forward. Ed did the same. "There's your river, Boss," he whispered.

Meadows wriggled up alongside the sergeant. From their location, the ground dropped off in a bluff, then levelled off again before reaching the course of the river. The stream itself was maybe 50 meters wide, then there was a sandbar on the other side, a little more water—10 meters, then the other shore, another bluff, and more jungle. Ed could see no one. The water looked clear, not muddy at all, and seemed to have a pretty strong current. He couldn't tell how deep it was, but rushing water could indicate some depth. To the north, their left, the river curved eastward, while to the south it took a westward course. There were a lot of weeds growing on the sandbar and they were brown, so if the river flooded, it hadn't done so for awhile. Meadows and Bushman spec'ed down the countryside for a good thirty minutes before Ed looked at his watch. It was all fogged up from sweat, but he thought it indicated 1800 hrs. Now he understood why the departing team all wore their watches in the button hole of their lapels. He also understood the short sleeves, for it was very hot. Meadows was getting ready to go when Bushman lined his weapon up on something across the river and spoke.

"You wanta see the enemy, Boss?"

"Yeah, where?"

"About half-way up that sandbar, on the bluff. There's two of 'em." Ed looked in the direction Bushman had indicated. Sure enough, there were two small figures standing just in the trees at the top of the bluff. "Want me to take them out?"

"No, wait, let's see what they're up to." They watched the two men for a few minutes. Ed could see that they were dressed in grey uniforms and wearing black berets. It looked like they were carrying Carbines. While they continued to observe the enemy troops, several more soldiers appeared over there to join them. Even though they were well out of shotgun range, Ed lined up on them. To their surprise, the enemy troops began sliding down the bank and entering the water. "Get ready,

Sarge, looks like they want to come see us." Bushman flipped the safety off the Browning. Just as the bad guys entered the water on this side of the sand bar, about fifteen of them, Ed noticed some movement on his side of the river. It seemed that some of the FAR troops were going out to meet the enemy. Either this was to be a shoot-out at the OK Corral, or something fishy was going on. The troops of the opposing forces met in the middle of the river and began to have a gay old time taking baths. There was giggling, and laughing, back-slapping and hugging—it was a sight to behold. Somewhere, in the recesses of Ed's mind, he remembered the words of an old song about down on the banks of the Hanky-Pank, where the bullfrogs jump from bank to bank, and he determined that this was exactly what he was seeing out in front of him, a lot of hanky-panky.

"C'mon, Sarge, let's go back to the team. This shit makes me sick."

"I could put a hurt on a lot of them if you want, Boss," said Bushman, reluctant to leave.

"Naw, be a bad way to start our tour here. Maybe we'll come back and fish this hole again sometime, like tomorrow night. Let's get back and see what Flag's been up to." Meadows wondered for the umpteenth time what he was doing here.

19

Snap, Crackle, Pop

Flagstone had deployed the men by twos in a line some thirty meters from the road. Eason had already set up the radio and attempted to communicate with the B Team with limited success. Riley and Beaudreau had strung their ponchos from the lower shoots of some of the bamboo, a thicket of which they were using for partial concealment, and Flagstone had done likewise with his poncho. Meadows' rucksack had been moved next to Flag's and Bushman's was next to Eason's. Ed was pleased to see that the hooches were paired by bug-out buddies. He and Bushman set about stringing up their ponchos with the mosquito bars inside to make for a nice, if temporary, shelter, while Flag gave Ed a rundown on what he'd accomplished. It seemed the tahans were less than willing to part with any grenades, but the guard roster had been worked out, in three-hour shifts, by bug-out buddies. Meadows and Flagstone had the first shift.

"Okay, Boss, now tell me what happened down at the river," requested Flag. "I can tell you and Bushman are both pissed off."

"Flag, no one's gonna believe this," began Ed. "These hot-shot Airborne troops of ours are something else. We saw a bunch of guys dressed in grey, wearing black berets…"

"Those are KL's," interrupted Flag.

"…anyway, they came down to the river from the other side and started across. I thought it was a patrol of theirs, and me and Bushman were all set to give them a surprise party, when a bunch of our tahans went into the river from our side and met them in the water. I didn't know what the hell was happening. Then both sides started playing grabass right there in the water with each other. It was like Old Home Week. They were giggling and laughing and hugging one another like a bunch of queers. Bush wanted to waste the whole bunch, and I halfway wish we had. It makes me feel real good to know Kong Le wants some American prisoners and the guys protecting us are such good friends of his. Kong Le could drive a company of troops across that river anytime, without anyone in the world offering any resistance. We got ourselves a problem."

"I figured it was something like that," said Flag. "Hey, Bush, you got anything to add?"

"It was like the Boss said. When we left them, they were still out there in the water farting around. I guess the KL's went back to their side, but there ain't no guarantee of that. They could be strolling up to waste our asses right this minute. We might wanta consider a 50% alert, at least tonight, instead of only a third."

"That's a thought," said Ed. "What do you think, Flag?"

"It's something to consider. We could provide a lot more security with three guys than two. At this rate, we're gonna be a pretty tired bunch in no time at all."

"I think three guys ought to stay awake. We'll try to let the late shift get some rest tomorrow," stated Meadows. "Eason, you stay awake with me and Flag for the early shift, and keep that radio set up. Who's cross-trained in CW (code)?"

"I am, Boss," stated Beaudreau.

"Okay, then you stay close to that key on the second shift. I think we ought to sleep with our clothes on and have whatever bug-out gear we need next to us. Now, listen up. We ain't playing this fucking hanky-panky game. If you have any doubts during the night, shoot first and we'll fill out reports later. We don't want no visitors tonight. What's for chow?"

"We ate a can of C's while y'all were gone," said Flag.

"Okay, I want everyone to eat something and drink a lot of water. You can take a leak while you're on guard, but if anyone else gets up, you damn sure better make sure the guards know who you are, or you're gonna grow some holes. We need a challenge and pass-word,

Sarge, you got any ideas?"

"What about, 'Oskie-Wahwah'?"

"Oskie-Wahwah it is. The first shift starts at dark, right now, as a matter of fact. The rest of you better try to sleep."

"One thing I need to mention, Boss," said Riley. "There are snakes around here, Cobra, King Cobra, and Krait, all poisonous as hell, neurotoxic; so if one of them bites you, you can kiss your old ass goodbye. Be sure you tuck the mosquito bar under your blanket to keep those fuckers out."

"Thanks, Riley, I needed that," replied Ed. "Okay, go to bed." Nothing happened that night.

The team was all up at dawn, but none of them had slept well. They tidied up their camp, ate more C-rations for breakfast, and performed what toiletries they could. About 0800, a little tahan wearing U.S. fatigues and an Old Ironsides cap came strolling into camp. He wasn't armed, so he was allowed to approach. "Are you the new team?" he asked in damn good English. "I'm Charlie, your interpreter."

"Hello, Charlie, we're glad to see you," said Ed. The guy looked awfully familiar. "I'm Lieutenant Meadows, this is Sergeant Flagstone, that's Bushman, Beaudreau, Riley, and Eason."

Handshakes all around. "Lieutenant, you look familiar to me," said Charlie.

"Same here. Have you ever been to the States?"

"Yes, I attended Ranger School there." That was it. In Ed's class back at Benning, there were three Thai Officers whom the Americans thoroughly disliked. The only words the Thai seemed to understand then were "chow" and "break." They were ignorant when you said "carry the machine gun," or "let's clean the weapons."

"I was in Ranger School in the summer of '60," said Ed. "We had three Thai in our class."

"That was when I was there," said Charlie.

"Your name wasn't 'Charlie' if you were in my class," laughed Ed.

"No, my real name is Lek Kongjarean. I remember you."

"You speak better English now." They both laughed. "We've been at a disadvantage without an interpreter."

"You have another one coming to join us tomorrow," said Lek, alias Charlie. "His name is Sam, and he's been to Ranger School, too, but not in our class." Meadows resented it being called *OUR* class a little bit. "Where is Colonel Khom? He speaks a little English, and a lot of French, if you speak French."

Meadows shook his head. "Does anyone over here speak Spanish?" Everybody laughed. Ed considered telling Charlie about the river event yesterday, but decided not to. "The colonel is supposed to get back from up on the river this morning. He spent the night with one of the companies there." The team and Charlie talked about trivial things for awhile, then Charlie noticed their poncho hooches.

"Do you know how to make split bamboo beds?" he asked. "It isn't a good idea to sleep on the ground here. There are a lot of snakes that like to get next to your body for heat. It's better to make a swamp bed with bamboo."

"We don't know about bamboo beds, but we're willing to learn," replied Ed. "I personally don't want a snake for a bed-partner." Charlie set about showing the men how to split lengths of readily available bamboo to form a platform that was tied over some poles cut from the nearby trees. Then the platform was mounted on legs about two feet off the ground. On top of this, the poncho hooch was re-erected. The men worked hard at their beds, and by noon, everyone's belongings were off the ground. A bonus was that there seemed to be a little breeze at two feet that didn't exist at ground level. While they worked, Meadows had two men at a time stand guard, just in case. All the men kept their weapons close at hand.

Early in the afternoon, the 3/4-ton truck came grinding up the trail as the colonel returned. Meadows saw the men on the truck, and he and Flag went out to meet them. Spying the man who was obviously the colonel, Ed walked up to him, placed his hands in the position of respect, bowed slightly, and said, *"Som ba de, Boi?"* which was supposed to be Laotian for, "How do you do?"

The colonel grinned broadly, and returned the greeting. *"Som Bai,* Let-ten-ant. Do you speak Lao?"

"No, that's about all I know. I am Lieutenant Meadows, this is my Sergeant, Flagstone, and we're here to help you."

"Good, good, we work well together. You teach me English, I teach you Lao. *Parlez vous Francais?"*

"Mais non, Monsieur. I have the English course to work with you on, if you wish. I also want to talk about some operations against the enemy. My men over there," he said, indicating the team members

back in the trees, "have a lot of ideas and experience in combat. We are anxious to help you with your patrolling, for instance." Ed thought he'd interject the idea of patrols as soon as he could.

"Yes, Let-ten-ant. We want your help. We also need some supplies that you can get for us. Then we are ready to fight, kill lots of PL. Now I go eat, then sleep some. Later I take you and your sergeant up to see positions on the river. My companies are very alert up there. Kong Le men across river, very tough, some of them trained with us. I go eat now. *Som Bai*, Let-ten-ant."

"*Som ba de*, Colonel. We'll be ready." After the colonel and his men left, Ed called the team together. He went over Flagstone's list, and they decided to send Eason and Bushman back to Savannahkhet on the daily chopper to get what supplies they could. If possible, they'd be back before nightfall. Charlie would go with Flag and Ed and the colonel, and Riley and Beaudreau would mind the radio. "Riley, one of you can sleep while the other watches, since you both had late duty last night. Charlie, I notice you haven't got a gun. Any reason why not?"

"No, Sir, I just don't have one. If you have an extra one, I'll be glad to have it."

"What do you want?" Charlie indicated he'd like an M-1, like he had in Ranger School. He damn sure didn't have a machine gun back then.

"Bush, bring him an M-1." Bushman nodded. "Flag, we both ought to get some sleep till the colonel comes. What do you think?"

"I think I want those grenades, Boss. I don't trust any of these guys. You're right, though, we ought to try and rest."

"Bush, you and Eason get going. We could stand some beer, and a Lister bag. And, please, get Flag his grenades."

"No sweat, Boss. You better bring the truck when we get back." With that, everyone set out on his assigned task.

The colonel came over at about 1500 hrs. Meadows, Flag, and Charlie were ready to go. There were about a dozen tahans with the colonel, and the troop moved in single file toward the river. All the tahans carried their rifles at the ready, very combat-looking. Six tahans led the way, then the colonel, carrying a carbine slung over his shoulder, then Ed with his Remington, Charlie, Flag, and six more tahans. Thinking of the scene at the river yesterday, it amused Meadows to see the tahans acting so warlike, glancing off the trail to either side as they moved, crouched over, rifles at the ready, it was so much *ke kwi*. There was a burst of gunfire from the front of the column, automatic weapons fire, and Ed hit the ground. So did the colonel, and Flag, and Charlie, and all the tahans in the rear. The tahans up front were all firing now, all standing, their weapons throwing out spent shell cases left and right. Ed pushed the button taking his shotgun off safety and looked for something to shoot at. He could see nothing, but he wasn't about to stand up, for he was taller than any of the tahans and would therefore make the largest target for any enemy gunman. As suddenly as the firing had started, it stopped, and the six tahans in front went tearing off the trail into the jungle, whooping and yelling. The colonel got up, so Ed followed, but he kept the safety off. Warily, they went after the tahans, and about fifteen meters off the trail they found them, hard at work picking up some dead birds that looked a lot like chickens. "What happened, Colonel Khom?"

"Tahans got us some supper, good. We eat at my place tonight." That was all the explanation there was. For Ed, the Russian-frogman-porpoise episode paled in comparison to this one. *I wonder how scared you can get for no reason at all?* The game all gathered, the troop continued toward the river.

When they reached the place where Ed and Bush had observed Old Home Week yesterday, the column turned left. They were walking behind the screen of dry vines that had provided cover for the two Americans on the previous evening and making a lot of noise on the brittle leaves beneath their feet. Some branches over Ed's head started snapping, jerking violently, and a couple broke off. *What the hell is this now,* thought the lieutenant, but the thought had barely cleared his brain when he heard the crackle of automatic weapons fire chasing the snapping, which was obviously caused by the supersonic rounds outrunning the sound of the guns. Everyone hit the ground at once, but Meadows noticed one of the tahans up front fell kinda funny. He was the tallest one up there. They heard the popping of semiautomatic weapons, and the snapping and crackling continued. Snap, crackle, pop. It was unreal.

Meadows wriggled around to face the river, poking the muzzle of the shotgun through the vines ahead of him. Some of the tahans were returning fire, and Ed saw Flag burning up the barrel of his M-1 as he fired round after round across the river. Try as he might, Ed saw nothing to aim at. It was a long way over there for a shotgun, but he decided to give it a try, anyway. Aiming at a clump of bushes on the bluff, he fired all five rounds from the Remington, then rolled on his side, dug some rounds out of his shirt pocket, and reloaded. There were a few more shots, then all became quiet. Cautiously, the colonel got up. So did Ed, and Flag, and Charlie, and all the tahans except the one who fell funny. He was lying there on the ground, very still, his face buried in the leaves, his feet turned inward. The carbine he had been carrying was off to his side. One of the tahans up front picked up the fallen man's wrist, then dropped it, and it fell awkwardly. Meadows followed the colonel up to look at the man: he was dead. No movement, no breathing, no moans, no theatrics, no nothing, just dead, snuffed out, gone. There was a small round hole in his right temple, but no brains blown out, no gore, very little blood. Ed thought he was going to be sick. It was the colonel speaking that saved him from vomiting.

"Those Kong Le bastards. They break their word. We go back now, Let-ten-ant. Tomorrow we start training for patrols. You get us machine guns, we kill Kong Le bastards." It took only a few minutes to reach the camp. The tahans were carrying their fallen comrade, and there was much weeping, wailing, and gnashing of teeth in the BP camp. As for the Americans, Ed was just glad there wasn't any vomiting going on.

20

Turn About's Fair Play

Back at the camp, Ed got with Flag and Charlie to see if they could figure out what had happened. Besides the obvious fact that they had been bushwhacked. Meadows opened the conversation, "I never saw anything, no muzzle flashes, no people, nothing."

"They had a bunker," said Flagstone, "and that's where they were firing from. At least one automatic weapon, sounded like a .30 calibre, and a couple of sharpshooters with probably SKS's or M-1's. I saw the bunker, but I don't know if I put any rounds in it or not. One thing for sure, they were aiming for the Americans. Did you notice they took out the first big man in the line? They were aiming for you, Boss."

"If that's so, then they knew we were coming down there."

"Oh, Sir," said Charlie, "they knew. They know everything we do and talk about. The only way we can surprise them is to plan while we're moving. They meet at the river every night and talk with the KL." Now Ed knew that Bush had been right in wanting to waste those troops the other night. First he'd stopped Pompeo from killing Young, then he'd stopped Bush from killing the traitors; it was time to stop saving lives—except his own, and start spending some.

"Flag, can we take that bunker out?"

"Not with what we got. Maybe a satchel charge would do it. We can ask Bush when he gets back. Why, Boss, what do you have in mind?"

"I think we ought to let these wise-asses know we can fight back. I think we ought to blow that damn bunker up and all them inside it. Probably ought to let Colonel Khom in on our intentions. Listen, Flag, if he's as torn up as he acted like he was, let's get on over there and see if we can't get him to commit to some patrols and a retaliatory action before he freezes up. Send Beaudreau up to the GM and see what he can find out about some explosives or,...no, wait. I have a better idea. Let's get Beaudreau down to the river and let him look the bunker over. Take some field glasses. Flag, you'll have to go with him. Riley, you come with me and Charlie. I wish that damn Bush would hurry back here."

"Oh, I meant to tell you. We got a message on the radio that they won't be back until the morning," said Beaudreau, who had joined the conference.

"Okay, then, look, Frank, you and Flag go on down there. See what it would take to blow that bunker, and we'll tell Bush to bring it back. Y'all get going." The two sergeants began gathering their gear. "C'mon, Hal, let's go talk to the colonel. Be back here at 1900 hrs and we'll come up with a plan."

At the BP Command Post, there was a lot of grieving going on. Colonel Khom had tears in his eyes as he was talking to some of his men over the dead body of the tahan. When he saw the Americans approaching, he waved them on over. "We are very sad," he said.

"Colonel Khom, we came to express our sorrow over your fallen tahan," said Ed. "We can certainly understand your grief, and we feel bad about it. I have talked with the other team members, and we think the enemy was trying to kill one of us, since they shot your tallest soldier. We feel very bad about this." The colonel hugged Meadows and cried out loud.

Ed continued, "We would like to make it up to you, somehow. If you don't mind, we would like to eliminate the enemy's bunker over on the other side of the river as a gesture of our friendship and solidarity." Charlie translated Ed's words into Lao just to make sure the colonel understood. The colonel was very touched.

"I am happy to hear these thoughts, Let-ten-ant. We are sad right now, and must make arrangements for a funeral. When do you plan to do this?" Meadows remembered the words of Charlie about the pipeline of information to the other side.

"Soon, maybe in three or four days," he lied, "but only with your permission." Ed intended to react against the bunker tomorrow.

"What will you do?" asked the colonel.

"I don't know, yet. Perhaps we could run a patrol over there with some of your men to show us the way and see what we need to do, after the funeral, of course."

"That would be good. Excuse me, now, I must join my men," and the colonel went back to the mourning. Waiting for a few minutes so as not to seem too anxious, Meadows, Riley, and Charlie went back to the American camp.

The radio was crackling, so Riley picked up the earphones and worked the key. It seemed that Beaudreau wasn't the only one cross-trained in code. There was a pause while Riley copied down what he was hearing, then he worked the key again and took off the earphones. "Nothing. It was just a commo check from the B Team to make sure we were still here."

When Flag and Beaudreau got back, it was getting dark. They'd seen the bunker and it was a pretty good one. Unless they could get around to the rear, only a satchel charge would suffice for destroying it. They had also looked for the nightly bathers, but there were none this evening. "It's gonna be tough, Boss," said Flagstone.

"Tough or not, we have the colonel's blessing, and I want to send a message to Mister Kong Le. We ain't got no satchel charges, so we have to think of something else. Frank, you're our weapons expert, what kind of gun would we need to do the job?"

"Damn, Boss, it would take a big one, like a howitzer."

"Flag, think, what else can we do?"

"I could try sniping with an M-1. If I got off a couple of rounds through the firing slit, it might get them. Otherwise, we could just go over there some night and capture the damn thing, then kill everyone in it. That would work, and we could pull it off with no sweat if the KL's are no better than our tahans."

"Nah, we would be too exposed, what with the pipeline. We'd probably get shot by our own tahans. I guess we could take some of them with us, but I'd sooner trust one of these cobras, right now. Think, men, there must be some way we could get at it." They all thought, and several more plans were offered, and each was rejected for some reason or the other. Then, about 2100 hrs, when everyone was tired of trying to solve the mystery of how to blow the bunker, Charlie spoke for the first time.

"Sir, I don't know if it would work, but they have a recoilless rifle at the 15th GM that might do the job."

Beaudreau perked up. "What calibre is it?" he asked.

"I don't know," replied the Thai interpreter, "but it only takes one man to carry it."

"That might work. It's got to be at least a 57 mm, maybe a 75 mm. A 90 mm or a 106 mm would be too heavy for these guys to carry. That might be it, Boss. That might work." Ed had fired all the weapons Beaudreau had mentioned at one time or another, and he knew the problem of back blast which these "reckless rifles" created.

"Just exactly who has this thing, Charlie?" Ed asked.

"It is always at the GM CP. I don't know who controls it."

"If we could get it, and I say, 'IF,' we would only get one shot. If we missed, they'd grease us. That back blast would show where we were like a spotlight."

"Ain't no problem, getting it, if it's there," said Flagstone." Let's talk this over. I think we may have something here." They modified, improved, changed, refined, and finalized their plan for getting even with Mister Kong Le until well after midnight.

The next morning, right after a breakfast of good ole C's, Ed went over to talk to the colonel. He asked if they might borrow the 3/4-ton vehicle to go meet their team members returning from Savannahkhet with supplies and some stuff for the BP. The colonel readily agreed. The "Time of Mourning" was in full sway in the Laotian camp. Riley had contacted the B team and found out that Hotel X-ray should be arriving at the GM about 1000 hrs with their men aboard. At 0930 hrs, Ed, along with everyone else from the FTT, loaded up in the vehicle and left for the GM. Once there, Meadows went to talk with Captain Johnson and tell him about the shooting yesterday. He intended to tell the Captain about the retaliation planned, too, but Flag had suggested he not do that. Too many cracks make a jug leak. Flag, Riley, and Beaudreau wandered around. When the chopper arrived a little after 1000 hrs, they all went to meet it. Bushman and Eason had a plane full of goodies for them. There was mail, groceries, not C-rations, a Lister bag for storing fresh water, cases and cases of beer, some ammunition for everyone, an M-1 for Charlie, and a whole case of grenades for Flag, both fragmentation and smoke. It was like Christmas. As they loaded the truck, Meadows found there was something else that hadn't come on the helicopter. There was a 57 mm reckless rifle and two rounds in cardboard containers lying under the seat in the back. He knew better than to ask where it came from, for "a good agent never divulges his source of supply." For his money, Meadows would have bet on Flag, but he'd have lost, for it was ole Medic Riley who had pinched the weapon. They drove back to their camp while Flagstone filled Eason and Bushman in on the plan.

Once at their camp, they unloaded the truck and returned it to its rightful owner. The beer was Asahi, Japanese, but it drank alright. They each had a couple, then they began the implementation of their plan, which they'd dubbed "Operation Upyours." Since it had been about 1500 hrs when the ambush had occurred yesterday, they planned to strike back at the same hour. They wrapped the "reckless rifle" in a couple of ponchos, then covered it with bamboo stalks like they intended to make another bed. So as not to alert any observing tahans, they wandered off into the woods one at a time and reassembled about fifty meters down the trail. Beaudreau was to man the gun, and Riley would assist him.

The plan was for them to make their way unseen till about 100 meters north of the trail, then approach the river through the woods at about the spot where the tahan had been killed. Meadows, Flag, and Bushman would go on down the trail to the river at the usual place. Eason was to return to camp with Charlie and stall anyone trying to follow. Just before reaching the bluff, the three troopers turned off the trail to the south and hid in the bushes. Time to wait and check their weapons. Ed had obtained an empty M-1 ammunition bandolier, and loaded the seven pockets with three shotgun rounds each. These, plus the five in the weapon, gave him over a box of ammo. Bush had his BAR, and Flag the trusty M-1. Frank and Harold were to be in position by 1500 hrs, and it was 1455 hrs now. The three men edged up to the bluff, still hidden by the vines. Flag pointed the bunker out to Ed and Bushman. There was someone moving around near it. "Good," said Meadows, "they're in it. Okay, are y'all ready?"

Flag and Bushman nodded. Ed felt his mouth getting dry. He could hear the watch on his lapel ticking: 1459. One minute. Right at 1500 hrs, Meadows began shaking the vines with his shotgun while still remaining prone, then Flag fired a couple of rounds at the bunker. Almost immediately there was the flash of answering fire and the vines started to snap. The crackle of the machine gun followed, then the pop of the sniper's weapons. All three men tried to become earthworms as the whizzing bullets hummed and zipped over their heads.

When the recoilless rifle fired, there was no doubt in anyone's mind that it had done so. The loud crash of the rifle was followed almost instantaneously by a resounding "Whump" from across the river. Cautiously raising his head, Ed sneaked a look. So did Flag and Bush. Where the bunker had been, there was now a cloud of dirt and dust rising from a smoking hole lined with torn-up sandbags. Bulls-eye! Ed raised his fist and cheered, but when he started to get up, Flagstone grabbed his arm. "Not yet, Boss. Let's just watch from here." To Ed, it seemed a useless precaution, for no one could have survived that hit. He stayed down, anyway. As he watched, there was a small figure who emerged from the hole that was the bunker. The man was holding his face and staggering, obviously stunned, *probably damn near dead, too,* thought Meadows. The doubt was removed when Bush opened up with his BAR. Ed couldn't see the rounds, but by the way the figure jerked and twisted, it was obvious he was being hit numerous times. He fell backward, sprawling on the dirt, and that was where he was lying when Beaudreau fired the second round from the recoilless rifle. There was a flash of orange and a big cloud of smoke, and when it cleared, the man wasn't there anymore. Meadows couldn't see any arms or legs lying around, just dust and smoke, and no body. Nothing. Maybe this was a lot more gore than yesterday, but Ed didn't feel the slightest bit sick. *Served him right,* he thought.

Winston Churchill once said there is nothing in life so exhilarating as to be shot at without result, and, after the previous day's events, Meadows tended to agree. The newly initiated lieutenant took the sentiment a step further, however: *don't get mad,* Ed thought, *get even!*

21

Burning Your Bridges

"Operation Upyours" had its desired effect. The atmosphere around the 11th BP Headquarters took on a much more military tone, and down on the river, the companies began 50% alerts every night—even mentioned the idea of patrolling. The 57 was returned to the GM by the same surreptitious means that it had been obtained, and the colonel asked the team if they could help his men improve their marksmanship and polish their patrolling skills. Meadows teamed Beaudreau and Eason together and they worked with the tahans to clear a combat-type firing range in the rear of the HQ, where a platoon at a time spent a day with the two Special Forces troopers in practice shooting. Calling it marksmanship would have been a farce, but at least they did shoot. Bushman and Flag worked with a platoon at a time on the principles of patrolling, and Riley held sick call every morning as well as working with the corpsmen of the BP on their emergency care of war wounds. It was a busy place.

LT Meadows stayed with the colonel, and Charlie was usually with them, too. Sam, the second interpreter did arrive, and he worked mostly with Flag and Bush, while Frank and Ricky hardly needed an interpreter. The Americans found out about the little man in Taket who had an old Singer sewing machine, and who would convert your long sleeved HBT's to short sleeved shirts for 20 kip apiece. They had all their shirts converted and they all purchased green western-style hats for 100 kip each. The last vestiges of the "Green Beret of the parade ground" disappeared when they donned these "go to hell" hats. Although at least one of them checked every day, there were no more meetings of the two sides in the river. Yessir, things were looking up.

From their position near Taket, Highway 13—about the only paved thoroughfare traversing the country, lay about ten miles west of, or behind them. It was too far away to be considered part of their area, but it was the only road linking their location with Savannahkhet and Thakhet. About a week after the team had joined the battalion, March 24th, there was a report that a unit of reinforcements was to arrive from Xeno. These were supposed to be Rangers who were to assist the battalion in their efforts at intelligence gathering, or, in the words of the Americans, patrolling. Maybe the colonel was serious about getting tough.

The unit was to arrive at about noon, and when noon arrived and the unit didn't, no one got excited. By 1800 hrs, the troops still hadn't shown up, so at the request of the colonel, Ed put out a message to the B Team requesting information about this unit. The reply was quick in arriving, but was not designed to bring smiles to the faces of the Laotian commander and his advisors. Hotel X-ray had witnessed the truck, that's all there was, one truck-load, being ambushed along Highway 13. Rangers or not, as near as the helicopter could determine, the ambush had been successful in eliminating the FAR unit. There was more. The PL, if that was who they were, had also blown two bridges along the highway, effectively cutting off the 15th GM and its units from any chance of re-supply or reinforcement by land for the time being. It didn't take a genius to figure out what was coming next. Someone up there along the river was about to be hit. It was time to buckle your chinstraps and sound off for equipment check. Gut-sucking time, gut check. There was another expression which described this situation; pucker time, and that's about what the members of FTT-19 did.

Ed looked at Flagstone, who looked at Ed. "Flag, we got a problem." Flag nodded, and lit a Camel. To the colonel, Ed said, "Sir, we simply must know what's going on over across the river. The line-crossers the GM depends on are simply not reliable nor timely. We have no longer the luxury of a choice, but we have to send patrols across the river and find out something." Charlie translated.

Colonel Khom listened to the whole translation without blinking, although Ed was sure he understood what he'd said the first time. LTC Khom nodded. "Yes, Let-ten-ant, we must send out patrols. I will have my company here take care of it."

For Ed, that wasn't good enough. He wanted some American involvement, otherwise there might be another Old Home Week. His mind raced to find a solution which wouldn't insult the colonel, but would, at the same time, ensure that some of his people were involved. "Sir, that's fine. I appreciate your willingness to take this action. I'd like some of my men to go along, if you don't mind. We need to see how you patrol in Laos, for all we know is what we learned in the States. We need to learn from you."

"Not this time, Let-ten-ant. Too dangerous for you. Later."

"Whatever you say, Sir. I just thought I'd have more luck getting those Thompson machine guns from Savan if we could say they were for us."

"What machine guns? How many?" (Ed noticed there was no need for Charlie to translate the words).

"Oh, at least six, since there are six of us, and maybe one for you, with ammunition, of course. It probably wouldn't have worked, anyway, they're too expensive."

"If you want to learn from us, the only way you can learn is to go along with us. We will be sending out a patrol tonight, after dark."

"I don't think I can have the guns by that time, but maybe by tomorrow. We could still learn tonight."

"No, my men will go tonight, to make sure it is safe. When we have enough machine guns to protect you, then you can go tomorrow." End of discussion.

"Nice try, Boss," said Flag. "I thought you were going to pull it off."

"Yeah, but I didn't. We've gotta get something he wants. I don't know if they even have Thompsons at the B Team, do you?"

"No, but we can find out. Send Bush in tomorrow. We'll know then."

When tomorrow came, after a night spent in alternating the guard every two hours, it was a tired bunch who gathered for the breakfast Riley prepared. Spam, fried or burned, hardtack, peaches from C-ration cans, and the "dreaded date-nut roll" from the same box. Tasted pretty good. The hungrier you are, the better Spam and date-nut rolls taste. There was a low ceiling and a drizzling rain that was a harbinger of the approaching monsoons. Hotel X-ray wouldn't be in unless this stuff cleared. The report from the patrol was that they had seen nothing the previous evening, but it couldn't be verified whether or not they had even crossed the river. Training was suspended, and the BP stood a full alert all day. Back at the GM, their two 105mm howitzers kept up a steady fire all day, the shells humming over the heads of the men of the 11th BP and exploding somewhere across the river, way across the river. Mahaxay, the Headquarters of the Kong Le battalions, was a little out of range for the 105's, but they must have been trying to reach it for the shells exploded far, far away somewhere. Meadows wondered if they knew what they were firing at. He was sure there were no Forward Observers, and from his days at Ft. Sill, if you didn't have FO's and a Fire Direction Center, FDC, you weren't going to do a lot of effective artillery fire with 105's. But, then, if all you had was two field pieces, you weren't going to do much barraging anyway. Better outgoing than incoming!

By noon, the rain had showed no signs of letting up, so Meadows gave up on the idea of his Thompsons. The colonel had gone up to the GM, and Ed hadn't been invited along, which meant Khom was going to talk business with the GM CO. Lao business. Monkey business. Ed fretted as he lay on his platform and watched the rain misting down. This was the pits. If he stayed here and got to feeling sorry for himself, what with their tenuous position in regards to their safety, Ed and the other team members could find themselves in a real funk without much trouble. He got up, grabbing his hat and weapon, and walked over to Flag's hooch. "Hey, Flag, let's go up to the GM. Maybe we can find out something, and the worst we can do is have a beer with the other guys."

"Be right with you, Boss. Hey, Bush!" he yelled at the sleeping figure of the other sergeant. The figure moved, and a sound came out.

"Hummm?"

"Get your ass up. Me and Boss are going up to the GM. You're in charge here. You hear me?"

"Uh huh."

"Let's go, Boss," said Flag, and he bounced out of his bed. There hadn't been enough rain to even make the trail muddy yet, but there had been enough to wash some of the dust off the leaves and make the walk up to the GM somewhat pleasant. Meadows had heard that during the growing season, bamboo grows at about six inches a day and can penetrate a quarter-inch of steel. They had to be back at camp in less than four days if he was to salvage his hooch. Time to sharpen the machete.

Ed didn't like the GM HQ. It was located in the middle of Taket, there was no kind of order around it, and there was always a bunch of women in the headquarters itself. Maybe they were female soldiers, but they sure didn't dress like soldiers, and they had some pretty weird duties: like stroking the commander's thigh, or lighting cigarettes for him, even combing his hair. One thing for the commander, he seemed not to mind all this attention, and it didn't deter him from his job—if smoking and eating and getting his thighs rubbed was his job. There was an important conference going on today, and the tahan guards ringing the HQ tent were stern looking. Ed was able to see that the commander had his staff with him.

Flag and Ed looked up the U.S. team, and found Pickett sitting on the porch of a little house, working on some little kid's foot. Seemed to have a splinter, or something in it. "Hi ya, Pickett," said Flagstone. "Where's the team?"

"They're around here somewhere. Captain Johnson and Bradley are in Savan, trying to get us some automatic weapons. They're all upset by this bunch who blew the bridges the other day, but I figure they'll get y'all before they get us, and I know my good buddies with the 11th BP wouldn't let me down. So how the hell are you?"

"We're fine. We need some intel, and this ain't the place to discuss it. Where's your team house?"

"It ain't no better than here, and I don't know anything, anyway. The Lao are having a big pow-wow and we weren't invited. One or two of the girls the colonel has hugging on him all the time will sell him out in a flash for a little roll of kip, so we ought to have some poop pretty soon. That's really what I'm here for, watching for our contact. There's a store, of sorts, down this street about a block where they serve some food called "Joke" and cold beer. Why don't y'all go on down there, and I'll come see you as soon as the meeting's over. If you finish before I get to you, come on back here and we'll wait together. I can't mess around with this worm forever."

So it wasn't a splinter, but a worm that was in the boy's foot. Enough to make a feller sick. The beer served was either Asahi or Kirin, take your pick, and the "joke" was pretty good stuff. Neither Ed nor Flag had any idea what was in it, but the dish itself consisted of some starchy paste with lumps of something throughout. Tasty. Of course, there was gummy rice and the hot stuff to dip it in, that goes without saying and comes without ordering. They'd finished their joke bowls and two cans from Japanese breweries before Pickett arrived. He was in a hurry.

"Hey, you guys, listen up. The 11th's gonna go get those guys who blew the bridges. Somehow, they think they know who it was and just about where they are. I don't know how many of the troops are going to be involved, but that's the skinny. I gotta go tell our guys. Take care." He left the two men sitting at their table.

"Hot damn, Boss, let's get back to the camp. We don't want to miss the fun. We gonna get us some slopes." While there were different slang words, most of them derogatory, for the different nationalities of Orientals, the common bond connecting them all for the GI's was "slopes." That's who Flag said they were going to get, be they PL's, KL's, Viet Minh, Chinese, or Cambodes. They hustled back to tell the rest of the team about their upcoming expedition.

A long time ago, Julius Caesar was fighting the Gauls, and the Germanic people from across the Rhine were harassing him. He tolerated it for awhile, then had his engineers build a bridge across the unbridgeable river, and he crossed and punished the pests to the point of extinction. Ed wondered how severely the 11th BP was going to punish the bridge-blowers?

22

The Quick And The Dead

By hustling back down the trail to their camp, the Americans were able to beat the Laotian commander back by a comfortable margin. He had to go through all the formalities of saying goodbye to the GM personnel, and he had no reason to suspect that the news of the 11th's upcoming incursion into Indian Country was already known to the FTT. "Indian Country" was the name of any disputed, unknown, or hostile territory. To the Laotians, it meant nothing, but to all the Americans, its meaning was perfectly clear. LTC Khom asked for Ed to come to his HQ for a talk shortly after he returned to the camp.

"*Som ba de,*" said Meadows, inclining respectfully to the colonel, and holding his hands above the level of his head, the ultimate sign of respect. "How are you this evening?"

"*Som bai*, my Let-ten-ant," replied the colonel. "Please to sit down. Beer?"

"*Cop koun mak*, thank you, yes."

Motioning to one of the tahans, the colonel ordered beer all around, and after a healthy draw from the bottle of Tiger Beer the tahan offered, Khom passed the bottle to Meadows and continued. "Let-ten-ant, the colonel at GM wants us to find and eliminate the band of PL who destroyed our bridge. We take one company from here and go get them. Your team is invited to go with us. Do you wish to go?"

"Yes, Sir," said Ed. "I think it would be a very good idea, but where are these PL, and how do you know who it was?"

The colonel smiled a wicked little smile. "We know. We leave in the morning, early." That could mean anywhere from before dawn till noon, for 'early' to the Lao was a strictly relative term. "I have a plan I would like for you and your sergeant to look at," and he proceeded to lay out his idea. Ed had Charlie go get Flag, and the team sergeant was soon at his side. They listened intently to the plan, nodded their approval, and promised to be ready at 0400 hrs, which was the current definition of 'early.'

It wasn't 0400 hrs when they moved out, but it was still early, just barely dawn the next morning. The members of FTT-19 moved out with three platoons of Laotian tahans up the road toward the GM HQ. They marched, or rather, strolled, in two single files down the road: one file on each side of the trail, one platoon in front, then the colonel and the Americans, then two platoons trailing. The village of Taket was quiet—sleeping in the morning mist when the combat patrol passed by. It was a rapid stroll, and Ed was both amazed and pleased by the march discipline displayed by the tahans. There was very little talking, not much jingling from equipment, and one reason for that was the Lao were travelling very light. Each man was carrying his weapon and a blanket roll over his shoulder, reminiscent of pictures Ed had seen of Russian troops during the Second World War. The Americans, on the other hand, were struggling under their heavily-laden packs, which contained all the goods from their camp. By the time the column reached Highway 13, about 0900 hrs, it was obvious that the big and relatively fat Americans were going to have their work cut out for them just in managing to stay caught up. At the highway, the colonel called a break and Ed called Flagstone over.

"Flag, this gear is killing us. We are going to be a detriment to this mission if we can't find something to do with it."

"Right, Boss," puffed the Sergeant. "We're up to our ass in stuff and these fuckers are nearly naked. The colonel plans to stop at the blown bridge site south of Ban Tung for the night, and if we can't do nothing else, I suggest we cache the stuff we don't need there. What do you think, Bush?" he asked the demo man.

"Shit, Sir, let's call the damn helicopter to come get all this stuff and take it to the B Team in Savan. We can pick it up later. If we cache it, these slopes will have it all gone and divided up before we even turn our backs."

Ed got out his map. Tracing their route and their intended destination, he spoke to Eason. "Rick, contact the B Team and tell them we need a Safe Hands chopper pick-up north of Phou Pongdeng, at the bridge, at 1700 hrs tonight." 'Safe Hands' meant only American personnel were to be involved.

"Roger that," said the radio man and he began unpacking the radio, stringing out the antenna. Beaudreau set up the generator, and in just a matter of minutes, the team in Savannahkhet had been informed of their request. They acknowledged in reply and the pick-up was set.

"Let's try to make like the Lao and carry some food and stuff in our ponchos," said Meadows. "Right now, however, we have got to make it through this day. I don't want the tahans thinking they can outwalk us. Divide up the radio gear and swap out on carrying it. Help each other out. I'm going to try and get the colonel to keep going and not take anymore breaks," he continued, remembering the painful lesson Ole Whiskey Bill had taught him in Florida. "I don't think these little farts have the stamina we have, but it's a cinch we can't keep up with them all day at this pace. Riley, get out the salt tablets and everyone drink a lot of water. It's gonna be a long day."

Ed proved to be a prophet without honor. The team struggled under their loads, and even though they frequently swapped the gear around, it seemed every load you gave up was lighter than the load you took. There was very little traffic along the highway, one or two rattle-trap trucks, and a couple of those funny-looking French cars with their hindquarters jacked up higher than their forelegs. Ed and the rest of the Americans had the impression they were under constant surveillance by unseen eyes throughout the day. The colonel agreed to a constant, if slower pace, but still, it was all the FTT members could do to stay with the column. By noon they had passed Ban Mouang Ba and were near the settlement of Ban Tung by 1500 hrs. If the Colonel's intelligence estimate was correct, this was the town from which the PL guerrilla unit was staging its operations against the bridges. He called a halt outside the village.

"My Let-ten-ant, I wish to talk with some of the villagers now. We wait here. I think it would be good if you did not go with me, for these villagers are not familiar with Americans."

Ed nodded a reply, but he was uneasy not knowing what was going on. An idea crossed his mind.

"Sir, I agree with you. Would it be okay for Charlie to go with you? He is familiar with our requirements for reporting to the B Team, and perhaps he could help you, and us." Charlie translated his request.

"Fine. We return in one hour," and Khom, Charlie, Watt—the colonel's body guard, and Captain Preseuth, one of the company commanders, went into the village. It was good to take the packs off, and Flag said it was a good time to smoke, too, and he did. So did Bush, Riley, Eason, and Beaudreau. *What the hell,* thought Ed, and he bummed a cigarette from Flag.

"Flag, I think we're gonna make it."

"Me, too, Boss, but we sure as hell ain't in no shape to fight. I don't know what's gonna happen around here, but we have been watched all day long. If there are PL's around, and I was commanding them, I'd knock off a few tahans right now, here on the road. Might even get an American or two. We better spread out and play soldiers."

"Good idea, Sarge. Riley, you and Eason go down the road a piece. Take your gear. Bush, you and Frank go a couple of hundred meters back the way we came. When we move out, me and Flag will wait for you here. Riley, y'all wait for us to catch up before you move out. Keep your eyes open. Saddle up and let's be careful."

The two-man teams moved to their assigned positions. Flag moved off the west side of the road and Ed took the east. They waited. It was a good hour before the colonel and his men returned. He spoke briefly to his men, waved at Ed, and the column moved out once more. Meadows called to Charlie, and the Thai came over. "What's going on?"

"Sir, the people say they know no PL, but they lie. There were no young men in the village. The KL took our positions this morning when we left. The BP now at Taket, but they have many wounded, some dead. We left just in time. I think this village is PL base, and I think they left just ahead of us, maybe this morning. We spend the night with the men repairing the bridge, but I don't trust them, Sir. You be careful." Sometimes, what Charlie didn't say was a lot more disturbing than what he did say. Bush and Beaudreau caught up, and the four of them joined Riley and Eason a few minutes later. Ed shared Charlie's thoughts with them all. Sam the Second had remained silent throughout the proceedings. Meadows had a funny feeling about Sam.

It wasn't that he didn't trust him, it was just that Sam seemed a lot different than Charlie, and different meant danger to the lieutenant.

Right at 1700 hrs, while still a couple of klicks north of the bridge, Hotel X-ray came guinea-wopping through the sky above them. The chopper made a wide circle, then set down in the middle of the road, much to the delight of the tahans, who hooted and giggled at the ungainly bird's presence. Crew Chief dismounted and motioned Meadows over. Above the roar of the engine, he shouted at Ed, "Safe Hands, Lieutenant, watch your ass," and he handed Ed an envelope. "Get the stuff aboard, we gotta go."

The men threw their rucksacks and duffel bags aboard, keeping only their weapons, the radio and generator, some grenades, and their ponchos. With a throbbing beating of its rotors, Hotel X-ray struggled into the air, did a 180 degree turn, and headed back for Savannahkhet. When it was out of ground effect and the dust had partially cleared, Ed opened the envelope. It had a message inside which read, "11th BP overrun with casualties. Your position in peril. Be prepared to escape and evade. Maintain contact every two hours beginning 2000 today. Failure to contact will result in activation of extraction assistance. Use Diana pads. Good luck. Burn before reading. Murphy." What can you add to a message like that?

When they reached the destroyed bridge, it was close to dark. Ed had alerted the men to the message, and they were now moving as bug-out teams, by twos. The company set up a perimeter of defense outside the camp of the engineers working on the bridge, and prepared to spend the night. It was going to be a long one.

There was no way Ed could justify a 33% alert after the message he had received from the B Team, but neither could they all stay awake all night, either. After consulting with Flag, they decided a 50% alert would suffice, but they also determined that the three men awake would be composed of one man from each bug-out team. That way, if something did happen, at least one man from each pair would be awake from the start and have an idea of what was going on. Flag, Eason, and Riley had the first shift, so Meadows took Charlie and went to talk with Colonel Khom. One interpreter was to stay awake, also. After the usual bowing and smiling, the colonel offered beer to everyone and they talked.

"Sir, we have received a message from Savannahkhet that the BP has been attacked and over-run. I have no information on whether or not the enemy is continuing his advance, but our people think this unit could be in peril," said the lieutenant.

"Yes, Let-ten-ant, I know that. When we finish this patrol, we go back and kick some ass," said the colonel, smiling at his knowledge of GI talk. "No matter, this side of river, that side of river, same-same. Tomorrow we catch PL, kick ass. Then we go back to take our position. I have sent some men to trail PL's. They will lead us in tomorrow. *Ba pin yang*, you see."

"How do your men know where they have gone?"

"They go to Ban Na Xoi. Villagers tell us. How did you enjoy walking today?" Khom asked with a big grin.

"It was okay. Tomorrow we'll do much better without equipment. What do you think of our position tonight? Will the PL attack us?"

"No, Let-ten-ant, sleep well tonight. PL's have run away. We have long walk through jungle tomorrow, time to sleep now." This was the colonel's usual way of terminating a meeting, so Ed and Charlie arose, did their *"som bai"* act, and returned to their comrades. All the Americans were still awake; only Sam the Second was sleeping.

"Flag, Bush, all of you. Colonel Khom said we could sleep well tonight, the National Guard is awake. I say bull-shit, or at least *ke kwi*. We'll keep our 50% alert. I want every man to sleep in his gear with his weapon. Flag, be sure everyone has at least four frag grenades and one purple smoke. Ricky, send the B Team a message at your next transmission that we'll be using purple smoke for identification if we need pick-ups We'd better try and sleep. If the FAR intel is any good, we should make contact tomorrow. Any questions?" There were none.

There was no sleep, either, at least not much. When Flag came to wake Meadows, Ed was already awake, and he could not remember sleeping. He rolled up his poncho and slung it over his shoulder, checked his loads in the Remington, and joined Beaudreau and Bush on guard. They talked a little, but soon spread out about ten meters apart to watch the remaining darkness. It passed slowly. There were lots of noises in the night: natural jungle sounds, the occasional clinking of metal on metal from the Lao on guard as they moved around, but nothing out of the ordinary. That made it even spookier than usual. When the sky began to grey in the east, it was a relief for Ed. Even though he had slept little, if at all, he wanted to get going. The sleeping guys didn't have to be awakened, they just joined those already up, and all of them gnawed some gummy rice for breakfast just like the natives. The Lao were up, too, and Charlie went over to find out what he could from the tahans. He soon returned with the word that the patrol was moving out. Having run a cold camp, there were no fires to be extinguished, so the company of troops began moving out.

They crossed over the bridge that had been blown at first light, and Ed saw that a more apt description would be a bridge which had been partially blown. One lane was missing, but no vital supports had been cut, so the structure was still useable. Bush said someone had done a piss-poor job of wasting demolitions. Maybe so, but as a result of this piss-poor job, they'd lost their positions on the Xe Bangfai and were now exposed like a dove on a wire. Ed hoped the PL were good sports about it all, and wouldn't shoot a resting dove. The column turned off the road on the south side of the bridge, and now, moving in single file, they followed a narrow trail through the dense forest. The sun was full up, but it was still twilight down on the forest floor. Dry leaves lying on the trail crunched at their every step, and Ed's senses were at their highest alert level. Any second he expected to hear the snapping, crackling, and popping he had come to associate with incoming small arms fire. *Small arms, hell, what was to prevent the PL from setting off a booby trap or two, throwing a grenade, ambush, anything. If we know where they are, they sure as hell know where we are!*

About noon, Ed received a thrill that was both a tension maker and a tension reliever. They were passing next to some rocky outcroppings, the underbrush had thinned out somewhat, and the colonel sent word back for Ed to hustle up to where he was. Grabbing Charlie, Meadows hustled up to where Colonel Khom was. The column had stopped, and the men had dropped off the trail in combat positions. It amazed Ed that the tahans could really perform as soldiers when they had a mind to. Must have been McKinney and his boys. Colonel Khom was grinning as he stooped in a crouch, and he motioned Ed up with his hand. "Look, look," he whispered, and pointed toward the rocks. Ed looked in the direction he had indicated, holding his weapon at the ready, all set to spew five rounds of double ought buck at someone. He looked and looked, but saw no one. Charlie joined him.

"Up there, Sir, on the rocks—a tiger." A tiger? What the hell kind of war was this? A tiger? Then Ed was able to make out the object of the colonel's attention. It wasn't really a tiger, but lying up there on the rocky shelf, intently watching what was going on below him, was a bona-fide leopard. A fucking leopard. They were supposed to be in Africa, but this one was evidently uneducated, or else they'd taken the wrong turn off that bridge back there. What the hell was a leopard doing here in Indian Country? Just resting, evidently, for he didn't seem to be bothered by the tahans at all. Khom laughed, got the column moving again, and Ed passed within twenty meters of the big cat, although he did so rather uneasily. Try as he might, he could see no bars between himself and the beast, no moat, and not much chance of Tarzan swinging by anytime soon. Meadows had no idea of how a 12 gauge would do against a leopard, but he was prepared to find out. The cat, however, was content to let the men go on about their business of seeking others of their own kind to kill.

The patrol crossed the Xe Noi River in the early afternoon, and when they closed on the village of Ban Na Xoi, the lead platoon spread out in a line in the woods. One squad from the trailing platoon was sent around to circle the town and take up positions on the far side, acting as a blocking force. At 1600 hrs, as Eason was contacting the B Team, they approached the village. It was eerie. There was no fire from the huts, no noises, no troops breaking for cover. There was nothing but a few women and some dirty kids. Colonel Khom set his troops up in a perimeter around the town, and sent for Meadows.

The enemy, it seemed, had been there that morning—about twenty men, but had left sometime around noon, moving north. They were evidently unaware they were being followed, although Ed doubted it, and had planned to go to Ban Sok Sa for the night. Colonel Khom planned to catch them there tomorrow. He was convinced they would spend a couple of days at Ban Sok Sa. Time to sleep now. Ed talked with the team, and they were in agreement to build a fire and at least boil some of the rice they'd gotten from the Lao, so they did. Once again they stood guard by split bug-out teams, but this time Ed had the first shift, and when he got off duty that night, he slept like a log. PL or no PL, a feller needs his rest.

Flagstone woke him up at dawn. They ate more rice, drank some more brackish water flavored with halazone tablets, and struck out for Ban Sok Sa with the company. It was a repeat of day one. Walking through the jungle in the oppressive heat all day, blocking positions on the other side, and advance by the first platoon, and a bunch of women and dirty kids to greet them. *Ke kwi*. Now the FAR intel said the PL had gone to Ban Kham Phuang, another village further north and west of their location, and on the banks of the Xe Bangfai, near the point where the 57mm attracted Kong Le's attention. Meadows went to talk with the colonel and took a map with him.

"Sir," Ed began, "either this unit is heading for Mahaxay, and hoping to draw us into an ambush, or else they're going home to their village of Mouang Ba or Ban Tung. If it's Mahaxay, we can't stop them; but if its the other way, then they're heading for Mouang Ba tomorrow. They are leading us in a circle. We know the KL and PL are north of us, but these PL may not know that. They may think we still control the other side of the river. I think they're heading for Mouang Ba. If we could take a direct route over there, we could be waiting for them when they arrive. I think it's worth a chance. We can't go to Mahaxay." Charlie translated. The colonel pondered, squinting his eyes, deep in thought. The plan had merit, no doubt about that. The only question was whether or not the colonel would buy it. If he thought it meant he was losing face, there was no chance of him agreeing, but if a way could be found to save face, he just might accept the suggestion. "Colonel," continued Ed, "it is the same plan you taught me at Taket. You used such a plan in Sam Nuea."

Colonel Khom's eyes brightened. He smiled. "You are correct, my Let-ten-ant. I did use such a plan, but I was not sure you remembered. It is what we will do tomorrow. Time to sleep now." (Ain't face-saving wonderful?)

Before they slept that night, Flag had a talk with Ed. "Boss, I think you hit the nail on the head with this plan. We ought to catch up with those sonsabitches tomorrow, so I want to talk with you. You might make a good officer someday, and there ain't no sense in getting your ass shot off over here. If we do hit those guys, no matter how well we set it up or how straight we shoot, we ain't gonna get them all. Some of them are going to break to the jungle, and the natural tendency is to chase 'em. Don't do it. If you got 'em in sight, okay, but as soon as you lose sight of them, stop, look, listen, and sneak back the way you came. They'll cut your balls off in the woods, and I can't stand a soprano Boss. Listen to me, Sir."

Ed could tell by the, 'Sir,' that this was serious, so he nodded assent and crawled under his poncho to let Flag take the first watch.

The rain started falling before dawn, and by the time the group got underway, it was pouring. No one wore their ponchos—they were for sleeping, and all the men were thoroughly soaked by the time they'd shaken off the night's sleep. Colonel Khom had sent out some additional men to try and find the enemy, and when they got to the Xe Bangfai about noon, some of these men reported in. The PL were heading west, had already crossed the river, but were heading further south than anticipated, toward Ban Na Deng. There were no villages between the river and Na Deng, so either they were going to try and reach the town tonight, or were spending the night in the woods. Their last reported position was less than two klicks away.

A bright gleam appeared in the colonel's eyes, and he ordered the scouts to get back on the trail of the PL. Motioning to his men, he ordered them to cross the river, and he increased the pace in hot pursuit. Ed would have felt better if they had shown a bit more caution, but he, too, was anxious to close on the PL. By 1500 hrs, the scouts reported the enemy was only one klick ahead, and the colonel called a halt. Ed joined him. "Let-ten-ant, they will not reach Ban Na Deng tonight. When they reach a clearing, they will stop for the night. Then we kick ass. Tell your men to be ready. We use the same method we use on the villages. Let's go."

The next hour was an eternity. Moving with caution now, the column wound through the jungle, weapons at the ready, the men breathing hard. It had quit raining, but it was still hot. Steam rose from the vegetation, and to Ed it seemed like he was walking through the Twilight Zone. At 1700 hrs, the report came back that the PL were making camp. The blocking squad moved out stealthily through the woods. The Americans joined Colonel Khom and the first platoon as they approached the camp. Meadows could see a look of anxiety on the faces of the tahans, not fear, exactly, but definitely anxiety. He hoped his own face didn't look like fear. Anxiety, he could buy, but, please, Lord, don't let me look scared. The platoon stopped, then silently began spreading out. Through the thin cover of bushes in front of him, Meadows saw the PL for the first time. There were about twenty of them, as reported, and they were cooking rice and preparing their beds for the night. Most of them were dressed in black pants and dirty white shirts, like the rest of the Laotian population, but here and there a complete dark green uniform was evident. Regulars. They were obviously unaware of the danger they were in, for there were no sentries out and the men were relaxed and horsing around, giggling, and chattering in their humming monotone of the native tongue. It would be dark soon. Meadows' mouth was dry, his hands gripping the Remington were soaking wet. He was wet; it was hot; but Ed was cold enough to shiver. It was like Ranger School, or an operation in Florida, or at Bragg, but the shells in his shotgun were real and these little men were real enemies. Kind of hard to believe.

At a signal from Khom, the men of the first platoon rose up and began walking forward, the GI's with them. Hearing the commotion, the PL turned to see what was going on, and then, realizing their predicament, they began grabbing for their weapons. At the first volley, about half the group fell. Ed heard the thum-thum-thum of Bush's BAR and the sharp crack of Flag's M-1. He aimed at one of the uniformed figures and fired a blast from the Remington as they ran forward, but he couldn't tell if he'd hit his target or not. Jacking another round into the chamber, he fired at a fleeting figure in black, but, again, he couldn't tell anything about the result. There was some return fire, more thum-thum-thum, crack, another shot at a ghostly figure, and then the patrol was upon the PL. Several bodies were lying near the fire, more were strewn in the grass nearby, Ed saw a couple of men with their hands raised. As he reached the vicinity of the fire, Meadows saw a figure in dark green running for the woods about twenty meters away. He blasted a shot off, but the man kept running with Ed hot on his trail. The figure reached the woods ahead of Ed and disappeared. Meadows dived right into the underbrush. He couldn't see the quarry, but he could hear him thrashing around up ahead. Ed pressed on.

Fifty meters into the woods, the sound stopped. Heeding Flag's advice, Ed stopped, too. He crouched down and listened, ears straining for a sound, eyes moving quickly back and forth, searching for the tell-tale movement of the enemy. Ed was breathing hard, the light was growing dim, and he was as likely to be the hunted as the hunter.

Making the decision to save his balls, Meadows began moving slowly to his left, where he'd noticed a trail previously. He heard, saw, smelled, nothing. Upon reaching the trail, Meadows paused before stepping out. When he did, he looked back toward the camp. There was no movement. Glancing to his right, Ed came face to face with the PL Regular, fifteen meters away. The man was holding a carbine at port arms, and he was just as surprised to see the American. The combatants looked at each other for a split second, then the PL started to raise his weapon. Dropping his right hand from the Remington, Ed grabbed at his Smith & Wesson, thumbing open the holster, cocking the hammer as he drew the weapon. There wasn't time to aim, but the hours of firing at Ft. Bragg paid off, and pointing the barrel at the center of the man's chest, he fired. He could hear the bullet hit, saw the arms throw the carbine away, the knees buckle, the head jerk back. The PL fell backwards, flat on his back, not moving, still. Meadows cocked the pistol again and crouched down, his eyes never leaving the supine figure in the forest.

At the sound of the shot, several tahans came running up the trail from the camp, weapons at the ready. Seeing Ed and the figure on the ground, they ran up to the body and began hooting and kicking at the figure. It lay still. When one of the tahans took out a knife and began cutting off the PL's ears, Meadows sheathed the revolver and headed for the camp. Flag met him at the clearing. He could tell at a glance that the lieutenant was badly shaken. Flag took out his smokes, lit one and handed it to Ed. Meadows took the cigarette and drew a long breath. The smoke made him cough, but he continued drawing on it anyway. "Boss, you done good." Of such things are friendships cemented.

23

Who You Gonna Believe?

Once the company had all gathered in the clearing, there was a great telling and retelling of how brave each of the tahans had been. Must have been several hundred PL's killed here, if each Lao soldier's story was to be believed. The colonel was obviously pleased by the action, and pleased by the way his men had performed in it. One enemy soldier, possibly two, had gotten away, or was at least lost in the bush, while seventeen had been killed and four captured. The most amazing thing was that there were no wounded, but when you took a minute to count the holes in each corpse, it was easy to see why there were no wounded. Few people can survive twenty bullet wounds, and none of these had. Colonel Khom let the tahans celebrate for a few minutes, then he posted his guards, told the troops to prepare for the night, and began the interrogation of the prisoners. Meadows sent Charlie over to 'assist' in the questioning.

Meanwhile, the really grisly part of their work lay ahead of the team. As Khom took care of questioning the living, the FTT members took care of questioning the dead. All seventeen bodies had been dragged out of the woods and away from the fire, and were now arranged in a neat little row of dead people near the center of the clearing. Meadows saw his uniformed tahan with both his ears cut off, and he walked over to take a closer look at the man who had walked into the Valley of the Shadow of Death with him, but had failed to walk out. He was a young man, maybe Ed's age, maybe a little older or younger, tough to say. Ed's bullet had hit him right in the middle of the chest, just above the nipple line. His uniform had a circle of dried blood ringing the bullet hole, but there was very little where his ears used to be. His skin had a waxy sheen, sort of a greenish-yellow, and his eyes were only half-closed. The black irises were clouded over and one of them had been poked out, probably by the tahans. Flag came up to disturb Ed's inspection of the corpse. "Boss, there ain't no sense in looking at him; he's dead, nothing but cold meat for the leopard. I sent Eason over to set up the radio and notify the B Team about what's happened. Beaudreau and Riley are cranking the generator. Let's you, me, and Bush search the bodies. I'll start with this guy; Bush, you start down at that end; Boss, why don't you start down there?"

Ed walked away from his former opponent's body and down to the corpse lying closest to the fire. This one had been hit in the face, among other places, and was unrecognizable as a person. His face was blown away, his head all crooked and misshapen. One arm was nearly off and his shirt was soaked with blood. He obviously hadn't died with the first shot. Meadows went through his pockets, found a plastic folder full of pictures, a letter—now blood-soaked, a handkerchief full of little Buddhas, and that was about all. The next body was that of a woman, much to Ed's surprise. She had a folded up packet of what looked like orders, or at least something official, a K-54 pistol tucked in her waistband, and a gold bracelet which joined the other items in the pile by Ed's knees. Bush must have gotten her, for she had a dozen or so wounds to her chest. Her hair had been pulled back into a tight bun, but it was now limp and strands were hanging down on her face. The third body had no pictures, no papers, no cards at all, but there was a Zippo lighter, made in USA, in his pocket. Before Meadows could start on the next body, Flag was already there, expertly frisking the body, searching even the cap where he found a single black and white photograph of a smiling woman holding a slant-eyed little baby. The woman was ugly, but the baby was cute as a button. Bush joined them. The three men pooled their findings, and Bush gathered all the stuff together. "We better send all this stuff back to Savan and let them work on it there. Looks like we may have gotten some good stuff. Couple of these guys were Regulars, no doubt about it. Did you see anything unusual on any of them, Boss?"

Ed told him about the woman and the Zippo lighter. Bushman seemed interested in the lighter. "Sonofabitch, Boss, which one had that? Could be he worked for the teams sometime in the past. Wish we had a camera."

"I've got one in my poncho, Sarge," said Ed.

"Really? Damn, Boss, let's get it and take their pictures for the B team. They might be able to identify them." Ed got the camera out, a little Petri, and handed it to Bushman. While he photographed each body, Meadows sat down and watched. He felt tired, exhausted, puzzled, sad, relieved, and a little bit satisfied.

"First man you ever killed, Boss?" It was Flag. Ed nodded. "I remember the first gook I killed in Korea, I mean, the first one I was ever sure of. It was a kid, younger than me, and he looked so little when he was dead. I wanted to bury him, but we were moving out, and I had to let him lay. Sorta like yours. Never did forget him." They were silent for a few minutes.

"Flag? You think there's a mother somewhere waiting for her son to come home?" Flagstone didn't answer. In the silence, the clicking of Bush's camera seemed very loud. He was shooting Ed's victim now.

"Naw, his mother probably died when he was born. Let's get some rice and stop all this talking. Almost time to get some sleep."

The patrol didn't break camp until the middle of the morning. They moved out down the trail toward Ban Na Deng, and as Ed passed the row of bodies, he saw that four more had been added. Guess they answered the questions wrong. Charlie had reported there was nothing much gained in the grilling by the colonel. Evidently the prisoners were all little tahans who knew very little about the activities of the PL group and had been with them only a short time. Or so they said. It hardly mattered now, for whatever else they might have known was locked away forever behind those half-closed eyes and cloudy pupils.

It didn't take but a couple of hours of easy walking to reach the village of Ban Na Deng. It was, as were all Laotian villages in this area, a dusty square surrounded by wicker or rattan houses with grass roofs. There were a lot of people here, at least there were a lot of women and kids, and even an occasional old man, but Meadows suspected that a sizeable percentage of the young men were lying back there in the clearing, rotting. A lot of the young men and one young woman. Much to the team's surprise, there was a hotel in this town. It wasn't much, a two-story bamboo and grass thatch structure with the second floor being open, and that's where the guests were quartered. All the Americans and the Lao officers chose to sleep there, so they dropped off their gear and went back downstairs and out toward the square to see about finding some place to buy some hot food.

The kids were everywhere, all about the same size, all seemingly very curious about these giants with round eyes. Sam the Second found them a place he said was a restaurant, and they were able to enjoy a bowl of hot soup and a wicker steamer full of hot rice for about 20 kip each. The soup was tasty, but Ed didn't know what kind it was. One thing you probably didn't want to know in Laos was what you were eating. When they finished their meal, Eason and Beaudreau went to set up the radio and call for Hotel X-ray to come pick up the intel they had taken off the dead bodies, "Safe Hands," of course. Meadows found the remains of a cigar in his shirt pocket and tried to light it. Soggy as it was, he still managed to get it to burn. He was sitting with Flag and Bush—Riley having gone back to the hotel to lie down for awhile, and it was obvious the troops were winding down from the previous day's excitement.

About that time, Let, the colonel's other body guard—a Lao Tung whom Khom abused horribly, walked up to one of the cows standing placidly by the restaurant and shot it right in the head with his revolver. The animal shook its head, rolled its eyes, and took off after Let. Taken totally by surprise, the tahan was thrown into the air by that first charge, but he hit the ground running. He ran alongside the beast and shot it again. Unfazed, the cow turned and swatted Let with her head. Down he went, but up he came almost immediately as the animal tried to follow up her advantage. The rest of the tahans had come to watch this extremely western rodeo, and they were whistling and hooting at the plight of Let. To Ed, it seemed the tahan was in some real danger, but the Lao didn't see it that way. There were weapons in abundance, but no one rushed to lend a hand. Dodging a flailing hoof, Let jumped aside and shot the cow yet another time in the side. It was like the rodeo clowns hazing the bulls in El Paso, but this clown had a .38 calibre pistol. Swinging its head wildly, the cow tried to locate the elusive Let, who was now starting to ham it up. He grabbed the cow's tail and ran along behind it as the animal ran in a circle chasing Let. Another shot in the head, and the beast started to show signs of tiring. She stopped running, shook her head, slinging blood everywhere, then looked for her adversary. He was right in front of her, so she lowered her head and tried to charge. The life was draining out of her, and the charge was a pitiful sight. She stumbled, regained her balance, staggered like a drunken sailor, then fell to her knees. Let grabbed one horn, pushed her head to one side, and shot her in the neck. The cow shuddered, lolled out her tongue, and rolled over on her side, dead at last. As the tahans began to butcher the carcass and carry off the beef for their supper, Meadows decided that he had learned one thing from Let's performance: don't hunt cows with a .38.

Hotel X-ray picked up the packet of pictures and papers and the roll of film at about 1500 hrs. Pilot set the chopper down right in the middle of the square, filling the air with dust and grit. Crew Chief took the package from Ed, held out his hands palm up to indicate he had nothing for them, and with a swirl of blades and a hot blast of exhaust, the helicopter was gone. Alone again with the Lao, the three senior members of the FTT sat on a bench by the square and talked about their adventures on the patrol. It had certainly been more exciting than sitting by the Xe Bangfai, and it wasn't over yet, for they had no home to return to; but for the present at least, they could "sort of" relax. Meadows had struck up a friendship with one of the Lao kids—a little girl with a coy smile who agreed to stand next to him for Bush to take their picture. Ed was still trying to get her to sit on his lap when an old woman made her way slowly to the center of the square from the row of huts on the other side. She stopped there and called out, "Let-ten-ant!"

Ed looked up. The woman was holding some flowers, and she motioned with them toward the Americans. "What the hell is this?" wondered Ed out loud.

"She wants you to come out there, Boss," said Bushman.

"Must be one of their customs, or something. Here, Flag, hold my shotgun, guess I better go see what she wants."

"Don't go out there, Boss," said Flag.

"Why not? She probably wants to give us some flowers as a gesture of friendship. I better go."

"Flowers, my ass. That was probably her son you killed yesterday.

Fuck her. I wouldn't go out there."

"Aw, Flag, she ain't armed. If you can't trust an old woman, who you gonna believe in this place?"

"Boss, don't go. She's probably lining you up for a sniper. To hell with her and her flowers." Meadows looked around. The rest of the villagers were watching him, waiting to see what he was going to do.

"Flag, if I don't go out to meet her, these folks are gonna think we ain't friendly. Cover me." Meadows set his shotgun down next to the sergeant and got up.

"Sir (this was serious), if you're determined to get your ass killed, then go ahead. But listen. If I holler at you, you hit the dirt, hard. Don't fuck around with her. Get down and stay down, fast."

"Okay, Sarge, I will." It was only about twenty meters out to where the woman was standing, but it seemed like a long trip as Meadows walked out to see her. She was smiling, and holding the bunch of flowers out toward the lieutenant. Ed pressed his hands together, chest high, preparing to give the traditional greeting, when the loud shout of the team sergeant rang out. Meadows dove head first onto the ground, flat on his belly. He heard the thud of the bullets hitting the woman's body just before the crack of Flag's rifle and the thum-thum-thum of Bush's BAR. The woman fell backward, sprawled out in front of Ed, spread eagled on the ground. Meadows lay very still as Flag and Bush warily approached. Bush continued to look around, paying special attention to the huts on the other side of the square, as Flag rolled the woman's body over. Strapped to her back was a canvas bag, and when he opened it, Ed could see clumps of C-4 explosive inside. "Sonofabitch," whistled Bush. "There's enough shit in there to blow this whole village up. Let's get the hell out of this place."

Meadows got up and dusted himself off as they returned to their side of the square. Russian frogmen were nothing compared to the real thing. He didn't bother to check the front of his pants, for he knew what he'd find. What Ed was worried about was what was in the back of his pants. The colonel commanded the rounding up of all the villagers, and his men soon had them all assembled in one of the larger houses, kids included. He started searching the people, and the huts, too, all semblance of friendship with the people of Ban Na Deng gone. While they were carrying out the colonel's wishes, the FTT members retired to the hotel. Colonel Khom was very apologetic, obviously embarrassed by this event, and he promised Meadows he would find the PL's and take care of them. The U.S. team stood a 50% alert again that night, but for Ed, the most pressing thing was to find a place to take a bath. While he was washing out his clothes after bathing his body, it occurred to Ed that he wasn't feeling sorry for the little dead man in the forest anymore. Fuck 'em. Fuck 'em all. Bring on the little fuckers, Killer Dirty Pants was ready.

24

Payday

They stayed at Ban Na Deng for two more nights. The colonel left and went to Savannahkhet, or somewhere, for a conference with his higher ups, and the patrol company was commanded by Captain Praseuth in his absence. There was no action, no word of the situation on the Xe Bangfai, no nothing, and all the GI's were getting antsy. Eason made his usual contacts, and on the morning of the fourth day in the village, the word came from the B Team that FTT-19 was to meet Hotel X-ray at 1100 hrs and to come to Savan for a stand-down. Ed wasn't too sure exactly what a stand-down was, but Flag quickly informed him that it meant they were being taken out of the field for awhile.

There wasn't a lot of gear to carry out to the chopper when it arrived, for most of their stuff had already been sent on when they first passed this way. H-X had a different pilot and a different crew-chief, but it sounded like the same old Italian engine as they took off and headed south for the B Team location. The same guy met them at the airport who had met them on their first day in-country, but he wasn't quite as cocky this day as he had been when they first arrived. It could be that Meadows just didn't notice his attitude today, but it could also be that a half-month in the field, with some periods of actual combat, had served to take the sheen off the swaggering trooper who was, in effect, doing garrison duty. Without their equipment, the team fit nicely into the 3/4 for the ride into town, through town, and on to the team house. It was a tired bunch of puppies who crawled out of that truck and trekked into the house, for the closer they got to other American forces, the more relaxed the FTT members had become. They were so relaxed now that they nearly went to sleep waiting for Major Murphy, who had left word that he wanted to see them when they arrived. He came walking out of his office with a big smile, his hand extended to Ed, and as the two shook hands, or "pressed the flesh," as the troops called it, he told them all to stand at ease.

"Welcome back to civilization," he laughed, "welcome back! You fellows have had quite a time, and with the BP pulling back to Xeno, we figured you could use some rest. We want to talk to all of you about what all has gone on up there, and I think we have some news, too, but it can wait. The sergeant major tells me we have hot water this morning, so I'm sure you'd all like a bath and a chance to relax first. We'll meet in the morning at 0730—your whole team, Lieutenant. My entire staff wants to talk with them. Ask Top for anything you need. The entire third floor has been cleared out for you, or you can stay downtown at the Safe House (Constellation—whore-house), if you wish. See you in the morning."

Major Murphy was a nice guy. Ed felt like a bath, or shower, was of much more importance than a debriefing right then. Flagstone pulled him aside. "Boss, don't let all this glad-handing fool you. These garritroopers have some shit up their sleeves or they would want to talk today. We better get together tonight down at the whore-house and talk this over. I'll have the other guys there whenever you say."

"Okay, Flag, we'll get together whenever you think. How about 2100?"

"We'll be there. Be careful, Boss, and don't talk to these mothers today. They're treacherous."

"Gotcha. I think I'll take a bath and get some sleep." Meadows' mental alarm clock went off right at 1900 hrs, and the day was beginning to cool off toward that humid, warm night in the tropics which was not unpleasant. He took another shower, shaved the week's worth of stubble from his face and splashed a handful of Old Spice on, which promptly burned like the very devil. The team members had retrieved their goods from the S-4 warehouse, including their civilian clothes, so Ed put on a pair of lightweight trousers, a short-sleeved shirt which, when worn out, hid the .357 he stuck in the waistband, and he was ready to meet the folks of Savannahkhet.

This time, though, he came as a veteran of the wars instead of the wide-eyed newby he had been previously. Shunning the wait for a ride (Why was there always a wait? Why wasn't there ever a jeep just going into town?), he started walking down the street toward the dusty air marking the location of the town. As he walked, Meadows thought about what Flag had said concerning the debriefing. The members of the B Team had treated them differently, no doubt about it, but he didn't detect any real hostility. Hard to figure out some things. What Ed didn't realize was that the B Team personnel had been following the progress of FTT-19 on their trip after the PL with a great deal of interest. They say war is like flying, which is like a lot of other things: hours and hours, or days and days of boredom interspersed with moments of sheer panic. Since the team had been in country barely two weeks now, they had experienced more action than many teams saw during an entire tour. The general feeling was that the young, used-to-be DASL and his men had acquitted themselves quite well. But, of course, Ed didn't know this as he strode through the streets of town toward the Constellation.

They didn't have a guitar player tonight, and it seemed the air wasn't quite as smoky, either. Maybe there was an anti-smoking campaign going on here. Flag and Bush were at a table in the far corner and they waved him on over. They also waved the waiter over and ordered some more beer, then they waved away the dancing girls who came with the waiter. "You look well rested, Boss," laughed Flagstone. "Been sleeping all day?"

"Just about. I'm hungry. Have y'all eaten?"

"No, but I wouldn't want to eat here. The other guys will be here in a few minutes. I think we ought to have a pow-wow first, then we can go over to the Ba Pin Yang Club for something to eat. Too many of the officers from the B Team hang out there for us to talk. Besides, Boss, I think you liked that Thai whore over there and we need your undivided attention for this conference."

"She was a damn fine-looking woman, I thought."

"Yeah, and she'll give you the damndest case of clap you'll ever have," added Bush. "They'll be damn fine-looking germs, though.

She's probably a Thai intel agent, the way she hangs around the pilots. Probably knows more about what's happened with the 11th BP than old Charlie does." The idea that the prostitute was an intelligence agent had never occurred to Ed, but it was logical. *What a waste.* Eason, Beaudreau, and Riley arrived, Bush shooed off the girls, and they got down to business.

"What's so important, Flag?" asked Ed. "Do you know something we don't?"

"I talked with a couple of people today, so did Bush, and we were right in our suspicions. Major Murphy and the rest of the big-wigs are all pissed off over that incident with the bunker. They considered it an aggressive act on our part which we weren't supposed to be doing."

"What did they think about the KL's shooting at us?" asked Ed in disgust.

"They know about that, too, but since none of us were hurt, they say it was a Lao-Lao shooting. Boss, I told you these sonsabitches at headquarters weren't to be trusted. Anyway, they plan to chew our ass out tomorrow. I don't know if they plan to do anything or not, but there's an A team coming in next week and there's talk of assigning them to the BP and sending us up to the BI that bugged out on the Americans a couple of weeks ago."

"What should we do?" It was Beaudreau who asked the question this time.

"I don't know, but I think we need to be very careful in what we say. Bush wants us to say nothing at all, but I don't think that would be wise. Boss, you're about half-smart, what do you suggest?"

"If this is as bad as you think, they've already decided what they're going to do, so the only thing we can accomplish with talk is to make it worse. What do they think those fuckers were shooting at us, water pistols? If this ain't the shits. We come over here to fight a war, fight one, and they tell us we screwed up. What did they want us to do?"

"I think it's cause they're jealous, Boss," said Bushman. "They sit on their asses and screw the whores every night, then they get pissed off when someone does something right in the field. But it don't matter why; the question is, what're we gonna do?"

"I suppose we ought to answer their questions, don't embellish anything, just give them the facts, and see what happens."

"I agree with the boss," said Flag. "The main thing is we don't go in there cold and get surprised. I don't want none of you guys talking to no one about it tonight. Boss, I think it would be a good idea for you to be careful, too. Do you agree?"

"I agree. Fuck 'em. We been in the boonies for two weeks, let's go have a few. What day is today, anyway?"

"Friday, March 30th, why?" asked Riley.

"Cause I ain't got much kip, damn few dollars, and I'm ready for payday. Besides that, if it's March 30th, it's my sister's birthday."

"Well," said Flag, "Happy Birthday to your sister. C'mon, I'll buy you a beer, let's down a few."

The major was prompt. Right at 0730 hrs, the sergeant major called the team into the conference room where the commander and his four staff officers were assembled. They questioned the team in a forum-type atmosphere about the BP, their patrol, small talk mostly, and Ed answered all the questions except those directly asked to one of his team members. He got the distinct impression they were just sparring around, and his answers weren't telling the staff anything they didn't already know. It was the major's turn.

"Tell us about what happened on the river with the bunker, Lieutenant." Good. The decks were cleared. Now they could get down to business.

He told them how they had been fired upon from the bunker and how the tahan had been killed. It was his idea, he said, that they do something to show Colonel Khom that they shared his grief over the dead soldier, so he'd come up with the plan to eliminate the bunker. Yes, it might be interpreted as an act of aggression, but at the time and under the circumstances, he rather thought of it as an act of friendship for the BP and solidarity with their emotions. No, there weren't any other details he had failed to relate. Yes, he would do it again if the circumstances were repeated. Yes, he felt it had been effective. Yes, the BP did send out patrols after that (so they said). Yes, Sir, he was prepared for the consequences of his act. Here comes payday.

"Lieutenant, I'm not sure you realize how serious your actions were. We feel that as a direct result of that attack, the PL blew the bridge."

And got their asses kicked good, thought Ed. "There is no telling how much damage you could have caused in our relationship with Kong Le." *Or how much damage Kong Le's bullets could have done to me.* "Some of the staff suggested we pull your team out of the field and replace them with a more experienced team, and I must admit I considered that course of action. However, since there was relatively little reaction from the other side, and since you did a good job on the retaliation patrol, I'm going to leave you with the BP. I'm taking away your weapons man, Beaudreau, to join the B Team and replace one of our personnel who had to return to the States. Besides, the BP is being pulled out by the Lao and sent to Xeno for some refresher training. They should be there in a couple of days. Until then, you and your team will remain in Savan. Lieutenant, watch yourself, because, I assure you, we are watching you. That is all."

A hand-slap. Shit. He'd rather have been court-martialed. They all went to the Ba Pin Yang that night, but if Suni came (that was the girl's name), Ed didn't know it, for he really tied one on. Hell, with $16 a day per diem burning a hole in his pocket, he could afford to. So did the rest of FTT-19, now numbering only five men. So what? How many men does it take to sit around and suck your thumb at Xeno? Fuck 'em. Fuck 'em all, the long and the short and the tall. What the hell kind of war was this, anyway? Nobody is gonna believe this.

25

Viva La France

Xeno is spelled, "Xeno," but is pronounced with an "S" and is therefore called, Seno. It was located about 30 miles east of Savannahkhet on Highway 9, which was paved at least that far. It was the paratrooper training center for this part of French Indo-China and had an excellent airstrip and several rows of quonset huts serving as barracks for the troops stationed there. It was the home base for the 11th BP, the 55th BP, and Kong Le's BP, although the latter was currently persona non grata. Now it was to serve as the home of FTT-19. There was already a full A Detachment stationed at this location from the 1st Special Forces Group (Airborne) out of Okinawa, attached to the Regimental Headquarters. When the members of FTT-19 arrived, it was like Old Home Week for the old heads, for they knew many of the members of the 1st Group. To the career NCO's in Group, as soon as they completed a tour of duty with one Group, they usually transferred to one of the other Groups: the 1st on Okinawa, or the 10th at Bad Tolz, Germany. Thus, no matter which Group you may be wearing the flash of on your beret, you usually knew many of the members of the other Groups. To a neophyte like Ed, and most of the other officers, however, a tour with a Special Forces Group was only one of the many varied assignments you could expect during your career.

Meadows and Eason, the youngsters, were like lost lambs among the wolves. When they unloaded their gear into one of the huts, they found a poker game in progress and a lot of people who spoke the same language. Much handshaking, backslapping, and coarse language. That was the common tongue. Captain Harper was the CO of this team, and they were currently without an XO, thus no lieutenants. Bushman and Flagstone seemed to know everyone, Riley knew most of them. They talked about "whatever happened to old shitface," and "where the hell is shithead," and other terms of endearment while the new people staked out claims on territory surrounding a particular cot. The huts were built to house a lot more men than were currently occupying them, so there was plenty of room.

In addition to their interpreters, the detachment here also had another indigenous person in their employ, a female cook by the name of Sue. She was a Cambode, and probably one of the ugliest women Ed had ever seen, but she fixed two hot meals a day and cleaned the place up. Her knowledge of English was about the same as the mynah bird they also had who could say, "fuck You" in nearly perfect diction. He also dropped little packages of excrement everywhere he perched for a minute, and he perched everywhere. Ed immediately hated him, but he belonged to the other team and was considered sacred. The days were filled with long hours of poker playing and the nights were occupied with playing poker. In other words, nothing of any import was happening at Xeno. Savan was only thirty jeep minutes away, so two men a day were usually in town doing whatever there was to do there. The rest played poker.

Ed learned the names of the other team's members and grew to know them. They were, oddly enough, very much like the members of his own team. The whole time spent at Xeno could be called a waste except for one event which affected the way Ed was to feel about Frenchmen forever. They'd been at the camp about a week and wore the *pak ko mas* of the natives, the skirt-like things, during the day time and their shorts at night during the formal poker sessions. One morning a couple of C-46 airplanes landed at the base. These were like the same aircraft Ed had jumped from in Florida, but instead of stars on their fuselages, they had the blue-white-red roundels of the French Air Force. No big deal. The planes taxied up near one of the warehouses Ed had visited, shut down their engines, and the crews got out. Meadows decided to go talk with the Frenchmen, his allies, but they weren't very friendly and kept strictly to themselves. Meanwhile, the Lao were busy loading the planes with uniforms taken from the warehouse, boxes and boxes of uniforms, then some small arms crates, several score, and cases of ammunition. *Must be for one of the American teams training troops at another location,* thought Ed. The planes were refueled with gasoline supplied by the base, which was supplied by the B Team in Savan. After a couple of hours on the ground, they fired up their engines and departed, heading north. Meadows called Charlie over to find out where they were going.

"Oh, Sir," said the interpreter, "they go to Mahaxay. This equipment for Kong Le."

"Kong Le? That bastard is on the other side!"

"Yes, Sir, I know, but French have always supplied Kong Le. This equipment given to Kong Le before when he was friendly. Now he wants back."

"I don't give a shit what he wants. Who does he think he is? Who said he could have this stuff?"

"Sir, French have always supplied Kong Le. *Ba pin yang*, no matter." End of discussion. Charlie walked back to the team hut.

No matter, my ass, thought Ed. He was seething. Weren't the French members of NATO, and SEATO, and all the other -TO's...aligned against the communists, determined to stop the spread of this cancer across the world? They were our friends, weren't they? What about Dien Bien Phu, and all the aid we had given them? What about the fact that France had received more foreign aid than all the rest of the countries of Europe combined? What the hell kind of place was this? Why were the French allowed to come around here at all, if they were supplying the KL? Did they realize that the bullet that killed the tahan up on the Xe Bangfai, and those others directed at Ed himself, could have come from this very warehouse? What the hell was going on? He decided to talk with Flag.

"Flag, do you know what the hell I just saw? Those fucking frogs just loaded up two planeloads of goods from our warehouse and took them to Mahaxay. Our stuff, from our camp, to the enemy. Can you believe it?"

"Boss, I ain't surprised at nothing the frogs do. They're still pissed off about Dien Bien Phu, and want to help anyone if it means we get our ass kicked like they did. Fuck 'em. Don't let it bother you,

Boss, they ain't worth getting excited about."

"Maybe so, but I am excited. I'm downright pissed. We could have been killed by rounds these slimy bastards supplied the KL. That would piss me off royally. Who do they think they are? Fucking frogs, I ain't gonna forget this." Ed fussed and cussed for the rest of the morning and on into the afternoon. He spent some time cleaning his weapon, cussing out Napoleon and all his descendents, until it was time for supper. Flag came over and invited him to go with Bush and him into the village of Xeno to a place called, Francois', where they served beef under the heading of something French, and mad as he was at France at the moment, he decided to go, anyway. It was only a short walk into town and the restaurant wasn't much further. They went in and eased up to the bar to have a drink or two before eating. The bar was well-stocked and Ed had a shot of Wild Turkey while the two sergeants downed a couple of beers. He'd just ordered another round when the French air crew entered the establishment.

Meadows bristled. Flagstone recognized how angry his lieutenant was becoming. "Boss," he whispered, "don't do nothing dumb. Ignore the bastards. Enjoy your drink."

"Those guys piss me off."

"I know they do, and me, too, but this ain't the time to do nothing about it. Ignore 'em. Maybe they'll go away." But, they didn't. There were three Frenchmen, and they gathered together at the end of the bar and started drinking. At first they were quiet and caused no fuss at all, but after just a few minutes, they started jabbering louder and louder in their native tongue, ofttimes gesturing toward the Americans and laughing. Ed was sorely tempted to gesture back, especially with the long finger of his right hand, but he bit his lip and tried to follow Flag's advice. Now the frogs were drinking toasts, loudly proclaiming something, then all of them toasting and downing drinks. Francois, the owner, namesake, and bartender here, brought the Americans refills. With a broad smile he announced they were compliments of the Frenchmen. Ed looked at Flag, who in turn looked at Bush, then all three of them turned to face the Frenchmen. One of the Frogs spoke in accented English.

"God Bless America."

Ed raised his glass of whiskey toward the spokesman, smiled, and said, "Fuck France."

On the way back to the barracks, Ed wiggled his jaw around to make sure it still worked. *That frog could really hit,* he thought. Of course, that was before he had kicked the Frenchman in the nuts and followed that up with a barrage of kicks to the man's head, chest, and midsection. Then he had pounded the Frenchmen with his fists until Flag and Bush had pulled him off. They'd finished off the other two frogs, and when they left the Frenchman's establishment, all three of their opponents were stretched out peacefully on the floor. The thought crossed Ed's mind that on successive occasions he had been screwed by the Lao, the Americans, and the French since arriving in this war zone. It was going to be one hell of a tour. Wonder what he'd do if he met a Russian?

26

Who Could Know Such A Thing

Meadows fully expected the major to come roaring over from Savan with a whole team to replace FTT-19 and banish him to Vientiane on latrine detail. It could even be so bad that they'd send him back to Ft. Bragg and make him an aide to B.B. Briggs, but since he'd become a first lieutenant, he doubted that. There *were* TO&E slots in the Group for first lieutenants. When the major hadn't arrived by noon that next day, Ed began to doubt the word had gotten back to him concerning the drinking of toasts with the frogs, but what he didn't know was that the word had gotten back and Major Murphy had a big laugh about it. Some of the other officers weren't so gleeful, especially the ones who coveted Ed's job and Ed's team, but they really didn't matter in this case. The poker game continued unabated; it never stopped, day or night. His jaw had a bruise on it from the Frenchman's knuckles, but it didn't swell very much and the abrasions on his own knuckles felt pretty good. Meadows felt pretty good. *What the hell, the frogs ought to pay SOMETHING for their arrogant attitudes.* Sue served dinner and supper, Riley and Eason returned from the big town, and another night at Xeno passed as thrilling as the others.

Early the next morning, Bushman and one of the men from the 1st, a fellow by the name of Eisenvald, who had formerly served with the Wehrmacht and the Foreign Legion, decided to visit some friends of theirs at Dong Heng. They invited Ed to go along and he jumped at the opportunity. Anything beat another day at Xeno. Dong Heng was about 30 klicks east of Xeno, and the road soon ran out of pavement and turned into dirt. This was disputed territory—Indian Country; so as they rode along in the jeep with Bush driving, Ed kept the shotgun ready and a round in the chamber, while Eisenvald watched from the back seat with his Thompson submachinegun. They passed a couple of poosows (women) struggling along the road with heavily-laden backs, but saw no tahans from either side.

The village of Dong Heng was like the village of Ban Na Deng, which was like the village of Thom Lai, which was like the village of Phong Song, which was like...ad nauseum. The only difference here was that an American A Detachment was living here. At first glance, their hooch didn't seem much different from the other houses in the row, but when you looked a little closer and spied the Claymore mines nestled among the sandbags hidden in the bushes, and the elaborate bunker network dug in under the elevated house, you got the impression these men hadn't always been sitting around enjoying the morning cool as they were now. More of the usual greeting routine, and it dawned on Ed that they, the Americans, weren't all that different from the Lao in their rituals of greeting. The Lao held their hands in the position of supplication, while the GI's took to backslapping and handshaking; the Lao said, "*Som ba de, ba,*" while the westerners said, "Sonofabitch." Eisenvald and Bushman introduced Ed all around, they knew every member of the team, and a certain pride filled the young lieutenant's chest when Bush declared that "he was young, but he's okay." That was as good as you could get in the world of the Special Forces troopers: okay. Cold cans of beer appeared, and a long morning of drinking and lie-swapping began. Everything went well until the beer was replaced by the cognac and brandy. Remembering the axiom from the Customs and Courtesies classes at West Point, "beer on whiskey, mighty risky," or was it "whiskey on beer, have no fear," or something to that effect, Ed stuck with beer.

Bushman didn't. Neither did Eisenvald, but Bush was the one who had his tongue greased by the libation. The more he drank, the funnier he got, and he drank a lot. Along about noon, he started describing to the team from Dong Heng all about their experiences on the Xe Bangfai and their subsequent patrol, and the guy should have been on TV, he was so funny. Ed laughed so hard he thought his side was going to split. Even though he had been present for most of what Bushman described, he'd had no idea it was so funny. Now, in truth, the sergeant did bend the facts around just a little bit to compliment his tales, but not too much—he just viewed things a little differently from the way they had seemed to Ed. Some of the details he could have omitted, like the part about the condition of Ed's trousers after that Woman-in-the-Square episode, but, although the team laughed heartily at the story, they didn't seem to hold it against the lieutenant that he was known to have a weak sphincter. Quite the contrary, they drank a hearty toast to Lieutenant Shit Pants and laughed some more. Oh, well!

They had dinner with the team, fresh roasted kwi, prepared especially for this occasion, green somethings that looked like beans but tasted a heap sight different, and even a dessert of date nut roll from the C-ration stockpile. After eating, and while Bush was winding up his story of the major chewing them out, Lieutenant Fortner, the team XO, took Meadows on a tour of their defensive capabilities. Inside the bunker beneath the house was a machine-gun, a .30 calibre M1919A6, a Bazooka, tons of grenades of every shape and description, adequate ammunition to repel a division, and the crowning jewel was the placement of charges beneath some barrels of jellied gasoline they had placed at several points throughout the village. Fougasse, alias napalm. Ed had seen it set off in demonstrations at Ft. Benning. It created a veritable Hell on Earth, but was a nice touch as a last line of defense if you were about to be overrun. They had done a good job, and Ed congratulated Fortner. "You have a nice set-up here."

"Thanks. I guess we could take out a few if the time came, but we ain't seen any action at all. I've been here five months, and ain't fired a shot in anger; you've been here about one month and got the whole place in an uproar. I'm envious." Maybe that look at the airport when they came in from Ban Na Deng wasn't imagined, nor the different attitude exhibited by the B Team members. *They were jealous, by golly, the veterans were jealous of the action Ed had been involved in. Sonofabitch, who could know such a thing?*

Returning to the house in the middle of the afternoon, Ed found Bushman still holding forth, but now he was so drunk he was having trouble finishing one of the tales he started. Eisenvald was no better.

Meadows' head was buzzing, but he realized he was the only one he was going to trust to drive them back to Xeno. He waited for a polite period, then said to his two travelling companions, "Say, Fellows, if we're gonna get back home tonight, we better get started. You're both too drunk to drive, and it won't be long before I join you, so we better hit the road." To his surprise, his men agreed. They said their goodbyes all around, cussed each other out as was the ritual, and staggered out to their jeep.

Bush crawled into the back, laid his BAR across his lap, and declared to the team before they left, "You guys stick around. With ole Boss around, we'll be back with some more stories in a few days." Subsequent events would prove him a prophet without parallel.

Eisenvald got in the rider's seat and Ed took the position behind the wheel. He was glad he had his International Drivers' License in his billfold, for he was certainly too drunk to drive with the New York license. The engine sputtered to life, he let out the clutch, and killed the motor without any trouble at all. On the second try, he did the same thing, but the third time was the charm and they were on their way back to Xeno.

Had there been any options about which road to take, the men from Xeno could have been in some trouble, but there was only one road and it led out of town, and that's the way they went. As the jeep bounced and jostled along, Meadows tried to clear his head and take stock of their situation. He was sure that every PL for miles around was aware of the fact that they had been to Dong Heng, and was probably aware that they were now homeward bound in a state not quite approaching fully alert. It would be an ideal time to capture or waste some Americans.

"Eisenvald, keep your eyes peeled over there. We don't want the PL to end our party out here in the boonies." Eisenvald grunted and pulled the bolt back on his weapon.

"Right, Sir, I gotcha covered." At least, that's what Ed thought he said. His words were so slurred it was hard to determine exactly what he did say, and it certainly didn't make Ed feel secure to know his flank was so covered.

"Bush, you okay?"

"Fucking A, Boss, I'm with you. You got no worries behind." At that moment, Meadows' biggest worry was the man speaking these words of reassurance. There were a couple of hours of daylight left, so if the jeep kept running, there was no reason they shouldn't be tucked safely in their beds at Xeno by nightfall. Well, if you considered a countryside of enemy soldiers no reason. So far, the jeep was running, and they were about halfway home before they saw anyone along the road. Eisenvald was the first to see them.

"Couple of troops on my side of the road, Sir."

"Right, I see them. Bush, you awake?"

"Snalridght, Boss, Gotshacoverrrsted." Right, wide awake.

"What's that they're carrying, Sergeant?" Meadows asked Eisenvald.

"Looks like crossbows, Sir, must be 'Yards from Viet Nam." The Montagnards over across the border in Viet Nam were a fiercely independent race of people who had been recruited by the various powers in Indo-China for years. They specialized in making and using a rather ingenious crossbow with which they were deadly accurate. We didn't have any teams training 'Yards in Laos at the present time, as far as Ed knew.

"Better keep an eye on them," said Ed as they approached the two figures strolling down the side of the road. He was glad to see that the men were wearing black pajama bottoms and white shirts; at least they weren't in the dark green of the PL. As the jeep neared, the two 'Yards looked around but continued their walking. Ed relaxed and turned his attention to the road ahead. It was probably dumb to suspect every local yokel of being the enemy.

Suddenly, one of the Montagnards dove headlong into the bushes bordering the road and the other turned to face the jeep. Meadows wasn't sure whether he was in the act of raising his crossbow or not, he could have been, but the question became moot as the heavy .45 calibre bullets from the barking weapon in Eisenvald's hands thudded into his body, knocking him sprawling into the bushes after his comrade. "Get the fuck out of here, Lieutenant," Eisenvald yelled. As Ed mashed the accelerator to the floor, he heard Bush open up with his BAR from the rear seat. There was the smell of gunpowder, a cloud of smoke, and the scene of the shooting was soon hidden by the dust plume raised by the jeep as they bounced down the road. Meadows could see Eisenvald replacing the spent magazine in the Thompson and he heard Bush doing the same in his weapon. For two or three minutes they drove on in the hell bent for leather pace before Meadows even thought of slowing down. He kept swerving the jeep from one side of the road to the other so as to present the most elusive target to anyone trying to draw a bead on them, and when they finally rounded a bend in the road, he slowed down to look over at the sergeant next to him. All evidence of an alcoholic haze was gone, Eisenvald was wide awake and alert as Ed had ever seen him. He glanced around at Bush and found that he, too, was showing every sign of the fully alert trooper.

"Hey, Eisenvald, how did you know those guys were PL?"

"I didn't. Nobody knows. They may not have been. You just can't take no chances with people like that. You just never know."

Meadows thought that statement over as they got on closer to Xeno. It was not realistic to go around killing everyone who looked at you funny, but one of those who did come upon you was bound to be after your hide. It must have been nice in World War II for the bad guys to wear those helmets with the ear covers and to be dressed in grey or black. This was the pits. You could wind up killing a good guy with no trouble at all, or, worse yet, you might let a bad guy go. Who could know such a thing? Ed thought of something else. He had been drunk a time or two in his life, and there were times when he was sure he could not walk a straight line, but never had he been so drunk that he did not know what he was doing. He suspected that other people were in the same boat. Now he was sure of it. As drunk as Eisenvald and Bush had been, and they had plenty of reason for so being, they had still recognized danger for what it was. Intoxication was no reason for a failure to accept responsibility for your actions. You might fail to react as quickly, and your reaction may be impaired, but you were still responsible for what you did or did not do. Meadows was going to remember that.

27

A Workman Is Worthy Of His Hire

As soon as the trio returned to Xeno, Ed looked up his team sergeant. Unfortunately, Flag was involved in the poker game, and matters of warfare and dying took second place to poker. When the current hand was finished, Ed requested that Flagstone excuse himself for a couple of hands and come talk with him. Reluctantly, Flag agreed. Ed went over the details of the entire trip, and sought his elder statesman's advice on what they should do about it. A failure to report a shooting was a serious breach of their standing orders, but FTT-19 had been so involved with the hierarchy at the B Team that Meadows was a little reluctant to stir up the fire anymore than was absolutely necessary. As long as the three of them kept their mouths shut, it was highly unlikely that news of the shooting on Highway 9 would get out. There were only two other persons who knew of it, and at least one of them was in no condition to report anything, perhaps neither of them were. On the other hand, assuming that the two other parties were hostiles, it would be foolish for them not to warn the team at Dong Heng, at least, for they travelled that road almost daily, and they needed to be appraised of all hostile acts thereon. Flagstone listened to the tale, then thought over what he had heard. It was a tough decision.

"Boss, let me go into Savan in the morning and talk to the sergeant major. I'll tell him our need to stay out of the spotlight and see what he has to say about it. He's a good head, he'll understand."

"Good idea, Flag. I'll tell Bush and Eisenvald to cool it and keep their mouths shut. We'll wait for you to get back here before we say anything." It seemed like a good plan, and it probably would have worked, except for the Lao. There was a patrol from the 11th BP out on the road from Dong Heng, and they had heard the sound of the automatic weapons fire that afternoon, but they had seen nothing. A little later they came across the two dead Montagnards, and, seeing no one else around, they had decided to take credit for killing the two alleged PL's. Early the next morning, before Flag had even started for Savannahkhet, they came into the camp at Xeno carrying the two corpses and bragging about their bravery in bagging these enemy troops. Colonel Khom personally congratulated them and made a big to-do about how alert and brave his troops had been. He paraded up to the Regimental Headquarters with the bodies and told his colonel all about his troops' exploits. It seemed this wasn't the first ambush some PL had attempted of late, and the FAR powers that be called a conference to see what could be done to make the highway safe for travel. Major Murphy was called in from Savan by the Regimental CO to participate in the planning, and late in the afternoon the conference began. Meadows volunteered the services of Charlie to Major Murphy, assuring him that Charlie was the best interpreter around, and instructing Charlie to remember everything that was said so he could report to Ed when it was over.

The conference lasted well into the night. It began with several score of Lao officials present, but bit by bit the participants were reduced until only Major Murphy, LTC Khom, the Regimental CO, and Charlie were left. They remained huddled together until well after midnight. When the confab finally broke up, Major Murphy came by Meadows' hooch and called him outside. "Lieutenant, we have big plans for the BP beginning in a day or so. I have some things to work out with my staff, and I need to go to Vientiane to meet with Colonel Suomi and get his approval on them. I want you to come into town day after tomorrow with your team sergeant and get with us, say about 1000 hrs. I can't say anymore right now cause the whole thing may fall through, but let me work on it. See you in two days."

"Yes, Sir, we'll be there. Sir, we have plenty of room here and you're welcome to spend the night rather than go into Savan at this time of night."

"Thanks, Meadows, but I'll be okay with my driver."

"We could spare a couple of men to go with you. We ain't doing much here."

"Well, thanks, Lieutenant, that might be a good idea. How soon can they be ready to go?"

"They're ready now. Excuse me a minute, Sir." Ed called Riley and Flagstone over and talked to them briefly. The two men got their weapons and crawled into the back of the Major's jeep. Ed saluted the departing major, and when they had driven out through the gate, Meadows went back inside.

"Charlie, get your Siamese ass over here and fill me in." Charlie smiled his sheepish grin and came over to sit by Ed. He told how the conference had started with lots of bravado and condemning of the PL, but after all the *ke kwi* was over and the bigwigs had gone home, they got down to talking about some action by the FAR. It had been decided to have the BP sweep the road all the way from Xeno to a place called Tchepone. Ed got out his map and located the town. It was almost on the Vietnamese border, not far from a village in that country called Khe Sanh. Sonofabitch! That was over 125 klicks of road to sweep! It could take a month. There was a U.S. team at Dong Heng, of course, and another at Phulan further out the road, but the next 75 klicks was definitely Indian Country, Comanche Country, hostile territory.

Tchepone was known as a staging area for the Viet Minh infiltrating both Laos and South Vietnam and sat on what was called the Ho Chi Minh Trail. Wow! This was big stuff. They were talking about a major operation into the heart of the PL country, and Viet Minh, too. Charlie continued. The commanders realized that an operation this big was bound to draw the PL's attention, so they planned on a quick strike to secure the airfield at Tchepone, land the rest of the BP, then take off into the woods, raise as much hell as possible, and make their way back to Highway 9 and come back west until they could be picked up by trucks. They were figuring on three days for the whole deal.

Ed studied the map and matched it up with his knowledge of American positions and suspected PL concentrations. This began to look like either a masterful stroke of harassment, or the sacrifice of the 11th Battalion Parachute and their attached American advisors. The thought of dying in Laos, or, worse yet, becoming a prisoner of Uncle Ho, was not at all appealing to him. The thought of striking a major blow to the cocky PL and the Viet Minh who "weren't really here" appealed to him a great deal, however. Meadows was anxious to talk with Murphy.

The next morning, Ed called a team meeting with Bush and Eason, the only other members there, swore them to secrecy, and revealed the plan to his men. Bushman smiled at the prospect and said he wanted to go to Savan and start getting some stuff together. For some reason, "stuff" sounded like "demolitions" to Ed. Eason was silent. He sat and listened, then said he needed to work on his commo gear. It was hard for Meadows to figure out what Eason was thinking. Bush was released to catch a ride into town where he was to brief Flag and Riley while he got his "stuff," then all three of them were to return to Xeno before dark. Ed figured Flag would have some poop from Savan that he needed to share before they met with the Major tomorrow.

Bright and early on Sunday, the 15th of April, the members of FTT-19(-) (the "-" was in commemoration of Beaudreau) were standing tall at the B Team house in Savannahkhet waiting for word from the sergeant major that the meeting with Major Murphy was on. It was, for 1000 hrs, just as the major had told them a couple of days ago. He had arrived back from Vientiane early that morning and was briefing his staff on the plan that was so secret only FTT-19(-) and the Lao Army knew of it. Plus the Thai, don't forget the Thai: Charlie's mother, poor lady, had to be visited right on schedule. Ed forbade any drinking by the team members, even of beer, for he wanted no excuse for the B Detachment's jealous ones to replace them. Top called them into the conference room at 1000 hrs (damn, but the major was punctual). They sat around on the chairs provided after going through the "Real Army" ritual of greeting—salutes instead of sonofabitches. Major Murphy announced that the smoking lamp was lit, so Flag, Bush, and Riley lit cigarettes as Ed fired up a Dutch Master President. (Here we go men, get ready for some really secret stuff.)

"Lieutenant, I want you and your men to understand this operation has been classified Top Secret," began the major, "and is on a need-to-know basis only. No one outside this room and the CO's office in Vientiane is to know about it. Even Ft. Bragg won't know until after the thing is well underway. I shall brief you in the overall picture, then we'll try to work out any problems you foresee with the staff here. This is the story. LTC Khom has informed the French Embassy in Vientiane that he and his 11th BP wishes to defect to the other side to join with his friend Kong Le in the third party power in this country. Since his battalion is located at Xeno, the only way he can get them to the other side quickly enough to avoid a fight is by air. The French have agreed to supply two C-46 aircraft flying two sorties each for Khom to get his men to Tchepone. He says that's enough. They'll leave Xeno this afternoon beginning at 1400 hrs for a flight to Vientiane, supposedly, but actually they'll fly to Tchepone. Our problem is to get your team on the aircraft without the French knowing it. They're happy as hell to smear egg on our faces by helping another battalion defect. Once on the ground, the 11th will conduct interdiction and harassing actions against enemy forces utilizing the Trail into Laos and Vietnam for three days, then pull back to Highway 9 and head here. At whatever point we can, we'll meet them with FAR troops and escort them back. Do you have any ideas about getting yourselves there?"

"I don't right now," replied Ed. "Do any of y'all?" Bush and Flag shook their heads. Riley started to say something, then shook his head. Eason, the 19-year-old hippie, saved the day.

"Excuse me, Sir, but why camouflage us? Why not just send us along? If the Frenchmen really want to embarrass us, what would be better than for a whole FTT to be captured?"

"Damn, Son, I like that," said the major. "Why didn't I think of that? That has a nice catch to it. We'll put you on the first plane with the colonel and you can act dumb like you don't suspect anything. That's a nice touch." There were some other "nice touches" they discussed, but since they wanted to be back at Xeno by 1300 hrs, the conference didn't last too long. "Are there any other questions?"

"I have one," said Riley as Meadows held his breath. You never knew what Harold was going to say. "What's to prevent Colonel Khom from really defecting once we're at Tchepone?" There was no valid reply.

On the way back to Xeno in the trusty 3/4, Ed talked with Flag and the other team members. They made a lot of plans, reviewed their bug-out preparations, and divided the team into one two man element and one three man: Flag and Ed, then Riley, Bush, and Eason. Bush showed them the stuff he'd gathered, and it was a lot of stuff, spelled d-e-m-o-l-i-t-i-o-n-s. "You know, Guys, I like the idea of the French flying us in. Those frogs ought to be good for something," Ed stated.

"They'll earn their keep one way or another," Flag replied. "Either we'll eat supper with Uncle Ho, or they'll catch hell from him for helping us kick some ass." The truck entered the base at Xeno and found the colonel waiting at their hooch.

"*Som bai*, my Let-ten-ant. How would you like to go with us to Vientiane?" All systems were GO.

28

Tweaking A Beard

There was something vaguely familiar about the loadmaster-crewchief on the French C-46 when Ed, along with 125 Lao tahans and Flag, boarded her that afternoon. The man avoided Meadows' eyes, but even from a mostly profile view, he strongly resembled another face Ed had seen in a restaurant in Xeno a few nights before. According to the aircraft facts stored in Ed's head, the C-46 normally carries about twice the load of a C-47, about 50 persons as opposed to 25, but here they were taxiing down to the runway with over a hundred well-armed tahans and the pilot seemed to have no cares at all. The plane swung onto the runway, revved up its engines as it accelerated down the strip, and lifted into the air without a hitch. The gear were retracted, the plane leveled off at about 3000', and the ride to Tchepone-Vientiane was a little bit bumpy. Meadows sat near the door where he could watch the ground slipping by beneath them. It seemed to be mostly unbroken stretches of verdant jungle.

As soon as the aircraft had cleared the ground at Xeno, the second of the French planes began its landing pattern. The plan was to have the aircraft spaced about thirty minutes apart, flying time to Tchepone, so that as one left to return to Xeno after delivering its first load, the second would be preparing to descend with its load. Therefore, when Ed's plane started slowing for the strip at Tchepone, the second plane had filled up at Xeno and was preparing to start up its engines. It didn't take long to descend from 3000′. The pilot lowered the gear, then the flaps, then he cut the engines and the big iron bird settled onto the runway at Xepone or, Tchepone, call it what you like, but don't call it the paved runway and modernistic terminal of Vientiane. The runway was hard-packed earth, or perhaps had once been macadam, but now it was rough. With a hard stand on the brakes and by reversing the props, the pilot was able to stop his craft within the confines of the field. Immediately, the tahans began "unassing" the cabin and Meadows and Flagstone joined right in. It was a long way to the ground, so most of the tahans and the Americans held onto the doorsill, did the last half of a pull-up and the front half of a PLF when they hit the ground. Ed did his usual butt-buster, scrambled to his feet, and followed the colonel in a sprint to the side of the field. Khom was very efficient as he dispatched his troops to secure the airstrip and the Lao troops moved out to form a perimeter smartly. Thanks again to K.K., the previous American advisor. Flag joined Meadows as they moved to the wood-line surrounding the field.

It was obvious this was not a defended installation, for the only people they ran across were a couple of "civilians" manning the fuel dump, which consisted of several 55-gallon drums of gasoline. Long before they had secured the strip, the airplane was on its way back to Xeno. When the second plane landed, Khom had his troops in a rough circle around the field, and he directed the second planeload to fill in the gaps in his coverage. It was 1600 hrs by the time the third load arrived, and the colonel directed this group down the dusty road leading east out of Tchepone. When the final load arrived, the colonel called all his men in and the entire 11th BP then moved east out of Tchepone. Patrols of ten men each were dispatched several hundred meters out in front, to the flanks, and behind the main body. These patrols were in walkie-talkie contact with his aide, Wat, and they had so far seen nothing. For a solid hour the troops moved at a brisk pace eastward from Tchepone before the colonel called a halt. He was smiling broadly when he came over to talk with Meadows.

"My Let-ten-ant, we have fooled the PL. Tonight we camp in the jungle near here, and tomorrow we find out where the enemy is and kick his ass." It was a relief of sorts to know that he said "kick" and not "kiss".

"Right," said Ed. "Colonel Khom, we are a little vague on what we're doing. Our orders were to get some prisoners, if possible, especially any Europeans, but we left in such a hurry that I don't know how we plan to do it."

"*Ba pin yang*, no sweat. We find him, we kick his ass. Lots of Viet Minh in this place. It is easy to hide in the jungle." That was an understatement. If you got off the road anywhere along here, you could easily lose a battalion of men in the first dozen steps. "I have been here before, with the French. There are many trails the Viet Minh use to send men to South Vietnam. Tomorrow there will be not so much jungle, then we find them. I must go meet with my officers now. We sleep not far away."

Thirty minutes more walking and the troops began fading into the jungle off the road to set up their positions for the night. The Americans stayed close to the colonel's headquarters. There were to be no fires, and the Lao were ordered by their commander to remain on 50% alert throughout the hours of darkness. The sun was still high enough in the sky to light the tops of the trees in the jungle canopy, but down here on the floor, it was so dark that visibility was only a few meters in any direction. The Americans stayed close together, and before it got so dark they couldn't see at all, Ed called them together. They reviewed the bug-out plans and distributed some of the stuff Bush had brought along. Each man got one green flare to be used to signal in case a bug-out was needed, and each man was empowered to call a bug-out if he deemed it necessary. Once it was dark, it was fully dark—I mean *really* dark. Flag stayed awake with Riley for the first shift, and they determined about four hours would be a good shift. Ed unrolled his poncho, then wrapped himself up in it, propped his back against a tree, and went to sleep.

The watch on Ed's lapel indicated it was 0430 hrs when Flag shook him awake. "Bothth," he lisped, "time to wake up. Buthh ith about ten meterth to your left and he'th awake. Riley and Eathon are next to him. I'll thleep right next to you. Be awake, Bothth, cauthe there'th been people with flathhlightth walking down the trail all night long. Everything elthe ith quiet. Wake me up in a couple of hourth." Meadows couldn't see Flag as he settled down to catch a few Z's, but his regular breathing told Ed that Flag slept quickly.

It was oppressively quiet and dark as Ed stared into the night around him. There were no sounds at all from the Lao nearby, but about fifty meters away he heard some scruffing on the road and saw the dim glow of a flashlight as it moved back toward the west. Probably some PL's, or Viet Minh, or Viet Cong, or some other shade of Viet going to Tchepone. For a few minutes it was quiet and then another group passed by. If they were looking for the battalion, they weren't doing a very good job, but Ed guessed, rightly, that these troops had no idea there were any FAR troops in the vicinity. Once they got to the town, though, and talked with the inhabitants, that would change. Working in the favor of the Laotian Battalion was the fact that these troops were not prepared to deal with infiltrators. They were young recruits who had recently finished training at one of the North Vietnamese camps and were on their way south to infiltrate themselves, and they had received no orders and no training on dealing with an aggressive enemy in their own backyard. As the light began to glow over their heads in the trees, traffic on the trail ceased. It was 0600 hrs. Meadows shook Flagstone.

"I'm awake. Anything happen?"

"Nothing but what you thaid. Troopth on the trail. That'th all."

"Let'th wake up the otherth and go thee the colonel," Flag suggested.

Colonel Khom was already up. He had a map spread on the ground and was talking with his four company commanders. "*Som bai*, Letten-ant," smiled the colonel. "Come join us."

"*Som bai de*, Colonel Khom. Thank you. What's going on?"

"We are here," said Khom, indicating an area just to the northwest of the town of Dong. "When it is light, we will capture the town. There is a valley (Charlie was translating) here to the north where the Trail runs through. I will put some scouts at the north of the valley to watch for some enemy troops. When they see them, we will make an ambush in the valley and kick their ass. Dong is where the Trail meets Highway 9 and there may be troops in the town. We'll get some prisoners there. Tonight we'll sleep in the jungle west of the valley, then tomorrow we go back toward Xepone. Pretty soon this place will have many Viet Minh, but we will be on the way home."

Ed nodded. "What if the troops that passed headed for Tchepone come up behind us?"

"*Ba pin yang*. We leave some men here to warn us. Let's go to Dong," he said as he folded up his map and handed it to Lek.

Ed turned to Flag. "Sarge, put Bush, Eason, and Riley with Captain

Praseuth's Company. We'll stay with the colonel. We'll get back together tonight. Charlie will stay with us, and Sam the Second will go with them."

"Done, Boss," said Flag as he left to tell the men. Captain Praseuth's company led the way as the battalion grouped on the road and headed toward Dong. As his three men filed by, Ed gave them the thumbs-up signal and received the same in return from Riley and Eason. Bushman smiled broadly and flipped the lieutenant the finger. Ed laughed. Bush would make a good clown in any circus. The colonel's group followed Praseuth's company by a couple of hundred meters, then the other three companies strung out behind. The jungle was thinning out and through the breaks in the trees, Ed could see they were approaching an area of population. Suddenly there was some gunfire up ahead, a few scattered shots, then some heavy firing, then a few more shots. Colonel Khom ran ahead, with Ed and Flag close behind. Meadows pushed the safety off the Remington as he ran.

Breaking into a clearing, Ed saw the village of Dong and the men of the lead company moving into it. Two bodies lay on the road, dressed in dark green uniforms, and when Meadows reached them, he saw they were quite dead. Lying next to each of them were Soviet PPs submachine guns. They didn't pause, but ran on ahead to the village where sporadic firing was continuing. He thought he heard the staccato thumping of Bush's BAR, but it was hard to tell. Outside one of the huts near the edge of town were several more bodies, including a couple of BP tahans. He passed a man sitting next to another hut with a bandage wrapped around his leg, blood-soaked, one of the BP tahans. In the village square, there were some dark green clad troops sitting with their hands tied behind them and several tahans standing guard. Khom chose a large hut on the square and set up his headquarters. He began dispatching runners from there as the other companies caught up, and Ed sent Charlie over to monitor what was going on. "Flag, see if you can find our guys and check on them." Flagstone waved, grabbed his rifle, and set out. For the next twenty minutes or so, there were people running all over the place. More prisoners were brought in until there were a score or more, and then some more wounded straggled in. The Lao medics began treating them, cutting away clothing and wrapping bandages around bleeding limbs and bellies. Gradually the firing dwindled away so Ed sought out the colonel and Charlie for an update.

Colonel Khom was listening to one of his runners. He looked over at Ed and managed one of his smiles. "Come in, come in," he said as he gestured Ed over. "We have secured the village. Viet Minh soldiers were here but they ran away. My men are chasing them. Patrols are out as we planned. Sit down, we have some tea, and wait for word from them."

"Thank you, Sir. What about the prisoners?"

"All Vietnamese, don't speak Lao. We talk to them in French. No officers, no Russians. Have some tea, we wait." Ed sat down.

Flagstone returned with Riley and Eason. They were okay. Bush was alright, but there were some huts filled with rice and an old vehicle which he was wiring with explosives. Something to remind the Viets of the BP's presence when they returned. Meadows dispatched Riley to help the Lao medics care for the wounded, and he told Eason to contact the B Team and tell them where they were and that they were okay. He sent Charlie and Sam to crank the generator.

"Flag, let's have a look around."

The two men spent an half-hour inspecting Dong. It wasn't much of a village, mostly thatched huts, but there were a couple of the stucco houses favored by the French during their days here. Tahans were busy dragging dead bodies toward the village square where some of the prisoners were put to work digging graves. All together, about fifteen men had died in the First Battle of Dong—eleven Viets and four tahans. What civilians there were had been shepherded to the square and were now clustered in a couple of the huts nearby. Tahans were enjoying themselves tormenting the prisoners and the civilians, and Ed didn't want to know what was happening inside those huts. He couldn't have done anything about it, anyway.

Standing in the square when they finished, Ed looked northwards up the well-travelled trail leading to North Vietnam. Highway 9 intersected the trail at this particular spot. There were lots of other trails through the jungle, of course, but as he stood there watching Bush wire the dilapidated Peugeot, it occurred to Meadows that he was standing astride the Ho Chi Minh Trail at this intersection, and the FAR owned the real estate for the time being. *How about them apples, Uncle Ho?* he thought. *We've cut your fucking trail. And you ain't seen nothing yet.*

29

And Away We Go

By late in the afternoon, Eason had contacted the B Team a couple of times and sent rather lengthy messages written by Ed describing their position and situation. They encoded the reports on the Diana pads, so even if the Viet Minh were monitoring their transmissions, they would be receiving only a bunch of five letter groups that would mean nothing unless you happened to have the matching pad at your reception station. Since there were only two of these particular pads in the world, one at the B Team and one with Eason, it was doubtful the communists learned anything. A direction finder team could probably have pin-pointed their location, but Ed gambled that such sophisticated equipment was not available nearby. It wasn't, but miles away in a location in North Vietnam, there was such equipment, in more than one location as a matter of fact, and the town of Dong was circled on one of their maps being studied through the olive-shaped eyes of a Viet Minh colonel. He issued some orders, and soon after the transmissions were intercepted, a tracker team of the North Vietnamese Army was dispatched toward Dong with all haste.

Meanwhile, a runner from one of Colonel Khom's patrols to the north arrived at Dong with word that a large body of Pathet Lao troops was arriving at the village of Ban Xiangbom and appeared to be preparing to spend the night. Khom and Ed studied their map. Ban Xiangbom was only 15 klicks away from Dong, an easy march even for a large body of troops. If they were spending the night there, it was a good bet they would be moving on toward Dong tomorrow. Flagstone came over to join in the discussion the officers were having. There was no way of knowing if the PL knew about the 11th being in Dong. In all probability, they did not. Radio communication among the troops moving out of the North was rare, and, unless someone from the day's battle had reached Ban Xiangbom after escaping from the FAR, news of the battle probably hadn't reached them yet. Flag said they needed a prisoner, to question him, and various plans for snatching one of the PL from Xiangbom were discussed. It could be done, of course, but getting him back here and finding out what they needed to know would take time, and could alert the PL. On the other hand, if they were unaware of the BP's presence, and if they were coming to Dong tomorrow, it would be an excellent chance to ambush them along the trail and wreak havoc with whatever large body of troops this was. It was getting dark, so a decision on what to do had to be made soon.

Ed spoke first. "Sir," he said to the colonel. "I think this is the chance we have been waiting for. I don't think they know we're here. I suggest we pull off an ambush in the valley you mentioned in the morning, shoot them up good, get us some prisoners, and head on back to Xeno. We can't stay here forever, and the longer they have to react, the worse our chances are going to be on the way home."

The colonel looked at Flag. The sergeant thought for a minute more. "I agree with the Boss, Colonel. I wonder if we ought to move up to the valley tonight, and catch them when they first come out of Xiangbom tomorrow." It was Khom's turn.

"Let-ten-ant, you are right. But I think my men need rest tonight. The PL will not start early for here. It is close, and they will wait until the sun is well up before they come south. We sleep here tonight and my men can rest. Early in the morning, we go to the valley. We will be ready for them when they get halfway here and we kick their ass." Charlie translated.

"What time do we start, Sir?" asked Ed.

"0500 hrs. No fires. 50% alert. We sleep now."

Ed, Flag, and Charlie left the hut and went over to where the other Americans and Sam were waiting. They decided to sleep on the edge of the jungle just on the north side of Dong. All of them were a little uneasy about this PL force, and if they were wrong in their belief that the PL were staying at Xiangbom tonight, they wanted to be near the woods to aid in their bug-out attempt. If it were needed. If the PL came. If the BP didn't defect. If the sun rose. No ifs, ands, or buts about it, they would stay on 50% alert tonight. Flag had been up most of the previous night, so Meadows let him skip the guard rotation. He and Eason would take the first three-hour shift, Riley and Sam the second, and Bush and Charlie the third. They ate some cold gummy rice with tabasco sauce sprinkled on, then each man found him a comfortable dirt clod and settled down for the night.

0500 hrs came early, as it does everywhere in the world. In the half-light of the greying morning, the BP tahans could be seen assembling in the village square. One company was going to remain in Dong as a rear guard, and to secure the battalion's prisoners. They would also try to keep any of the civilians from getting away and taking the word to Xiangbom. An advance element was sent out to prevent any surprises, and the colonel told Ed of his plans. They seemed sound. By 0600 hrs, only a few soldiers could be seen in the streets of Dong, the others either on their way to meet the PL, or under the cover of the huts of the town. To any passing aerial observer, of which there were none, things would have seemed pretty normal in Dong, Laos.

About ten klicks out of town, the trail began a gradual rise which culminated in a rather precipitous drop into a shallow valley. The east and west sides of the valley were low ridgelines which gradually petered out into the savannah where Xiangbom was located. One company of Khom's men turned right at the top of the rise, made their way along the reverse slope of the ridge on the east, and took up positions at the crest of the ridge facing west. The second company performed a similar maneuver on the western ridge and wound up facing the east. At this point, the ridges were about 200 meters apart. LTC Khom and his headquarters joined the third company which took up positions right on the top of the rise blocking the trail. Bush, Eason, Riley, and Sam the Second went with the company on the western ridge. Flag and Ed stayed with the colonel's group and Charlie stayed near Ed. Meadows found himself a position just west of the road and settled down in the lush grass growing there. Then Charlie lay down, and Flag was to Charlie's left. The waiting began.

From Ed's viewpoint, he could see the entire valley. The walls of the jungle to the west were a good hundred meters away, while to the east there was nothing but rolling grassland for miles. This was his reason for sending the other element of the team to the western slope. The old bug-out plan, you know. He could barely see the location of Xiangbom, but it was too far away to make out any details. He wished for the field glasses he had left at Xeno, but they remained at Xeno. Although he knew where the rest of the troops were, there was nothing moving, no smoking, no hint of their presence now. The troops of the 11th BP could do some things surprisingly well. As he studied the landscape, Ed began to make out some troops on the trail coming out of Xiangbom. From this range, they looked like a column of ants, just little dots on the trail, but as he looked and waited, the column got longer and longer. He estimated that the forward elements were a couple of klicks out of town now, and still there was no end of the column. Sonofabitch! When the scouts said a large body of troops, they meant a *large body*. Another klick covered by the lead troops, and still the column didn't end. They were walking two and three abreast, Ed could see, and the line was stretching for a good three klicks. There must be at least a battalion, possibly even a regiment, heading their way. It was too late to pull the 11th out now. The FAR soldiers were going to have to rely on the element of complete surprise to pull this trick off. What had seemed to be a good plan to wipe out a company of enemy soldiers was beginning to look like a very tenuous plan to disrupt a regiment of bad guys. The action hadn't even started yet, and already it was getting scary.

Meadows could see the PL clearly now. They were dressed in what appeared to be U.S.-type fatigues, compliments of the French, no doubt, and were carrying rifles. Most of the FAR tahans carried carbines with a few M-1's. Ed wished they had some automatic weapons, maybe an hundred BAR's like Bush's. He could see the PL troops were sweating as they toiled up the hill toward the top of the rise. They weren't carrying much equipment, a small pack on each man's back, nothing heavy. One more thing caught Ed's eye. Each of the PL soldiers had an orange cloth wrapped around his left sleeve, the saffron-colored cloth the Buddhist monks wore back in Savannahkhet. That seemed strange. He checked the Remington, making sure the safety was off and a round was in the chamber. Colonel Khom was to initiate the ambush, and with the first troops barely fifty meters away, Meadows wondered when he was going to start the ball rolling.

Forty meters. They couldn't let the PL pass, for signs of the BP's passing were all over the trail behind them. Thirty meters. Just the right range for the OO buckshot in the shotgun. Twenty meters. Colonel Khom wasn't defecting, was he? The thought hit Ed in the pit of his stomach and began to gnaw a hole there. Ten meters. I ain't gonna let these guys walk all over me, thought Ed. From the distance of five meters, even the grass no longer concealed the hidden troops, and one of the PL saw something in the trail ahead of him. He pointed his finger and started to say something, but the colonel's carbine rounds stifled his words and ended his life before he could speak.

Firing all up and down the line broke out immediately. Meadows shot at one of the first PL, saw him fall, jacked another round into the chamber, and fired at another figure. He, too, fell. The mass of targets which had been present only an instant before had dwindled to only a few fleeing figures now, but Meadows picked one out, shot at him, and when he continued to run, he fired again. Rising to his knees for a better view, Ed shot at another man, then heard the hammer click on an empty chamber. Digging into his bandolier, Meadows stuffed five more rounds in the shotgun and took stock of the situation.

The ambush of the BP had worked well. There were dozens of bodies strewn over the trail for a distance of four or five hundred meters and the firing was continuing from the ridgelines unabated. The first elements of the PL column had been wiped out, and the rest were seemingly in a headlong retreat. Just out of range of the carbines, there was a great milling about in the PL ranks as their leaders tried to get them organized. Flag was lying on the ground about ten meters away sniping at the retreating PL, and Ed moved over to join him. "We got 'em pretty good, Flag."

"Boss, we're in a world of shit. If those guys get organized, they're gonna be back up here to kick our ass. We need to keep 'em running." He fired another round.

"I'll go get the colonel to chase 'em," said Meadows as he ducked off to the right. He found the colonel sitting in the middle of the trail, wreathed in smiles, firing his carbine ineffectively at the PL half a mile away. "Colonel, we need to go after them, keep them on the run."

"No sweat, my Let-ten-ant. Let them come back. We kick their ass again."

"Sir, there's too many of them. They can over-run us."

"We have good positions. They can't beat us. We stay here until dark." Maginot Line thinking. French thinking. Fucking frogs. Ed hustled back to Flagstone's position.

"He thinks we can hold them off till dark, Flag. I hope he's right."

"We'll find out soon enough. Look at those fuckers down there. See that big one doing all the traffic directing? He's a Russian or a frog, I'll bet a month's pay. I been trying to knock him off, but he's too far away for more than luck." Ed looked as directed. He estimated the range as about 500 meters, a long shot, but not impossible.

"Try again, Flag, you might hit him." Flagstone squeezed off another shot. One of the troops near the European fell, but the taller figure kept working to turn his troops around.

"No use, Boss, he's too far. Maybe he'll come closer. Let's wait." They waited. The PL had stopped running and were beginning to get organized. They set up a machine gun and began exchanging fire with the troops on the eastern slope. A line of troops was stringing out across the valley in a "V" shaped formation, several deep, and it was obvious they intended to come back up here for another go. Ed looked at his watch. It was 1400 hrs. Another machine gun was set up to engage the troops on the western slope and it began doing its job. To the rear of the "V," yet another body of PL soldiers was formed up and began moving toward the other side of the eastern ridgeline. More troops arrived and they were dispatched toward the west. *Sonofabitch,* thought Ed, *a double pincer movement with a frontal assault. Somebody down there knew his business.* If the troops on the ridgelines held, they'd be okay, but if they were flanked, or broke and ran, this was going to be a very undesirable place to be located in a very short period of time.

"Boss, they're coming back," said Flag. "Better get down and get that blunderbuss of yours ready. Charlie, use that fucking weapon for something besides a club." Meadows watched the PL start up the valley toward them again. He couldn't see the flanking troops anymore. As the PL advanced within range of the FAR carbines, the firing from the ridges picked up again. Troops were falling in the PL ranks steadily, but on they came. When they were about a hundred meters away, Meadows joined in the fusillade with the Remington. He fired two full loads of five rounds each while the PL kept coming. There was firing from everywhere now, and some of the PL had reached the FAR positions. He saw two enemy soldiers advancing on Flag's position and downed them both with a single blast of the shotgun. Flagstone rose to his knees, hurled a grenade with an overhand, lobbing toss, yelled "Grenade!", and Meadows hit the ground. A muffled thump and a quiver of the ground signified that the bomblet had gone off, so Ed jumped up, looked around, and saw there were orange arm bands everywhere. He pulled the flare from his belt, reversed the cap, and hollered at Flagstone.

"Flag, get out of here! Head for the woods! Bug out!" So saying, Meadows hit the flare with his hand, there was a flash of white, and the green arc into the sky told the other Americans the game was over and it was time to go home. If there were any other Americans left. If they saw it. No time to worry about that now. Flagstone threw another grenade, and when it had gone off, both men jumped to their feet to head for the woodline.

Meadows looked for Charlie. He was lying right where he had been all along, between the two Americans, but now he was lying on his back, smiling, wrapping a piece of orange cloth around his left arm. Not even pausing to take aim, Ed fired at Charlie from a distance of about two feet. The heavy load of lead hit the small Thai just below the rib-cage in the middle of his gut. His body seemed to mash into the ground, then it just lay there. He was still smiling, but the life had left the smile and it was now a macabre grimace. Ed jacked another round into the chamber and ran after Flag. For fifty of the required hundred meters, they ran toward the woodline, but by zigging and zagging, they made the distance at least double. Flag stopped, dropped to one knee, and faced back the way they'd come. Several PL were hot on their trail. Between Flag and Meadows, they downed three of the pursuers and the others hit the ground themselves. Flag yelled at Ed to throw a grenade, so Ed pulled one from his belt, yanked out the pin, and threw it as far as he could. It landed in the middle of a group of three PL and they got up to run away from it. 4.2 seconds is not a long time, and from the time Ed released the spoon until the grenade went off, that's all the time that transpired. It took a couple of seconds for the grenade to reach the PL, another for them to see it, another to get up and start running, and you just can't run very far in 0.2 seconds. The fragments from the exploding charge hit the troops in their backs, their legs, their heads, and they gave up the chase.

Flagstone told Ed to throw his smoke grenade out in front of them and the sergeant did the same with his, but off to their right. As the purple smoke billowed forth, it provided them with a small screen from the other PL, so the two Americans ran like hell for the trees. Ed reached them first, not bad for a guy with fat thighs who stopped a few yards short on the PT run. He went into the trees a few yards, then waited for Flag, who was right behind him. Together, they moved a hundred meters into the dense jungle, then found a tree with big roots they could hide in and squatted down.

Both of them were breathing hard. Each of them was scared. They waited a few minutes, ears open, eyes open, mouths open, but sphincters, gratefully, closed. Ed whispered, "Do you think they'll follow us in here?"

"I don't think so. Not right away. Let's wait a minute to make sure, though." They waited. Nothing was stirring. There was no wind, no breeze, no movement, no nothing. They could hear some shots out in the savannah, but they were dull and far away. More minutes of their lives passed.

"Flag, I shot Charlie."

"I know. I saw it. Forget it, Boss, fuck the little shit. I hope he's roasting in hell right now. To hell with that shit-head. How much ammo you got?"

Ed checked. "I've got eleven rounds for the shotgun, a hundred, no, ninety-nine, for the pistol, three grenades. That's it. And a knife, my Kabar."

"I ain't much better, got three clips for the M-1, eight shots for the pistol, and no grenades. We gotta get out of here."

"Did you see any of the other guys, Bush, or Riley, Eason?"

"No, but don't sweat them. If they were alive, they saw your signal and they're somewhere in these same woods right now. C'mon, Boss, we got some tracks to make before it gets dark." "Tracks" was an unfortunate choice of words.

30

When The Going Gets Tough...

With Flag leading the way, the two men left the relative sanctuary of the big-rooted tree and headed deeper into the jungle. They went north because, as Flag had explained it to Ed and Ed agreed, the PL expected them to go south. By now it was no secret they had landed at Tchepone, so that was one place they intended to stay away from. Both of them wanted to look for the other FTT members, but there was no sense in that at all. Even if they found them, and they were captured, or dead, they couldn't help. They could all die together, of course. Had the situation been reversed, they wouldn't want the other guys hanging around looking for them. Flag set a fast pace, considering the terrain they were in. With only an hour or so remaining before the oppressive darkness of the jungle surrounded them, they had to get as far away from their pursuers as possible. They avoided the temptation to follow a streamline, or to walk in a streambed, because the vegetation was too dense in the former case and they were too exposed in the latter. Flagstone moved carefully, despite his haste, and Ed tried to keep an eye on their trail, despite his hurry. They covered about two miles in that hour. It was too dark to do anything but blunder into trees now.

"Boss, we may as well stop here for the night. I figure we're about due west of Xiangbom, and this ain't where they'll be looking for us, if they even care."

"Yeah, I agree with you. If they got the other guys, I don't think they'll mess with looking for us very much. Three Americans would be enough of a prize; five wouldn't make much difference. I hope those guys got away."

"They probably did. Bush ain't gonna get captured. He may get killed, but he ain't gonna get caught. Neither will Riley. He's a good head, even if he does bitch a lot. I don't know about the kid, Eason, but if he's with them, he'll do okay. We got enough problems to worry about. Tomorrow is gonna be the critical time, so we better get some rest tonight. You want to watch or sleep first?"

"I'd rather watch. I'll wake you about midnight."

"Okay. If you gotta take a leak, or move around for any reason, wake me up first and let me know. I'd hate to shoot my favorite lieutenant for pissing in the jungle."

"Right. Same here. How we gonna handle this watching, I mean, where are you going to sleep while I watch? You want to split up?"

"Hell, no, Boss," said Flag with conviction. "You sit right where you are and I'm gonna sleep glued to your ass." That's the way they settled down for the night, side by side, the sergeant soon sound asleep and Ed wide awake.

There were gibbons in this part of Laos—apes that lived in the trees and loved to make a lot of whooping noises. Their cries were both welcome and frightening, for as long as they were whooping it up, there was probably no one moving on the jungle floor below, but whenever a new song began, it scared the hell out of Ed. He had stopped sweating and was now sitting there in his drenched uniform providing a feast for all the insects who happened along—and a lot of them happened along. At first, Meadows tried to shrug them off, he wasn't about to slap at them, but his shrugging disturbed Flag, so he stopped that and just sat there offering his body as a living sacrifice to the bugs.

He could see nothing, of course, but he hoped any errant PL would be kind enough to shine a light if they came his way. Before long, even the gibbons got quiet and only the hum of the mosquitos and the croaking and chirping of the lesser forms of life broke the stillness. Meadows tried to analyze their situation. There wasn't a whole lot to figure out. They were out here in the middle of Indian Country, alone, miles and miles away from any assistance, and the B Team wasn't even going to start worrying about them for at least another day. Once they started worrying, there was little more they could do than worry. If every member of the White Star team came looking for them, there was a good chance they wouldn't find them. No, it would be up to him and Flag to find a way to contact their own kind, or else they'd have to walk back to Xeno, or Dong Heng, at least. That was only about fifty miles of jungle and angry PL's away. *Gotta think of another plan.*

Due west of them was the Xe Bangfai area where Kong Le was anxious to come up with some American prisoners. Zero percentage of survival in heading that way. To the east was Vietnam. That was out. No U.S. teams to the south until you got down to the Plateau de Bolevens, and that was a couple of hundred miles of PL infested jungle away. North, well, there was nothing friendly about the north. The situation was grim. No doubt, once the B Team started looking for them, they'd use Hotel X-ray, and maybe the other two helicopters in country, plus some of the other air assets available. What he and Flag needed to do was to get to a safe clearing where they could signal any airplane that flew over. The problem there was that the PL would probably be trying to make every clearing unsafe. Oh, well, they'd cross that bridge when they got to it.

Meadows figured it was about time to wake Flag, so he carefully raised his hand to his lapel to sneak a look at his watch. It was 2100 hrs. He had three more hours to stay awake. Ed thought about the other guys. He wondered what they were doing now, or if they were doing anything at all. The PL would have spotted Bush's position early in the fight, because he had that BAR, and they'd want to silence it as soon as they could. If any of the team was dead, Bush was the most likely candidate. Then there was Riley. He'd probably be okay, he lived a charmed life. Eason, well, he hoped Eason was okay. If he got out, he'd have made contact with the B Team by now and would speed the search party up. As for Sam, he could make it or not, Ed didn't really care. That damn Charlie. Why would he pull such a stunt? Ed really liked Charlie. He was a cute little fellow who had served them well. They had talked about Bangkok, and what all they were going to do when they visited there together. He would have been a lot of fun in his own city, showing the team around. Like Ed would have shown Charlie around Memphis, if he'd ever visited there. *I guess people do strange things when the going gets tough.* Meadows remembered the words of Coach Strickland at South Side High School when they were trailing Messick in the best football game in which he had ever participated. Coach said, "When the going gets tough, the tough get going," and the Scrappers had come back in the second half to down the Panthers, 28-20. He had felt tough that night, and by golly, he was still tough. He knew they may not survive this experience, but he intended to go down fighting, scrapping for every breath. If only there weren't so many of those damn PL out there!

At midnight, he shook Flag into consciousness, and reported to him that there was nothing going on. Closing his eyes to the hum of a million asiatic insects, Meadows fell asleep. He had hardly started breathing deeply, it seemed, when Flag woke him up. "It's a new day, Boss, time for us to wake up." A look at his watch confirmed Flag's words. 0500. Time for the tough to get going. They ate the last of their gummy rice, checked their weapons, and got up. Ed's legs ached from sitting cramped all night, but after a few minutes walking, the circulation returned and he felt a lot better. The men moved just a couple of hundred meters away from where they had spent the night, then Flag stopped and hunkered down. Ed joined him, but both of them kept a sharp lookout while they paused. "Boss, I did some thinking last night, and I want to see what you think about it. Lemme tell you what I figured out, then you tell me what you think about it. First off, we're in a world of shit. They ain't gonna find us out here. The way I figure it, we've gotta get back to our guys on our own, and we've gotta avoid any contact while we're doing it. I think we've lost any pursuit, so we've got plenty of time. The worst thing we could do would be to go running back toward Tchepone, or running anywhere else. It don't matter how long it takes us to get back, the Army keeps paying, anyway. We have canteens and there's plenty of water. I think we can find enough stuff to eat to stay alive (he sounded like ole Chubby Cheeks in Florida, "Survive!"), and as long as we don't get sick or split up, we oughta be okay. I figure in a couple of weeks, we can make Phulan or Dong Heng. What do you think?"

"I ain't got any better ideas. I thought about it last night, and I couldn't come up with anything better. We might get lucky and get spotted by some airplanes; I think they'll be looking for us."

"Oh, hell, yes, they'll be looking, but we gotta be careful about going out in the open. You can bet your ass the PL will be looking, too. I think we can make at least ten klicks a day with no problem. How's your water holding out?"

"I need to fill my canteen at the next stream we cross, but I'm okay for now. Hey, Flag, what's that?" asked Ed as he heard the sound of something beating the air. They listened. There was no mistaking the sound of the blades of a helicopter stirring up the air over the canopy of the jungle. It seemed to pass somewhere close by, then they could almost tell that it was settling to the ground. The whishing of the rotors lessened, as though the craft had landed, then it increased in tempo and disappeared from their hearing.

"I'll bet my ass that was the other guys getting picked up. That's good. They wouldn't be landing for any other reason," mused Flagstone.

"Right. Listen, give me your canteen and I'll go fill it up at the stream back behind us. We may as well start with a full load." Flag passed Ed the canteen, and Meadows started back the way they had just come. It was about two hundred meters to the swiftly flowing brook, and it took Ed a few minutes to reach it. He eased up to the water, watching the woods all around him for anything out of the ordinary. There was nothing. Dunking the water bottles into the water, he let them gurgle until they were full, then screwed on the caps and prepared to leave. Something moved in the underbrush on the other side of the creek. Ed lay down and watched. Some fifty meters away, there was a man in a khaki uniform studying the jungle floor. Behind him were several other men, similarly dressed. They were intent on whatever it was they were looking at on the ground. Ed could see the rifles they carried at the ready, and a couple of them had PPs's. No doubt about whose side they were on, but the khaki uniforms were new. Now the man in front was gesturing, and he started walking toward Ed, moving slowly, still with his eyes fixed on the ground. They were following the Americans' trail. Sliding backwards silently on the ground, Ed moved away from the stream, rose into a crouch once he was sure of a screen of bushes hiding him, and moved quickly back to where Flag was waiting.

"Sarge, get your ass in gear. We're being followed, and they ain't far behind. We gotta move. Follow me," and Meadows tossed the canteen to Flag, who was on his feet and ready to go. They stepped out quickly, heading west.

■ ■ ■

The phone rang in the house at 5155 Windham Road, in Whitehaven, Tennessee. Dr. Meadows answered. The voice at the other end of the line said, "Dr. Meadows? How are you today? This is Major Thurston, from the Special Warfare Center at Ft. Bragg. I'm calling about your son, Lieutenant Meadows. He was in some action over in Laos, and he and his men were separated from the friendly forces. There were five of them, and we have picked up three, so far. LT Meadows and the team sergeant, Flagstone, are still missing in action. We think they are alright, at least the other members of the team said they saw them get away into the jungle, and we think we know about where they are. They don't seem to be in any immediate danger, and we're confident that with the training they've had, and their own ingenuity, they'll come out of this in good shape. The area they are in is mostly heavy jungle, so we are having some difficulty in locating them to extract them. I know you will be worried, and there is cause for some concern, but I want you to know that everything possible is being done to insure their safe return. We'll let you know as soon as we find out anything more, and if it's okay with you, we'll be calling you daily to keep you posted on what we're doing." Ed's dad hung up the phone. He called his wife—Ed's mom, and told her what the voice from Ft. Bragg had said. Together, they knelt down and began a prayer vigil that would last until the end of this trouble, no matter what the outcome might be.

31

...The Tough Get Going

For a good two klicks they headed due west while keeping a brisk pace. Ed filled in Flag on what he had seen at the stream, especially the part about the khaki uniforms. Flag wanted to know if they were Asiatic troops, and Ed told him that as far as he could tell, they were all Southeast Asians, short, dark, and definitely Oriental features. They made a right angle turn and walked toward the south for a klick or so. Flagstone was very anxious to see who it was following them, and he figured if they headed south, as the PL would be supposed to expect that they would, they could double back after awhile and sneak a peek at their hunters. Meadows was as anxious as Flag to learn exactly who these trackers were. The day was young, and it was a good idea to get to know their enemy long before it got critical. Besides, if the hunters got a little careless or sloppy and strung out, perhaps he and Flag could pick off a couple of them and lower the odds. Flag asked for one of the three remaining grenades which Ed surrendered without a murmur. Turning west once more, they crossed a stream, refreshed their canteens, then headed north for several hundred meters. From their present position, they could see the path they had made on the other side of the creek a little while earlier. Flag found a place of dense brush behind which they could hide and they sat down to wait for the trackers. The wait wasn't very long.

There were two men out front of the main body now, one studying the trail, the other keeping a sharp lookout as they moved along. They were walking pretty quickly, confidently, and about ten meters behind them came the rest of their party, walking in single file, all dressed in khaki, all armed with either SKS semi-automatic rifles or PPs submachine guns. Meadows counted twenty-five of them in all. Once the last man had passed, the two Americans waited a couple of minutes to make sure there were no trailers, then they crossed the stream to the east and walked back north the way they had come. By their maneuvering, they had alerted the trackers to the fact that they were aware of their presence. When the head tracker saw where they had watched their platoon pass by, it would certainly cause them to slow down and exercise more caution as they moved. The game was on, hunted versus the hunters versus the hunted.

Right now, the hunted were both getting pretty hungry. They had nothing left to eat, and the small portion of gummy rice the previous day was not much to live on. Flag set a brutal pace, explaining to Ed that while the trackers were temporarily slowed down for fear of an ambush, the hunted had to get as far away as possible. At noon, they finally took a break in a stand of bamboo. Remembering his survival training axiom that chewing was sometimes as important as eating itself, Ed cut a couple of shoots of young tender bamboo and passed one to Flagstone. They gnawed on them as they rested and decided on a plan. Going further north was not wise, for safety eventually led to the west and south. If they headed east, they would soon run out of jungle and into the hornet's nest of angry PL created by their ambush the previous day. The only logical thing to do would be to head west, for right now the trackers were south of them. Except, that's what the trackers were no doubt expecting them to do. They determined to go on north until dark, heading west if they encountered a clearing or a village of some type. Also, if they passed a good place for an ambush, or some type of terrain where they could set some booby-traps with the grenades, they would avail themselves of the opportunity to do so. Meadows led the way with Flag forming the rear guard.

Instead of walking in a straight line, Ed wandered back and forth a couple of hundred meters each way, keeping under cover all the time, choosing rocky soil whenever he could find it. They swapped places every two hours, but neither of them ever caught sight of the trackers. Flag found a mango tree at one point near a small stream, and they each filled their pockets with the softest fruit they could find. The light was failing when they came to a good-size stream gurgling through the jungle.

"Boss, this thing is running roughly west, and the bottom seems to be pretty firm. By the time the trackers get here, it ought to be good and dark, if they haven't stopped already. We're going to have to take some chances somewhere along the way, and I think now is the time to do it. Let's walk in the stream for as long as we can see, and put as much distance between them and us as we can. Maybe we'll find a good place to spend the night." Ed was too tired to argue. Instead, he waded out into the cold water until it was past his knees, then went downstream. Flag followed.

The stream ran relatively straight for the first few meters, then it wandered slowly to the south. They stayed within ten meters of the shoreline, so they could gain the safety of the woods if the occasion demanded, and even though the sun had full set and the jungle walls on either side of them were black, they still had enough light to keep going if they stayed in the water. Of course, any hidden eyes watching them from the jungle also had enough light to see well enough to pick them off, if the owner of those eyes was so inclined. He wasn't, if he existed, for they walked a good three kilometers down the stream before fatigue forced them to shore. They chose the south side of the creek, and finding a big-rooted tree in the dark, they thrashed around to scare off any lurking snakes, then settled down between two large roots and tried to get comfortable. Ed was feeling very, very tired.

"Flag," he panted, "I don't know how I'm gonna stay awake to watch tonight. I'm about done for."

"Me, too, Boss. Maybe we could take two-hour shifts. We gotta do something, cause we ain't gonna last very long at this pace. I'll stay awake first, but before you go to sleep, we need to make some plans. I think we may have lost them with this river walk. The only way they could find us would be to walk both sides of the river and find out where we came out, and they could only do that if they were damn good. They don't know which way we went, upstream or downstream, so they're gonna have to split their force to check both sides. In the morning, soon as its light enough to see, we'll head out in the water again, find a place to ambush them, and go on past it a ways, then come back to the place on land and wait for 'em. They may not come, and we can spend the day resting. What do you think?"

"Sounds okay to me." Anything including the concept of rest would have sounded okay to Ed right then. "Wake me up in two hours, if you can." The last words were barely mumbled, for the lieutenant was fast asleep.

Flag was a good sergeant, and good sergeants know how to wake the troops. He succeeded in rousing Meadows about 2300 hrs. "Boss, I ain't seen nothing. Goodnight. Get me up at 0100." Ed wriggled into a sitting position where he could see over the roots forming the walls of their temporary home. He yawned, stretched, moved his legs around to call them back to consciousness, and checked his weapon, then the grenades on his belt. Everything was okay. He silently counted the rounds in his bandolier. There were eight. Five more in the shotgun. Eight and five, thirteen. So far, so good. He took out a mango and chewed on it. It was a little tart, but not too green. He had discovered some time ago that eating green mangos tended to pucker you up and dry up your mouth. Finishing the fruit, he ate another as he watched the night pass. There was some splashing out in the creek, very brief, and he figured it was a fish. They did have fish in these waters, he guessed, but he couldn't remember seeing any.

There was a moon out, although he couldn't see it, but it made the surface of the stream shimmer and sparkle in its reflected light. The gurgling of the water had a hypnotic effect on Ed, and his eyes kept wanting to close. He shook his head, got out his canteen, and splashed some water on his face. That helped. He tried to work some math problems in his head, mentally plotting out the coordinates of a formula for a hyperbolic paraboloid. He liked the saddle-shaped figure the Memphis airport had chosen for its new design. That was going to be a beautiful building, if they ever got it finished. The Interstate was going to be nice to bypass the congestion of Poplar and Summer, if they ever got it finished, too. He wondered what Denise was doing right now. It would be about noon yesterday there, and she would be at Memphis State going to class, he guessed. What day of the week was it, anyway? They had left Xeno on Sunday, spent that night in the jungle, then the First Battle of Dong was on Monday, the Valley Ambush on Tuesday and they'd spent last night in the woods, or was it night before last? This would be Wednesday night, or Thursday morning, the third day, no, still the second day that they'd been separated from the BP. What the hell, it didn't matter. The Army was not going to stop paying him just because he couldn't remember the day. At 0115, he woke Flag and reported that nothing was going on. He didn't even mention the airport or the hyperbolic paraboloids. By 0116, Ed was asleep.

Even a good sergeant like Flagstone had trouble waking Ed at 0300 hrs. "Boss, wake up. I've had it. Are you awake?" Not waiting for a reply, Flag reported. "Nothing happening. As soon as you can see, wake me up and let's move out." He was lost in slumber before Meadows could reply. They say that the night is darkest just before the dawn, but what they don't say is that it's hardest to stay awake just before the dawn. Ed poured some water over his head, disturbing the mosquitos, but shocking himself awake in the process. He stood up and leaned against the trunk of the tree. Wrong thing to do, it was too comfortable. He crawled up onto the root and straddled it, figuring that if he went to sleep, he'd fall off and that would wake him up.

The moon had set, and in the utter darkness he could hear the sound of the water rushing by, but he could see not a thing. He tried the old math trick, but the only formula he could remember was that $x+y=$ anything you wanted it to equal, and you needed two equations to solve two unknowns. No good. You couldn't build a building without an equation. How about the problem of the trains that left the station two hours apart, the first travelling at thirty miles per hour and the second at forty-four miles per hour. Let's see, that would be $30x + y = 44x + y$; no, it would be $44x + 30x = y$; no, it was ...Ed caught himself falling off the root. He regained his balance, blinked his eyes, ate another mango. To hell with the airport, and the trains, too. Wonder who the engineers were for the Interstate? Denise would be out of class now and going to work at Kellogg's. Did she work on Thursday? Was it Thursday? He looked out at the last known location of the stream, and was surprised to discover that he could see the other side now. He crawled down from his perch and woke Flag. It wasn't easy, but finally the sergeant sat up, up, blinked a couple of times, and smiled at Meadows. "Good morning, Boss, is the coffee ready?" They both laughed. Gathering their gear, such as it was, they moved to the edge of the water and looked both ways. Seeing nothing amiss, they waded out into the stream and followed its downward course.

For the better part of two hours they waded along before they passed some rocks rising from the streambed and forming a ridge running into the jungle on the north shore. "This looks like a good place for us to wait for the bad guys," said Flag. "Let's keep going a couple hundred meters, then get out over on the other side, head into the jungle a ways, and come back here." Ed nodded and kept wading. They rounded a curve in the river's course, crossed over to the north side, and entered the dense vegetation. After a few steps, the vegetation thinned out, so they turned back to the east and reapproached the rocky ridge from the backside. Ed found a spot between two rocks where they could see the river plainly, both sides, yet they could exit back into the jungle without exposing themselves to anyone wading in the water. They settled down to wait.

"Boss, we need to talk about something. It's about what to do if we get hurt, or if the bad guys get to us. I don't want to be taken prisoner, wounded or otherwise. I want you to promise me you won't let that happen. Save a few rounds from your pistol, no matter how much we have to shoot. If they look like they're going to get me, you take me out. Two shots, in the head. Don't let those little fuckers capture me. I mean it."

Meadows wasn't shocked by the request. He nodded his head. "Okay, Flag, and you do the same for me. I want your hand on it." They shook hands. "When we get back to Xeno, I'll buy you a drink."

"Shit, Boss, when we get back to Xeno, I'll buy you Francois', if you want it." They laughed. As the sun rose to its zenith, both men caught themselves dozing off. The heat wasn't too bad as they sat there not moving very much, and every so often, a little breeze served to make the air stir a bit. Kinda like being on a picnic, except there wasn't any food. They conserved their water, sipping a little occasionally, and one at a time they slipped back into the woods to take a leak. All the mangos were gone, but they found some thick grass behind their outpost and chewed on the stalks. It tasted a lot like grass, but it was something to do. The sun had started its afternoon slide when they saw the figures moving slowly down the stream toward their position. The enemy had, in fact, split his forces, and there were about a dozen of them coming their way. Ed could see six men on this side of the river, then he made out six more on the other side.

They were wading slowly through the water near the banks, the first man in each file watching the sides of the stream for signs of the Hunted's exit, the others keeping wary eyes glued to the green walls on either side for signs of the Hunted's presence. Flag whispered. "When the first couple of men get past us, throw a grenade at the guys on the other side. Lob it up into the air and try for an airburst. Then you take the last three guys on this side with your shotgun. Don't fire more than one load. I'll do the same, then I'll take the first three on this side. One quick strike, then we'll run like hell back into the jungle. These guys are good, but they ain't perfect. No noise now, get ready."

Meadows settled down on his stomach and eased the shotgun out in front of him. He took a grenade and pulled the pin almost all the way out, then clasped it in front of him. Flagstone had done the same thing. The trackers were barely fifty meters away now. The sunlight was making the stream too bright to look at, so Ed concentrated his gaze on the men on the far side. He avoided looking at any of the faces of the trackers, for if a deer can sense your presence by your staring at him, he figured that a tracker could, too. The first men were even with the ambush position now, barely twenty meters away, on this side of the river, some forty meters away on the far side. Two trackers passed, then three, and Ed looked at Flag for a signal. Barely nodding his head, Flag winked at Ed and slipped the pin the rest of the way out of his grenade. Meadows did the same. Both men lobbed their hand grenades at the same time, and the steel objects described smooth arcs into the bright sunlight.

A couple of the trackers on the far side saw something flying through the air and they paused briefly to figure out what it was. Briefly was all the time they had, for Ed and Flag had both grabbed their weapons and were lining up on the trackers closest to them. Meadows hit the fourth man in the column in the side of the head with his first blast, pulverizing his brain and flinging his body sideways into the middle of the creek. His second shot slammed into the fifth man's side, and he seemed to come unglued as he collapsed. Flag's M-1 was barking, and the number three man was down, number two was falling. Just then the grenades went off, and everyone on the far side was down, some diving for cover, but others hurt and dying as they fell in the water. Ed instinctively flinched at the explosions, and his third shot missed man number six, but the fourth caught the tracker as he dived for cover on the creekbank and stopped him in his tracks. Flag was already sliding backwards out of the cleft of the rocks, his job done. Meadows was close behind him. They scrambled down the backside of the ridge and reached the jungle floor. Flagstone took off running into the shadows with Ed only a meter or so behind him. The sound of shots coming from the river let them know that they hadn't gotten all the trackers, but, by golly, they'd gotten a few. The odds still favored the Hunters over the Hunted, but it was getting better. Now it was time for the tough to get going.

32

A Winner Never Quits...

They didn't even try to be stealthy as they ran through the surrounding jungle. Except when they had to detour around a tree, or a patch of especially dense brush, their path led due west, with Flagstone showing the way and Ed trying to keep up and at the same time keep an eye on their trail. Running was not either man's forte and after some 400 meters—about a quarter-mile, they slowed to a fast walk. There was a patch of bamboo that swished against their legs and barked their shins, then more tangle foot that grabbed at their feet and sapped the remaining strength from the tired Hunted.

Flag turned north when he reached a stream and paralleled its course for some distance, then entered the water and walked back the way they'd just come. He stayed in the stream until a clearing appeared on the north shore. Here, he got out on the south bank and stayed out of sight in the woods. The village in the clearing had about a dozen huts, and several fires were burning as the women of the tiny town prepared supper for their families. The smell of boiling rice and roasting meat wafted across the creek and tormented Ed and Flag with its fragrance. Some villagers were down at the water's edge filling their pots and laughing and talking in the soft murmuring tongue of the Lao. Ed thought they ought to risk a foray into the town to get some food, but Flag was adamant that they should keep moving.

He selected a new route to the south and they swapped positions to let Meadows lead for awhile. It was getting dark in the forest now, although the light was still pretty good out in the clearing. They couldn't go much further unless they got in a stream or came on some hills with less dense canopy above their heads. Ed had no idea where they were although he knew they were still north of Highway 9 and west of the savannah where the ambush had taken place. He pushed on for a couple of kilometers before they stopped to rest by mutual consent. "I need a break, Flag. I'm spending more time getting up from the ground than I am walking."

"Me, too, Boss. Let's catch our breath and have some water." Out came the canteens, and down went the last of their water. "We hit them a pretty good lick back there. If they keep after us now, they want us awful bad." Meadows nodded and wished that the trackers would give up the chase, but somehow he knew they weren't going to do so.

"Where do you think we are, Flag?"

"I dunno. Let's take a look at the map and see if we can find ourselves." Although Ed's map was sweat-soaked and limp, it held together well enough for them to study it in the failing light. They traced out the streamlines and took a couple of compass readings and decided they must be somewhere in the vicinity of Ban Katep, about forty klicks as the crow flies from Phulan. Trouble was, neither of them were crows and they weren't even sure they were where they thought they were. "This is close enough for government work," stated Flag. "If we head southwest, with a little luck we'll run into the Houay Tin Gnalong River, which runs into the Xi Xangxoy, which runs by Phulan. I think we got a chance to make it if we can get something to eat and if we don't have to run anymore. You got any other ideas, Boss?"

Meadows had been studying the map, too. He was, by his own admission, a whiz at map reading, and he could back up his claim with performance. After all, he was the one who found the missing grid square on the map at Ft. Sill which they had been using for years in their Artillery training. He decided they were further south than Flag believed, closer to the village of Ban Nathou, and if they kept going toward the southwest, they'd run into Highway 9 before they hit any streams depicted on the map. It really made little difference; the main thing was that they were getting away from the troops frequenting the Trail area and closer to some friendly positions. If only those damn trackers would get off their asses. Somewhere around here, there ought to be a pretty good-sized trail, big enough for the cartographers to draw it in, so they had to be very careful. Anywhere there was a trail, there would be troops, or at least civilians with loose tongues, and they didn't need anyone else trying to lift their scalps.

"I'd like to find the trail that runs through here. The Lao don't move around much at night, and we might be able to make some good time. I don't think we've crossed it, so it has to be somewhere west of us. Let's see if we can find it before dark." He got up, urged his rebellious legs into action, and walked toward the west rather slowly. Flagstone followed. They were both tired, and the unrelenting chase was taking its toll on them. Not much more running was left in them. If they could just rest for a day or so, get some food, and sleep, and tank up on good water, they'd be ready to play some more, but for now, they were close to exhaustion. Meadows had put Halazone tablets in every canteen full of water he had filled up on, but Flag had been a little negligent. Already, there were tiny eggs of liver flukes circulating in his bloodstream, and if he survived, he'd have to contend with them. From sitting on the root at night, and lying on the damp ground for the ambush, Meadows had picked up the hitch-hikers known to the biology people as Strongiloides stercoralis, a relative of the hookworm, and he would have to contend with that parasitic infestation. If they survived. If they didn't, who cared?

It was a little after dark when they found the road. Since it was too dark to see, they were simply stumbling along, keeping in motion so they wouldn't go to sleep, and they heard the sounds of the road before they actually came across it. Both men had been wrong in their estimates of their location, for they were not as far west as they had thought. It was a common mistake among tired men, to think you're closer to home, or to friends, than you really were. Right now they were just a few klicks northeast of the town of Ban Khokkate, and the road they were approaching was Highway 23. The sounds they heard were coming from a Russian-made truck grinding its way slowly to the south, stopping every few minutes, then grinding southward again.

When Ed got within ten meters of the edge of the woods bordering the road, he kneeled down and waited for Flag to join him. They could see the headlights on the truck about a quarter-mile off to their right, and they watched it roll noisily in their direction. Both men lay down flat on the ground when it got nearby. There was scant chance of the personnel in the vehicle seeing them, but once they were flat on the jungle floor, there was even less chance, and the less chance there was, the better off they were. The truck ground to a halt just a few meters away from their location, and in the light of the truck's headlights, they could see some men walk out of the woods and climb into the back of the truck. On southward it continued.

The men coming out of the jungle probably constituted a patrol that was being picked up. There were a lot of reasons the PL could have for patrolling the roads in this area, but there were two very valid reasons hiding there in the jungle watching the pick-up. Ed lisped to Flag, "That looked like a patrol. Onthe they're out of thight, thith might be a good plathe to crothth the road."

"Right," Flagstone lisped back. "Let'th wait a few minuteth and go on acrothth." In the silence following the truck's passing, Meadows went to sleep, but when his head fell onto the ground, it woke him up with a start. He nudged Flagstone.

"Tharge, let'th go." It was an effort to get to his feet, but Meadows managed, then dropped quickly back to the ground. Flagstone, who was only halfway up, did the same. They had both seen the glow of a cigarette which someone was smoking in the darkness on the other side of the road. It seemed that not all the men had gotten into the truck.

"Bothth, we better eathe on back the way we came."

"No, let'th head north. If we go back, we'll jutht be lothing ground to the trackerth." They crawled a few meters to their right, then rose in a crouch and carefully picked their way through the bushes. Flag was leading, and he not only headed north, but also a little east to get further away from the road. They pressed on until midnight when it became impossible for either of them to go any further. Flagstone called a halt. They sat down on the damp ground, not thrashing around for any snakes and not concerned in the least with liver flukes or hook-worms.

"I think we ought to get some sleep, Boss. It'll be light in a few hours, and we need to take stock of our position. We ain't accomplishing nothing here in the dark." They sat back to back, and even if they had tried to stay awake, it wouldn't have done any good. Both of them were asleep inside of a minute.

For eight hours, they stayed there leaning against each other, sleeping the sleep of total exhaustion. Meadows was the first to awaken. For a minute, he was unable to determine where he was, and it was terrifying to be sitting out there somewhere not knowing where you were or what you were supposed to be doing. He tried to get up and have a look around, but when he moved, it woke Flagstone, and Ed remembered exactly where he was. This was at least as terrifying as the previous feeling had been. Meadows scanned that portion of the jungle he could see while Flag went through the wake-up process. When Ed could see he was conscious, he spoke. "Hello, Sergeant Flagstone, how are you today? Your mission for today will be to find a way out of these woods for yourself and your companion. You are a Special Forces trooper thoroughly trained in the art of Escape and Evasion, aren't you?"

"Where you getting all the humor, Boss?" growled Flag. "The last I remember, our ass was in deep shit and the PL were about to wax us good. Must have been a bad dream, huh?"

"Wasn't no dream, Sarge, and we ain't out of the woods. I guess our plan to head south and west is about over, don't you think?"

" 'fraid so, Boss. Looks like the bad guys are covering the roads like a blanket. We gotta come up with a new plan somewhere. You had any ideas while you were sleeping?"

"No. I didn't even dream. We musta slept a long time, cause it's after 0800 now. If the trackers are still after us, they may not be very far away. What do you want to do?"

"Well, I don't figure we have much choice. We have to get past the road to get back to civilization. If we go stumbling around in the dark again, they're gonna nail us. Let's go have a look at that road in the daylight." They took their time in getting up, but it was still a chore. Very carefully, they made their way toward the west. Ed spied a little brook trickling through the bushes, so they drank about a quart apiece and filled their canteens.

There had been no movement at all that they had seen. The road wasn't more than a kilometer away, and they found a place where they could see in both directions down it for an hundred meters or so. No one was moving on it that they could see, but they waited, anyway.

While they were checking out the road, they heard the sound of some voices behind and to the south of them. The voices were speaking Lao. Ed wriggled around so he could watch in the direction of the voices. He watched and listened intently, and before long he saw a slight, khaki-clad figure slipping through the woods. He was moving toward the northeast, toward the place where the two men had spent the night. Just a few steps behind him were more figures—a dozen more, and they were looking all around, trying to pick up any movement. Ed watched for a minute or two more to make sure that they were continuing toward the east, then he turned back toward Flag.

"It's the trackers, and they're following our trail from last night. Those guys are good. They'll be coming this way soon. We gotta do something."

"I ain't seen a sign of life on the road. Let's make a run for the other side right now." It was about thirty meters to the woods on the other side of Highway 23, and they almost made it undetected. Just as Meadows entered the jungle with Flag at his heels, one of the PL soldiers doing road-watch duty spied them, and he started firing his SKS at the departing figures. His aim wasn't even close, but the sounds of his shots woke up all the other PL strung out along the road, and they all began firing wildly. A couple of rounds zipped overhead as Ed and Flagstone pushed into the woods, but they were soon far enough away from the firing to not worry about it. What they were worried about was the fact that the trackers must have heard the firing and they'd be coming right along. Meadows turned north to try and stymie any headlong pursuit by the PL, and they kept going for an hour. Finally, he stopped. They listened with all they were worth, but they didn't hear anyone moving in their vicinity.

"Maybe we ought to shoot them up a bit and try to slow them down again."

"Too risky, Boss, we're too tired to run away and we sure ain't gonna take them all out. We need to try and find a hole we can crawl in and let them pass us by. You still got your grenade?"

Ed felt at his belt. It was still hanging there. "Yep, I still have it."

"You got any string?"

Meadows dug out the length of suspension line he carried in his chest pocket to tie knots in when he was pacing out a distance. "I got this suspension line. What do you want to do?"

"Let's find some thick bushes and crawl through them. I'll set the grenade in our path, and if the trackers follow us, maybe they'll hit it and hurt themselves. Find us some good bushes, Boss." Meadows began walking toward the west again. He looked all around as he walked, and soon enough he saw the signs of a creek-bank with the vegetation growing in matted blankets along it. He crawled into the brush on his hands and knees, forming a little tunnel as he went. Flagstone followed. Reaching the creek, Ed splashed some water on his face, looked both ways briefly, then slipped into the water on his belly and crawled across. Once on the other side, he squirmed into the brush there and waited. It was getting late in the afternoon, and the gibbons were tuning up. There was one especially deep throated one which must have been the ruler of the pack, for when he sounded off, he drowned out the other hooters. *Probably doesn't even know there's a war going on down here,* thought Ed.

Flagstone joined him in a few minutes. "All set, Boss, let's get the hell out of here." Meadows continued his tunnel-making until they were once again in the less dense jungle undergrowth. He got up and was somewhat surprised to find that his legs were quivering as he stood erect.

"Flag, we gotta find some food of some type. I'm getting weak."

"Not now, Boss, we gotta keep moving. In another couple of hours it'll be dark and we'll have to stop. If we run across some mangos or something then, we'll pick them up. I got a hunch those trackers ain't far behind us at all." There was a clearing just a couple of hundred meters in front of their location, and when they reached it, they had to skirt the edge, heading south in a large circle. Flagstone came across a trail, just a footpath, but it caused him to stop, look, and listen. While they were watching, they heard the muffled explosion of the grenade going off behind them. The trackers were not far behind. Hopefully, some of them wouldn't be coming any closer. A man came hustling down the trail, a stick across his shoulders, and a basket of vegetables hanging from each end of the stick. It was too much of a temptation to pass up. Meadows jumped the farmer when he got in front of them, and Flag hit him in the back of his head with the butt of the M-1. They didn't know if it killed him or not, but there was no time to check on that. They filled their pockets with things that looked like turnips and some other things that looked like carrots.

This entire episode took only a few seconds, and then they were off into the jungle again. There was no point in hiding the body, for the trackers would find it for sure, and it would only take time that they could use in putting distance between themselves and the Hunters.

As they walked on, both men stuffed themselves with the flat-tasting, but juicy turnips and the dry carrots. It would soon be dark, and they felt like they had to get away from the body as far as possible. They were probably a kilometer away before it was fully dark, but even in the failing light, they could make out the other road they had stumbled upon. There were troops standing in the road, milling around. "Boss," whispered Flagstone, "this looks like a good place to spend the night."

33

...And A Quitter Never Wins

Despite the fact that they were so tired they couldn't have run away had a cobra come after them (well, maybe they would have run if it were a large cobra), there was very little sleep for Flag and Ed that night. Traffic was not heavy on the road, but it was busy all night long. Troops could be seen walking in both directions on both sides of the thoroughfare, and at least hourly there was a vehicle, either a 3/4-ton truck, or a jeep driving slowly by. Many of the troops carried flashlights, and it gave the appearance of a convention of lightning bugs as they switched them on and off as they tromped around.

Ed didn't see any khaki uniforms, he didn't expect to, for the trackers were probably getting a good night's sleep as they rested for the labor facing them tomorrow. Flagstone and Ed took turns trying to sleep, but the best Meadows could manage during his shift was a fitful dozing off. There was little conversation, but in the few words spoken, each man expressed his feeling that tomorrow was going to be the climax of this chase. Either they would find a way to get through the enemy and into the relative safety of the jungle closer to home, or...well...they'd buy the farm here in Laos.

That thought alone was enough to keep a fellow awake. As it began to get light along the road, Flag and Ed got out of the depressions they'd found for resting, checked their weapons, and moved out in the only direction left open to them—the north. A little bit at a time, they eased over toward the east to try and get away from the PL-controlled road, but they couldn't ease too far because of the other road behind them. What was it that the Light Brigade had faced, as into the valley of death, rode the six hundred? Cannon to the right of them, cannon to the left of them. Ed could appreciate those horsemen more than ever before. PL to the right of them, PL to the left of them, trackers behind them, and who knows what in front of them. They would soon find out.

When Ed checked his watch at 0800 hrs, they had moved far enough away from their roost of last night that they were feeling a little better now. Even though their legs reminded them constantly that they were reaching the point of total wipe-out, their brains told them that every hour which passed without running into any enemy troops increased their chances of getting out of this thing with their top-knots intact. Meadows was in the lead, so he was the first to spot the clearing when they approached it. Not only was it a clearing, but it was full of enemy soldiers, at least a company, complete with tents and lots of firearms. Great. They could see the road entering the clearing to their left, and it looked like the troops were forming up for something. They paused to see what was going on, and as they watched, it was very discouraging to see the enemy soldiers were spreading out across the clearing and preparing to conduct a sweep of these very woods. There was no choice left but to head east, and fast. They tried to run, but the life was gone from their legs, and it was all they could do to walk fast.

Meadows heard some shouting behind him, and he reasoned that the trackers were hot on their trail. The vegetation was thinning out now, and it was obvious they were running out of jungle. It was 1500 hrs when they came to the end of their road. There was no more jungle in front of them, there were excited voices behind them, and there were dead legs under them. Out to the front, across about two hundred meters of rice paddies, was a rather high hummock of a grass-covered, rocky outcropping. The rice paddies were dry, so crossing them would present no problem at all. "Ed," said Flagstone, calling him by his given name for the first time in his life, "let's you and me go out on that hill and make them come and get us. We may as well make them pay for their sins."

There was nothing to be gained by trying to run. Flag and Ed walked side by side out to the hill and made their way to the top. From there, they could see for several hundred meters in every direction, so they lay down on the summit, checked their weapons, and waited. Meadows hadn't been very faithful in his praying during his stay in Laos thus far, but he made up for some of it as he waited. Pretty soon, the trackers appeared at the edge of the woods. They milled around, looking at the hillock, but apparently a little reluctant to make an approach. Then their leader, a short man with a pith helmet, made some gestures, and they fanned out and started across the paddies. Flag sighted down the barrel of the M-1 as Meadows got out his .357 and checked the loads. There was no reason to check the loads, he knew there were six rounds in the chambers, but he needed to do something. From this range, neither the revolver nor his shotgun was very effective, but he had a lot more rounds for the sidearm than he had for the Remington. He noted there were eleven trackers left, and since they'd started with twenty-five, the Americans had already extracted a price.

"Let them get to the middle of the paddies, then try to chase them back," said Flagstone. Meadows lined up the sights of the Smith & Wesson on one of the persistent enemy soldiers, steadied it with both hands, and hoped for luck. When the khaki figures were out in the open and fully exposed, Flagstone squeezed off the first shot. Ed followed that with all six of his in the revolver. The troops had hit the ground, so it was not possible to tell who was hit and who wasn't, but as Meadows reloaded and Flagstone continued sniping, those troops who were able began to run back toward the wood-line. Three of them couldn't run, and one of those was the man Ed had first fired at. Of course, Flag may have shot at him, too, and he had a lot better chance of hitting with the M-1 than Meadows had with the .357.

Once the troops gained the woods, they began some sniping of their own and while most of their rounds were high and passed harmlessly overhead, there were a few causing Meadows and Flagstone to flinch. Ed looked up at the sky, noting that it was a sparkling blue, cloudless—a beautiful day to be outside in Shelby Forest north of Memphis, with Denise. He looked to the west, and far, far away, there was a little black speck that seemed to be moving. He blinked his eyes to make sure he wasn't dreaming, and looked again. It was still there, and it wasn't an insect.

Down below them, along the wood-line, the khaki troops had been joined by some of the PL who had been sweeping the woods. They were deploying along the edge of the rice paddies, and it was obvious they were getting ready for another assault. Their firing had also increased, and now there was the rhythmic rattling of automatic weapons' fire. Flag rolled over on his side. "Boss, I'm gonna have me a last smoke. You want one?"

Meadows shook his head. His mouth was dry, and he didn't miss the significance of Flagstone's remark...that bit about the 'last' smoke. He faced away to the west as Flag fired up the short Lucky Strike. If Flag was gonna take him out, he was gonna make it easy by presenting the back of his head for a target. Fishing the metal signalling mirror out of his shirt pocket, Ed peeked through the sighting hole and began wiggling the mirror at the black object which seemed so far away. He flashed and flashed, but the only thing that happened was that the object seemed to stop moving. Flag's cigarette was growing short, and the bad guys were forming up. Ed was sure the object was getting larger, so he told Flagstone about it.

"Flag, I think I see a plane heading our way. I've been flashing at it, and I'm sure it's getting bigger. Look over there to the west." Flag dutifully followed the direction of Meadows' pointing. There it was, no doubt about it, there was an aircraft heading their way. There were also enemy troops heading their way.

"You keep flashing that thing at the plane as long as you can. I'm gonna engage these guys and try to slow them down, but I'm about out of shells. When I tell you to start shooting, forget the plane and use your weapons." Meadows kept wiggling while Flagstone fired on the advancing enemy. Not only was it a plane, but it was a helicopter, an H-34—probably Hotel X-ray, and it was definitely heading right toward them. Ed put the mirror back into his pocket and took up his weapon. The enemy was at the base of the hill now, and some of them were starting up. Meadows fired five times with the shotgun, and it did have the effect of causing the troops to hit the ground and dive for cover. As he stuffed more rounds in the magazine, Flag remarked, "I'm out of ammo, Boss, so don't let up."

The helicopter was lining up for a landing just behind the hilltop, and the PL had seen it by now. They started running up the hill, ignoring the fire from the shotgun which knocked a couple of them down. The gun clicked on empty, so Ed drew his Smith out again.

Flagstone punched him. "Let's go, Boss!" and he was up and running down the back side of the hill. The helicopter was about ten feet off the ground when Meadows caught up with Flag, and he could see the crew-chief blasting away with his Thompson at the PL just now cresting the hill. They reached Hotel X-ray together just before his gear hit the ground, and they both dove through the open doorway, throwing their weapons in ahead of them. Ed grabbed for something to hang on to as the craft took off again, and his fingers found the tie-down rings in the floor and held onto them for dear life. Flag was doing the same thing. Their legs were hanging outside as the pilot jerked and swerved the chopper around in an attempt to disrupt the PL's aim, but they heard the metallic sound of a couple of rounds striking the tail boom, anyway. Nothing vital was hit, and in a matter of seconds, they were dodging across the tops of the jungle trees, out of sight of the PL.

Crew Chief helped Meadows and Flagstone crawl the rest of the way into the cabin, and when they were safely inside, he slid the door shut. He grinned down at them as they sat on the cabin floor and gave the thumbs-up sign. Ed smiled back. He looked over at Flag, and found the sergeant looking at him. Meadows put an arm around Flag's shoulders, then threw the other arm around him and hugged him. Flagstone hugged Ed back. They laughed, and Flag leaned over to put his mouth close to Ed's ear so he could be heard above the roar of the engine. "Boss, your Right Guard ain't working!"

The airways were filled with transmissions. Hotel X-ray called the B Team to tell them what had happened. The B Team called Vientiane. White Star called the Special Warfare Center. Major Thurston called 5155 Windham Road, and the message was the same in every instance. "We've picked up a couple of stray dog-faces, and they are alive and well. That is all, out."

At the field in Savannahkhet, Major Murphy and the rest of the brass were waiting for the chopper. A lot of other people were waiting, too. The craft landed, settled onto its gear, and the transmission was disengaged. As the blades slowed down, Crew Chief opened the door, and several people rushed up to help the returning troopers off. What they saw when they got there were two very dirty, very smelly, very lucky men, lying on the bare floor of the cabin, sound asleep.

34

Story Tellers

Major Murphy gave Ed a ride back to the B Team house in his jeep. Meadows kinda missed the old 3/4-ton truck. Flag sat right beside Meadows in the back seat as they rode through the peaceful streets of Savannahkhet. Nothing seemed different at all about the town, nothing had changed, no one was more nor less excited among the population then they had been the last time Ed was there. You wouldn't expect anything to be different, for we only react to those things we care about. The Lao weren't reacting to Ed.

The Americans, on the other hand, were jubilant. They had been long-faced around Savan for the last few days, but now, their comrades who were lost had now been found, and better yet—they had been picked up all in one piece with nothing but scratches to tell of their ordeal. Everyone, including Major Murphy, was anxious to hear their tale, but everyone, including Major Murphy, could see they would have to wait. Even though he was a first lieutenant now, and there was a TO&E slot for him in the Group, Meadows was ill-at-ease around majors, especially B Team commanders, so he stayed awake during the ride. It would be rude to sleep while the major was talking.

At the team house, there was a lot of hand-shaking and congratulations, then the two men were ushered to the third floor where Bush, Riley, and Eason were also quartered, and informed that there was hot water for showers. Meadows peeled off his uniform for the first time in a week, including his boots, and he discovered that his Odor Eaters weren't working, either. As he looked at the pile of clothing lying there on the floor, he was appalled at the sight. He wouldn't have put those clothes on under any circumstances he could imagine. The hot water of the shower had such a soothing effect that he promptly dozed off while the spray rinsed his body, and he probably would have stayed there all night if Flag hadn't hollered at him to hurry up. Ed towelled off with a clean-smelling, dry white towel, put on some clean shorts, and shaved the week's worth of stubble from his face. His shaving and Flag's weren't the same, for their beards were considerably different. Ed's was not very thick. He lay down on the cot and tried to listen to the questions his team members were asking, but halfway through the first one, his eyelids met and he was gone.

Flagstone wasn't far behind. He talked for a minute with Bush and Riley, but only for a minute. Before he went to sleep, he looked over at the form of his lieutenant and said to his fellow non-coms, "Boss did a good job, he couldn't have done better. If I ever get in another situation like this one, I'll take him. He's a good head." As every trooper knows, there are no higher words of praise that a sergeant can bestow on his officer.

The next morning, there was a breakfast of bacon and eggs and sausage and toast and coffee and orange juice and pancakes and syrup, just like they fed you in Ranger School when you got in from the five-day patrol in the mountains. Ed remembered the sign they had in the mess hall up there near Dahlonega, Georgia, which said, "Take all you want, but eat all you take."

Meadows took a little of everything, and he ate what he took, and then he vomited all he had eaten. It seemed his stomach wasn't quite as ready for a return to reality as his eyes were. Alligator eyes, but a jay-bird ass. Flagstone tried to eat, too, and he also vomited. They finally were able to keep some Cokes down, and if they let them go flat first, they sat right well on the abused stomachs. The major informed them they were to go to Vientiane that morning for their debriefing, and he would be going along, in fact, all the men of FTT-19 were going.

At the airfield, Red was waiting with his trusty C-47, and with little ado, the engines were cranked up and they were off to the big town. Flagstone wanted to talk with Ed, but they couldn't seem to get together. No matter how they swapped their seating around, there was always someone from the B Team close by. Major Murphy's instructions to his men were that they were to listen in on everything the two men said until the de-briefing. It was common practice. Meadows looked at Flag a couple of seats away, caught his eye, and slowly nodded his head. He understood. Be careful in what you say, for you never knew how these guys were going to interpret your actions. He had already decided that Charlie had gotten separated from them when they first bugged out, and he hadn't seen him again. Had no idea what happened to his excellent little Thai interpreter. The flight was smooth enough, and it didn't last much more than an hour. Red banked the bird into the pattern at Vientiane, touched the wheels down right at the end of the runway, and the plane settled down to a sedate roll without even a hint of a bounce. *Must be an inspector watching Red,* thought Ed. They climbed down the airstair to the tarmac and found LTC Suomi waiting for them. He shook hands with Meadows and Flagstone in his formal fashion, bowing slightly, and spoke to all the members of the FTT.

"Welcome back home, men. We were concerned about you. I wasn't worried, because I know what kind of men you are, but I was concerned." Then he laughed. They all laughed. Meadows really liked Colonel Suomi. As they climbed into the jeeps and trucks assembled to take them to White Star Headquarters, Ed looked around at the Vientiane airport. Not far from where they sat was a brand new terminal building, two stories high, yellowish stucco, with a red tile roof, and nearly as large as the one at Bangkok, but this one was obviously not in use. There were no roads leading up to the terminal, no asphalt around it for planes to sit upon, no electrical lines hanging from its eaves. Weeds were growing right up to the sides of the building, and it was obvious that either the project wasn't finished, or else it was abandoned. Either way, it looked like a waste of someone's money, and Meadows was willing to bet it was probably Uncle Sugar's bucks being squandered.

The trip from the airport to the town took a few minutes, but even from a distance, Ed could see that Vientiane was a different breed of cat from Savannahkhet. There was traffic on the roads, people everywhere going everyplace, lots of new permanent buildings, and lots of fountains along the street. These folks must have been queer for fountains. The main drag was quite a large street, and straddling it at the far end was a huge structure surrounded by bamboo scaffolding which looked for all the world like pictures Meadows had seen of the Arch de Triomphe, in Paris. This was incredible. The USOM compound was right around the curve from the Arch. "USOM" stood for the United States Overseas Mission, and Meadows never was sure just exactly what their function was. There were always a lot of long-haired civilians around who weren't concerned very much with money, for they always seemed to have a great deal of it, but what they were supposed to be doing, Ed didn't know. White Star Headquarters was located in the USOM compound; otherwise, Meadows would have had nothing to do with the USOM personnel, who were, he imagined, the epitome of the accursed Ugly American label.

Colonel Suomi led the way into his conference room which had been arranged as a board room, sort of. There was a big table that ran nearly the length of the room, and the members of the FTT were directed to sit on one side while the commander and his staff occupied seats on the other side. More than just Suomi's staff was present, for there were some people from MAAG-Laos—legs, mostly, and some civilians from one of the Intelligence agencies over there. It was a big deal. LTC Suomi began the proceedings by announcing to the FTT members that the purpose of this de-briefing was to get their thoughts on what had happened, hear their stories, benefit from their recommendations, if possible. Everyone here was a friend, and they should speak freely. He was very proud of the men for beating the best efforts of the PL to capture them, but he was anxious, as were the others in the room, to hear the true story of what had happened to the FTT. The floor was now open for comments. No one said anything. The assistant S-2 Officer broke the silence. "Lieutenant Meadows, I'm Captain Young, the assistant S-2 for White Star. Why don't you begin by telling us what happened after you landed at Tchepone?" It was Whiskey Bill Young, himself. *Friends, my ass,* Meadows had better friends than this at the village of Dong.

Ed told the story very matter-of-factly, hitting all the high points, but trying to leave his thoughts out of his relation. He was interrupted frequently by members of the audience with questions, but the atmosphere was friendly, despite Young's presence, and as they talked, the others members of the team joined in. It lasted for several hours. They took a break for dinner, but the FTT personnel were isolated from everyone else during this time. In the afternoon session, Meadows and Flagstone learned what had happened to the other guys. They had seen the signal when the flare went up, and their situation had become quite uncomfortable, too. All three of them made it to the tree-line and into the woods without any trouble at all. Sam the Second had escaped with them. They spent the night in the jungle near there, Eason contacted the B Team, and Hotel X-Ray picked them up the next morning. No sweat, we do it everyday. *Sure you do*, laughed Meadows to himself. Bushman told a good story. It made Meadows want to hear what really happened.

Flag and Ed told their story next. They had gotten very similar impressions on what had happened to them. Even at this recent date, the chronology of some of the events were getting jumbled. Colonel Suomi told them not to worry about that, but to continue with their story. When they'd finished, silence filled the room. One of the civilians broke it. "Lieutenant, I think you and Sergeant Flagstone have something to be really proud of. From your description of the trackers, it sounds like you were being chased by one of the NVA anti-recon teams, some pretty sharp cookies—the best they have to offer. You beat them at their own game, and I think you are to be congratulated." Meadows nodded and smiled. He appreciated the compliment, but he knew better than to believe the part about beating them. They had escaped, true enough, but beat? Naw, they didn't beat them. Maybe a draw. Or maybe the Americans were saved by the bell.

The S-3 had an interesting question. He asked the team about their choice of weapons. If they could have the ideal weapon for this type of operation, what would it be? Ed thought that one over. He really liked Bush's BAR, but it, and its ammunition, was so damn heavy that it couldn't be the ideal thing. The M-1 was also heavy, but was very accurate. It had the problem of heavy ammunition, too, and its rate of fire was too slow. The shotgun was great in the jungle, but was absolutely useless at ranges greater than 100 meters. Not a very good choice. Carbines? In Ed's opinion, carbines weren't worth a tinker's dam. "I like the Russian AK. We fired it at Bragg, and it has a lot of stopping power, it can be fired full automatic, and it isn't all that heavy. I guess that would be my choice."

"Are you familiar with the AR-15, Lieutenant?"

"Yes, Sir, they had one on the range at Bragg and I fired it."

"What do you think of it?"

"I didn't like it very much. I don't see how a .22 round can be very effective, even a souped-up one. Besides, it looks like a Mattel toy and it's plastic."

The S-3 nodded. "If you could design a weapon that would be ideal, what would you design?"

Meadows thought that one over. "I guess I'd design a light-weight AK with a grenade launcher on it, and some tiny grenades. I think it is important to be able to fire grenades further than you can throw them. I don't know, but I feel very strongly that for the operations where a small team is going to be out on its own without help available, you need the ability to fire automatic, if only for short periods, and you must have some way to break contact. Grenades will do that for you, but they are so heavy that even with the new baseballs, you can't carry very many. The BAR would be nice, it it weren't so heavy. It can certainly make people dive for cover. To tell the truth, Sir, I don't know what I'd recommend, but I also know we haven't got it. I'm sorry but I don't have the answer."

The S-3 nodded. "I hear you, Lieutenant, and I'd like to tell you that we are working on exactly what you're talking about. Maybe the next time you get in a bind like this, we can help you out."

"If it's all the same to you, Sir, I'd like to pass on the next time." Everybody laughed. The conference broke up, the FTT was released to enjoy the sights and sound of night life in Vientiane, and they were to return to Savannahkhet in the morning. For Ed and Flagstone, night life in Vientiane consisted of a meal of soup at the USOM mess hall and a cot with a mosquito bar attached in the USOM Visitors' Quarters.

35

Among The Hmong

Early the next morning, LTC Suomi called the FTT in for another meeting with him and his staff. They had discussed the situation as it concerned the 11th BP and FTT-19, and it was the consensus of opinions that the amiable working relationship between Ed and his team and the BP had been effectively destroyed by the incident on the Trail. For this reason, sending the team back to work with LTC Khom would, they felt, be counter-productive. There was a rumor that the FAR intended to send the BP into Nam Tha, as reinforcements, in a situation the CO felt was untenable. It might be a good time to switch Ed's team to a new role and to save face at the same time. Simply detaching the Americans from the Lao battalion now might cause their hosts some embarrassment, and could provide the impetus for Khom to go ahead and join his friend Kong Le. But, if the team were withdrawn because of a pressing need elsewhere, and if Colonel Khom bought the idea, then detachment from the 11th would be palatable. Exactly what this new assignment was to be, he wasn't at liberty to disclose right then, but they were to return to Savannakhet and thence to Xeno and inform the good colonel of the need for them to be switched to a new group. It might work.

Red piloted the trusty C-47 back down to the south where the men were then given a ride out to Xeno. Khom was in his Headquarters, but when Ed and the rest of the FTT members arrived, they were not ushered right in. Instead, it seemed there was a flurry of activity inside, and Meadows could hear the rustling sound of paper being gathered up, as though the colonel was hiding some maps, or something. After a minute, the Americans were welcomed inside.

Som bais were exchanged, beer was produced, and the usual amenities were gone over before they got down to talking about the purpose of FTT-19's visit. Ed introduced the subject. "Colonel, we have had a bad time. The raid on the Trail has covered the 11th BP with a great deal of praise. If we hadn't encountered a vastly superior force (Sam was translating), there is no doubt we would have come back here as a complete unit with no shadow of doubt hanging over our actions. You are to be commended. It is also obvious that your command is ready for whatever comes your way. For this reason, my commander at White Star has determined that there are some units who need our help much more than the 11th BP. He would like to change us from this assignment to another, if it is okay with you."

Khom listened intently to Sam's translation. Sam's Lao wasn't as good as Charlie's had been, and he frequently had to search for the correct phrase in changing from his thinking in Thai to his speaking in Lao, similar though the languages were. When he finally finished, Khom nodded and smiled. "My Let-ten-ant, I think your commander has heard of our plans to go to Nam Tha. He doesn't want to lose you on a futile effort, and I agree with him. We are going to die at Nam Tha, if we go there, but it is my duty to obey my orders. I have enjoyed having your team with us. If we survive, I may someday go to the Command School in the United States, and perhaps we'll meet again. It is sad to see you go. I regret we cannot have a party to celebrate your leaving, but our time for planning is very short. Goodbye, Let-ten-ant, and I wish you and your men well."

Meadows hugged the small officer, and Khom hugged back. The other members of the team either shook hands, or hugged, or both, and then they took their leave. Once outside, Meadows said to Flagstone, "He's a pretty sharp character, Flag. Too bad he's not in charge of the whole Lao Army."

"You're right, Boss, but it seems like that's always the case. The ones who are good become the ones who are expendable. Let's collect our shit and get back to Savan. I don't like Xeno anymore."

There wasn't a lot of stuff to pick up, either at the hut in Xeno or when they went through the S-4 warehouse in Savan. They had never really gotten unpacked since they'd been in the field so much of the time. The supply officer agreed to let them take their weapons with them even though they were leaving his sector, and each of the men was glad of that. Breaking in a new weapon was uncomfortable. They ate dinner at the B Team where Major Murphy told them they were to go to Vientiane on the afternoon milk run and to take everything with them. He concluded by addressing them all: "You men have certainly livened up this military region with your exploits. I can't say it's always been fun keeping up with you, but it has always been interesting. I'm glad I didn't have twelve, or even six, teams like yours. I think you'll like your new job. Good luck." For Ed, that beat the hell out of Briggs' farewell, "Don't fuck up."

There were the same fountains in Vientiane which had been there a couple of days before, the same Arch in the same state of construction, the same USOM personnel with the same length of hair, only a couple of days' growth longer, and the same cots with mosquito bars in the visitors' quarters. It seemed to Meadows that living and fighting in the woods was a lot easier than all this flying around. Flag called it "fiddle-de farting around." The team ate supper in the mess hall, which was sparsely populated, then Bush and Riley left to renew recent acquaintances at the Lido Club, the White Rose Bath House, and other houses of repute, ill or otherwise, in Vientiane. Ed dug out his writing stuff and caught up on some correspondence, watched a movie USOM furnished in the Mess Hall, and went to bed. He'd gotten a message from Colonel Suomi that the team was to gather in the conference room the next morning to learn about their new job, but there had been no hint of what it was. The time spent on running away from the Trail and the Trackers still constituted a sleep deficit for Meadows, so when "Tammy and the Bachelor" ended, Ed sought out his cot. Already, the memories of the experience with the Trackers were growing dim. *Wonder what they were doing tonight? Wonder if we'll ever meet again? I hope not,* thought Meadows in his last conscious thought.

Whereas they had spent the better part of a week in the Cage learning about the Lao and the 11th BP, FTT-19 spent about two hours in the White Star Conference Room learning about their new assignment, a place called Site 20, or Sam Tong, if you preferred a name rather than a number for an address. It was located north of Vientiane about an hour's flight away by Helio Courier or Dornier Skymaster aircraft. Their mission was to be changed as well as their location, for they were to be training members of the Meo, the mountain people of Laos, in Unconventional Warfare—Guerrilla warfare, the ultimate goal of all Special Forces troopers.

Ed could hardly believe his ears, for this seemed too good to be true. First they had been assigned to a parachute battalion, the best the FAR had to offer, and now they were going to work for an organization known as CAS, for Confidential American Source, and everyone knew who that was. They were actually going to work for the Agency—the Company—the Customer. Fantastic! Site 20 already had a full A Detachment from the 1st Group out of Okinawa there, but the plans were to develop the Site into a major training base for the Meo in their war against the PL on the Plain de Jarres. Supporting them with air assets would be Byrd & Sons Construction, a cover name for one of the many Agency mini-airforces in this part of the world. Both the Helio and the Dornier were STOL aircraft, Ed knew, but the latter was a twin-engined bird while the former had only one windmill.

They would still be under the control of White Star, but their operations would be planned, supported, and directed by CAS. The CO of Site 20 for the time being was a Captain Thomason, but he was an interim commander, for a major was slated to take over the operation as soon as enough of the site was developed to warrant the increase in power structure. The members would be flown up one at a time with all their gear on the routine resupply runs so as not to give the impression of a major buildup too quickly. As the commander, Meadows decided he should be the first to go, and he'd be leaving within the hour. There was a lot more information delivered in the attempt to prepare the FTT for their assignment, but it was mostly organizational and supply info, and Ed took only a passing interest. When the conference concluded, Meadows gathered his gear together for the ride out to the airport.

The Helio was an unpainted aluminum aircraft with no markings save the number "555" on each side of its rudder. It had a high wing, no struts, and sat on conventional landing gear made of tubular steel. The engine compartment was long, sticking way out in front of the main gear, and at the front was a large, three-bladed prop with a conical central spinner. The pilot, a civilian by the name of, "Ed," said "Hello" when Meadows arrived, but then said nothing else. He directed Meadows to store his gear as far forward in the cargo bay as he could, then he pointed Ed to the right-hand seat while he performed his pre-flight inspection. There were large slats on the leading edge of each wing, the entire length, and tremendous flaps drooping from the trailing edges. The engine, Meadows was informed when he asked, was a 500 hp of some variety which was described by a lot of numbers and letters that meant nothing the him, but it had a loud noise when it started up and it had no trouble turning the big prop. They didn't even make it to the runway as they took off directly from the parking area. As the rice paddies surrounding Vientiane slipped by beneath their wings, Meadows could see the mountains of Meo Country looming to the north.

Ed thought over what he'd heard about the Meo. They were called the Hmong, the Mung, or several other lesser monikers, and they were strictly mountain dwellers, living in a society of slash-burn agriculture where they raised poppies for the extraction of opium. The men smoked opium in pipes and the women chewed betel nut which colored their teeth black and their gums a fire red. They were supposedly very warlike and loved a good fight, much opposed to the placid nature of the lowland Lao. There was a Colonel Vang Pao, the King of the Meo, who was the rallying point for the tribes and was being used by CAS in an attempt to gather the Meo on our side. The PL, actually, the Viet Minh, were trying to convince the Meo to join with them, so there were wars within the war. It sounded exciting.

When the plane reached the first of the mountains, all signs of civilization below them ceased. There were no roads to be seen, no villages, no cultivated fields. It was some of the most beautiful country Ed had ever seen, and reminded him somewhat of Yosemite National Park that he'd visited once in California. The hills weren't as high nor as craggy as those in Yosemite, but they were high enough. Deep valleys marked the countryside, and waterfalls hundreds of feet high could be seen nearly everywhere. They flew over a big river nestled in one of the valleys, then the terrain took on a slightly wilder appearance as they passed limestone karch formations sticking up like big fingers in the sky. Meadows was enthralled.

After some time, Ed the Pilot tapped Ed the Passenger's shoulder, and pointed down to a valley coming up ahead of them. "Site 20," he yelled above the engine's roar. Meadows looked down. All he could see was a tiny dirt airstrip with a hill at one end of it. Pilot Ed fiddled with the controls, the pitch of the prop changed, the sounds of the engine were modified, the flaps came down, the slats came down in sets of two, and the aircraft lost altitude in a hurry. Not that there was that much to lose, cause they had been barely skirting over the highest peaks, but the wheels hit the runway with a thud in no time at all. That was good, also, for the runway was very short. Pilot Ed directed the plane to the left side of the strip, wheeled it around to a perpendicular heading with the runway, and shut down the engine. "Welcome to Sam Tong," grinned Pilot Ed to Passenger Ed.

Meadows looked around. There was nothing here. No people, no town, what the hell was going on? Pilot Ed crawled out and left the door open, so Meadows climbed out, too. The air was cool and brisk, felt like an Autumn afternoon in Fayetteville, and the sky was a cloudless, sparkling blue. Whatever was going on, this was a beautiful place to have it. After a few minutes of solitude, a soldier came walking toward them from out of a small valley behind the plane. Ed could see he was an American dressed in fatigues, and wearing a camouflage bush hat. He carried no weapon, but strapped to his belt was a big revolver that Meadows was willing to bet was a Smith & Wesson in one of the Magnum calibres.

"Hey, Ed," yelled the soldier, "you and your passenger come on down. We're eating, come join us. Leave all the shit on the plane; we'll get it later."

Pilot Ed said to Meadows, "Come on, Lieutenant, they tie on a good feed bag here."

"What about all this stuff?" Meadows protested, pointing to the cargo bay. "You gonna just leave it here?"

"No sweat, it'll be okay. You're among the Hmong now. If they like you, they won't steal nothing. If they don't like you, we'd be dead already." Meadows trailed after Pilot Ed. From all he had seen, being among the Hmong was akin to being alone. What the hell was going on around here?

36

Rice

The campsite the Americans had established at Site 20 was spread under the branches of a grove of trees several hundred meters and one valley away from the airstrip. It took them a few minutes to walk over, and the first sign of the camp was a wooden arch leading into a single-strand rope corral. There was a piece of wood hanging from the apex of the arch upon which someone had branded the name, "O.K. Corral." Trudging up the hill that followed, they entered a squad tent with the sides rolled up that was also named. It was obviously the dining facility and was called the "Longbranch Saloon." Enough tables sat under the tent awning to handle a considerable number of men, but there were only ten present. As Meadows looked the people over, he was very surprised to see Frank Terrell, a Classmate of his from the USMA Class of '60. *Well, I'll be a sonofabitch. There wasn't any telling who you would run into in this country.* Terrell saw Ed at about the same time, and he stopped chewing in mid-bite. Getting to his feet, he said, "Well, I'll be a sonofabitch. There is no telling who you're going to run into in this country! Ed Meadows! We heard you were captured by the P.L.!"

"Not hardly," said Ed in his best John Wayne tone as the two men shook hands and embraced. "They made a good try, but when the going gets tough, it's time to Go Like '60." They laughed at the usage of the Class Motto.

Terrell introduced Ed to Captain Thomason, an older fellow for a captain, ancient to the 24-year-old Meadows at 35, and the captain grinned broadly beneath his fiery red, handle-bar mustache. "Pleased to meet you, Meadows, and happy as hell to see you got away from whatever it was they were doing to you down in the flats." His pleasure seemed genuine as did his smile, and Meadows was cautiously prepared to like the captain. That, in itself, represented a change from his usual attitude toward ranking officers.

The non-coms sitting at the tables were introduced next, and Ed knew it would take him some time to learn all their names. They were your usual assortment of Eastern Europeans, a Latin or two, and the rest Gringos. They all wanted to know what had happened to Ed and Flag, for while they had learned that FTT-19 had experienced some difficulties, they had not heard of their ultimate escape. Meadows gave a brief synopsis of their adventure against the Trackers. One of the men had gotten the two Ed's some food on Mel-Mac plates just like the ones at Bragg, and the food looked a lot like some variety of stew. He explained to Ed that they ate stew three times a day up here because that was all their Meo cooks could make from the C-rations they were furnished. It tasted pretty good.

When they'd finished eating, the cooks came in and cleaned the tables while Captain Thomason briefed Ed on what was going on at Site 20. Their major effort at present was the building of the camp and the enlargement of the runway. There was a Meo village—mostly refugees from communist-occupied towns in the surrounding mountains, who had agreed to work on digging out the strip in return for rations, arms, and training. The training would have to await the building of a longer strip so that planes larger than the Helio could utilize it, but the rations were in the form of rice doled out daily in return for their labor. The rice arrived per air-drop from CAS planes on a somewhat irregular basis, and the administration of the rice was causing the team more headache than it was worth. The captain thought the next officer who arrived should be put in charge of the rice detail, the storage, payment, and dispensation of same, and the next officer to arrive happened to be Ed. Meadows nodded and agreed. He had no idea what would happen if he ever disagreed with his superior officer's suggestions, but now wasn't the time to find out. Terrell offered to help Ed gather his stuff from the airplane, as Pilot Ed was anxious to get back to Vientiane, so he took him to a cot in the tent next door which was labelled, "Marshall Dillon's Place." Evidently the BOQ. Ed set his Remington down on the cot and they went to unload the Helio.

Rice Officer, thought Ed when they were done with his moving in and Terrell had gone off to continue with his project of the construction of a warehouse. *One minute I'm a Team Leader with responsibilities and duties, then I come up here to work with the vaunted Central Intelligence Agency, and they make me a damn Rice Officer! It takes all kinds to run a war, so I guess I'd better get out there and learn what this rice is all about.*

SSG Post was the current Rice NCO, and it made Meadows feel even better to know he was replacing an E-6. Fantastic. Post was a cheerful enough fellow, and was absolutely delighted to turn the rice over to Meadows. Before he could hustle off to the war, however, Ed informed him that the captain had directed that Post was to remain as Meadows' NCOIC. Post was almost as thrilled as Ed had been at his assignment. "No offense to you, Sir," said the sergeant, "but when I found out I was going to work for the Agency, I had no idea they were going to take me out of my job and make me a fucking rice dispenser."

"I don't take offense, Sergeant, but since we're going to be the rice people, we may as well be the best rice people around. Tell me all about how you're getting the rice, what you do with it, and where you keep it." The rice, explained Post, arrived from the sky like the feces of a bird whenever a C-123 flew over. They double-bagged the rice and packed the bags only half-full so they wouldn't burst when they hit the ground. Then the plane flew over and dropped a pallet at a time—about forty bags, which fell like bombs and would kill you for sure if they hit you. The Villagers collected the bags and brought some of them over to the camp where they were simply stacked up and stored outside in some convenient place. Then Post would fill up whatever container the villager had with rice and that was it. They were supposed to work on the strip first, but not much work was getting done. The Meo, like the Americans, liked to fight, but didn't much like to dig dirt for an airstrip.

Meadows took Post down to the airstrip where they watched the work being done. It wasn't much. There were several women, some with babies strapped to their backs, wielding primitive adz's and chopping away the topsoil to create a relatively level surface of the hardpack underneath. At the rate they were going, they ought to have a long enough strip to accommodate a C-123 by the Year 2000, perhaps somewhat later. From the strip, they walked over to see the warehouse Terrell was supervising. It was a large building, bamboo poles for supports, roofed over with thatch, and the plans were to construct woven sides for it. When completed, it would keep out all but the worst weather. Meo women were involved in building it, too. Ed was impressed at how small these people really were. It was getting on toward supper stew time when they got back to the Long Branch, so Ed and Post went in for an early meal and Meadows then went to his hooch to work on a plan.

The team had a generator here, and wiring to each of the buildings, but there were no lights, as yet, and they didn't like to run the generator, anyway. It made so much noise that you couldn't hear anything else and when night fell, it was time to go to bed, anyway. Night fell early, so Ed was without light in pretty short order. That, too, was okay, cause he was a pretty tired young man, and the cool mountain air made the thought of sleep under the GI blanket on his cot quite inviting. After his first day as a worker for the Agency, it was easy to fall asleep. *Wonder what the Trackers are doing tonight? Wonder if I'll ever meet them again? I hope not.*

When the breakfast stew dishes had been cleared away, Ed went to Captain Thomason and asked for a meeting. He and SSG Post, he said, had a plan for the rice that might get more work out of the Meo and take less of the team's resources to administer. Thomason sat down where he was. "I'm ready for anything, Lieutenant, speak."

"Well, Sir, here's our plan. First of all, we need more work done on the airstrip and the warehouse. Second, we need better control of the rice. Third, we need some formula for handing the rice out that rewards workers and ignores watchers. Do you buy this?"

"You got the floor, Meadows, let's hear it all."

"Okay, Sir. I guess we don't have much control over how the rice gets here, but we can do better with the gathering of the bags when they fall. The Americans could gather it, or maybe only certain Meo, but both those plans take even more of our time than the one now. Could we get the C-123 to tie a parachute onto the pallets, a G-13, and kick out the whole pallet still bound up? The chute might not support it, but it would slow the load down enough to keep from killing anyone, plus heaping it all in one pile. They might not even have to double-bag it. We could hire us some Meo, for pay with rice, to tote it up to LT Terrell's warehouse, where we could keep an eye on it. Then, we could make an agreement with the Meo that we'd issue one kilo of rice per man per day's work on one of our projects. That's the usual ration for a Lao tahan, and they're bigger than these guys. If a lot of people work, they get a lot of rice; if no one works, we keep a lot of rice. It would only take a couple of our men initially, and after the project got going, maybe only one man could handle it. What do you think, Sir?" Ed was hoping that the one Rice-Lord would not be him.

"Sounds good, Meadows. Take your men as they arrive and do it. I need Post on another project, anyway. Our CAS contact, Roger, is supposed to arrive up here today, and I'll tell him about the chutes. He won't care, he's for anything. Have at it."

The next drop was that very afternoon, and Ed collected about 50% from the total dropped. The rest disappeared in the direction of the Meo village. Bushman arrived that afternoon in a Dornier, so Post gleefully bade them adieu. Bush enthusiastically adopted Ed's plan, as did Roger when he learned of it at dinner-stew. From now on, all rice would be delivered by semi-drop rather than free-fall. Bush had some other ideas, such as booby-trapping the stored supply to prevent pilferage which he was sure would follow. That Bush did love to booby-trap things. They agreed it would be necessary to have a pow-wow with the village Headman and the Meo Elders to explain the new system, so that was their project for the afternoon.

Captain Thomason's interpreter was a young Meo named Kom, who had been educated by some French missionaries in both the French and English languages, so the two men borrowed him for the afternoon and set out for the Meo village. It lay on the other side of the valley, about a mile away from the camp. It was a beautiful day, and the walk was pleasant. Their presence in the village caused some excitement, and by the time they had reached the Headman's hut, it seemed that every kid in the village was following in their wake. Meadows felt like a Pied Piper.

Kom explained to the Headman the purpose of their visit. He called the Council together in the meeting hut, they passed around a jug of fermented rice which everyone sipped with a straw, and Ed was offered the opportunity to speak. He told them his plan for rice distribution, and, to his surprise, they accepted without any objections. It seemed like a good meeting. More rice juice was sipped, it tasted like hot mush with a decided afterbite, and the meeting was over. The didn't say *"Som Bai"* up here, since they didn't speak Lao, but instead held up their right hands like the Indians of the old West, and said, *"Yo Yunga."* After his *Yo Yungas* were repeated all around, Lieutenant Meadows—Rice-Lord of the Sam Tong Valley, and his Assistant, Bushman the Rice-Duke, returned to the Special Forces camp. It was time for supper-stew.

The next three days were spent in gathering and storing rice, for the CAS planes arrived every day. Flag also arrived, as did Eason, and, finally, Riley, and FTT-19 was in the rice business. Only trouble was, there wasn't enough work for all of them to do, so Meadows released all but his Rice-Duke to join the team in preparing training facilities for future Meo soldiers. They had agreed that the plan wouldn't go into effect until Sunday, the fifth day following the Meo meeting. By late Saturday afternoon, they had several hundred bags of rice, weighing about 40 kilos each, stored in Terrell's recently completed warehouse. The time for implementing the rice system was here, "Project Work-or-Don't-Eat" was ready to commence. What a laugh. From running from the Trackers to hoarding rice in a single week. They said you could expect different assignments in your Army career, and this was a different one. Ed and Bushman drank a couple of Kirins as they sat on the warehouse floor and viewed their bank of rice bags. Ed had obtained the permission of the captain for FTT-19 to stand guard over the rice at night, and it was getting close to Ed's turn to pull the first shift. "Bush, you ever been a rice guard before?"

"Shit, Sir, when you been in the Army as long as me, you been guard over damn near everything. I don't know of any rice I've guarded, but I've guarded shit that ain't even been made yet. I'm going to supper-stew; you coming?"

Ed got up and followed Bush out of the warehouse. He'd have to admit that he'd never guarded "shit that ain't been made yet," but he still didn't think guarding rice was an ordinary assignment.

37

When Your Hair Stands Up On End

It was Sunday morning in the Sam Tong valley, a day dawning not unlike any of the other days in this virtual pristine valley. For Meadows and Bushman, it was a very special day, for this was the day they expected to reap the beginning of rewards from their plan for labor among the Meo workers. They ate breakfast-stew with the other members of the team who were aware of their plan and many of whom were doubtful of its potential; then they went down to the airstrip where the work of digging was already begun. Such a crowd of diggers they had not previously seen. Although the vast majority of workers were still women, there must have been well over a hundred people wielding adzs and shovels and picks and hoes out there in the early morning light. It was a sight to make the heart glad.

The Headman was there, clad in his finest attire—a dark green suit that looked a lot like a PL uniform, complete with black oxford shoes and a snap-brim hat. Since the Meo were almost exclusively a barefoot people, the shoes were the most striking part of his get-up. He was bustling around issuing instructions and sweating like a real worker. Ed and Bushman exchanged *Yo Yungas* with Headman, all three of them smiling. Kom, the interpreter was present, and through him, Ed told Headman how delighted he was to see such a response to the call for workers. Headman responded by stating that he expected over two hundred people to be out working today, and Ed replied that they were going to cost him a lot of rice. Headman nodded. Meadows next instructed Kom to perform a head count and try to come up with the exact number of workers actually present. He also instructed Bush privately to check on Kom's figures. Kom may speak a little English, but he may be tempted to count in Meo.

Leaving them at the strip, Ed walked up to the warehouse where there was also a beehive of activity. Eason had the warehouse detail today, and he was supervising as the sides were being tied onto the structure. It was gonna be nice. Terrell had been released from the project as it had been transferred to the Rice Lord and his Duke, and Eason fell among those who worked for the Rice Lord. Meadows told Rick to perform a count of all persons present at that time, and again after the noon break. It wasn't the noon-hour break, but rather the noon break, for the Meo took a couple of hours off in the middle of the day, sometimes three or four, but that was okay with Ed. If this many people worked even the better part of a day, every day for a week, they would be able to get a C-123 in here, maybe, and then they could get at least a front-end loader or a little tractor, perhaps even a little bulldozer, and then the project would really take off. Meadows was excited.

With all the peace and tranquility around the valley, Ed had stopped carrying the shotgun everywhere he went during the day, but he still carried his side-arm, as did most of the team personnel, and all of the FTT-19 folks. Peace is fine, and all that, but there was still an enemy out there somewhere, and the Americans were sure he was aware of their efforts to lengthen the airstrip. Captain Thomason had an alert plan with which everyone was familiar, and they had arranged for a Reaction Force of Americans to respond to a call for help from any of the locations where work was going on. Still, it was an awfully peaceful place. With work in full sway, Meadows didn't have much to do, but he felt like he ought to be around in case of any disputes and to mainly be seen by the workers and let them know he was interested.

Back at the strip, Headman had presented Bush with his figures for workers present, and Bush handed it to Ed when the lieutenant returned just before noon. There were marks all over a scrap of paper and then a figure at the bottom with a circle drawn around it. The figure was 256.

"The guy's a damn liar," explained Bush when Ed whistled at the figure. "Me and ole Kom here counted 139 out there on the field. I don't know how many there are at the warehouse, but there can't be all that many."

"There were 34 this morning," said Ed. "I told Rick to count them in the morning and again after the break. We may have missed one or two, but our total of 173 is a lot less than 256. Where is Headman? Maybe we ought to have a little talk with him."

"Shit, Sir, he left right after we got here. Probably went back to the village to stir the rice pot and smoke a little dope since he's gonna get all that rice. What're you gonna do, Boss?"

"I hate to call the guy a liar, but if this project is going to work, we've got to establish our credibility somehow without him losing face. Let's go eat some stew—and think about it." They walked across the draw and on to the Long Branch, Bush filling Ed in on what all had gotten done that morning. It was a lot, for the women were hard diggers. They lunched on stew—yellow stew today, then had a beer with Flagstone and discussed their dilemma. Flag listened to their talk earnestly.

"Why don't you wait and see what happens this afternoon? Maybe the old fart is gonna bring out the whole village and put them to work. Are you going to pay for half a day's work the same as a whole day? What if you get 500 this afternoon? What will you do then, Boss?"

"I'll handle that problem when I come to it. There is no way they can come up with 500 people unless they get the PL from the PDJ (Plain des Jarres) to pitch in. Who's in charge of our rations here, anyway?"

"Kendall, guy from the 1st. He's out with the cooks. Why?"

"I'm going to talk to him. Bush, you and Kom count again when you get back to work. Riley," Meadows said, calling the medic over, "you go to the warehouse with Eason this afternoon. Both of you take your weapons with you, kinda casual-like. Keep them out of sight, but nearby. Flag, you join us when we knock off for the day, and bring Bush's BAR up to the warehouse. I don't think there'll be any trouble, but I want to be safe rather than sorry. Bush, does Eason know how to set off your charges up there?"

"I don't know. Maybe him and me better swap places this afternoon."

"Good idea. Tell him about it. I'll be along." Ed got up and headed for the kitchen in search of Kendall. He found the sergeant easily by following the sound of a string of expletives being shouted by a lean American and directed at a diminutive young Meo who was washing dishes. "Sergeant Kendall?" Meadows asked.

"Yes, Sir, what can I do for you? We ain't got no steak, the menu for supper is red stew and hot coffee. Anything else?" Meadows laughed. Typical mess sergeant.

"Naw, Sarge, I'm just after some information. How much beer do we have on hand?"

"Hundred cases, more or less. Depends on how much you guys have stolen today. Why?"

"Could you spare a couple of cases for the Meo if I asked for them?"

"Who's gonna replace them? If I run out of beer, my ass is grass, and it takes a lot of Helios to replace beer. What you got in mind, Sir?" he asked hesitantly, realizing that this could result in all kinds of precedents mess sergeants hate.

"I might need a couple of cases, just occasionally, not everyday. I'll talk to Roger and make sure they get replaced. It might mean we can get a C-123 in here sooner so you can have some steak for the troops and all the beer we can drink in a month."

"Promises, promises. Okay, Sir, I can let you have two cases, but only Asahi, no Bud, and only one time." Meadows thanked the sergeant and stopped by the BOQ to pick up the Remington. Then he walked down to the warehouse.

Bush was fiddling around with his demolitions control panel when Meadows arrived. There were about a dozen Meo tying sheafs of straw to the sides of the warehouse framework, no more than that. "How's it going, Bush?" asked Ed.

"Oh, Boss, glad you're here. Let me show you what I've done. I put a cap in every bag of rice in this frigging warehouse and connected them all to this button," indicating the first in a line of switches on his panel. "That'll blow open every bag of rice in here in a flash. Then I've got a charge under every stack that's controlled by this second button. If you want to blow the place to smithereens, that'll do it. The third button sets both the caps and the charges off together. That'll put each individual grain of rice in the air about a thousand feet and seed the whole damn valley. Over here," continued the sergeant, obviously enthralled with his work, "I have a little stack of rice bags that we could use for a demonstration, if you like. Not much, just a couple of pounds of C-4 and some caps. That's button four. Finally, I put out a few Claymores around the hut, and if you want to kill everybody around but save the rice, hit the fifth button. What do you think?"

"I hope we don't have to use it. Is that all?"

Bushman grinned. "How'd you guess? Naw, I got a few other things. I got each stack booby-trapped so they'll go off if someone decides to take the rice without our permission. See these little strings here?" indicating a small strand of twine at the corner of each stack. "You pull the twine out and it safes the charge. If you don't pull the string out, you better not steal no rice. Okay, Boss?"

"Be sure to pull the strings out when we issue the rice. I'm going down to the strip. By the way, how many workers you got this afternoon?"

"Eleven."

At the airstrip, the crowd was a lot smaller that afternoon, too. Eason reported a count of 87, a big improvement over the preceding days, but a lot less than Ed had hoped for. Headman was not around. The women were dutifully chopping at the soft topsoil, and every hour that passed brought the C123 about two feet closer. They needed about 1000 more hours. Meadows hung around the airstrip until 1700 hrs, when the sun was still well overhead, but the shadows were longer. He noted that many of the Meo women had umbrellas which they held with one hand while they chopped with the other. It was a quaint sight. Headman had not returned all afternoon, but as Ed was getting ready to leave, he saw the Headman walking up the trail with Kom. Ed waited for them to arrive. Yo Yunga. Nice day. Hot sun. Hard work. Many people. All that good shit. Finally Headman handed Meadows a slip of paper. The number 345 was circled in the center. Ed looked at Headman.

"This is a large number. Where are all these people now?" Kom translated, waited for the Headman's reply, then translated back.

"Headman say that all from morning too tired to work rest of day, so more come. Everyone must be paid." Ed did some arithmetic. There were 173 that morning, 98 more that afternoon. That was 271. 345 minus 271 equals 74. Say 80 kilos, two extra bags of rice. 271, say 280, divided by 40 equals seven. It was hardly worth the effort to argue, but they had to establish credibility.

"Tell him I can pay only part for the half-day workers. I will give him eight bags of rice, 320 kilos. Plus, tell him I am very thankful for all his help today, and I have for him two cases of beer as an expression of my gratitude." Kom translated. Headman smiled and nodded, but his heart was not in either the smile or the nod. He didn't like the deal. Ed wrote a note for Bushman and dispatched Eason to deliver it. Issue eight bags, no more, and he hoped to hell the Meo who went with Eason didn't try for an extra bag. He didn't want to seed the valley.

On Monday morning, the Headman was back making his rounds on his workers bright and early, but there were fewer of them today than yesterday. Eason counted 112 at the airfield, while Bush had 23 working on the warehouse. By noon, the warehouse was virtually finished, so those laboring there were dispatched to the strip. Headman reported, by yet another slip of paper, the number 279, with a circle around the number. In the afternoon, the count was only 86 by Eason, but when quitting time came, Ed was faithful to issue one kilo for each of the morning total, 135, rounded up to 160 for ease in issuing four sacks. No beer, this time. Headman was displeased, but said nothing audible. The atmosphere surrounding him and Ed was charged with electricity. Headman took his sacks of rice and went home, so Meadows and his men went up to supper stew. The lieutenant felt it was time to tell the captain about the inflated personnel counts and his intent to stick by the bargain he'd made with the Headman. Even with the problem, they were still getting more work out of the Meo villagers than before. Captain Thomason listened to Ed's story and expressed his whole-hearted support. For that, Meadows was grateful. He said he had liked the captain all along, didn't he?

Tuesday morning, and the number of workers by actual count was 59. The circled figure was 231. This was getting ridiculous. Through Kom, Headman asked how much rice Ed intended to issue, and the Rice Lord of the Sam Tong Valley replied that he intended to issue one and one-half bags, 60 kilos. Headman then told Kom that he and the village council wished to have a meeting with Ed and Kom after lunch. That was okayed by Ed, who then informed the captain. Thomason told Meadows to be cautious, but he didn't see anything wrong with the meeting. Meadows ate his dinner-stew, and at 1300 hrs, he and Kom began the long walk to the Meo village. He considered taking the Remington, but decided against it as he felt it would be too aggressive. Bushman said that he and the rest of FTT-19 would be at the airstrip with all their guns strapped on if Meadows needed any help.

When they arrived at the council hut, a long table was set up and about a dozen of the elders were seated along one side. Ed and Kom took their seats opposite Headman in the center of the table. *Yo Yungas* all around. Kom whispered to Ed that he didn't like this set-up, and he felt they should be very cautious. The mood of the council was evil, he added. This was just great. Ed could think of only ten or eleven thousand places he would rather be right then. He wondered what the Trackers were doing about then. Headman began the proceedings. He informed Ed through Kom, that the Meo were unhappy with the rice distribution. They weren't getting enough to feed all the people in the village. Meadows tried to express surprise, and said he was trying to stick with the agreement the council and he had reached a few days before. Headman replied that they had other things to do besides work for the Americans. It was their rice, and they wanted to handle the distribution of it from then on. Meadows carefully explained that the rice was a gift from the United States Government, in exchange for help on the airstrip so they could get even more aid for the Meo to fight against the communist Viet Minh and Pathet Lao who wanted to enslave the Meo.

Headman wasn't satisfied. He told Meadows they were going to take over the rice warehouse and issue the rice themselves. Ed replied that he owned the warehouse, and he intended to keep it. Headman shouted that he had enough troops to capture the rice, and he intended to do so. This was a bad situation getting worse. No, said Meadows, he wouldn't capture the warehouse, for Ed's men were guarding it and they would fight. Headman said the Meo would kill the Americans and take the rice. Meadows was searching for a way out of this predicament, but no exit reared its head. The rice, Ed explained, had been booby-trapped by Bushman, and if the Meo tried to take it, he would blow it all up and then there would be none for anyone. Headman consulted with the council. The mood was, indeed, evil. After a rather heated argument, during which Meadows saw many evil glances thrown in his direction by the council members, Headman said that if that were the case, they were going to kill Meadows right there and take the rice before Bush knew something had gone wrong. For some reason, Ed believed him. Holding up his left hand to indicate he was doing nothing wrong, Meadows drew the Smith & Wesson from his holster and laid the heavy revolver on the table. Talking directly to Headman, without waiting for Kom to translate, Ed said,

"It is true you can kill me right now and there is nothing I can do about it. But before I die, I will shoot you right in the face," pointing his finger in the face of Headman, "and you," pointing in the face of the man to Headman's right, "and possibly you," the face on Headman's left, "and maybe even you and you," the next two faces in line. "But I guarantee you I will kill *you* before I die." The finger was once again on Headman. The table was silent. Ed's words needed no translation. Headman was sweating. Meadows was *REALLY* sweating. Headman looked nervously at the pistol next to Ed's hand. He licked his lips. Without taking his eyes off the revolver, Headman said something through clenched teeth. Meadows expected a bullet in the brain. Kom whispered, his voice cracking. Headman wanted to discuss Meadows' proposal with the council. Ed nodded, leaving his hand next to the Magnum. All the council members jabbered excitedly, then Headman smiled and looked back at Ed.

It was a test, Kom translated Headman's words, to see if Ed could be scared. They weren't going to kill him, they were just joking. *Joking, my ass,* thought Meadows. They were as intent on Ed's demise as the Trackers had been, but they gave up more easily. They were going to talk some more about a new plan for earning the rice, and they would present it to Ed tomorrow. He could go now.

Meadows got up from the table, picked up his weapon, and slid it back into the holster, leaving the snap undone. Raising his right hand, he *Yo Yunga'd*, motioned to Kom, turned around and walked away. He had heard about the Last Mile, and what a condemned man thought as he walked to his doom, but he would no longer wonder what the condemned thought about. They thought about the bullet, or the shock, or the fumes, or the jerk on the rope that would end their life, for every step Meadows took he fully expected to be his last. It was a long, long way down the hill and over toward the airstrip. It took an eternity to reach the halfway mark, and Ed wasn't sure he had the strength to make it all the way.

At the little valley separating the strip from the village, he thought about hitting the ground and trying to crawl the rest of the way. It took all his will-power to keep from looking behind him. Then he saw the most beautiful mirage he had ever beheld. Sitting there in the draw were four men—the nicest, cleanest, most handsome men he had ever seen. Bushman was lazily looking up the hill at the Meo village, his BAR lying across his thighs. Flagstone stood with the M-1 lying in the crook of his arm. Riley had a grease-gun resting on his hip, and Rick Eason was cradling a .30 calibre machine-gun with a belt of ammo glistening in the sunlight. They were gorgeous.

"Hello, Boss," said Flag. "You look like you've seen a ghost. Everything okay?"

Meadows nodded, trying hard not to kiss Flag right there in front of the men. Bush spit on the ground and said, "We thought you might need some help. The Reaction Force is right on top of the hill. Let's just stroll on up there and join them." As they walked, Flag explained to Ed that the captain had learned from Kendall, who had learned from the Meo cooks, that the Headman intended to kill Ed at the conference. Thomason had thought it wise to alert the team, and they had deployed the Reaction Force. It might not have saved Ed's life, but they would have at least been able to retrieve his body. What a comforting thought. Ed was delighted that his body would not have to worry about being retrieved. The team reached the strip, and there they saw that the other team had deployed some machine-guns on this side of the field, had Claymores stuck in the ground, and were dressed for war. Even though it wouldn't have saved his life, it might have made the decision to kill him harder for Headman to swallow. Ed turned to the FTT-19 members.

"Thank you, all of you." They smiled and nodded.

38

Vang Pao

The entire detachment at Site 20 spent an uneasy night. No one was sure exactly what the Meo would do now. Captain Thomason was very supportive of Ed's actions, and, quite frankly, he was as tickled as shit at the way the lieutenant had extricated himself from the village. Ed had diarrhea, but he was able to control it until he reached the latrine at the American camp. That represented an improvement over some of his previous episodes. The boy was growing up. Some said he was grown.

The captain ordered a full-scale alert, and sent a message for Roger to get his ass up there the next morning. Those were his exact words. The Meo did nothing that night, or, if they did, it wasn't obvious to the Americans. And right at first light, a Dornier landed on the strip with Roger's ass sitting in the co-pilot's seat. Captain Thomason and Meadows took turns telling the field operative about the Great Rice War and the actions of the Rice Lord. Roger (he didn't have a last name, or if he did, it was a closely-guarded secret) listened intently to the entire tale before he said anything. He nodded a couple of times, smiled at the story of, "I'm going to kill you before I die," then nodded some more. Finally he spoke.

"I don't see how you could have handled it any differently, under the circumstances." Ed liked Roger. "But I don't think we can continue like this. Obviously, Lieutenant Meadows is through as the Rice

Lord, but I don't want it to seem that he's been relieved. I agree entirely with his plan. I think we need a new Headman in the village, and I know just the man to get it done. Colonel Vang Pao hasn't been here in a while, so I think it's time for him to check up on this place. I've sent him a message to come, and with any luck at all, he'll be here before dinner. He'll take care of the Meo side. I want him to meet Meadows and hear his side of the story first, so we'll have him up for the mid-day stew, if you don't mind, Captain." Thomason said he didn't mind. "Good. I would suggest that Sergeant Bushman stay on as the Rice Boss, and I have another assignment for Meadows, if you don't need him." Captain Thomason said he didn't need him. "Okay, Meadows, get with me after dinner, and I'll tell you what I want you to do."

The morning was spent in waiting for Vang Pao to arrive and at the same time keeping a wary eye on the Meo village. Roger went over to talk to the elders and the Headman and tell them of Vang Pao's visit. Ed sat on a small hill overlooking the strip with Bushman and Flagstone, and they reviewed all the things they had heard about Vang Pao. The guy was a legend, no doubt about it. They said (the ubiquitous "they") that every village he visited, the elders gave him a couple of wives, and the good colonel spent a lot of time servicing his entourage. He also had quite a reputation as a fighter, though, or at least as a leader of fighting men. The story was well-known that the colonel visited a village once right after the men of the village had captured a bunch of Meo aligned with the PL, fifteen of them, to be exact, and all the people were anxious to see what Vang Pao was going to do with the prisoners. After all, he was the King of the Meo, and these folks were supposed to be loyal to him, not them (the PL).

The day he arrived in the village, he had the prisoners line up in a row, then he walked along the row in front of them, saying nothing. When he reached a spot determined only in his mind, he pulled out the little snub-nose Smith & Wesson that he carried, pointed it in the face of the captive, and blew his brains out. Then he holstered his revolver, told them to put the rest of the prisoners back into confinement, and went on about his business of serving the needs of his people. The next day he repeated the performance, walking down the row of POW's, stopping in front of one of them, drawing his weapon, and splattering the poor guy's brains all over the sky. The rest were sent back to confinement. So the process had continued for eleven more days until on the fourteenth day, there were only two poor souls standing there in front of Vang Pao when he made his rounds. By this time they were pretty much resigned to their fate, so they were standing with their faces to the ground as the colonel approached. He drew his Smith, then pointed it at the ground and expended a round at their feet. Replacing the revolver in its holster, he told the two survivors to return to their village and tell their people what happens to Meo who line themselves up with the PL. There was a karch formation nearby—a vertical wall of limestone which would take experienced mountain climbers all day to scale, but they said the two Meo ran straight up that wall of rock and disappeared over the top.

Meadows believed it. Hell, he imagined he would have scaled a wall to get away from the Trackers. Lots of other stories abounded about Vang Pao, but when he arrived, he didn't look like a legend. He came in a Helio with two aides, and he wore the infamous Smith & Wesson, but aside from that, he looked a lot like the other Meo. Until you got up close. Then you saw that his khaki uniform was of tailored gabardine, he flashed a lot of gold teeth when he *Yo Yunga'd*, and he had a uniform cap with scrambled eggs and gold braid. If he wasn't a legend in his own time, he sure dressed like he thought he was.

The dinner-stew had an additional side dish of gummy rice that day, prepared by the Meo cooks, and Meadows was introduced to the colonel. Vang Pao spoke nearly perfect, if somewhat stilted, English and he told Meadows that he was unhappy with the Headman for trying to obtain the rice without working for it, especially since he had made the deal with Ed. After they ate, Vang Pao paid a visit to the village with Roger, and when they returned, he brought with him the new Headman. It was the Number Two man on Ed's hit list of the preceding day. Meadows wondered how many rounds remained in Vang Pao's side-arm, but he didn't ask. Vang Pao paid his respects all around, then the same Helio that brought him in whisked him away to places and parts unknown. None of the team ever saw Headman again.

Roger was getting ready to go, too, but he took Ed aside and talked to him about his new job. There were a lot of camps where the Meo were getting supplied by the CAS, and Roger needed someone to be a liaison for him with these camps, someone who was an American, someone who understood military things and could observe what he was directed to observe, and report what he was directed to report. Someone, it seemed, named Ed Meadows, Lieutenant, U.S. Army. Starting tomorrow morning, Meadows would go along with the Helios and Dorniers, whichever they happened to have working out of Site 20, and learn where these camps were, what they were about, and carry out Roger's orders with respect to the camps. There would be Americans at some of the camps, other nationalities at some of them, but there would be an English-speaker at all of them. Regardless of who they might be, Ed was to keep close-mouthed about what he saw and what he did, and was to report directly to Roger, get his orders from Roger either in person, or in the form of a Safe Hands message delivered by the pilot each day. With a wave of the hand, Roger boarded his Dornier and left the strip. Meadows watched the plane depart. Wonderful. Once upon a time he had been a leader of men, engaged in a struggle, as he saw it, to keep the world safe for Democracy, then he became a Rice Lord, and now he was to be a messenger boy. Fantastic. Ed walked up to the Long Branch and quietly got stuporously drunk.

39

Air Boss

The pilot who arrived the next morning was a fellow known as, Morris, who had been into Site 20 on several previous trips and was well-known and well-liked by the team members. This particular morning he had a manila envelope with him that had "SAFE HANDS" stamped in red ink all over it. He presented it to Meadows when Ed approached him and said, "Here you are, Lieutenant, I has done my duty. I hate delivering those fucking things. It always seems like it contains the Crown Jewels, or something. You got some coffee?"

"Up at the Long Branch. I'm going to stay here and read the orders. What are you going to do, Morris?"

"Hell, Lieutenant, I'm at your service today. Imagine that—I used to be a fucking major and here I am serving a Lieutenant! I'll be at the coffee pot." He made his way toward the camp while Ed unfastened the clasp on the envelope, ripped open the seal, and drew out several sheets of paper. Roger, or someone, had hand written the message. It began by saying, *"Good morning."* The text of the letter was as follows:

"1. Take the load on the Helio over to Xat Bo and deliver it personally to a man who will identify himself as, 'Falcon.'

2. Take whatever Falcon gives you to Xing Dat and deliver that package to a man who will identify himself as, 'Vulture.'

3. Pick up two or three prisoners at Xing Dat and bring them to

Site 20 where I will meet you. Don't let the prisoners hurt themselves.

4. If anything happens other than what I said, have the pilot contact Pepperbox and ask for Eagle. That's me. They can reach me."

The other sheets of paper were blank and served as a filler. This was going to be even more exciting than playing Rice Lord, for Ed could see he was being groomed as a keeper of birds. Maybe he should send home for his Field Guide to North American Birds. On second thought, there weren't a lot of North American birds around here. Okay, he'd get a Guide to Asiatic Birds. Whatever happened to the war he was being paid by the Army to fight? Meadows made his way up to the Long Branch and told Morris he was ready to go. The pilot finished off his coffee, got up and started toward the plane. "Where to, Boss?" Ed was surprised to hear that old name, but decided it probably didn't mean anything. Just a name Morris chose to indicate his status as a server rather than a served.

"Xat Bo is first," replied Meadows.

"Sonofabitch!" exclaimed Morris. "The last plane in there was shot down a couple of days ago—a Beaver; killed a buddy of mine. I don't like that place."

"Where is Xat Bo?" asked Meadows.

"It's about twenty minutes west of here. The Viet Minh have been active in that area trying to cut-off Luang Prabang from Vientiane. It's a pisser. Where do we get rid of the gear I got on board?" They had reached the aircraft by this time, and Ed was crawling in while Morris checked the plane over.

"We drop it off at Xat Bo. What are you carrying, anyway?" he asked, indicating the tarp-wrapped bundle behind the seats.

"Damn if I know. Something that don't move is all I know. I don't mind the quiet stuff, but the stuff that talks or ticks scares the piss out of me." The propeller started its jerky spinning as it waited for the engine to roar to life, and the engine followed in order. Right away the prop blades were only a blur as the herky-jerky motion settled into a smooth arc. Morris taxied out onto the strip, looked all around in the sky, revved up the motor, released the brakes and lowered the nose. It seemed that they rolled only about a hundred feet or so and he eased the wheel back. The Helio left the ground and picked up speed. Instead of climbing out of the valley, Morris banked the plane steeply over the Meo village and headed west, just above the treetops.

He looked over at Ed, smiled, and said something. Ed couldn't hear a word he said, so he cupped his hand behind his left ear and shouted, "What?"

"No sense in letting them know we're coming before we get there. We're going in low and fast. Less time for them to react."

"Do you really expect trouble?"

"Damn right. We nearly always get shot at here." End of conversation, for now Morris was intent on dodging tree-tops as they crested the ridgeline around the valley. Once over the crest, he immediately pointed the nose of the aircraft down the slope and they picked up speed as they dove. Ed watched the air speed indicator needle as it swung to 120 knots, about 150 miles per hour, at a height above the trees of approximately three feet. He decided that Morris must have been a major in the air commandos at Hurlburt and he made a note to ask him if they survived this flight. Now Morris was twisting the little plane back and forth, not only above the trees, but through them.

Ed had never had any kind of motion sickness in his life, and he didn't feel sick now, at least not to his stomach. His soul kinda hurt as he contemplated hitting a stray tree at 150 mph and the plane coming apart in pieces with a piece of Ed attached to each major fragment. It wasn't a good feeling. Suddenly, the trees stopped and they were over open rice paddies, heading for a dirt strip that was rapidly approaching. Morris pointed out of the side window, gesturing determinedly with his finger. He shouted at Ed.

"See those tracers?" Meadows looked in the direction the finger was pointing. Sure enough, there were tiny little streaks of fire flashing from the woods and disappearing before they got to the plane. "Fuckers misjudged the elevation," hollered Morris. "We were lucky this time." Their wheels hit the runway, no flaps, no slowing down, just bump, down. Morris dropped the tail, cut the engine, and stood on the brakes. The plane shuddered, yawed, raised up on its left gear like it wanted to turn over, then banged back onto the runway and stopped. It wasn't like American Airlines at all.

The engine had hardly died when a man came running up to the plane followed by three little Meos, or Lao; Ed couldn't be sure. The man wasn't American, for his hair was cut funny and he had a very blonde face and hair. "Hallo." Guttural sound, long "A's," probably Nordic. "I'm Falcon. Have you a package for me?"

"Ya," mimicked Meadows. "Have you something for me?"

"No-o-o-o, but you are welcome to stay awhile."

"No, thanks," butted in Morris. "We got a schedule to keep. Besides, I want to get out of here before those guys have a chance to change crews to one who can shoot," indicating the direction from which the tracers had come. "Where to, Lieutenant?" The natives were lifting what must have been a heavy load from the cargo door of the plane.

"Xing Dat."

"Xing Dat? You really are a glutton for punishment. That's the end of the earth."

"Where is Xing Dat?"

"North of here about thirty minutes. It ain't too bad, but I want to see what you think of their runway."

"By the way, Morris," said Ed as the pilot started up the engine again, "How do you plan to get out of here with that gun crew waiting for us?"

"Fly right at 'em. Scare the hell out of the bastards." He turned the aircraft around, locked the brakes as he increased the throttle to full, then released the brakes, increased the pitch of the blades, and the craft whisked down the runway. They were airborne in even less space than they'd used at Sam Tong, since they'd been relieved of their load, but Morris was flying *REALLY* low now. Except for the fact that the plane wasn't bumping its wheels on the ground, Ed wasn't at all sure they were flying. Morris began twisting the plane now, popping up a few feet, banking left, then right, then back down as he headed straight for the location of the gun. Meadows didn't see any tracers, but decided that if they were coming right at you, you wouldn't be able to see them. They were almost to the tree-line, the air speed had reached 100 knots, and they were going to cut some trees down in their death throes if they didn't get up pretty soon. Meadows saw the gun emplacement on the edge of the trees, and he saw the gunners looking at them as they seemed destined to commit suicide. Morris jerked the wheel back, kicked the right rudder all the way in, twisted the wheel to the right, and they banked as they rose, missing first the ground, then the trees, but neither one by very much. He levelled out at tree-top altitude, adjusted his heading to the north, and they escaped from Xat Bo. Bring on Xing Dat.

After a few minutes, Morris directed the airplane to climb, and they gained altitude faster than the terrain, which was also rising and becoming much more mountainous. At 6000′, he slowed the engine to cruise, and they flew leisurely along for the next ten or fifteen minutes. The countryside beneath them was beautiful, virgin, no sign at all of the rapist of the world, man. Morris pointed ahead of them, mouthing the words, "Xing Dat." Meadows looked ahead. Holy Cow! That couldn't be a runway! It looked like a couple of small peaks with their tops cleared off and connected by a trestle. Surely Morris was jesting, they weren't going to land on that! They were. The flaps came down as the airplane slowed, then the slats came out of the leading edges of the wings, and their approach was made at about 35 knots. There was a horn sounding somewhere in the cabin which meant nothing to Meadows, but is the stall warning for pilots. Had Ed known the meaning, he might have been excited. Morris set the plane down on the first peak, they shuddered across the trestle with no room to swerve, and stopped on the second peak. Ten more feet and they would have been airborne again, ready or not, for the end of the runway was the beginning of a several hundred foot drop. *Wonder if I could make peace with the Meo and pass out the rice again?*

Meadows got out of the plane and helped Morris lift the tail and turn it around within the very narrow confines of the tiny trestle-strip. They had it pointed back in the direction from which they'd come before a couple of Europeans appeared at the mountain peak. The taller of the two, speaking English words but with French pronunciation, said, "Bonjour, how are you today? I am Vulture, and I have for you a package, two packages. Have you for me anything?"

Meadows didn't like frogs anymore up here than he did down in the flats, but now wasn't the time to debate this man. "We have for you nothing. Where are your packages?" The man turned around and beckoned. About a dozen Meo tahans came struggling up to the plane, carrying two well-tied and blind-folded prisoners. The POW's weren't Lao or Meo, Ed was sure of that, but he wasn't sure exactly what they were. Probably Vietnamese, he guessed. No time for musing, they stuffed the men into the cargo compartment, tied them down, and prepared for take-off. Even as loaded as it was, the take-off was easy, for as the plane reached the end of the second peak and rolled off, they were two hundred feet in the air. Morris pointed the nose down, going with the flow, and gaining airspeed, then brought the craft under control and levelled it off. They flew at 6000' all the way back to Site 20. As they approached the valley, Ed was amazed at how long their runway actually was. Compared to where they had been that day, it looked like Memphis International. Morris lined the nose of the plane up with the imaginary center-line of the strip, put all the flaps down, the slats came down, and they were nearly home free.

The engine stopped. No warning, no flashing lights, no nothing. Morris flared the plane as it settled into the trees at the east end of the runway, but they were still going 40 miles per hour when the nose plowed into the upper boughs of the first tree. There were limbs and branches and leaves everywhere, then there was a sudden stop which wrenched Ed around in the harness and slammed his head into the instrument panel. He felt his left leg break—it snapped and he thought he even heard it, but he didn't feel or hear when his unprotected head hit the roof of the cabin. All he knew was it seemed that all had gotten very quiet, they had stopped moving, and the lights were out in Sam Tong. Then it seemed like it all got very warm and pleasant. Time for a nap.

40

Med Evac

Ed was only unconscious for a minute. He missed the thrill of the airplane falling to the ground at the base of the trees, and then the trees falling down on top of them. As the blackness cleared from his brain, he was aware that something bad had happened, but he wasn't sure exactly what. The last thing he remembered, he had been flying in a Helio, and here he was in the woods hiding in the trees, he guessed, for there was foliage all over him. Instinctively, he reached for his weapon in case there were any PL around, and discovered that he wasn't exactly free to move. There was a strap across his waist and he seemed to be confined to a seat of some kind.

Not only that, but there were other people around somewhere, for he heard breathing. It was hard to focus his eyes on anything, but he was sure there was someone close by on his left. So close by, in fact, that he was touching Ed, and whoever it was was moving around, not paying any attention to noise discipline at all. Couldn't have been Pompeo or Flagstone; they were never so noisy. The Person Next Door was banging on something like he was trying to open it, but he wasn't having much luck. What he did seem to be adept at was cussing, and he was really cussing, in English, so the situation wasn't as grim as it could have been. There were now the sounds of people running up, and Ed wished to hell the Person Next Door would knock it off so they could check out these folks. It might be the Trackers; those fuckers never gave up. Someone grabbed Ed's arm, and he turned, or tried to turn, to see who it was. He couldn't reach his revolver, he couldn't turn around, and he couldn't see. The hand which had grabbed him was shaking him, hard.

"Boss, Boss, can you hear me?" Meadows recognized the voice, but he couldn't quite place it. Must be one of the team in Laos, for they called him, "Boss."

"I hear you, but I can't see very well and I can't move much. What the hell has happened?"

"Your airplane crashed. It's busted all to hell. We gotta get you out of there, there's fucking gas all over the place." It was Flag, for the way he described the gas was with a Boston accent.

"Flag, is that you?"

"It's me, Boss, no sweat. Wipe the blood off your face and see if it helps any." Ed wiped the blood off his face and it made a world of difference. For one thing, it allowed him to see. There wasn't much to see, just a bunch of trees waving and wiggling, but he felt no breeze.

"Flag, why are the trees moving?"

"We're trying to get your ass out of there. Morris is already out, he ain't hurt, and there's two dead slopes in the back. Can you move at all?"

Ed tried to move. "No."

"Then be still, we'll have you out in a minute. Riley, get your fat ass up here and look at the boss. See what's wrong with him." Riley's face appeared in Ed's limited field of vision. He was smiling.

"Hello, Boss, fancy meeting you here. Do you hurt anywhere?"

"I hurt everywhere, but my left leg feels the worse. I think it's broken."

"By George, I think you're right. It sure is crooked. You got a cut on your head that's bleeding like hell, better let me put a dressing on it. That's all I can see, Flag. Want me to give him some morphine?" Ed could neither see nor hear Flag's reply, so he spoke up for himself.

"I don't want no morphine. I want out of here." Riley swabbed off the exposed right forearm of his lieutenant and stuck the needle in the muscle. "Damn it, Riley, get me out of here!"

"No sweat, Boss, you ain't gonna have a care in the world. Just relax and we'll get you out of this tree."

"Flag, am I in a tree?"

"Just a little bit, Boss. Problem is we can't get a grip on anything. What we need is a monkey, and Bush is on the way."

"Bush? He'll want to blow the tree down. Help me out, Flag."

"You're gonna be okay, Boss. Try to relax." Ed tried to relax and it was easy now with the morphine. He felt himself being pulled out of the plane, which now resembled a broken pile of shiny aluminum and not much else. Flag held onto his hand as they lay Meadows out on the ground and he saw a lot of familiar faces over him. Riley was splinting his leg, that hurt a little, and Bush was there and Eason, and Captain Thomason, and some Meo. He looked for Headman, but didn't see him. He was probably up at the warehouse stealing rice. Riley started an IV in ED's right forearm as they placed him on a litter and about six of the Americans carried it up the hill. They set him down beside the runway, and Flag told him there was a Dornier on the way to take him to Vientiane. Doc Holmes was there, the only American doctor in the whole country. It was getting harder and harder to concentrate, and Ed decided there was something in that IV. "Hey, Flag, will you take care of my stuff till I get back?"

"Boss, you ain't coming back. I'll go pack your stuff for you and we'll send it with you."

"Flag, lemme whisper something in your ear." Flagstone bent down. "Listen, Flag, I been keeping a diary, and you know that's against the law. Get it for me, will you?"

"We know about the diary. I'll take care of it. Be back in a few minutes. Bush, take care of the fucking Boss." With that, Flag was gone. Ed heard Bush say something, but it was far away, and then Ed was far away, too.

They loaded his litter on the Dornier and strapped both Ed and the litter to the floor in the cargo compartment. Meadows said goodbye to everyone, and there were tears in his eyes, tears in their eyes, tears all around. Flag turned to the pilot. "You get him safe to Vientiane, or you better die in the attempt. Fly that fucking airplane carefully; there's one hell of an *Officer* on board."

In Vientiane, Holmes put a cast on Ed's leg, changed the IV to something else, they cut all his clothes off and put some pajamas on him, then shipped him, complete with all his gear, by C-123 to Bangkok. He spent two days in the American Hospital there where they put him to sleep and set his leg. They also casted it and sewed up the cut in his head. A C-135—military equivalent of the Boeing 707, flew him from there to Hawaii, where they kept him for two days at Tripler Army Medical Center, then another C-135 flew him on home to Pope Air Force Base and Ft. Bragg. He was sleeping when they admitted him to the hospital, Womack Army Hospital.

■ ■ ■

A month had passed. Lt. Meadows was attending his first formation at B Company, 7th Special Forces Group (Airborne). Since he still wore a cast, he stood in the back of the formation. There was a young-looking 2nd lieutenant standing in front of him. When the formation was dismissed, everyone went somewhere, but the 2nd lieutenant didn't have anywhere to go. "Hey, Lieutenant," said Ed. "You busy?"

The man seemed scared. "No, Sir, I'm not."

"Well, would you like a cup of coffee?"

"Yes, Sir! That would be nice."

"Well, come on, let's go over to the mess hall. By the way, my name is Ed Meadows, and you don't have to call me, 'Sir'."

"You're Meadows? Sonofabitch! We've heard all about you. Aren't you the guy who beat the Viet Minh for five days, single-handed? You were one of the original DASL's, weren't you?"

"I was a DASL, but I didn't beat any Vietnamese. Come on, I'll introduce you to some of the old heads."

"Sonofabitch! Ed Meadows! I'd like to hear all about your tour in Boogey-land, sometime."

"Maybe some day I'll write a book, and you can read all about it."